About

Neil McLocklin was brought up in Dorset and enjoyed visits to the Purbecks and Corfe, something he continues to do with his wife and family. He has enjoyed a career in business consulting and real estate, but has written a number of books in a diverse range of genres, mainly written on his commute to London. *A Nation in Ruins* is the first to be published and he is now writing a sequel, following the fortunes of the Bankes and Harvey families through to the end of the Civil War, the execution of Charles I and Oliver Cromwell's rule as Lord Protector.

A NATION IN RUINS

NEIL MCLOCKLIN

A NATION IN RUINS

Vanguard Press

VANGUARD PAPERBACK

© Copyright 2022
Neil McLocklin

A CIP catalogue record for this title is
available from the British Library.

ISBN 978 1 80016 253 2

*Vanguard Press is an imprint of
Pegasus Elliot MacKenzie Publishers Ltd.*
www.pegasuspublishers.com

First Published in 2022

**Vanguard Press
Sheraton House Castle Park
Cambridge England**

Printed & Bound in Great Britain

Dedication

I would like to dedicate this book to my wife Sandrine for her love and kindness and for those moments that we have shared in Corfe and the Purbecks, forever and beyond.

"There is in the Isle of Purbecke a strong castell called Corffe Castell, seated on a very steepe hill, in the fracture of a hill, in the very midst of it."

Mercurius Rusticus — 1643

"There is nothing Civil about a Civil War."

Axl Rose — Guns and Roses

Preface

As a proportion of the population, more people died in the English Civil War than in any other conflict, before or since, in British history. The same is true of civil wars in America, Ireland, South Africa, Spain, Yugoslavia, Rwanda and Syria. When a nation turns on itself, and families and neighbours start fighting amongst each other, the hatred and intensity of conflict and atrocity has no limit. Fuelled by misunderstanding, class and religious intolerance, the impact of the English Civil War on a small village in Dorsetshire is no exception. Through the anxiety and destruction, Lady Bankes and a young lieutenant, Tom Harvey, had the strength of character to hold things together, despite losing their respective reasons to fight, as friends and lovers are lost in the conflict and the village is left in ruin. Having fought against each other, they now have to build a new future from the ruins and a world of shared understanding and tolerance; a lesson for us all in modern days.

Much of the story takes place on a peninsular in Dorsetshire surrounded by sea on three sides, called the Isle of Purbeck. To help readers I have provided a map of the Isle, showing Corffe Castell at its heart, and its strategic position between West Hill and Nine Borrow Down.

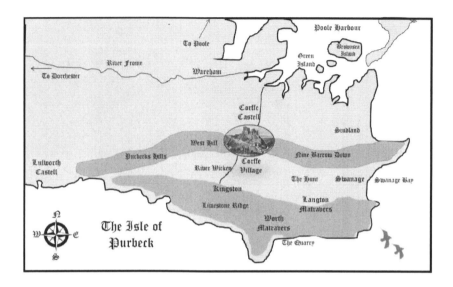

A more detailed layout of Corffe village and the Castell is also provided as well as an image of the Castell drawn in at the time of this novel.

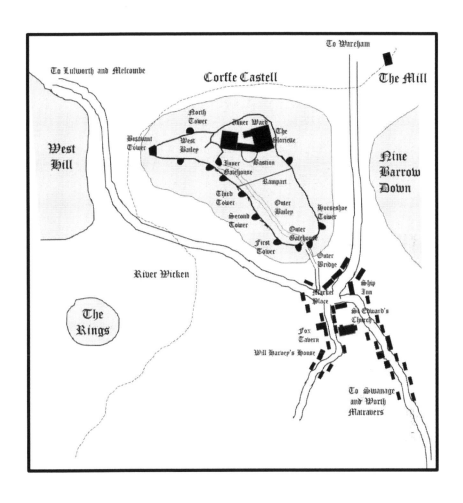

To Lulworth and Melcombe

To Wareham

Corffe Castell

The Mill

West Hill

North Tower

Inner Ward

The Gloriette

Butavant Tower

West Bailey

Inner Gatehouse

Bastion

Rampart

Nine Barrow Down

Third Tower

Outer Bailey

Horseshoe Tower

Second Tower

First Tower

Outer Gatehouse

Outer Bridge

River Wicken

Ship Inn

Market Place

St. Edward's Church

The Rings

Fox Tavern

Will Harvey's House

To Swanage and Worth Matravers

Chapter I
The Hunt and the Harvest

The woods outside Corffe — Dorsetshire
21st September 1634

Tom and his friend Francis ran through the thick, summer-forest undergrowth, desperate to keep up with the men and the hounds ahead in the boar hunt. The dogs had picked up the scent of the quarry five hundred yards back and were now frantically barking to let their masters know they had trapped the animal. It looked like the plan to drive the beast into a trap that the boys had helped to erect, as dawn broke that morning, had worked. It consisted of some temporary willow fencing that had been placed around a tight cluster of elm trees. The hounds had to harass and harry the boar into the trap and then keep it cornered while the hunters, including the two boys, caught up. Tom and Francis had to ensure that they reached the enclosure before the hunters made the kill. Their hearts pounded, fired up by excitement, anticipation, trepidation and fear. They had never been on a boar hunt before, and it was very unusual to allow boys of thirteen to join what was such a dangerous exploit. A fully-grown boar, with large tusks that can easily impale a man, can weigh three hundred pounds. The hounds can be equally as unpredictable and even more ferocious. The boys' parents had been reluctant to allow them to join the hunt but Captain James Cleall had reassured them that he would take care of them. The captain was just a few yards ahead of them, supervising the hunt, running with his sword drawn.

The baying of the dogs was increasing with every stride, and their frenzy echoed through the forest. All other living creatures kept themselves well hidden in the ferns and bracken that carpeted the woodland as they anticipated the kill. The boys were now running through familiar territory and joined the cries of their fellow hunters as they checked their speed on approach to the willow trap. Ned and Jed

Parfitt had been first on the scene and as serial hunters, they approached the prospect of the finale to the hunt with caution. The brothers were themselves boar-like in structure, both with barrel-shaped chests and bulging biceps that paid testimony to their work as quarrymen, but today they were armed with six-foot long spears, rather than picks. Besides them was Alfred Smith, with a long bow, arrow already set and the bowstring partially drawn by his muscular blacksmith's arms. It was a hunting arrow, three feet in length with a sharp, iron tip designed to pierce the hide of pigs or deer.

Three other villagers, one with another bow, one with an axe and the third with a spear, formed the second row that entered the coppice trap. The captain and the boys brought up the rear — the captain with his cavalry sword, and the boys with spears that dwarfed them. The long shafts of ash had fire-hardened points, and the boys gripped them, both-handed, with all their might. The captain was as pumped up as anyone was. He was now in his mid-thirties but his physique remained in peak condition; he had dark features, strongly set cheekbones, and almost wild, shoulder-length hair. He was a man of adventure and risk and since retiring from the cavalry, hunting had been his only release. He had been trained to kill and many men had met their end by the thrust of his blade, and this was something that could not simply be turned off. The real pleasure was a horse-mounted deer hunt but that pleasure depended on an invitation by the nobles, so a boar hunt was the second-best thing.

The two boys were like brothers, spending as much time together as they could negotiate with their demanding parents with their endless lists of chores. Tom was the curious and adventurous one; he could be as impulsive and enthusiastic as any teenager but maintained a likeable and warm character. He had hair to match his nature: a mass bundle of mousey hair that had been bleached at the tips by the summer sun. Grey-blue eyes and a permanent smile set between dimples in his cheeks completed his features. Tom was a couple of inches taller than Francis, who was definitely the follower of the two. Francis had an enthusiastic and kind nature, but lacked Tom's intellect and ambition. He had a simpler view of the world. His hair was a few shades browner but totally straight, although normally, like today, ruffled and with the front palmed back and sticking up with sweat.

Now the boys could see their prey for the first time, their blood racing. The animal was about three feet tall, and could have butted up to the chests of the boys. It had a thick bristly coat with underlying brown pelage and a ridge of longer hair growing along its spine. It was snorting loudly through its nostrils and was clearly frightened, despite being armed with two-inch tusks each side of its long, narrow snout. Its seemingly under-sized ears stood erect as it faced down the five hounds that had it cornered. The barking was frantic. Seeing the dogs close up, the pig obviously did not rate its chances. It suddenly turned and charged the willow fence behind. Its snout seared through but the limited momentum it had did not allow it to progress any further. It thrashed its head around to try to break the fence but only succeeded in searing its left eye, and a stream of blood flowed down its check. It tossed its head again and with a piercing squeal, followed by an almighty snort, it freed its head and staggered backwards. One of the hounds jumped on the boar's back and buried its teeth into its hindquarter. But the pig was too big for him, and with surprising agility spun around and sent the hound flying off into the wooden palisade. The four remaining hounds barked, growled, yapped and howled. This boar was going nowhere.

Ned Parfitt briefly turned to the captain. "He's gonna charge!"

The captain hollered, "Put him out of his misery, but mind the dogs!"

With these words, Smith and the other villagers released their arrows, one hitting the boar on its right flank and the other on its left. As the second arrow found its target, the boar started its charge. Its trotters drove the huge body mass forward, ramming into the middle hound who was sent staggering back, but the remaining three dogs mauled the swine from both sides. The momentum of the pig's drive took it forward to the waiting Parfitt brothers, who lunged their spears into the creature's back. Whilst the rest of the hunting group parted to avoid the charge, the two brothers kept hold of their spears and used them to break the advance, before falling on the swine, weighing it down into the ground, so it came to rest right at the feet of the captain and the two boys. Smith and one of the other villagers pulled the hounds off by their collars, while the pig lay on the ground, hemmed down by the two quarrymen with a spear projecting from each side; snorting, belly pulsating and head thrashing. Tom instinctively raised the shaft of his spear and plunged it into the belly of the pig, realising just how tough it was. The pointed end penetrated barely an inch. Francis followed the example of his friend but with no better result.

"You will have to do better than that to kill this one, boys," said Alfred Smith, who took out a ten-inch blade from a sheaf on his belt and cut the pig's throat, finally ending its struggle. The blacksmith stood up and everybody stood around the kill, eyeing up the beast.

"Must be three hundred pounds," said Nat.

"More, I say," replied Alfred.

The captain cried out to the remaining three men. "Give the dogs their reward, lads!" and two of the villagers pulled out five rabbits, hunted earlier. They tossed them to the frenzied hounds who shredded them into meat. Tom realised he was still panting from the chase. The dogs were chomping their prizes in the background, but otherwise it was a moment of calm, quiet and reflection, with the rest of the forest completely still, as if mourning the passing of one of their elders. Tom had hunted many rabbits and fish, but this was an altogether more magnificent trophy. Yes, a family of pigs had lost their father, but Tom knew that this roasted hog would bring joy to the whole village after the hard labour of bringing in the harvest. Chicken, rabbit and fish were regular treats to the diets of the villagers, but pork was a real treat and the highlight of the harvest celebrations.

August had been one of the warmest and driest in living memory and the good weather had continued into the first two weeks of September. With a bumper crop and nearly all of it safely stored in Sir Edward Coke's barns, Captain Cleall, as custodian of the Castell and the estate while Sir Edward was away, had decided a hog roast would be an appropriate reward for the labourers and villagers. There were plenty of wild pigs and deer on Sir Edward's sixteen-thousand-acre estate in the Dorsetshire countryside, with Corffe Castell at its heart. This was just one of the noble's estates, with others in Buckinghamshire and Norfolkshire, as well as property in London, and the villagers had not seen their elderly lord, in fact, for five years now.

Ned broke the moment of reflection. "Need to get this pig roasting pretty sharpish if it is to be eaten tonight."

The hunters grunted in acknowledgement, the captain issued a series of orders and the troop dispersed in different directions. Tom and Francis's assignment, along with the Parfitt brothers, was dismantling the temporary wicker fences. The ropes that tied the fencing to the elms were quickly untied and carried back to the cart, positioned eight hundred yards away on the main track between Corffe village and the coastal bay of Swanage, earlier in the morning. Meanwhile, the captain supervised the other villagers retrieving the boar, which had been rolled on to a stretcher and carried back to the cart. It was lifted on top of the fencing stacked in the cart and covered in old cloth to keep flies and hounds at bay. The hounds were leashed on a lead tied to the front of the cart. The cart horse, that had been tethered to a tree in the forest shade nearby, was put into its harness and Alfred Smith mounted the cart ready to go. Francis joined him at the front with one of the Parfitt brothers, whilst two other villagers sat on the back of the cart, and the rest set out to walk by the side of the cart. The captain had mounted his cavalry horse, a gelding named Thunder; a magnificent animal that had been reared on oats for strength and agility. Thunder had been the captain's horse for five years now and they were a perfect pair together. The captain called over to Tom. The boy only came up to the captain's boots as he towered above him, but he leaned down and pulled him up by the arm, mounting him in front of him. Tom was overjoyed being on the back of such a magnificent beast, a real destrier cavalry horse, eighteen hands tall and as black as the night.

The captain had taken a liking to Tom over the last couple of months, which the village boy had relished and thought about as they started the journey back to the Castell and village of Corffe. It was mid-morning now, with the sun rising in a brilliant blue sky. The early morning dew had disappeared, and it promised to be a magnificent day. On each side of the track, the trees hosted singing birds. The main woodland was to the left, and to the right above the tree line rose the chalk ridge of Nine Barrow Down. The road followed the foot of the Down until it reached the Corffe village, which was nestled in a gap in the Down, no more than two miles down the track. This was Tom's homeland. He was born in Langton Matravers, a mile up the track, but had lived in Corffe village, since he was six, with his father William and stepmother Elizabeth.

Tom's mother had died in childbirth, when she could not stop bleeding after his delivery. His mother had been a nun at the priory in Wareham, the nearest large town. She had met William's father when he had an accident and had been carried to the small hospital in the Benedictine nunnery. Sister Jane nursed him through three months of recovery and during that time fell in love with William. She left the nunnery for her soul mate and moved in with William, but died twelve months later. Many said that it had been God's revenge on her turning her back on her convent and her Benedictine vows.

Elizabeth, who was a widow, almost immediately stepped into his mother's shoes. It was an arrangement of convenience: William needed a mother for Tom and a housewife, whilst Elizabeth needed a bread winner for herself and her six-year-old son, Daniel. The convenience turned into a love of a kind, and the two were married in 1627, two years after Tom had been born, and six months before the arrival of Tom's half-sister, Beth. William was the estate manager for the Corffe estate, a prestigious position in the community which he had earned through hard graft, self-education and being attentive to the needs of his master. The estate stretched from just south of Wimborne in the north, to the east of Wareham, across the River Frome and all the way around the southern half of Poole Harbour to Studland and Swanage in the east, Steeple and Kimmeridge in the west and Kingston and Worth Matravers in the south. A dozen or so families had acquired their houses from previous lords, but the majority paid rents, which all had to be collected. The tenants were also under obligations to keep their property maintained, and this had to be enforced. Protecting fishing rights along the River Frome and overseeing the quarrying on the limestone ridge were also important duties. The estate also had rights to the cargo from wrecks along the rugged coastline, and barely year went by without some kind of dividend.

William had a lot of responsibility and was respected as he was considered fair and straight, as well as hardworking and a man who knew everything there is to know about this part of Dorsetshire. He was now in his mid-thirties, and the tips of his brown, curly hair and beard were turning grey. He was a big man, five feet eleven inches in height, and he kept in good shape with his constant activity around the estate; riding, walking, climbing, repairing, even harvesting, for he was a man who could not stand by and let others do all the toil. He now resided in one of the larger houses in Corffe village; one of only a handful that were of two-storey construction, made from Purbeck stone, with a thatched roof, glass windows and a fire place and chimney. There were two rooms downstairs, the kitchen and the parlour, and two sleeping rooms upstairs, one for William and Elizabeth, and the other for Tom and Beth, while Daniel was now living in Worth Matravers, as he was working in the quarry.

Tom often travelled with his father around the estate. He was developing his father's physical frame and features, three to four inches taller than boys of his age. However, it was said that his mind was more akin to his mother's. His father knew what had to be done and made sure he did it, with a great practical ability to resolve problems along the way. Tom was far more inquisitive, asking why things happened, not just what needed to be done. Folks said that was another reason why his mother had left the nunnery. As a novice, she had been constantly questioning everything she was being told, whether it was in respect to theology and faith, or medicine and care. Why was there so much suffering, injustice, poverty, unfairness? Why were prescribed medicines not working, and why did prayer not always work? The answer that it was God's will, was not convincing enough for Sister Mary.

Then William came into her life, providing even more questions, and shook all the foundations and reasons why she had entered the nunnery in the first place. Tom, like his mother, could not stop asking questions until he truly understood the reasoning behind everything. Sometimes he would drive his father to despair as he asked questions on subjects that ranged from building engineering to agriculture, from astronomy to mathematics, from physics to theology, from geography to geology, and he was now just starting to take an interest in politics and King Charles' Ship Tax. William's position did provide Tom with access to other, more educated residents of the Castell, who were better able to feed his insatiable appetite for knowledge, most notably Captain Cleall and Sir Edward's daughter, Charlotte, a widow in her later thirties who had taken a liking to the boy when she visited.

The labourers on the cart began singing and sharing around a flask of ale. Could life be better, thought Tom — a beautiful day, the prospect of a hog roast to celebrate an abundant harvest, and riding on the back of a cavalry horse.

"Thank you for taking me on the hunt," Tom said to the captain, and then started quizzing him about hunting: what were the biggest boars and stags he had killed; what were the different hunting techniques; what was it like hunting in France?

The captain responded to the questions but wanted to give the boy something more to think about.

"The lesson today, Tom, is that killing a boar is similar to winning a battle. The boar is as big as any of us and with tusks that could easily kill any man. But we are able to hunt and make the kill because we create confusion for the boar and have a plan to kill it. In battle it is the same. In the confusion of battle, it is a plan that gives you the edge; not the sword."

Tom pondered this for a moment before bombarding the captain with more questions. While the boy loved and respected his father, the captain was more worldly and had experienced places and countries that Tom could only dream about. He wanted to learn everything about everything and his inquisition could have continued all morning but before long, they had reached Corffe village.

"Well, Tom. I think your questions will have to await another day. We have to prepare for the festivities tonight. I also have a surprise for you," the captain said.

"What is it? Please tell," Tom pleaded, but the captain would not divulge it.

The main street led them passed timber and cob single-storey cottages, two rooms — at most — inside each. The larger houses, built of the local grey limestone, congregated along a parallel street in a newer part of the village and that is where Tom lived. As they approached the market square, there were more Purbeck limestone buildings, including the Ship Tavern and of course, the church, named St Edward the Martyr, after King Edward of Wessex who had been murdered at the Castell, but whose body was found by a local blind woman and in doing so, her sight was restored. The bells were ringing from the church tower, and people were milling around the market square. A few stalls had been erected in the market square, which was unusual as it was not a market day but people were anticipating some custom in advance of this evening's festivities. When people feel good, they are prepared to spend more and one stall offered cloth and lace, another offered cider and apples, and a third cheese. The bells were not the typical peal of bells inviting the villagers to service on a Sunday, and in any event today was a Saturday. They tolled out a far merrier sound, more akin to a wedding celebration, presumably getting people into the spirit of the day. The captain pulled up in front of the church.

"Take the boar to the Castell outer bailey, where Jack Miles should have the charcoal white-hot by now and be ready to skin the beast," the captain said to Alfred.

As Tom looked up at the tower and the bells, Father Jerome, in his habit, came out of the large oak doors of the porch adjoining the bell tower. He was in his early twenties and had his hair shaved on his crown which made him look older. He was looking anxious.

"Why are the bells ringing?" the captain asked, avoiding the normal pleasantries.

"It gives the ringers some practice and gets the village in a merry mood for the festivities tonight."

"Good idea. Everybody is looking forward to some fun and dancing after working so hard to get the harvest in. We have just hunted a boar to make a nice hog roast. Anyway, I had better get back to the Castell to see how Povington is doing with the arrangements. Good day, Father."

With that, the captain spurred Thunder on towards the Castell, which rose in all its splendour before the riders. It occupied one of the best defensive sites in England, positioned between two cuts in the Purbeck Hills, made by the Rivers Wicken and Byle Brook since the beginning of time. This resulted in a pass or 'corffe' around a residual steep hill between the two water courses, on top of which was perched the Castell overseeing any movement through the passes below. The current Castell had stood guard for over five hundred years, since William the Conqueror discovered the location. The ramparts circled an inner keep and gloriette of aged and weathered Purbeck stone, so that the edifice looked almost as natural as any of the limestone cliffs along the Dorsetshire coast. But its prominent position provided it with a formidable status to travellers. The walls seemed to rise out of the patchwork grass and stone slopes of the hill, which on three sides were almost sheer, making any attack from that direction very difficult. From the village, the slope was gentler but the Castell was separated on that side by a deep ditch, filled with water from the Wicken. For the local community the Castell was fraternal, providing security, employment and authority, and had seemingly always been there. It was a short distance across the market square and up to the Castell. Thunder trotted across the drawbridge and through the outer gate in no time.

"Tom — take Thunder to the stables and rub her down for me and give her some oats. I need to talk to Ralph Povington about the arrangements for tonight." The captain, a tall man, strode pass the tents and tables that were being prepared in the outer bailey for the festivities. His long legs marched swiftly up the path to the inner gate and into the gloriette, the heart of the Castell that contained the staterooms from the days when it hosted kings and queens. The inner ward around the keep and the gloriette contained ponds and a wonderful garden of roses, which were a marvel of colour in the September sunshine. This was testimony to the previous owner, Sir Christopher Hatton, Queen Elizabeth's notorious Lord Chancellor, who had started modernising the building, a process continued by Sir Edward Coke. However, the truth was that both men spent most of their time at court and few of their plans to convert the gloriette into a stately home, rather than the medieval facilities of a Norman Castell, had come to fruition.

The captain opened the large oak door of the gloriette and was greeted warmly by a servant who was sweeping the floor.

"Where is the house master?" Captain Cleall asked. He did not need to await a response because Ralph Povington was in the state room and saw the captain enter the great hall. It was a three-storey room which had been the focal point and reception room of the Castell for the last three hundred years. A huge fire place with oak mantle was the focal point, and the grey Purbeck stone walls had been softened on one side of the room by wooden panelling and on the other by a tapestry depicting the crusades and a battle for Jerusalem. A staircase to the right of the entrance led up to a first-floor gallery, which led to a series of doors: bedrooms for the master, family and guests. Ralph Povington was the man who was the head of household, managing the staff and arrangements for the absentee Sir Edward. He walked quickly towards the captain across the oak wood floor.

"Oh, I am glad you are back, Captain Cleall. I have some bad news. Sir Edward has passed away. Here — I have the letter from Lady Elizabeth," said the house master in a flustered voice.

The mid-thirties man was a tall and wiry in stature, well dressed in a close-knitted dark blue tunic with white stockings, and black shoes complete with a ribbon. His mannerisms were often effeminate and he was more often than not in a flap about something. The captain took the letter and read it quickly. It confirmed the Castell's Lord had passed away peacefully on 3rd September and would be resting in state at his manor in Norfolk until the end of the month, and begged for payers for his soul. Other than that, the note did not say anything: what more could a grieving widow say immediately after her husband's death?

"What shall we do, Captain? We have the harvest thanksgiving and what should we tell the villagers?" There was a knock at the door behind, which was opened by the servant, and in came Father Jerome. He was informed of the situation and then Captain Cleall suggested the three of them sit down and devise a plan of action.

"We have three things we need to address. Firstly, what we tell the villagers and how we pay respects and commemorate the life of their lord. Secondly, what we do with the harvest thanksgiving. Thirdly, how we find out what is to happen to the estate, as people will be worried and will want to know. My suggestion is that we address the first two together. We should make a service of thanksgiving at the church this afternoon and the harvest festivity can be a thanksgiving for the life of Sir Edward. Father Jerome, what do you think?"

The priest looked a little concerned but he recognised the pragmatic approach proposed by the captain.

"It is right to have the service before any festivities," he replied. "God has provided us with a lord whose long life and work provided the land that enabled us to reap the harvest. It would not be a full requiem — we do not have time to prepare — but a service that will help people come to terms with the loss, before any celebrations. There is still the harvest service tomorrow for further reflection. Captain, would you be happy to provide an account of the lord's life during the service? You have known him as long and as well as anybody."

"Yes, I can do that," the captain responded. "But we still need to address people's concern about what will happen to the estate. I can see no option but to go and see Lady Elizabeth. I suggest Ralph and I set out tomorrow to Norfolk. It will be a hard ride and take a couple of weeks, but people will be assured that something is happening."

Ralph Povington's face visibly paled. While the captain would relish the prospect of the undertaking, the planning, the responsibility, the ride, the adventure and even the danger, it was a bleak prospect for Ralph. In truth, he had rarely ventured outside of Dorsetshire; even the Purbeck Isle. He was a man who attended his lord and lady's wishes that banquets were planned and prepared with the right selection of food and dished out with the etiquette of the day, the Castell was kept clean and tidy and the gardens looked spectacular. A journey to Norfolk meant the prospect of travelling on inclement days on unknown roads frequented by outlaws. It would mean staying in rowdy or unclean taverns at best and sleeping rough at worst.

"But if I go, who will manage the Castell? I could not possibly leave — there is so much to do," Ralph said, self-protectively.

"If you do not go, then you may not have a Castell to manage, Ralph," the captain retorted. Ralph opened his mouth in response but failed to think of a reply. "We need to communicate with the village elders as soon as possible about what we are going to do," the captain continued. "Ralph — can you send messengers out to them to meet us here in one hour?"

Ralph nodded agreement to the edict from the captain and the three men dispersed before the elder meeting.

Within an hour of sending out messages, most of the elders had assembled in the hall. There was Will Harvey, the estates manager and Tom's father; Thomas Moreton, the publican; Josh Miller, who leased the water mill; Tom Mason, who had repaired and renovated much of the Castell; Jack Morris, who would normally have been fishing in his boat had it not been for the festivities; and Sam Ash, who farmed one of the larger tenancy holdings. Father Jerome, the captain and Ralph Povington joined them, all seated around a large, dark oak table at the far end of the hall. The head of the household opened proceedings, thanking people for coming and informed them of the sad news. As expected, the news was met with a whole host of questions and concerns. Thomas Moreton opened the response by declaring that Sir Edward Coke's death was expected, as he was in his eighties and had not been to Corffe for five years or more. But this started the expected surge of questions that were mainly focused on what it meant for the village and their individual wellbeing. Who would take over and what might happen to the Castell and the estate? What about the Thanksgiving festivities?

The captain let the assembled men have their say, as he would with any troop under his command, but then stepped in to provide direction and leadership.

"I would like to say a few words, as a friend of Sir Edward." He did not wait for his request to be acknowledged but stood up to reinforce his command of the room. "Yes. Sir Edward has been absent for some years, but this was partly due to ill health and not being able to travel at the age of eighty-two, but also the calls and demands on his time from king and country, despite his retirement. I do know he did have a special place in his heart for Dorsetshire, and especially Corffe and its villagers. I also know that, throughout England, people will be mourning his death and every village in the land will regret his loss, for he has given so much to this country. I was here in Corffe fifteen years ago when the Bill of Rights was passed, and the bell in this very village church, along with churches up and down the country, tolled out in celebration. I do not know the workings of Parliament and our King, of policy making and legislation, but I do know that they are fraught with danger, risks and frustrations that would drive an ordinary man spare. Sir Edward was no ordinary man — he was extraordinary in his drive and determination and his legacy should live on. First and foremost, we should thank God for Sir Edward's life, and pray that his soul will be well received in heaven."

The captain paused, but he was far from finished. He wanted to gauge the room. Nobody said anything. The men were all looking at him intently. He carried on.

"To this end, Father Jerome has agreed to conduct a service of thanksgiving for the life of your Lord. This ceremony will take place an hour before dusk. It will precede the thanksgiving festivities which Ralph

Povington has confirmed will continue thereafter, but as a festival to celebrate Sir Edward's life, as well as the bountiful harvest that the Lord God has granted us."

The captain paused again as his audience nodded silently in agreement.

"Then tomorrow, Ralph and I will set out to Norfolk on behalf of you all to pay our respects to Lady Coke. We understand Sir Edward is to be laid in state until the end of the month, when the funeral is arranged, and so we have no time to lose. We can also find out what she and their eldest son, Harry, plan for the Castell and the estate. We may have to spend some time with Harry working out the details. It may take us several weeks. If anybody wants to join us, they can."

Ralph was looking more and more worried as he contemplated the prospect of such a trip, but the rest of the gathering were reassured that the captain would take up their cause.

Will Harvey spoke up. "We are much appreciative of your counsel and leadership, Captain Cleall. We know you be a good friend to Sir Edward and we also know you will seek out the reassurances about the future that us from the village would seek. But I have worked for Sir Edward nigh on twenty years now. As the estate manager, I would also like to join you to pay respects on behalf of the village and estate. If that be all right with you."

"Why, Ralph and I would welcome your company, Will. We now need to brief the crier and spread the word about the service at the church. I will see you all there later."

The church was packed. Every inch of pew had a bottom squeezed on it, and the entire internal perimeter of the church was two-deep in villagers standing. The crier and the messengers had done their job, reinforced by the bell-ringers who had turned the merry peal into a single toll that haunted the village for most of the afternoon. The people needed reassurance at this time, and Father Jerome delivered a sombre but comforting service. He was a timid man but his timidity was lost as soon as he entered the pulpit and with God's authority he declared the need for gratitude for the Almighty's servant, Sir Edward Coke, his eighty-two years on this earth and the good work he did. He then asked Captain

Cleall to make the eulogy, sharing his gratitude and some experiences of the life of his friend and the Castell lord.

Many people were not alive, or would be too young, to appreciate the importance of the Petition of Rights, the most important bill that impacted people's rights since the Magna Carta. Sir Edward was its author and instrumental in making it law. The rights included habeas corpus of free Englishmen and freedom from taxation without parliamentary approval. The current tension between Parliament and monarch was because the king could no longer just do as he wished and this was because of Sir Edward, a true man of the people whose legacy would live on.

The captain described the man's dedication to his cause and principles, his energy and drive and his intellect and political nuance. Yet underneath all this was a family man; one who relished the time he spent in Corffe with his wife Elizabeth, his children, now all grown up, and the grandchildren. Throughout the service, the captain's and Father Jerome's words were met with a lot of appreciative nodding and 'yeahing' in agreement but as the captain closed, with the direction to the congregation that Sir Edward would not only have wanted them to remember what he had done, but also celebrate it in the festivities that followed this service, there was applause. The congregation then rose from their seats and started to make their way out of the church and back to the Castell outer keep.

It did not take long to get the party going with the mass of people already assembled for the service. The smell of the hog roast and several chickens was an irresistible draw, and before long everybody was assembled around hay bales and a big fire, armed with good wholesome food and jugs of ale and cider. It would be an hour before the sun would set, but dark shadows fell across the assembly. William and Francis were first in line to taste the meat from the boar that they had proudly played a hand in killing; something they made sure everybody else in the queue was aware of. The pig had now been raised high above the white-hot coals that sizzled with dripping fat as the flesh was carved. The aroma of the roasted pig permeated throughout the outer bailey and made the boys ever more ravenous. Other people waited at various stalls that had popped up around the grounds, where chickens, eggs, cheeses, bread, apples and cakes were all available at the expense of the late Sir Edward Coke, who was surely looking down on his old estate, happy to see so much joy.

The boys clustered around the fire along with everybody else and enjoyed their supper and their companion jugs of ale, chattering about their extraordinary day — the hunt, riding on the captain's destrier, the death of Sir Edward and now the celebrations. Tom had learnt that his father would accompany the captain and Ralph Povington on a long trip to Norfolkshire to see Lady Coke tomorrow. It would take them weeks to get there and weeks to return, a trip that Tom could barely imagine in terms of what they would see — towns, different landscapes, outlaws and other dangers along the way. He wished he could join the adventure and had asked his father to take him, but was told that his duty was to look after the house, his step-mother and sister. The importance his father placed on this role was a partial compensation for Tom but he still yearned for the adventure. On a couple of occasions, he had been to Poole in the east and Melcombe in the west, the two main ports, as well as Dorchester. These towns had given him a glimpse of places that were different to his tranquil and quiet Purbeck life. True, they did not have a Castell but they had markets selling wares from far-off places and magnificent buildings — guildhalls, customs houses, grand churches. But his father had told him of places further afield, boasting cathedrals with towers that touched the sky and housing tens of thousands of people in street after streets of houses, and taverns, and stores selling everything from guns to garments; places like Winchester and the capital London, where King Charles himself resided.

Whilst the boys chatted, Jed Parfitt had got his fiddle and was joined by his brother Ned on a drum, and they started the music. Singing and dancing would take the party into the night, as the sun bade farewell in a crimson sky and the first few stars came out, whilst several braziers around the Castell were ablaze to provide light for the celebrations. After a warm-up by the fiddlers, the villagers egged on Elizabeth, Tom's step-mother, to start the singing. She frequently did as she had a good voice and would often sing something quite mellow to get the singing started. However, as always, she would pretend to be reluctant before finally getting up to join the musicians. They waited for her lead and rested their

28

bows and sticks while she looked down at the ground in contemplation, before taking a deep breath, and then her voice rose quietly and floated over the shushed audience.

"Lavender's blue, dilly, dilly, lavender's green,
When I am King, dilly, dilly, You shall be Queen.
Who told you so, dilly, dilly, who told you so?
'Twas my own heart, dilly, dilly, that told me so…"

As she increased her volume, she raised her head, and grabbed the hand of her husband, who was sitting on a make-shift seat to her right.

"Call up your men, dilly, dilly, set them to work,
Some to the plough, dilly, dilly, some to the rock;
Some to make hay, dilly, dilly, some to cut corn…"

Elizabeth now had a beaming smile on her face, which radiated in the firelight, and her voice was joined by rhythmic hand-clapping, as well as the fiddle and drum.

"While you and I, dilly, dilly, keep ourselves warm.
Lavender's green, dilly, dilly, lavender's blue,
If you love me, dilly, dilly, I will love you.
Let the birds sing, dilly, dilly, and the lambs play.
We shall be safe, dilly, dilly, out of harm's way.
I love to dance, dilly, dilly, I love to sing.
When I am Queen, dilly, dilly, you'll be my King.
Who told me so, dilly, dilly, Who told me so?
I told myself, dilly, dilly, I told me so."

The massed voices of the village joined her for another rendition of the last few lines, and everybody was now in full festive spirit. The captain started distributing a half-dozen song sheets he had acquired for a penny each, when he had recently visited Winchester. They were quickly passed to the few folk who could read, which included Tom and his father. Cohorts of villagers assembled around each of the readers, and

29

the folk quickly learnt the verses of songs that told tales of courtships and infamous murders, of battles far away and chivalric adventures. Then each cohort took it in turn to go up as a collective to share his or her rendition. This process continued and was then repeated, so the entire village became familiar with the new verses and joined in the singing. Interspersed with the new songs were the old favourites, each led by a villager who called it their own. The singing voices were oiled with a continuous supply of jugs of ale and cider, and before long the singing was accompanied by dancing, which would carry on until feet and legs were too tired.

As the night wore on, Captain Cleall launched his surprise. Earlier, he had secretly arranged for one of the cannons to be mounted on the bastion, which projected from the Castell's gloriette and overlooked the festivities. During a short interlude in the music and dancing, he brought it to life with a roar that boomed like thunder, echoing off the surrounding hills, and bringing shrieks from the women and momentary anxious looks from the men, but then laughter as they all realised what it was. The cannon had been directed on to the neighbouring slope of Nine Barrow Down and as soon as it was fired, Tom and Francis decided to scarper and seek out the ball. They made their way as fast as they could run out of the Castell, across the village and then climbed the Down before any other children had the same idea. But it was much darker than they had expected on the slope, deceived by the brightness of the Castell fire and the braziers all ablaze. Alas, the cannon ball would have to wait until the morning to be found. The boys sat perched on the hill, enjoying the sound of laughter and singing floating up to them. They could see a few lights in Wareham, as well as Poole in the distance, but nothing in comparison to Corffe below. What a perfect day; indeed, the best Tom could recall in his thirteen years. What a great place to live, having a Castell, wild boars to hunt and eat, and a real captain who fired cannons for fun. He was truly grateful he did not live amongst the puritans of Poole but said a silent prayer for his father's safe return and that nothing would change. Yes, please God: just keep this world as perfect as it is.

Chapter II
Oxford Reunion

25th September 1634

Captain Cleall led the trio from Corffe Castell down through the Chilterns, tightening his coat as the wind picked up and the day started to draw to a close. They could now see the spires of Oxford in the distance. Thunder, his trusted destrier, trotted along the old Roman road; she had made it an easy journey from Winchester, where Ralph Povington, William Harvey and the captain had stayed the night before.

He let his fellow travellers draw up alongside him.

"Now, there is a great city. You thought Winchester was grand but wait until you see this. I was stationed here in the army, but that was before the disaster of La Rochelle back in 1627."

He reflected on the events of La Rochelle for which he still blamed King Charles, who had come to the throne two years earlier. Charles had never really meant to become king but his elder brother, Prince Henry, died from typhoid fever before he could succeed King James. Charles' father did not help him too much in his hasty apprenticeship, and indeed made things worse by allowing the Earl of Buckingham to have influence over him. Buckingham set about finding a wife for Charles, and the two of them arrived in Spain together, in disguise, seeking the Spanish Princess as a prize, to the astonishment of Philip IV, and of the English ambassador. Charles was infatuated with the princess, but he and Buckingham were both badly equipped to negotiate her hand. Charles had an awkward stammer, was uncomfortable in the presence of women and lacked courting prowess. Buckingham preferred the male sex, and was rumoured to have had a relationship with King James. But their political ignorance really made this a total farce and after six months the two of them realised the folly of their adventure and returned home, empty-handed.

It was another Catholic, Henrietta Maria, the fifteen-year-old sister of France's King Louis XIII, who Charles did marry two years later. This did not stop Buckingham's influence and his meddling continued. There was a lot of anxiety, particularly in parliament, about the influence of the Catholic queen: she sensed it and with her foul temper, she made her feelings known. Persuading her husband to relax some of the anti-Catholic penal laws still did not make her happy, so Charles sent much of her household back to France. Her brother, Louis, responded by arresting British citizens in Calais. Buckingham wanted to retaliate and came up with a plan to strike the French at La Rochelle, where Louis's forces were besieging the Huguenot garrison. Captain Cleall was still livid about this episode. It was appallingly planned, and had a poor cause and purpose. Buckingham's leadership was cavalier and not worthy of the British standard. From the outset, the captain and several of his colleagues had protested to such an extent that they were threatened with court marshalling. He had expected to be promoted to colonel that year, but his defiance had ruled that out, despite being proved correct. In the end, only three thousand soldiers returned from the eight thousand who left for La Rochelle; one of Britain's greatest humiliations.

The captain reflected on the loss of life from that expedition — many good friends and comrades and all so pointlessly. He questioned what he was doing serving king and country to such an end. He stood down from his commission and welcomed Sir Edward Coke's offer to be his guardian of Corffe Castell and the estate. The only saving grace was that one of Cleall's colleagues, Captain Felton, felt so angry that he assassinated the Duke of Buckingham in Portsmouth. Many other colleagues at the time left the army and became mercenaries on the continent in the many wars waged between Catholics and Protestants. This was something that Cleall considered, but he was glad he had not followed this course. He was a man who needed purpose and conviction to fight. It was not about money, even although he very much enjoyed the professionalism of his officership. He would never get over La Rochelle, and something he often talked about with Sir Edward was whether or not he could ever serve the king again.

The captain's thoughts consumed the final few miles. He then led the travellers over a bridge that crossed the River Thames and through the Westgate on a road that led straight up to the Castell guarding the city. Instead of preceding into the Castell, he followed a road south around its walls and into the heart of Oxford. His companions, although weary from the long ride from Newbury, felt refreshed from the anticipation of entering this famous city. They first passed St Ebbes, a modest medieval church standing above some tumble-down housing, obviously a poorer part of the city. But this led to Pembroke College, the first of many magnificent buildings that created a vibrant city scene in the Castell's shadow. The College had recently been constructed from local Cotswold stone and proudly wore a shield depicting its coat of arms comprising three lions, a rose and a thistle above an open-gated entrance, guarded by a man-at-arms. The coat of arms signified that King James 1 of England and V1 of Scotland had founded the College a few years earlier. The travellers could catch a glimpse of the grassed courtyard, and the heart of the College within, with colourfully dressed students milling about inside in the late afternoon autumn sunshine.

They turned north into the cobbled South Street, which was even more of a bustle than Winchester. The captain started recalling some of his old haunts in the city but for William and Ralph, every step their horses took was one of awe and amazement: the grandeur and variety of the buildings, colleges, churches, two- and even three-storey houses of the gentry. These were interspersed with taverns and cottages that would not look out of place in any Dorset village, as well as artisans producing or tradesmen selling their wares in stores, makeshift stalls or adapted buildings. Tailors, butchers, smithies, tanners, tinkers, weavers, cutlers and cobblers, to name but a few, paraded their wears amidst a cocktail of smells, cries to attract business, signs and sounds. A crier bellowed the news of the day, while horses and carriages jostled for passage through the mayhem.

The captain pulled up outside the Cock Inn and dismounted. A boy came from the tavern and took hold of the reins. His two companions followed suit, Povington complaining of the soreness in his buttocks and aches in his legs before trailing after the captain inside. The main room opened onto the street and was busy with travellers and tradesmen eating and drinking, with the smoke from clay pipes and the tallow candles fermenting with the smell of the food, ale and so many folk crammed together. It did not take long before the captain found the landlord and secured a room for the three of them to share. As he concluded his business and was about to be shown the lodgings, the captain was almost knocked off his feet as a hand slapped him suddenly on the back of the shoulders.

"Cleall, you old dog! What brings you back to this splendid city?"

Recovering his balance, the captain spun round to find a man of equal size and stature, but dressed in black, academic robes. Long brown and grey curls crowned a head that was smiling from ear to ear. It was Henry Catchpole, a friend of the captain's from his Oxford days.

Cleall's tired face was refreshed by a welcoming smile. "Ah, Henry, what a great surprise. I was hoping to find somebody to share a glass with in this godforsaken city."

"Sir Henry to you now, my friend."

"What king would grant somebody with your manners a knighthood?"

"King James, just before he died, in recognition of setting up Pembroke College. That means it must be over ten summers since we last saw each other. That is a lot of drinking to make up. How long are you here for?"

"Alas, just the night. We are on our way to Norfolkshire and have no time to lose."

"Why then, you must dine with us at the College tonight. We have some other guests I am sure you will like. Let's say eight o'clock but I must rush now or I will not be ready for it myself."

Sir Henry patted the captain on the back and the two friends embraced before parting.

The three travellers were shown through an arched carriage entrance into a courtyard behind the inn with stables on one side and guest rooms on the other. It was a busy establishment and drays were coming and going as visitors arrived and others were departing. There was just a single room left but it had four small beds taking up nearly the entire space. There was a fireplace at one end, with wood stacked up ready to light, and at the other end a table with bowl and water jug for washing. The three men each claimed a bed, and dropped their travel bags on the fourth. The captain told his companions how he had befriended Henry when stationed at Oxford. They were people from very different backgrounds — army and academia, middle class merchant and wealthy aristocracy — but they shared an ability to make each other laugh, especially over a bottle of wine or brandy. The ten years had not dampened the friendship and the captain was looking forward to the forthcoming evening. His two companions agreed to take a walk through the city before they would find a place for a hearty meal ready for the next day's travel, while the captain readied himself for dinner. Cleall smiled to himself: he had been the fulcrum in conversation over the last couple of evenings, and he wondered how his companions would fare alone. Will Harvey did not have much to say other than what needed to be said, and in contrast, Ralf Povington had a lot to say about nothing.

It was not long before the captain heard one of the city clocks chime a quarter to the hour, the hour being eight o'clock, and he set off from the tavern to the College. Darkness had gripped the city now, but the main street was lit by lanterns hanging out from the windows of every tenth building, as he carefully avoided clumps of horse dung. He had only seen lighting in parts of London before and was impressed how the city had developed over the last ten years. He soon reached the gates of the College, but they were now firmly closed. There was a door within the gate, upon which he knocked, and a porthole within the door opened to reveal a squirmy face and lots of whiskers.

"What is your business?" challenged the face.

"My name is Captain Cleall and I am dining with Sir Henry this evening," the captain responded, with authority.

Just then a carriage pulled up at the gate. It was no normal carriage but one of style, rarely seen outside London. It was drawn by two black horses and had a driver and footman up front. The lantern above the gate provided enough light to see that the carriage doors were adorned with a coat of arms and that the vehicle had some very elaborate décor and detailing. The footman jumped down and joined the captain at the door.

"Lord and Lady Bankes to see Sir Henry Catchpole."

The face behind the door coughed and spluttered to get his words out and before he could, he let the porthole close and began to open the gate. The captain waited for the wheels of the carriage to trundle through, allowing him to catch a glimpse of the man and woman inside — an aristocratic couple in fine dress. The gatekeeper grunted that he should follow the carriage and the captain wondered what sort of night his friend had set him up for. He had a clean pair of breeches, shirt and jacket; clothes he had brought with him for when he was to see Lady Coke. He had polished his boots, but he felt quite puritanical in comparison to the haughty dress of his apparent fellow guests.

The carriage had drawn up at the far end of the quadrangle. The captain consciously slowed to allow his fellow guests time to be received by the servant, who escorted them into the College building. The night sky above him was clear with only the last fragment of a moon to provide light. The scent of the courtyard grass and clean freshness of the river mingled on the light breeze. The captain arrived at the steps to hear the servant within announce his guests, and a few seconds later, he returned.

"Good evening, sir," the servant said and bowed his head as he did so. He was dressed in better attire than the captain, making him feel even more self-conscious. The man was not in the livery of the normal servants but in a plain black suit and white shirt with a small, discreet frill around the collar. He was obviously the butler, or the College equivalent.

"Good evening. Captain Cleall for Sir Henry Catchpole."

"Of course, sir. Please follow me." The man led the captain up the stairs, into the College, and turned into an impressive, ornate room on the left. He stepped aside to allow his new guest to enter and announced the captain.

It was a magnificent reception room with high, carved ceilings and dark oak-panelled walls, a large silk crimson tapestry hanging from the far wall. The fire place was the focal point in the room, made from large Cotswold stone blocks that were ornately carved to justify its status, a blazing fire within, the heat from which was reaching out to the captain. He cast an eye over the guests who had already arrived, gathered in small groups across the room, nine in total, all of whom glanced around at the captain as they conversed. Contrasting with the men's black and grey doublets, three women sported opulent and brightly coloured dresses of silks and velvets of a variety of hues — a deep red, an emerald green and a golden yellow. The low-cut dresses were complemented with jewels that shimmered in the dancing light shining from the candles on the wall sconces around the room. The lace and frill of the gents' shirts showed that they were a match for the female finery, and two of the menfolk, one of whom the captain instantly recognised as his friend Sir Henry Catchpole, had academic gowns over their doublets. Sir Henry stepped towards him, smiling warmly.

"Ah, Cleall — you made it. Let me introduce you to everybody," he said, patting the captain's back. He guided the captain by his arm, firstly towards the two guests whom he recognised from the carriage that preceded him.

"Let me introduce you first to Lord and Lady Bankes, who are frequent visitors to Oxford but reside in London. Lord Bankes has just been made attorney general to the king so we must all be well behaved tonight. Captain Cleall is a good friend of mine, but I have not seen him for many years and to my delight, I just bumped into him in the city this afternoon."

The captain dipped his head in greeting, and the two guests nodded in response as they traded pleasantries. Lord Bankes was a man Cleall guessed was a little older than himself, perhaps early forties, and of equal height. He was dressed in an elaborate embroidered doublet, but with a modest-collared shirt beneath. His face, with its high cheekbones and thin lips, set a courteous but slightly disinterested expression. The captain detected a man of importance, but a man who had other things on his mind than being entertained by an academic. In contrast, Lady Bankes' demeanour was far more engaging. Her radiant smile, with full lips and soft, blue, almond-shaped eyes instantly made the captain feel more comfortable. She must have been at least ten years younger than her husband — late twenties or early thirties — with pale skin. She was dressed in a very becoming emerald green, with pearls dangling above her cleavage, and with strawberry-blonde locks of curls dangling down either side of her face.

"It is an honour to meet you both," the captain said, before Sir Henry took him on to his next introduction to two men and a woman in red standing by the window. The guests were soon revealed as Visconte and Viscontessa de Medicini from Florence, and a student, who could only have been seventeen or eighteen, by the name of Robert Boyle. The Visconte, apparently, was the younger brother of the powerful Grand

Duke, whose reputation was well known to the captain. He was a handsome gentleman, in his late forties or early fifties, with a head of curly, silver hair, neatly trimmed with a beard to match. He spoke perfect English and had apparently studied in the city. His much younger wife was clearly less conversant, but her dark features and beaming smile spoke for her. Sir Henry informed the captain that Robert Boyle was visiting the College from his school at Eton and had been invited to dinner in recognition of exemplary academic achievement at his school, whispering to Cleall that they were hoping he would continue his studies in Oxford. Boyle looked nervous but managed a polite greeting to the captain.

The final threesome of introductions incorporated John Hampden, a man dressed in the Puritan style with modest white collar with the merest hint of lace and plain black tunic that dropped to his knees, but of a quality of fabric that confirmed he was a man of status. He lived south of Oxford and had been the parliamentary representative for Wendover, when it was last sitting. He was with Sir Henry's wife, Elizabeth, whom Captain Cleall knew well and was pleased to see again, and one of the Masters of the College, William Adams, a Scot from Edinburgh.

The captain was given a glass of claret by one of the waiters and entered into conversation with Sir Henry about how remarkable the College looked. He was offered a tour if he could spare the time. He explained to his old friend the purpose of his journey and the death of Sir Edward, before a bell sounded and the butler announced dinner. The guests were led into an adjoining room, much smaller but with another roaring fire and a table set for dinner with white cloth, candles, china and silver cutlery, a setting of such luxury that it said as much about the status of the College as anything the guest had so far observed. A portrait of the late King James hung on the wall opposite the fire, and even he would have been comfortable in this stylish room with its modern décor. The invitees were individually escorted to their pre-arranged places, a process which separated the couples and meant that the captain found himself seated between Lady Bankes and the student, Robert Boyle. As the rest of the guests were finding their seats, it was the young Mr Boyle who started the conversation between the three of them.

"Pray sir, are you a naval or army captain?" he asked, disclosing a slight Irish accent.

"Cavalry. Never been one for water."

"And have you seen much action, sir?" the youngster enquired.

"Enough. I have fought the Spanish and the French, and the Habsburgs, but prefer hunting stag and boar now."

Overhearing the response, Sir Henry butted in.

"Our Captain here is oh-so-modest. This country owes him so much and he would have been made a colonel by now were it not for his ability to speak his mind. James, tell Master Boyle the truth behind La Rochelle."

The captain looked slightly awkward and side-stepped the challenge.

"I am sure Lady Bankes would not want to discuss such unpleasantries at the start of what promises to be such a wonderful dinner, Sir Henry." As he spoke, two waiters came in armed with their first course of a green soup. "Do you have ambitions to serve in the army, Master Boyle?"

"Alas, sir, my interests are not in the battles of men but in studies of the heavens — the stars and the physics of how planet earth was formed. The works of Galileo inspire me."

"Why, God made the earth. Surely that is simple, is it not? And which part of this planet do you come from Master Boyle. I detect an accent," Lady Bankes asked.

"Ireland, my Lady. County Waterford in the south east of the isle."

"I have always been fascinated, when I travel, that the dialect and words themselves change so much across our nation. In London, a 'codder' is a person who makes saddles whilst in Lincoln it means a person who picks peas. Who is right? And have people been wronged or confused by these differences? Would it not be a good idea to write all the words down and define them so people would know the different meanings?" Lady Bankes continued.

"Why, what a splendid idea," replied the student. "Like a bible of written meaning covering all of England. One version of the truth, bringing some scientific discipline to language. I love the concept, your Lady. I think you may have something there. I believe language reflects the diversity of our nation. London is so vibrant: a melting pot of cultures, trades and classes. It is fast and furious and people in the streets speak the same way. Even within London, around the quays of Southwark, a much harsher dialect is spoken. In Waterford, where one finds such peace and tranquillity, and nature blossoms with such variety and beauty, no wonder the dialect and words are softer and I would say more wholesome. Whereas here, in Oxford, nestled between the Chilterns and the Cotswolds, people speak in a much more considered and thoughtful way."

Master Boyle's passion and enthusiasm was infectious.

"You are so right, Master Boyle, and Captain, you must have encountered many different strange words and dialects in your travels." Lady Bankes directed the conversation between them with natural charm, as if she were the hostess.

The captain nodded. "Indeed, I have, and your observations are correct, my Lady. One reason why the army is organised in regiments from different parts of the country is so the soldiers can understand each other. I have, indeed, travelled around Europe, in France and down the Rhine, but the battles detracted from the beauty of those places. There are certainly many places that are close to my heart, and that includes the people, their dialects, the food and the customs, as well as the landscape. One of them is where I am fortunate enough to be residing at present: Corffe Castell in Dorsetshire. It is wild with natural beauty, where you can ride high along rugged cliffs above the waves crashing into rocks below, or splashing along sandy shorelines. Do you know Dorsetshire, my Lady?"

"I have heard about the beauty of the shire, but I have never had the opportunity to visit. I have often suggested to my husband that we should have a place close to the sea, where the children can benefit from the healthy air. Our main residence is just north of London and I am sure it is not as healthy. Please, Captain, tell me about your Castell. It sounds so wonderful."

"Alas, it is not mine, but that of my late friend Sir Edward Coke. It is a wonderful Castell built on a hill in a gap in a chalk barrow. It provides splendid views to a beautiful harbour, with islands and sandy beaches to the east, and to the west is a limestone escarpment leading down to sheer cliffs and the sea, which can be as gentle as a mill pond one day and hell's fury the next. The countryside between is rich and plentiful, providing delightful fresh food as well as a great hunting and riding terrain. It is an idyllic place."

"It truly does sound sublime," Lady Bankes commended and was about to continue, when Sir Henry interrupted.

"Did I hear you mention Sir Edward, Captain? May I propose a toast to the late Sir Edward Coke?"

"I would second that. I worked closely with Sir Edward in developing the Bill of Rights, which I believe is testimony to the progressive outlook of this country," John Hampden added.

The proposal was greeted by several mumbles of acknowledgement and the party in unison took their glasses and toasted "Sir Edward."

As Cleall drank from his glass, he reflected on how much he enjoyed Lady Bankes' character. Most women were timid and would barely have an opinion on anything other than the weather. But Lady Bankes was the opposite and Cleall found it very refreshing and thought Sir John a very lucky man. He, in contrast, seemed to be a very thoughtful man, with few words. Indeed, as Cleall watched him, Sir John seemed to be deep in thought on which potato to eat next, and was indeed a slow diner, as the rest of the guests had finished. But with Mary as his wife, perhaps there was more time and opportunity for contemplation, Cleall thought, with a smile to himself.

John Hampden broke the brief pause for reflection after the guests had taken their wine.

"I fear Sir Edward will be a major loss in keeping our sovereign on the right path. He has dissolved parliament now for six years, and there are very few people who truly reflect the views of the British people and have the ear of the king." He paused, remembering the king's attorney general was in the room, and added, "With the exception of present company. And now he is starting to raise taxes without Parliamentary approval, which goes against the Bill of Rights that this country celebrated with all the church bells across the land tolling."

Cleall hoped this interjection would not ruin an enjoyable evening. From his experience, religion and politics were definitely subjects to avoid in groups of this size and, indeed, diversity. His fears seemed to be justified when Lord Bankes responded by challenging Hampden.

"The king needs to raise taxes to protect this country and its ships from foreign forces and piracy, Mr Hampden. But sir, what is the right path that our King should take, in your view?"

"Well, he certainly should be listening more to Parliament and the representatives of his country, rather than his Catholic Queen. We watch on the sidelines as Protestant states battle it out with France and Spain and the personal rule of the king keeps us at bay from where our obvious interests lie. We should also be supporting the broader Protestant faith in this country and support the energy behind the Puritans. The energy and enlightenment of this movement has the potential to make this country great. It is a movement that transports us beyond the Catholic and Protestant wars of the past and is a force for good for the working classes, as it educates and disciplines, creating a strong work ethos for the glory of God."

Cleall's fears were coming to fruition as smiles dried up and eyes diverted to china plates, sensing the impact of Hampden's inconsiderate and confrontational statement on the guests around the table. But that did not stop the Puritan, as he continued.

"The Sovereign's narrow, high-Anglican view is alienating the Puritans, and his recent appointment of the new Archbishop of Canterbury will inflame matters further. I fear that English Protestantism is being segregated and weakened for the benefit of Catholicism, but more importantly, humanity."

Sensing the tension, and worried about the direction the conversation was taking, Sir Henry intervened.

"In Oxford, and especially Pembroke College, we believe that strength is created by developing understanding of different cultures and religions, current and historical, and through this understanding we can create a better world. Too many lives have been lost already in the name of Christ. Why, Visconte and Viscontessa de Medicini are here precisely in that cause."

The Visconte was still taken aback by Hampden's diatribe, but saw the opportunity to develop the discussion in a more considerate way, as Sir Henry was clearly intending.

"Thank you, Sir Henry, and I commend this College and city on its investment in academic institutions which share much in common with those of my own in Florence. I travelled many weeks on a Genoese boat to London, with the Viscontessa, with the aim of coming to Oxford to enjoy the free debate within these buildings. Why, you ask? There are two answers. Firstly, a boat is safer than crossing Europe where Catholics and Protestants are at each other's throats. But I still wanted to make this journey and this is the reason. I am, of course, from the country where the Pope resides and indeed, I am a Catholic. But I fear that popes, kings, princes, Catholics and Protestants are more focused on their differences than their similarities. Why? In not all cases — but many, I fear — the answer is greed and personal ambition. This is not the teaching of Christ in any denomination but it is played out every day across Europe. In my travels I see many un-Christian acts in the name of Christ, and many hypocrisies. I have been to Spain and witnessed inquisitors finding any excuse to question and torture honest, hard-working and Godly people. In France, there are many similar stories and of course the Huguenots have been massacred in towns like Toulouse and Cissy. To what end, I ask? It is certainly not the promotion of Christian Catholic values, for what goes on behind the closed window shutters of southern Europe is a far cry from that preached at the pulpits. Calvin sought to make Geneva not only a Protestant enclave, but of social righteousness and commercial morality, which I can applaud."

"It sounds as though you want to become a Puritan," Hampden interrupted, with a scathing tone, eyebrows raised.

"Please, let me finish. I do believe there is less hypocrisy in Geneva, Amsterdam and Oxford, and fewer shutters to hide what does exist. But even this doctrine of openness and righteousness has been taken too far. I can only commend promoting virtues over vices, but when militant doctrinal virtues start to battle against everyday virtue, this is not good. I have been to Geneva, Amsterdam and London, and witnessed Catholic suppression. This is intolerant and un-Christian, Mr Hampden." The Italian was looking straight at the Puritan with all the authority of his position. "But I now see Puritans in these Protestant places denouncing many of the pleasures in life — the theatre and playhouse, even meeting and eating with friends, such as we are tonight. Such extreme is hardly distinguishable from the worst practices of orthodox Catholics of Spain, France or Italy."

"The playhouses celebrate the failings of men's character, as well as attracting drunkenness and other vices," the Puritan butted in again.

"But sir, did not Christ himself teach us righteousness through parables and stories? Did he not attend wedding celebrations and provide wine for the guests?" The Visconte banged the table. "I have seen plays by Shakespeare and Marlowe when I studied here. There is no harm in them but much can be learnt. I must say your comments are reinforcing my views. It would seem the more extreme the denomination, the less the distinctives but the more powerful the venom of the rhetoric that is preached. When I come to places like Oxford, I am welcomed by Sir Henry and meet fine ladies and gentlemen such as those around this table, and I enter into constructive conversation, and discuss both academic, theological and even political topics of mutual interest. If we had more travelling, talking and understanding in Europe, it would be a better place; a more Christian place."

Behind his neatly trimmed beard, Hampden's face was reddening, burning with rage, and the guests held their breath ready for his retort, but it was Lady Bankes who broke the tension from the other end of the table, surprising everybody.

"Bravo. Well said, Signore," she said.

This was no ordinary lady, Captain Cleall thought, as she continued.

"I would also like to add that the popes, kings and princes are all men, and I am sure the Viscontessa will agree that a little more maternal feministic influence would also help to make Europe a better place," continued Lady Bankes. "As Mr Hampden will know, it was Queen Beth who created more tolerance in England and stopped the burning of so-called heretics. Not being married meant she was not influenced by the political fights for power amongst the male nobility at the start of her reign. Furthermore, Mr Hampden, I would like to suggest that, in recent years, our Queen has been a calming influence on the king. We are no longer embarking on foolhardy missions like we did at La Rochelle, under the influence of the Duke of Buckingham. Surely good can come from a strong Catholic queen married to a Protestant king as a model of tolerance for us all?"

"As a man who fought at La Rochelle, I entirely agree with you on that one, my Lady," Captain Cleall interjected, eager to support her mission to calm the situation before Hampden could muster a response. Lady Bankes acknowledged his comment with a warm smile.

But Hampden's fury was still bubbling and he rose from his chair.

"Sir Henry, I fear you have invited me to dine with overt and closet Catholics and—"

"Sir, let me respond to your original challenge on behalf of the king, before you make a fool of yourself," Sir John Bankes commanded.

Hampden stood speechless, trying to swallow his fury. Sir Henry's wife placed a hand on his am, which seemed to quell some of his rage, and he sat back down as the guests turned to Sir John in expectation. He spoke very slowly and calmly, in contrast to the recent outbursts.

"I recognise much of what has been said tonight. I do have the ear of the king, but he is also his own man. He believes strongly in the divine right to rule. I also believe that God chose Charles, our King, to rule over us, but I do believe the style of reign should be more consensual and Parliament provides the king with the means to do this, as you correctly stated, Mr Hampden. I do hope I can use my influence to heal the divide between King and Parliament and also that, collectively, we can build a nation that is more inclusive and understanding, as the Visconte and my dear wife suggest. Why, in this very city, the Oxford Martyrs were tried for heresy and burnt at the stake by Queen Mary. Bishop Hugh Latimer, Bishop Nicholas Ridley and the Archbishop of Canterbury Thomas Cranmer were amongst them. Their fate and those of many others are shared amongst us all in the Book of Martyrs, which can be found in churches up and down the country. This book has created a strong anti-Catholic sentiment within this nation. It is my view that we must remember the martyrs not as Protestants but Christians, and as a reminder of the bad things that can be done in the name of religion."

The audience around the table was listening intently. Sir John was clearly a man of knowledge and position and this was as close to hearing the king himself as one could get outside the court.

He continued. "We must recognise that we are going through a revolution with the printed word, which — like all change — has good and bad influences on our lives. In the old days, our people blindly followed monarchs and priests for they did not have access to their own knowledge. But now the word of God is printed in bibles and available for more and more to read for themselves. I strongly believe this is a great thing, as it is encouraging people to learn and develop and think for themselves. But I see the risks. There are people who are taking sections of the bible and re-printing them out of context to spread their own version of God's word, and even printing false news stories about the queen and or king to the same aim. The cartoons and images that accompany the printed news are targeted at even those who cannot read. This is truly heretical and false witness to the word of God and truth itself. We must recognise the risks of this and stamp down on it, for it could undermine our whole society and could lead to very bad ends.

"We must learn how to live together as one nation that can embrace different views and faiths — Protestants, Puritans, Catholics, Presbyterian, and Jews — and use the written word to promote tolerance and the true word of God. There are many ways to truth, as the Visconte and Mr Hampden have shown. But this is easy to say and much harder to accept, given the bloodshed of the Tudor times on all sides and the lies that seem to be spread far and wide before the truth gets to the printing press. Given this, I fear we are becoming more segregated and not less, with divides between Protestants and Puritans, let alone Catholics and Jews."

"Well said, and let's toast to tolerance," Sir Henry replied, and all the guests raised their glasses, including Hampden as he mastered his anger.

As the guests lowered their glasses, Captain Cleall joined the conversation once again.

"On the battlefield, in the moments just before the battle commences, when fear swells the minds of even the hardiest of veterans, there are few men who are not praying to God and few times when God is needed more. That is when faith is stripped of all distinctions, and few could tell men apart on grounds of religion. But to get men to the battlefield in the first place, and certainly to fight with passion, they must have belief not only in their God, but their king and country. For me, sadly, the latter is lacking. I am not sure what my country stands for, and I am certainly dispirited by my king when he surrounds himself with advisors like Buckingham in the past, clearly with the notable exception of present company."

He raised his glass to Lord Bankes, who responded.

"Thank you, Captain. Indeed, I must be honest with you all, for I also fear for these islands of nations. The captain is right: it is not as straightforward as I just set out. I was speaking with my heart and not my head, and this head has lost much sleep knowing that I am an advisor to the king. I pray every day that I have the ability to advise him on the right course but I see only rough seas, rocks and sandbanks ahead. The king is his own man and I will not comment on his character, for God chose him to be our sovereign, not I. I will, however, paint a picture of the complexity of the situation that vexes me. We have discussed the religious tensions that face these nations and the rest of Europe, but these are also mixed up with politics. And the combination of politics and religion is as volatile as gunpowder, and in both matters, people seem to flock behind dogma like sheep and with a similar level of intellect and blindness to consequence."

The waiters collected dishes and served fruit and cheese in the background, adding a log to the fire which crackled in appreciation. The attorney general spoke softly but in a precise manner and style which held the full attention of the table, as he continued.

"Let me explain for the benefit of my Italian friends, Visconte and Viscontessa de Medicini. There are four forces at play — the union, the monarchy, religion, and the English Parliament. Firstly, the union. The king's father, James, was the first king of England, Scotland, Ireland and Wales: a union. Easy to say, but having a shared king and a new flag does not create a union of nations. Nations need to be built and people need to believe in a shared destiny, culture, belief and values, whilst reconciling histories full of bloodshed, discrimination and hardship. In my view, this process has barely started. But the starting point must be to gain a better understanding through conversation. I overheard Master Boyle talking about the power of the written word, and I applaud this — I think you spoke about developing a book that would define the meaning of words. A wonderful idea. Sir Henry, please ensure the College champions this aim for the benefit of humanity and collective understanding."

"Thank you, sir," Master Boyle graciously responded, while Sir Henry nodded.

"Yes, a common language and meaning of words will break down barriers and build unity. We have different languages in Scotland, Wales and Ireland, as well as a multitude of dialects. I see many issues in Ireland and Scotland and given that it was not too long ago that the English executed the last Queen of Scots — Mary, the king's grandmother — there is much to be done. We must help to heal the wounds of the past and build a future together. Which brings me to the second factor: the monarchy. Our King believes in his divine right to rule and sees his position as Head of the Anglican Church as almost one and the same. He exercises as much power as the head of the church through the bishops as he does as monarch. Yet Scotland is a nation of Presbyterians, and Ireland of Catholics, neither of whom recognises the king's role as a spiritual leader. The Scots have all signed a covenant — a document that states that they have a direct line to God and need neither a head of the Anglican Church nor pope as a route to the divine. Indeed, the king's father, as James VI of Scotland, signed this covenant. This infuriates the king. The Irish, clearly look to Rome for leadership with as much passion as the Visconte and Viscontessa, but are part of the union. The king and his father's response to that has been to encourage the settlement of Protestants in Ireland, the long-term repercussions of which I fear, unless there is a strong drive to build understanding between these two sides."

Cleall was in awe of how Sir John had defused the situation, involving all around the table, and breaking down the issues one by one. No wonder he was an advisor to the king and hopefully the monarch was listening as attentively as his audience around the table.

"Finally, we get to England and Parliament. How is Parliament viewed in Scotland, Mr Adams?"

"Why, it has no relevance for Scotland as the Scots have no representation," William Adams replied. "The clans have their own parliament, sir."

"Ah, the clans. That is another level of complexity of which, as an Englishmen, I have little understanding, but sadly nor does the king, despite being born in Scotland. But Mr Adams is correct, as Westminster is just a parliament for the English and Welsh, not the other nations. Mr

Hampden has rightly pointed out that Parliament is essential for the king: without it, he cannot raise taxes ever since the Magna Carta, and most of the taxes are paid by the wealthy gentry, who are represented in this Parliament. It has not sat for many years and the pent-up feeling of frustration, and even anger with the king, over their lack of voice, is all too apparent to me. These four pillars — the union, the monarchy, the religion and the English Parliament are all connected and I fear are all fuelling a breakdown, rather than the unity we all wish for in our nations. I do not know where this will lead and I wish I had the wisdom to know how to counsel the king on how to act for the best. To be honest with you all, I feel as though I am sitting on the seat of a runaway carriage approaching a cliff's edge, with no control of the four wheels."

The long, insightful speech was met with reflective silence. The guests could sense Sir John Bankes' heartfelt exasperation and Sir Henry sensed it was time to bring this particular conversation to an end. He suggested that the guests all retire to the anteroom for a brandy.

As the guests took their leave, Cleall found himself with Sir John Bankes and Sir Henry Catchpole.

"It was getting a little tense in there, was it not?" Sir Henry acknowledged.

"But I think you both managed to steer a course through it, in the end," the captain confirmed. "What you said, Sir John, made a lot of sense. You also have a wonderful wife," he offered.

Sir John bowed his head in acknowledgement. Lady Bankes was engaged at the other end of the room, persuading the Visconte of the merits of hosting the young Master Boyle in Florence, where Galileo was still living.

"And when are you going to find yourself a wife? No eligible young fillies in Dorsetshire that take your fancy?" enquired Sir Henry.

"Plenty of hunting of the other type keeps me busy. And I am not sure I have given up my fighting days yet. I just need something, or someone, to fight for. Until I have definitely decided to hang up my sword, I will not settle down and afford the distraction of a wife," the captain responded.

The conversation continued around the growth of Oxford as a city, and the current building projects, as well as the king's works in

Whitehall, before the captain declared that he needed to retire as he had a long ride the following day. He said goodbye to his host and fellow guests, and enjoyed a reflective walk back through the city to the tavern. He had enjoyed the evening, mainly the conversation with Lady Bankes and seeing his old friend Sir Henry again, clearly enjoying his life and his status in the new College. He wondered if William Harvey and Ralph Povington had such an interesting night. He would have to wait until the morning to find out, for both were snoring away. Whether they were sleeping off their travel aches and pains, or had consumed too much beer was impossible to tell.

Chapter III
The Funeral

The next morning brought with it a day of incessant drizzle. All three travellers would have preferred a few more hours in bed or better still, avoid the journey altogether. But it was the captain who ensured that they were up and leaving the city shortly after daybreak, and were the first to go through the East Gate after the guard unlocked the great oak doors. They were heading east to Bedford, the longest leg in their journey. An onion pie, bread, cheese small flat cakes and flasks of ale accompanied the travellers, but it would be a few hours before the captain would allow them time to have a break for this sustenance. Before then, there were only the remnants of last night's meal and alcohol in their stomachs to keep them going.

The road meandered across the Cherwell valley and into Bedfordshire through open countryside and then into woodland. Povington led the way, with Tom Harvey bringing up the rear. A sharp wind accompanied them, whilst the rain was malevolent as they passed through some woodland, where the leaves were already starting to turn into their autumn colours. Ahead, a figure seemed to be staggering towards them along the road. As they approached, it appeared to be a beggar stooped over his staff, with ragged clothing, head bowed beneath a hood, facing down to the puddles surrounding him. As Povington's horse approached at a walking pace, a hand was raised and a shrill voice cried, "Alms for the poor…" But as Povington's horse drew level, the beggar's head was thrown back and the man stood up straight, grabbing the rein, and out of nowhere a knife was drawn, raised and pointed at Povington's chest, who let out a shriek as the man shouted, "Hand over your purses or this man gets it!"

What happened next was most probably a moment that would be replayed in all the participants' minds for many years to come. Cries came from both sides of the pathway, as two men — one from each side, similarly dressed to the man with the knife, but carrying an assortment of pikes and clubs — came shouting from the undergrowth. But no sooner had they started their assault, than they were stopped in their tracks by an almighty scream, the terror of which would go through any man. The captain, in one seamless manoeuvre, had drawn alongside Povington, his sword having been unsheathed under his cloak as soon as he spotted the man ahead, but was now raised and came down in a single action to cut through the outlaw's knife-bearing hand. It was this man, whose assertiveness had evaporated and was now shrieking in pain. The knife was dropped, and his other hand grabbed his cut hand as blood was already pooling in the soaked ground. By now, the captain had turned and was facing the two nearest bandits who had stopped in their tracks. His destrier reared up and kicked both front legs towards the two men, one of whom stumbled and the other quickly turned and sped back into the wood. His colleague gathered his footing, and followed suit, alongside their blood-covered leader, who was still screaming and holding his hand.

Povington, visibly shaken by the incident, just wanted to be back behind the secure ramparts of the Castell, where the biggest crisis would be an over-cooked duck. Those outlaws could have killed him today, and his cloak was sprayed with blood but for once, he could not muster any words.

"I suggest we get the hell out of here before they return with greater numbers," said the captain. With that, he lashed Povington's horse with the flat-side blade of his sword. The horse reared momentarily and then galloped away, followed by the captain and William Harvey. Only when they had made enough ground did the captain allow them to drop their pace to a trot, and it was an hour before he let the horses rest by a stream, by which time the drizzle had abated. The captain suggested that they drink and eat as it would steady their nerve, but Povington could not be persuaded to have more than a few gulps of water.

"Who were those men?" he finally managed to ask.

"Outlaws. I am surprised we have not come across others along the way. That is why we must stay tightly together along these wooded roads," the captain responded.

The travellers set out on their way with more purpose, but the journey gave them plenty of time to worry, both about their immediate safety as well as the longer-term wellbeing of Corffe, following Coke's death. They had a long way to go to make it to Bedford before sunset, and they certainly were more wary of the open road now. Povington had stopped complaining about his saddle soreness and the aches in his joints. The horses soon took them into open countryside and through fields stripped of their harvest, but with workers still packing bales of hay onto carts ready for the forthcoming winter. The hard ride continued through the afternoon, but it was softened by a blue sky with the sun popping out from behind a constant stream of fluffy, white clouds. By the time the captain could see the spire of St Paul's church in Bedford ahead, the sun was low behind them and long shadows galloped before them.

The town was nestled in the wide vale created by the River Ouse, which meandered around the settlement. A variety of boats had journeyed up the river and were tied up to a wharf at the entrance to the town. It was clearly not as large as Winchester or Oxford, and nor could it boast the architectural splendour of those two cities. As the three riders entered the town, other than the church, the only other building of note was a ruin of a Castell, which had clearly been ransacked by the locals as the very same stone had been used in the walls and foundations of the predominantly timber buildings that lined the streets. The town appeared vibrant, with many people still going about their trade, and a market in front of the church where traders were now busy packing up their wares.

The captain spotted a tavern on the far side of the square, with a big red lion sign above its door, denoting the name of the hostelry. They dismounted and Povington gave a penny to a teenage boy to stable the horses for the night. Seeing the boy, William Harvey thought of his family back at home, the stable boy being about the same age as Tom. He was already looking forward to the day when they would turn west and head back to Dorsetshire. He was happy managing the estate, seeing people and countryside he knew.

The travellers deposited their bags in a room upstairs at the directions of the lady of the tavern. She was a woman who appeared equally proportioned in all dimensions — width, depth and height — clad in a large soiled apron, but she was full of life and spirit, laughing and joking with the men. She suggested they might want to eat outside, at the back, as the tavern overlooked the river, where there was a collection of wooden chairs, benches and barrels for that very purpose. The three were tired but having ridden all day, they stood around a barrel, drinking ale from the wooden mugs the landlady had brought out to them.

A young boy was sitting on an upturned pail a few yards from the men, watching the river. He was no more than seven or eight, with long, curly blond hair and black tunic, denoting a family of the Puritan set. William walked over to him and asked what he was doing.

"I am waiting for my father. He is a tinker from Elstow and will be returning shortly before we go home."

"Is it far, your home?" William asked.

"Why no, just a mile away. I thought everybody knew where Elstow was," the boy replied. The other two joined the conversation.

"Can you see fish in the river?" Povington asked the boy.

"I can see many things in this river but not fish. I can see my reflection. My father says one should look at one's reflection, not for vanity but to see yourself in God's eyes and ask yourself is this a good person that you see. I also see the water flowing in the river on a journey for God's purpose. This reminds me of what my father says: I need to find God's purpose for me in my life."

All three men looked at each other in turn. This was a boy of some maturity for his age, holding a conversation with three strangers and talking with such authority. The boy picked up a stone and threw it into the river.

"Look! Look at the ripples the stone creates. One stone can create that. I pray that I can be that stone and that God will guide me to make a good splash on the world, and the ripples will benefit many."

William asked, "What is your name, boy?"

"I am John, son of Daniel Bunyan. John Bunyan."

"You speak wisely for somebody so young and have learnt well from your father. What purpose do you think God has for one so bright?" the captain asked

The boy grabbed another stone and threw it into the water. "That is the problem. I do not know yet. I am sure it will be revealed to me in some way. I sense it will be to follow this river but I have no idea where it will take me, nor what God's purpose for me will be when I get there."

"We have been travelling all the way from the sea on the southern coast. We have been through Winchester and Oxford."

"I have heard of these places. Winchester is the ancient capital of England and from where Alfred the Great beat and converted the pagan Danes into Christians. There is a great cathedral there, where many kings and queens have been married. I would like to visit this city. What is it like?"

"Ah, it bustles with traders, and people from many backgrounds, rich and poor, like many cities and towns. But it does have a magnificent cathedral, as you say: a true glory to God. I am sure you would like it," the captain responded.

"And Canterbury — have you been there? I will go one day and of that I am certain," the boy added.

"No. I do not believe any of us have had the pleasure of visiting Saint Thomas Beckett's city. But I am sure you will," the captain replied.

Just then a man arrived, dressed in a long, black cloak and with grey, curly hair. The boy was clearly a chip off this block: there was no mistaking his father.

"Good evening to you, sir: Captain Cleall, Ralph Povington and William Harvey at your service. Your son has been keeping us entertained and is clearly a witness to your good character," Captain Cleall greeted the man.

"Why, thank you, sir. I hope he has not been too much trouble. Come on, John, we must make haste. I bid you all a good evening," the tinker said. The boy jumped up and reached out for his father's hand before they both headed back to the town square.

"We will see you one day in Canterbury, Master John," Captain Cleall shouted out. The boy looked back and gave him a wave. "If a boy so young can have such clarity of mind, it vexes me that the whole of Europe is fighting each other over things that to me matter so little."

He thought to himself that the boy would have made a good contribution to the conversation the night before in Oxford. Just then, the landlady returned with three wooden dishes of rabbit stew. The travellers sat down and ate the offering heartily, discussing the relative merits of Oxford and Winchester.

The next day brought a magical autumnal morning, with a golden sun peering over the horizon and transforming the strata of cloud into pinks, violets and smoky greys against a bright eastern sky. Pockets of mist settled in the vales and hollows as they journeyed through a still landscape, where birds were starting to chatter and a last screech of an owl could be heard. The landscape flattened and became easier-going as they migrated into East Anglia. There were still workers in many of the fields, tidying up after the gathering of the last few weeks. Others were herding cattle, or minding sheep. The everyday life of England continued, people focused on the basic needs of life, preparing for whatever the winter would send them. Captain Cleall reflected that the religious wars of Europe and the four wheels of Sir John Bankes' out-of-control cart seemed to have no meaning in this setting. In the everyday, life was very simple for many folk and mainly focused on growing and gathering enough food to live and enjoy the splendour of God's world.

The journey to their final destination passed without incident, and by late afternoon they arrived in Godwick in Norfolkshire. It was the relatively modest home of Sir John and Lady Coke, a manor house in a small hamlet. They had far grander residences across the country, many occupied by their children, and of course, Corffe Castell. But in the last few years they preferred to enjoy the tranquillity of this brick-built house in the countryside. The travellers were shown into a drawing room, with large windows overlooking the fields, and adorned with portraits of many of the Coke family. Lady Coke was sitting in a chair by the fire, wearing a black dress, with the smallest of white lace trim around her neck and cuffs, matching her white hair. She looked up and smiled to see and greet her visitors. Captain Cleall approached her and kissed her hand.

"Captain — thank you for coming and it is so good to see you. And you both, Mr Harvey and Mr Povington. You must be tired from your journey." She turned to the house servant who had shown then in. "Smithson — fetch us some tea, please."

"We were deeply saddened to hear the unwelcome news of the loss of your husband, my Lady. Indeed, we bring condolences from the whole of Corffe."

"James, I thank you. But I can only be grateful for the life he lived, and right to the end. He was eighty-two and died with an active mind and body. He was truly content with the life he had led: what more could a wife desire for her husband? My husband's body is still in state and you are welcome to pay your respects."

"Elizabeth, you know the respect I had for Sir Edward. He was an inspiration for me; for us all. This country is a lesser place for his departure and his legacy can only live on. But how can we help you and support you at this time?" the captain replied.

"Thank you, James. The funeral is planned for two days from now and please be my guest until then. We need to discuss the future of Corffe while you are here, but not today. You must refresh from your journey and all three of you join me for dinner tonight. Harry and Charlotte are here. My other children will be returning over the next two days but have been a great comfort since Edward's departure. I have also received so many letters of condolence, from the king and Queen, and from nobles and Parliamentarians across the land. But I would like his funeral to be a more intimate affair, for the family, and in that I include our friends and household of Corffe. I have many good memories of Corffe — the Castell, the views, the air, the sea, the village and all the community. I inherited it from my father, Sir Christopher Hatton, who was Queen Elizabeth's Lord Chancellor. My father cherished it, and Sir John and myself enjoyed so much of our live together there. I am saddened that Edward and I have not been able to visit for so long, but in the last few years, fragility of body overcame our will. We reminisced so much over the last few years about our time in Dorsetshire. I know I will never be able to return and I am deeply sorrowful about that. But I know my husband awaits me in the afterlife and — God be willing — that is to a place called heaven. I thank God that our life on earth has granted us the pleasure of living in Corffe."

"Elizabeth, we thank you for your kindness and your gracious words," the captain replied.

"Yes, my Lady," Povington and Harvey said together.

At that moment, Smithson returned with the tea. The travellers sat themselves down and they were all served with tea in china cups. Ralph was feeling as though he were back in Corffe; at last some civility and refinement. In contrast, Will Harvey was struggling with the concept of a cup and saucer but was desperate to make a good impression. Lady Coke enquired about news from Corffe. Will reported that the harvest was all in and it had been a good one. Ralph informed her about some plans he had for the garden terrace within the Castell, and the captain told her about the memorial service for her husband. Smithson then showed the visitors to their rooms and they each prepared for dinner in their own way — Ralph enjoying a bath-tub wash, Will going for a walk around the grounds, and the captain cleaning and sharpening his blade, as well as ensuring the horses were being well stabled.

Dinner was at seven. The travellers arrived in the best clothes they could muster, whilst Lady Coke retained her mourning dress. Harry, the eldest of the Coke's children, and Charlotte, one of the daughters, joined them. Harry was very unlike his father, in his mid-forties and overweight. He was dressed very flamboyantly and it was clear to everybody from the rose tint of his cheeks that he had already indulged in a few pre-dinner brandies. He was also loud and condescending. Sir Edward had confessed his disappointment in his son to Captain Cleall on a number of occasions. He feared that his own devotion to his work and the state of the nation had been at fault, for his eldest son had no interest apart from gambling, drink and social gossip. Sir Edward feared that his son struggled to live up to his father's reputation and achievements, and so ended up doing nothing. It troubled him deeply but he knew not what to do about it. He had confessed that he had to bail his son out from some considerable gambling debts and he feared for the future when he had gone. Harry Coke had not visited Corffe since he was a young man and apparently disliked the place, but Sir Edward did not know why.

In contrast, Charlotte, although quiet, was very empathetic and engaging, almost selflessly concerned with the needs of others. She was short and slight and had maintained a pretty figure, with light-brown hair tinged with grey, her warm, blue eyes overshadowing her mourning dress. Her husband had died in a horse-riding accident, and her only child had died at the age of two from the sweating fever. She somehow funnelled the love she would have had for her lost family into care for others, her mother and many other friends and acquaintances. She had been a regular visitor to Corffe with her parents and not only enjoyed her stays there but made a good impression on many of the villagers. It was she who escorted her mother to dinner, taking her by the arm.

"So how are you looking after King John's torture chamber, Mr Povington?" Harry asked, taking Ralph off guard. He was being his naughty self, throwing his weight around and needlessly upsetting people. King John had owned the Castell and indeed imprisoned and starved to death twelve French nobles during his reign.

"Eh… Eh, Corffe is in good order, sir," Povington responded.

"Good order for what? What is the purpose of a Norman Castell these days, with cannons and gun powder? And what is the good of one in Dorsetshire — it would hardly deter the French. I have no idea why father bought it," Harry continued to taunt.

"Brother, it is an idyllic place. Maybe it has outlived its original purpose, but the sense of history, the views and the air. We have had some wonderful times there, have we not, Mama?" Charlotte said.

"Yes, and Mr Povington and Mr Harvey have always ensured we had everything we needed. Come, let's all sit down," Lady Coke added and the diners took their seats.

Lady Coke continued. "I must be frank with you all. I am in my seventies now and cannot see myself travelling to Dorsetshire again. With my husband gone, there are many expenses to take care of. Harry will inherit most of my husband's estate, and we have discussed the future of Corffe."

"There is nothing for it but to sell it," Harry interjected, in an effort to demonstrate his authority as the new head of the household. But it backfired as everybody in the room turned back towards Lady Coke, who graciously continued.

"That is right, Harry. We have no choice but to find somebody to take over the property and cherish it in the same way as my husband and I did. Mr Povington and Mr Harvey — can you confirm that the estate continues to self-fund the Castell's upkeep?"

"Yes, indeed that is the case, my Lady," said Povington.

"Right then. I would like you and Mr Harvey to travel to London to see our family lawyer, Mr Edwards, in Holborn Chambers. I would like you to share with him the details of the Castell and his estate so he can prepare the process of disposal."

"But who will purchase it and what will happen to us all?" Povington asked.

"I do not believe that you should have cause for concern. I will write a letter for you to take to Mr Edwards that will confirm Harry's and my instructions. One of the conditions that I will include is that we should seek a purchaser who will ensure the Castell is maintained and the staff and tenants are looked after. I also expect it will take some time before it is sold, given that there are not too many people looking to purchase a Castell; they are a little passé these days. But if there is somebody out there looking for one, I am sure they will be connected in some way to London and Mr Edwards will find them."

"Elizabeth," the captain interjected. "And Harry," he added, respectfully turning to the man at the end of the table. "While we were in Oxford, on the way here, I dined with an old friend of mine, Sir Henry Catchpole, who is the principal of Pembroke College. He had invited several distinguished guests and we all toasted the memory of your husband, father. Lord and Lady Bankes were amongst the guests, and I believe they may be interested in purchasing a residence such as Corffe Castell. Would I be at liberty to write to them to let them know of this possibility?"

"The quicker we get rid of it to somebody mad enough to buy it, the better. Please do, Captain," Harry replied, in an attempt to reassert his authority. His mother just nodded to the captain with a smile.

The rest of the evening was taken up discussing, to the annoyance of Harry, news from Corffe, including the recent harvest festival and Tom Harvey's growth and development at school. He was a favourite of Charlotte's, who could not believe he was so grown that he was joining the captain on boar hunts. She was sorry she had not been to Corffe recently, but glad that Tom had remained as inquisitive as ever.

Harry eventually managed to turn the conversation around to his family and then bored everybody with his views on subjects ranging from wine, cards and his horses. He clearly had a narrow perspective on life

— the exact opposite to his father. The captain recalled, in his mind, Sir John's comments about his son — his shallowness and gambling habits, which Sir John feared were just to antagonise him. When the dinner finished, the guests retired to the drawing room, where Charlotte treated them to a recital on her mother's harpsichord, an ornate wooden box on beautifully carved legs. She played one piece of music before being encouraged by her mother to accompany one of her pieces with her voice, which floated over the resonant and rich sound of the instrument like a song bird. Harry tried to entice the men into a game of cards, but all were weary after their long day, and soon retired for the night.

The following day the three travellers paid their respects to Sir John, whose body was lying in a guest room, upstairs. It was a cursory visit, suggested by Lady Coke and out of respect for her husband, for the body was clearly not in a good condition after three weeks and the smell in the room was quite strong. The undertakers were already waiting to close the coffin, ready for the funeral the next day, and it was a relief to the three men that they could leave Lady Coke to say her final goodbye to her husband.

The three prepared to leave Godwick Manor to go to the small, nearby village of Tittleshall. The rest of the Coke family would be arriving that day and would reside in the manor, but the men of Dorsetshire were quite relieved to get away from Harry. However, before they left, they bumped into two other members of the family; Elizabeth, who was the eldest daughter and always a delight to be around, and George, the youngest sibling who was still in his early twenties and had been taught to hunt and use a sword by Captain Cleall. Elizabeth was now married to a very wealthy banker who had accompanied her and lived in Cambridge, while George had studied at Cambridge and after travelling in Europe, had returned to practise medicine. He had become a Puritan and worked in London, but mainly amongst the poorer families, where he said the need was greatest and so were the rewards in terms of appreciation. Both Elizabeth and George were a credit to their father's memory.

The three travellers stayed in the only tavern in Tittleshall. Indeed, there was not much else in the village, other than St Mary's church where Sir John would be laid to rest the next day. The three chatted at length over their bread, ham and potage dinner, accompanied by a wooden cup of ale, a stark contrast to the cuisine and refinery of the previous evening but far more enjoyable, given the fact that the obnoxious Harry was not in their presence. He and the Coke family were the focus of much of the conversation. Sir John had twelve children, one of whom died as an infant and another who died in late childhood. Between the three of them, they had known the other ten fairly well. It was amazing that the same husband and wife could give birth and raise children who varied so greatly from the loathsome Harry all the way to Elizabeth, George and Charlotte: nicer and more gentile people you could not meet. They feared for Sir John's legacy, given that most of the estate would be vested in Harry, but took comfort from the fact that his dislike for Corffe would mean that he would be unlikely to journey down to see them. They must hope for a quick sale to a good family who would cherish the Castell and its estate. As the beer flowed, William confessed that he knew one reason why Harry hated Corffe.

"Was twenty years ago or more now. Harry was at the Castell with his family and one night, after he had obviously had a few too many glasses of wine for dinner, he came down to the village for some more at the Ship Tavern. After a couple of cups of ale and some brandy, he started making a fool of himself. Joseph Painter was the landlord at the time and Harry started shouting at him, asking where the whores were, and he needed some tits."

"That does not surprise me. His father said his son was frequently whoring."

"It was a difficult situation given his status," William continued. "Joseph suggested that he had had enough to drink, which infuriated him. He demanded more brandy or said he would close the tavern down, so he was given another glass. By and by, he went out the back of the tavern to the ditch by the stream to relieve himself. On his way back in, he bumped into the landlord's daughter, Daisy. She was fifteen at the time and had been washing up plates and mugs. Harry grabbed her, shouting 'Titty!' and then dragged her into the stable. We heard the screams — that be myself, Joseph and the Parfitt brothers. We rushed out and found him with his breeches down, bent over her, one of her breasts already exposed as he had ripped open her shift and tried to stop her screaming with his hand over her mouth. After we pulled him off, her father's anger boiled over. He turned around and punched Harry, first in the stomach and a second blow to the head, which knocked him out cold. Daisy had been bruised and scratched but — thank God — that was all.

"There was a lot of discussion about what to do next. We were afraid of the consequences. But Harry would not be coming around for some time, that was sure. We left him in the stable with his britches down and his manhood there for all to see. Ned Parfitt fetched one of the aldermen, a man named Roland Garret, who passed away shortly afterwards, and he came in and laughed at the sight of Harry. It was he who came up with a cunning plan. They would let Harry sleep until morning and then bring all the maids in the village to give him a surprise awakening. And so that is what we did. Just after sunrise, there must have been twenty maids in that stable, witnessing Joseph Painter throw a pale of water over him but before he did so, somebody put a sign around his neck saying 'Little Lord Harry'. And with the splash of the water, he awoke to the sound of the maidens greeting him. 'Morning, Little Lord Harry' and all pointing to his manhood. See, it was very little. He quickly pulled up his britches but as the laughter died, Joseph Painter told him, 'Now, Little Lord Harry — you may be wealthy and powerful but if you touch my daughter again, I will kill you. And if you return to this village, remember that everybody here will be whispering Little Lord Harry behind your back. I suggest you sneak back into your Castell and fake an illness for a few days whilst your bruising heals, but do not return to the village, ever. Whenever you come back to your Castell, stay within its walls, and even there be on your guard.' Harry got up with tears in his eyes, sick with embarrassment as much as drink, and staggered back to the Castell before his family awoke."

"Great story, William," remarked Captain Cleall. "Well, not for poor Daisy but at least the village got a fitting revenge. A toast to Little Lord Harry."

"Tis not finished. Before mid-morning, everybody in the village and Castell knew of the story, apart from his family. The folk in the Castell continued the nightmare for him when he found an engraved 'LLH', which stood for Little Lord Harry, above his bed, and the same letters started to pop up everywhere in the Castell — in the water closet, in his books, on his saddle and even carved into a potato on his dinner plate. The man became paranoid and within three days had left the Castell, apparently to visit a friend in Winchester, but was never to be seen again."

Povington and Cleall both laughed.

"You sure he did not recognise you last night?" Povington asked.

"Yes, I am sure. Twenty years have passed and I was very much a bystander. I was tempted to make a reference to LLH but far too risky here in his domain," William replied.

"It would have been worth the risk, just to take that smug grin off his face," Povington said.

The next day was grey and rather heavy. The men of Dorsetshire made their way over to St Mary's church, through the soggy graveyard and into the building, which was already filling up with mourners. There were many local villagers but clearly wealthier and more important visitors had also arrived to pay their respects, as evidenced by the carriages outside. The three took a pew towards the rear of the church that was not that big for such an occasion, having consideration for the infamy of Sir John but also the size of his family: ten children, nine of whom were married, and nearly thirty grandchildren.

Just after the three had got comfortable, in walked a man and his wife who created a stir amongst the congregation. He was well known in Norfolkshire and Cambridgeshire, his home being St. Ives, but even the men of Dorsetshire recognised his face from news pamphlets and posters that were commonplace in bigger towns, but occasionally made their way to Corffe. It was Oliver Cromwell, a Puritan and outspoken Member of Parliament, who managed to have a voice despite the fact that the king had dissolved Parliament. Dressed all in black, appropriate for the occasion but the norm for any Puritan, he marched up the aisle arm-in-arm with his wife. He was in his mid-thirties, with shoulder-length brown hair, a distinctively large nose and a rounded face which had an air of authority and was focused on the altar ahead. He took a pew three from the front. He was followed by the first of the Coke children, Elizabeth, and one of her sisters and their respective husbands, who sat at the front.

The church continued to fill up, as other members of the local aristocracy filed in, as well as the Coke family, including Charlotte, accompanying Lady Coke, who wore a black hat and a heavy veil. Cleall noticed a young man at the back dressed in city clothes but clearly from a much poorer stratum of society. He stood out as he was neither local nor nobility, and furthermore he seemed to have a small notebook and pencil. He could have only been late teens or early twenties, with adventurous dark hair and eyes that darted up and down the congregation. Cleall wondered what he was doing but his thoughts were interrupted as Harry Coke and his wife, a pale and rather frail-looking woman, entered the church with their two eldest sons, both in their late teens. Cleall turned to his colleagues and wriggled his little finger, mouthing "Little Lord Harry…"

After the service, the coffin was carried to the back of the church by Sir Edward's sons and dropped into a stone family vault. The words 'Sir Edward Coke, 12 Children and 13 Books' were already inscribed above. As the service drew to a close, the congregation filed out of the church to find the sun had broken through and shed a brighter ambience on the closure of the ceremony. Time to move on for family and indeed nation. Invited guests made their way back to Godwich Manor, where drinks and food were provided, an exquisite spread served on china and with silver cutlery. A tight circle of local dignitaries chatted freely amongst one another, whilst the three men from Dorsetshire looked on. They were joined by George Coke, who intimated that he would prefer to be elsewhere. He detested the gossiping, pretence and show of 'polite society' and preferred the 'real people' of London, with whom he worked. The captain enquired when he would be returning to the capital and when he replied, "As soon as possible", they agreed to travel together, leaving the next day.

The four left at the break of day, leaving from the tavern in Tittleshall, where George had also slept the night. It was another grey day, but at least it was dry, as the riders headed south. It was just over a hundred miles to London and the travellers were hoping to do it in just two days, which was really challenging, and the captain advised that they would have to keep to 'cavalry pace' to make it. The goal for the first day was to reach Cambridge. George had studied at Peterhouse College and was confident he would find lodgings there for them, and it was lucky he did, for when they arrived it was Michaelmas, the 29th

September, and the city was heaving. This was the day of the hiring fair when hundreds of temporary and nomadic workers were hired by farmers from the surrounding countryside, typically for a year, to supplement their stable workforce of tied labourers who worked with them permanently, often through generations, living in houses on the farm. It was important for the un-tied workers to secure employment at this time because it was hard to find other work during winter and often families starved if they were not successful.

At the hiring fair, the labourers, individuals or indeed whole families, as children were expected to work as well, would stand on a platform and then be looked over by the hiring farmers in search of people who were healthy and strong but also of good character. They would be quizzed on their experience and skills and of course their daily rate, which would be largely determined by the going rate through good and hard times. All the business had been done that day but many farmers from further afield and their new hands had stayed in the town before making the journey home the following day. The farmers had also brought with them much produce, including wheat and barley, vegetables and firkins of butter. Some of this came by road but also by the River Cam, where merchant boats transported produce from the agricultural lands to the north, to be unloaded in the town to complete their journey by road to London.

It turned out that George's friend at Peterhouse College was a professor of medicine, and he was able to find two rooms for the four to share. The professor joined them for a hearty meal in a local hostelry and told them about the troubles in Cambridgeshire over the last few years, as the gentry had started enclosing land, to the detriment of the poorer classes who relied on access to common land. More land was now being enclosed and turned from arable use, which required lots of labour, into pasture for sheep and wool, which required much less labour. Wool was where the money was. There had been many violent uprisings against these enclosures, fuelled by the economic impact and resentment of the labouring classes.

After a few cups of ale, George opened up about his concerns for his family legacy and his brother Harry. He hoped his mother would not survive too long to see what he believed was the inevitable sale of not only Corffe but nearly all the estates. Harry was a compulsive gambler, who often frequented London's card tables and then, after losing, would console himself in the whorehouses of Southwark. George feared that his debts were excessive and he himself had bailed him out a couple of times, when Harry risked being brought to account by some unsavoury characters in the capital. He knew his father had been troubled by his son's character and behaviour. The only rays of hope were that, perhaps, his new position as head of the family would make him a little more responsible, whilst the growth in puritan influence in the capital was making both gambling and whoring much more difficult.

As George was talking, Cleall spotted somebody whom he seemed to recognise enter the tavern. As the man looked around the room for a place, the captain realised he was the man who had sat at the back of the church taking notes at the funeral, and so he excused himself to approach him.

"Excuse me, sir, but did I not see you at Sir Edward Coke's funeral yesterday?" said the captain.

The man looked startled at being approached in an unfamiliar place, but quickly pulled himself together.

"Yes, that is correct. My name is Milton. John Milton, at your service, sir. I am the Parliamentary reporter for The Morning Chronicle newspaper in London and I am writing a feature on Sir Edward Coke's life, as well as the funeral."

"Captain Cleall. The honour is mine. Why not come and join us at our table? We are friends and employees of Sir Edward and indeed, one of our number is his son, George."

"Are you sure? I am quite happy to eat by myself."

"Yes, of course," the captain said, and turned and introduced his table to the young Mr Milton. The enquiring young man was keen to learn more about Sir Edward, the man, and retrieved his notebook from his coat pocket to write copiously as the captain and George painted a picture of the statesman. George showed him a medallion he kept in his waistcoat pocket, within which was a miniature portrait of his father. The writer asked if he could make a sketch from it, which surprised the doctor but he could see no reason why not, and within a minute the journalist had captured an uncanny likeness of the portrait in his book, which astounded all the men.

"I am but a young and inexperienced journalist, but I sense with the parting of your father, sir, a chapter is turning in the history of our country," Milton said to George. "I am a Parliamentary journalist, which is strange at a time when Parliament has been dissolved by the king, but there are many Parliamentarians in London who voice their dissatisfaction to me, and without Sir Edward Coke's diplomacy between King and Parliament, I am not sure what the future holds."

The professor responded and talked about the rising resentment amongst local gentry, particularly William Grey and Oliver Cromwell, towards the king. The dissolution of Parliament had just made the Parliamentarians more concerned about some of the king's actions, their fear of the French and Spanish, as well as the Popists in this country.

"When it was in session, Parliament gave them a place to let off steam, and in some cases, this frustrated the king, but dissolution has just meant that their opposition has been exacerbated," the professor exclaimed.

The captain agreed and added that the king had his hands tied anyway, because he had so little money after the thirty-year war with France had devastated the Exchequer, with no return whatsoever.

George followed up. "I see the everyday poverty in London amongst the poor; children with barely any clothes and certainly no shoes, malnourished and forced to beg, steal or sweep chimneys for a mere crust of bread. This is the real consequence of the war and to these children it is hard to see God's grace, whether the Catholic or Protestant version. They are often unloved and uncared for and have very little hope. Their battle is to survive the next twenty-four hours, but for what? Another fight through hardship to survive the following day. However, amongst these children I see incredible resilience and spirit. I see children looking after children by whatever means they can and I see them adapting to their dire circumstances in all sorts of ingenious ways. If the king or the Parliamentarians could capture this spirit, we would surely be a great nation, and for me a great nation is one that looks after its poor, which I am sure would be the first priority of Christ rather than whether the nation is Catholic, Protestant or Puritan."

"I understand what you are saying. I have first-hand knowledge of poverty. The experience was my biggest motivator to help me excel at school, when I was fortunate enough to return. I wonder if I could capture some of the spirit you talked about in words and if I did, who would read it?" Milton asked.

"I urge you to do so, sir. And to do so would be a greater obituary to my father's memory: there are few in influence who share such views. Indeed, while my father did and I am like-minded, my own brother Harry believes repression of the artisans, labourers and poor is the right approach and advocates the most extreme measures to maintain what he calls 'the rightful order of society'."

The conversation continued until all the tallow candles had died, and the city residents and travellers parted company. It was still a hard ride to reach London the next day, but the captain reflected on the pleasure of travel and meeting people from all walks of life as he made his way upstairs to retire. As one travelled and talked, one heard different perspectives and feelings that were pumping through the veins of the nation: people's every-day worries for their livelihood, the harvest, taxation and the price of wheat were intertwined with religious theology, politics, national identity and even fashion. Cambridgeshire appeared to be a county rife with riot and disorder against the enclosing of common land for the profit of the few, and he wondered whether such discontent could spread.

The make-up of a nation was highly complex and the different currents and counter-currents provided a dynamic balance, but this could easily be upset, creating turmoil and risk for all. The captain concluded that it must be God's will that kept it in balance, and people's own sins, such as greed, ambition, and hatred, controlled the drive into disorder or conflict. He prayed that God's will would prevail and that his soldering days would be behind him, but he feared — from what he was hearing on his travels — unrest may not be too far away.

The next day the three men from Dorsetshire, George Coke and John Milton set off at dawn, southwards, on the London road. It was an uneventful trip, although there were many travellers in both directions.

As they rode down the Thames valley, they could see the mass of the city before them, like no other, bigger than all the other places they had visited put together. The spire of St. Paul's Cathedral stood high amongst smoke and the mass of streets and houses that spilled out way beyond the historic city walls. The din of the city dampened the sound of the nature around them and as they approached, more and more people were either coming or going. Neither Povington nor Harvey could comprehend how so many folk could live together without suffocating.

They headed to the western end of the sprawl, to Lincoln's Field, outside the city gates, where George Coke lived and he offered two rooms in his house for the travellers to stay. These were gladly accepted, while John Milton headed to his own residence, a little further west. George lived in a small but newly constructed house built of brick and timber frame, with lead-lined windows, but it barely reflected his family's status and standing. He said he rented rooms in the city and Southwark where he employed a nurse and conducted surgeries for the poor, in addition to his visits to his wealthier clients. He lived modestly, with a cook and housemaid, which enabled him to help the poor and needy. He asked the cook to prepare supper for him and his guests when he arrived, but she looked taken aback, complaining that she was not a magician. As she disappeared, George assured his guests that she would be able to conjure up something. Sure enough, the guests were soon presented with a bowl of vegetable potage, followed by ham, potatoes and cheese. A bottle of wine helped wash it down.

The Coke's family solicitor, Mr Edwards, had a residence not far from Lincoln Fields, and George escorted the three travellers there the next day. They were greeted by a servant and shown into a parlour. Mr Edwards came in and welcomed them, dressed in Puritan black and grey, but of a high-quality cloth. He was in his late forties with curly white hair and bushy sideburns, and supported himself with the aid of a black ebony stick. He had a very direct manner and gesticulated often with his stick to reinforce his point. There were very few pleasantries other than inviting everybody to sit down. He apologised for not being able to make the funeral after his gout flared up following his trip to see Lady Coke and Harry in Cambridge two weeks earlier.

"There is no need to apologise, for my father knew that you had served him well, Mr Edwards, and we are sure that he would continue to service the needs of the family in the future," said George.

The captain handed over Lady Coke's letter and Mr Edwards looked at it thoroughly, first checking the seal before opening and then reading it slowly, muttering to himself at appropriate intervals.

"I see Lady Coke would like to sell Corffe Castell in Dorsetshire, and I understand that Mr Povington and Mr Harvey would be able to help me in this task in pulling together the requisite details." Mr Edwards said, looking up.

"That is correct," Povington responded.

Edwards got up and repositioned himself behind his desk in the corner of the room. He picked up the quill and started writing, talking as he did so.

"One Castell, in Corffe, Dorsetshire. Can you provide me with a few more details, such as how many acres, rooms, number of staff, yearly income, please, sirs?"

Povington and Harvey recalled as much as they knew about the Castell and the estates and the captain offered a few additional details. Mr Edwards then provided them with a list of further information for them to collect and send back to him when they had returned to Dorsetshire.

"I am aware of a family who may be interested in the Castell and its estate. I have mentioned this to Lady Coke and she bade me pass this name on to you," Captain Cleall said.

"Very well, Captain. Who is this prospect?" the solicitor said, without looking up from his desk

"Sir John and Lady Bankes," the captain replied.

"Ah." The solicitor put down his quill. "I do indeed know of them, as Sir John is the attorney general. Mr Pumphrey conducts their affairs and he lives just two doors away. I will share the Castell's details straightaway. Is there anything else we need to discuss, sirs? If not, I will bid you good day."

With that, the four men got up and departed. It was apparent that Mr Edwards was a man of business and had little time for pleasantries.

"Gentlemen, let me take you to the city. I need to go to my surgery there, anyway, as there will be patients waiting, but you can see St Paul's and the Tower."

"Splendid," Captain Cleall responded, although more for the benefit of Povington and Harvey, for he had frequented the sites several times before.

Before long, they were walking up Fleet Street, which lived up to its name, crossing the River Fleet, which flowed into the Thames and took with it much of the waste of this congested part of London, although the smell remained. George explained that it was a very popular part of London, particularly for the printing presses that were required by the lawyers nearby. It was so built up now that new building was banned, and the men from Dorsetshire could see why, as there seemed to be building on top of building, mainly made from timber. Amongst them were the magnificent churches of St Bride's and Temple Inn, as well as some equally splendid residences which George pointed out as homes to various bishops, with gardens down to the riverbank. The men paid more attention where they stepped as they entered the city through Ludgate, as the streets narrowed, with an open drain in the middle of the thoroughfare and overhanging buildings. William Harvey was wondering how people could breathe, given the stench of waste, but they could now see St Paul's ahead, with its magnificent spire pointing up to heaven. George took them to the western entrance, to view a new façade designed by Inigo Jones. Its magnificence highlighted the poor condition of the rest of the building.

"The king is spending enormous sums of money on his new hall in Whitehall, whilst the capital's cathedral falls into decay," remarked George.

"And more printers have established themselves here, as well. I cannot believe it would be possible to read all the material that can be produced in London," William observed.

Cleall recalled Sir John Bankes' words the previous week in Oxford, and pondered the power of the printed word. With so many printing presses, perhaps he was right to be concerned. They carried on passed the cathedral and into West Cheap, which was a market street lined with stalls down the centre, and stores either side, the number of which could not be counted. The bustle of people and the shouting of the merchants promoting their produce — whether butchers, bakers, tailors, ironmongers or furniture makers — was so loud that it was difficult to talk. There were aristocrats and artisans, apprentices and paupers of all colours and creeds squeezing passed each other.

"They say this is the busiest street in the whole world!" shouted George to his followers, who were quite grateful when he took them off to Mylke Street, where the physician's rooms were located. As predicted, five people were waiting outside, all looking in need of help, and amongst them two frail children.

"You can see, gentlemen, that my work is never done. I fear I will have to say goodbye, but I know you are keen to depart for Corffe, and I dare say I cannot blame you. I do hope I will be invited to visit the old Castell by whomever takes it over, as I do have so many fond childhood memories there."

"Let's hope so, George, as long as the right new owner can be found. And thank you for your hospitality," Cleall replied.

The three departing men shook hands with the doctor.

Within the hour, the Dorsetshire men were back in Lincoln's Fields, packed up and mounted on their horses, with some bread and pork pie provided by George's cook, ready to head west, out of the capital. They took the Strand, which would take them passed the Whitehall Palace and then across the river in the direction of Richmond. As they trotted down the Strand, they passed an open carriage that was drawing up outside a large, modern brick residence. The carriage had two children and a lady inside; a lady Captain Cleall instantly recognised as Lady Bankes. He told his companions to wait, while he pulled up his rein and turned back, dismounting in front of the carriage.

"Lady Bankes — what a pleasure to see you again."

"Why, Captain Cleall, how delightful. Meet my eldest two children, John and Alice."

"Pleased to meet you, sir," the two children said, in tandem. John must have been a similar age to Tom Harvey, and Alice perhaps a year or two older. Both were immaculately presented and dressed as young aristocrats, whilst Captain Cleall thought Lady Bankes looked even more radiant in the light of day. She was wearing a white lace shawl over a turquoise dress, and carried a parasol, not that the early October sun warranted it.

"Children — Captain Cleall lives in a wonderful Castell down in Dorsetshire and protects us from the French and Spanish. See his shiny sabre?" Lady Mary said, in a motherly voice. "But what brings you to London, Captain?"

"Strangely, the very Castell to which you refer. The Cokes have decided to sell and we have been meeting their lawyer to discuss the details of the sale. I have taken the liberty of mentioning you and Sir John as potentially interested parties. I hope you do not mind?"

"Not at all. I would love to see details, and if it is half as wonderful as you describe, Captain, I can see it as a perfect home for us. I want the children to spend more time in the countryside. I may have to persuade Sir John, but a woman has her ways."

"In which case, I do hope you can visit Dorsetshire soon. We are on our way back there now."

"I will, I am sure. Bon voyage, Captain."

Captain Cleall reflected on his second meeting with Lady Bankes as they continued their ride west. She was like no other woman he had met, not that he had been drawn to many in the past as he had been wedded to the cavalry. He found the way she spoke tantalising, and she had the strength of character so rare in a woman of society, most of whom were trained to be seen and not heard. She had maintained her good features despite being in her thirties, but it was her energy and the radiance of her smile that he found so attractive. He hoped she would come to Corffe and he would be delighted to show her the beauty of the county. If only she were not married.

Chapter IV
A Woman's Home is her Castell

5ᵗʰ December 1636

Sir John and Lady Bankes had just arrived at Corffe Castell. It could not have been a better day for the prospective owners to visit the Castell and decide if they wanted to make it a home. They brought with them their two eldest children; Alice, who was fifteen and John, who was thirteen. The other five children had remained in Middlesex. It was a cold winter's day but with a perfect blue sky that accentuated the Castell's definition on its hill. There was a lot of excitement in the village as news that the visit was taking place had spread like wildfire. Captain Cleall had told everybody that the Bankes were a good family and very close to the king. Povington was in a mild panic, having heard about the pending visit only three days before. He had been organising a thorough clean and refresh of the living quarters within the house, ensuring that the wine cellar was restocked and the kitchen larders had all the ingredients for a variety of menus he had created. Fires in all the rooms were alight, day and night, in an attempt to warm up the old stone fabric, and scented petal-water refreshed the air. Meanwhile, William Harvey was out repairing fences and clearing debris around the estate. Captain Cleall watched on but was confident that the Castell and the estate had never look better in living memory. The Bankes had certainly been impressed as they arrived and were greeted to a light lunch before they embarked on a tour of the Castell and its grounds. Lady Bankes and the two children were bubbling with excitement, reliving days of old, and lapping up all the tales and stories of the past that Povington had a remarkable ability to recount. Sir John listened on, taking a more pragmatic view of the building and its shortcomings in a world where Castells were being converted into residences for living, rather than battle.

By the time the tour had finished, it was getting dark and the Bankes were tired. Captain Cleall suggested that they retire and rest for a while before dinner, and the next day they could tour the estate and village. It was agreed that Lord Bankes would tour the estate with William Harvey and review its upkeep and management, whilst Lady Bankes would take a ride to the coast with Captain Cleall. Alice and John Bankes would be introduced to Tom Harvey and a few of his friends and explore the village and surrounding countryside in the way only children can do.

Tom Harvey, Francis Trew and Joseph Cobb met the Bankes children at the Castell gate in the morning, which was another very fresh but sunny, blue December day. The five children had all been wrapped up well, although the Bankes' furs underlined their status, compared to the local boys' fleeces. There were few words shared between the children before Tom suggested they climbed the Barrow — the chalk down that overlooked the Castell to the east. He sped off, closely followed by Francis and Joseph, before anybody had time to decline his suggestion. Alice and John followed and soon caught up with the others as they took a rest on the lower slope of the hill. They were already level with the outer fortifications of Corffe Castell on the hill opposite them, and as they caught their breath, they could see the daily activity in the grounds and horses being readied for the respective Bankes' tours.

"Let's see who can reach the top first."

John Bankes laid the gauntlet down to the others, and they all continued their ascents as fast as their legs would take them. It was the taller boys, Tom and John, who set the pace, and were neck and neck as the down flattened out at its peak. Both eager to win, they looked at each other and made a strenuous effort to dig deeper and outrun their opponent, but in doing so they both simultaneously lost their footing on the dew-covered grass and both collapsed on the ground in fits of laughter and panting as they recovered from the challenge.

"A well-earned draw," John said, between laughs.

"Indeed, it could not have been closer," Tom replied, as he recovered from the exploit.

The others had caught up with them, and all collapsed on the ground gasping for breath. Alice and John marvelled at the view. They were now higher than even the gloriette of the Castell and could see all the activity

76

within, as well as in the village beyond. The local boys had made this climb more times than they could count. Perched up here, they escaped from the everyday — where they were the minions in a world ruled by parents and grown-ups — to a world where they felt omnipotent. The activity within the Castell looked ant-like in scale. The vista below and beyond provided no better place to see the beauty of this pocket of Dorset. Alas, it lacked the colourful summer coat of the meadows ready to harvest and wildlife in full marvel, but even with naked trees and bare-soil fields, the landscape was alluring and brought a smile to the visitors' rosy faces. To the west was the harbour of Poole with its islands that had been known to provide a haven for pirates. But for the Corffe boys, it was a paradise of adventure as all the ships avoided the shallow water of the islands nearest to the Purbecks to sail to the port of Poole, or up the River Frome to Wareham, the long-established Roman trading port, just four miles from Corffe. To the east of Corffe was the limestone ridge, on which the villages of Kingston and Worth Matravers sat, and beyond them, at the foot of the rugged escarpment, the waves of the English Channel would normally be pounding out of sight of the children. But today, the children could be assured that there were no waves, for the sea was a perfect millpond of emerald greens, merging into the fading blues on the horizon. A trading ship, with a full complement of sails, made its way from the west to perhaps the markets in London. They guessed what was stowed on board and where it came from — sugar from the Caribbean, olives from Spain, or spices from the East? Or perhaps it was a pirate ship?

"Are your parents going to buy the Castell?" Francis asked John.

"I think so. Well, at least, I hope so," said John.

"Mother is very keen," Alice continued. "Father is too busy in London to be bothered with Castells. He says that they are a relic of the past and we should build a family house in the country to a modern style. But Mother likes the history that comes with a Castell. But I hope it is not haunted."

"I think the dungeons may be, but the main keep is free from ghosts, I am sure," Tom replied.

"Yes. Povington told us about French nobles being captured and starved to death in the dungeons," John confirmed.

"And King Edward was murdered here. That was before William the Conqueror built the stone Castell. He was only sixteen. Fancy being a king at sixteen…" Joseph added. Joseph was a bright boy, inquisitive like Tom, but much smaller and actually quite frail and certainly a lot less adventurous that Tom or Francis.

"Captain Cleall has been telling Mother how wonderful Dorsetshire is and we cannot wait to explore it. We will still have our house in Middlesex but that does not have the sea," Alice added.

"Why do you need two houses? Isn't that greedy?" asked Francis.

"We actually have a third one in London, as well. Father needs that one because he has to be near the king, whilst the Middlesex one is close to our schools. But I hope we spend most time here. There seems like so much to do," John enthused.

"The Castell will need updating. The rooms are very basic and Mother says that she would want to make them more in the French style," Alice said.

"But it was built by William the Conqueror. Can't be more French than that," Tom replied.

"Three houses. You must be very rich. What is it like to be so rich?" Joseph asked.

"Mm. I guess we have always been wealthy so it is hard to describe it. We do certainly have privileges but at the same time it is not always easy. I do not want to sound condescending but your lives appear much simpler to me and that certainly has some merit," John continued.

"What do you mean? Are you calling us simple?" Francis said, with a raised voice.

"No. I meant no offence — indeed I was trying to just describe our lives in comparison to yours. What does your father do, Joseph?" John asked.

"My father passed away when I was young, but my uncle is a miller. And a very good occupation he has. He grinds all the flour for Corffe and villages beyond. I will become a miller, too," Joseph replied, with a sense of pride.

"Exactly. Being a miller is something you can be proud of, for we will all starve without bread. And no doubt your uncle's father was a miller too?" Joseph nodded as John continued. "Well, my father is the attorney general to the king — I do not really understand what that means or what he does and so can hardly explain it. What I do know is that means I hardly see him, which makes it hard on our family and our mother, in particular. It also means it is very difficult for me to follow in his footsteps. We need lots of millers and will always need bread. There is only one post for an attorney general to the king and those footsteps are much harder to follow, especially if you do not see your father or understand what he does. I am sure you know the world of being a miller inside out already and help your uncle on a daily basis. I have never been able to help my father. Instead, I am sent away to school to learn Latin and Ancient Greek and subjects that seem to have very little relevance to anything, and Alice has similar studies at home with her governess."

"Indeed," added Alice. "Why we are happy to come and hopefully live in the Castell is because it already seems more real. We will be living with the people in the Castell and on the estate — blacksmiths, farmers, masons, carpenters and millers — who are part of a community; a real community. We would like to be part of that, too. We would also like to learn about nature — the trees, the rock formations, the sea, and the animals, wild and domesticated."

"Why, we can teach you that. We know all there is to know about that, don't we, Joseph and Francis?" said Tom and with nods from his co-villagers, he continued. "And perhaps you can teach us a little you learn at that school. Our schooling is just two mornings a week, and it is difficult to learn with half the children of the village crammed into a room. But my father says that education is the key to our future. I know my letters and my numbers but I'm not sure what to do with them. Apart from the bible at church, I have not even seen a book," Tom said.

"I think that is a deal — let's shake on it," John responded, and all five children got up and held hands together.

"Well, we can start with a nature lesson. Have you ever seen an adder?" Tom asked.

"You mean a snake? Why, no," John replied.

"Well, I know where there is one. Let's go and find it," Tom said, and led them along the top of the barrow.

The children had a wonderful day, getting to know and enlighten each other with their respective knowledge. After finding the adder, Tom led them down the Poole Harbour side of the down and onto a marshy heathland, where they found toads and sand lizards. They also visited the Devil's Anvil, a rock twenty feet in height, standing on a small mound. Tom explained it had been thrown by the devil himself from the Isle of Wight with the intention of destroying Corffe Castell.

"Why, he did not even get close," Alice declared.

"Lucky the Isle's far enough away, or you would not have a Castell to buy," Francis replied.

John was carrying a pack strapped to his back, which contained a lunch prepared by the Castell's cook. As lunch time approached, the children had reached the inner shore of the harbour and found two logs which they sat down on and shared out the food. The emerald-green sea was very still and gently lapped onto the shore, close to where they sat, although it was certainly chillier closer to the water. One of the islands in the harbour, known as Green Island, because of its covering of pine, was just a few hundred yards out to sea. The local boys often visited the island using a small rowing boat hidden in the heathland and they invited their guests to join them.

"Who owns the island? Are we allowed on to it?" Alice asked, in her role as the eldest child.

"It is deserted. Many years ago, people lived there making pottery but nobody does now. We go there often," Joseph replied.

"What an adventure. An island of our own," said John.

"All right. If you are sure we will not get into trouble," Alice said.

In no time at all, the Corffe boys had found the boat and dragged it to the shoreline and into the water, taking it in turns to jump in. It made its way deeper into the cold sea, bringing a shock of reality into the boys' young hearts. Alice did not want to get wet, so between them, Tom and John carried her to the boat. Tom took the oars and in no time at all they had made it across the narrow stretch of water, and moored on a small, sandy beach that skirted around the pine woodland beyond. The children trudged through the earthy loom of the pine-needle floor in search of anything that would appeal to their juvenile curiosity.

They soon came across a dilapidated wooden building, which at one time must have been a home to somebody. It comprised two rooms and a further gallery in the eaves of the roof but had been stripped of anything other than its pine fabric. Around the back was another shed and inside it, a brick kiln, which had been used by the potters who had inhabited the island. Scattered around were many broken pieces of clay pots. Two further buildings in similar conditions were situated a few yards further on, as well as a clay pit, which had been the source of the raw materials used for the pottery products. To the rear of the buildings, another beach was found with a boat jetty, with a few missing planks, but that did not stop the boys from venturing to its end, whilst Alice watched and asked them to be careful. There were crabs amongst the patches of seaweed and sand in the clear water beneath the jetty legs. Joseph wanted to catch some but Tom pointed at how low the sun was in the sky, and that it would take over an hour to get back to the Castell. So they found the boat again and set off back to the Castell, with a few diversions along the way, chasing a rabbit, skimming stones into the sea, and normal childish activities. The Bankes children would certainly sleep well tonight, even if the rooms were a little draughty. They had never had so much fun and adventure in a single day before.

Meanwhile, Captain Cleall had been looking forward to showing Lady Bankes the delights of Dorsetshire. He had mapped out an itinerary, which set them off through Corffe Village and then up the winding track that led up to the village of Kingston on the limestone ridge. From there they would ride along the ridge to Worth Matravers and then onto the ragged coastline of the Purbeck, with its abundance of headlands and coves, sea stacks and arches and dramatic cliffs, some rising three hundred feet above the waves that would usually be crashing at their feet. He could not have hoped for a better day in December to show off the beauty of the coast, although it would be chilly.

Lady Bankes was well dressed for the ride, with fur hat and a lady's dark-blue riding coat that covered her and the top half of her horse. As they set off through the village, the place was already a hive of activity, but nobody was too busy not to notice the lady who accompanied the captain as they trotted passed. The captain exchanged pleasantries with many of the locals as he led the way: Josh Miller, who had a cartload of grain that he was taking to his mill; Ned Parfitt, who was helping Josh

Painter offload barrels of ale at the Ship Inn; and Elizabeth Harvey, William's wife, amongst others. He knew they would be leaving behind a trail of gossip about Lady Bankes as they headed out of the village, and this was only to be expected given that the potential of a new lord and lady at the Castell was news as big as one could get. Lady Bankes rode side-saddle, but with confidence, and she kept a good pace as soon as they left the village.

At Worth Matravers, they stopped for a drink in a cottage that was part-time tavern, where a widow named Agnes had opened up her ground-floor room for this purpose, selling beer and gin she made herself. She lived in the only other room, in the eaves of the reed roof. The widow greeted her visitors with reverence. She was not expecting any custom at this time of day and could never imagine hosting gentry at anytime. She was dressed in a soiled apron that, at one time, may have been a creamy white, and a matching bonnet that clearly hid a mass of unkempt, greying hair. She was short and rotund in build but had a sparkle in her eye and a cheery smile, despite the loss of a few teeth. She flapped around to find the best seat for them and made a futile attempt to tidy the room up, shooing two chickens out, whilst the captain begged her not to go to any trouble. A couple of chairs were positioned by the window, where there was an old barrel positioned to act as a table. The window provided a candle, for the room was very dark with walls that were almost black from clay pipe smoke, as well as a smoky fire that smouldered in a hearth at one end. Agnes brought two small jugs of gin and excused herself, saying she would be in the yard at the back and to call if she was needed.

"You take me to the best places, Captain," Lady Bankes said, when they were alone.

"Of course. Only the best and I am sure you will enjoy the gin," the captain smiled, whilst pointing to the door and cupping his hand around his ear, confirming that he suspected Agnes would be eavesdropping.

"Gin is not a beverage in which I typically indulge, but when in Rome, Captain. Your good health!" Lady Bankes raised her jug and the captain followed suit.

Lady Bankes said she had enjoyed the ride and appreciated the captain's time and company. She loved the landscape as it reminded her so much of her upbringing as a child, in Devon. The captain enthusiastically assured her that the best was yet to come, and the couple chatted about life in Dorsetshire.

"She is a remarkable woman, Agnes, the landlady. People say she has 'the sight', and that she can communicate with those who have parted this earth to the other side, as well as foreseeing the future."

Lady Bankes raised an eyebrow and whispered, "She is not a witch, is she?"

"No, of course not. She just has a gift of more senses than you or I," the captain replied, in an equally hushed voice.

As they finished their drinks, he called Agnes to settle his bill, and at the same time asked, "Tell me Agnes, what does the future hold for us?"

"Captain, sir — I have been troubled in recent months as I see a black shadow coming over England. It is still not clear to me what it is or what it means but I am sure it is not good," she replied, with a gloomy face.

"Is it war with the French? Maybe I will be of service to my country once again," the captain probed but Agnes's face remained disconsolate.

"I cannot tell but it troubles me greatly. I see fire and fighting. I fear it is not good for any of us."

"Well, if it is the French, I am sure we can defend these isles."

He handed her an extra coin in remuneration for her foresight, and the couple continued on their journey.

The ride down from the village of Worth to the cliff line was dramatic. They followed a stream that meandered through a valley, and the horizon line of a green-grey sea between the grassed hills either side invited them on, with a freshness in the air. There were few trees, just hawthorn bushes, limestone walls, lush green grass and mud where the stream had overflowed. The trees that did grow had been moulded into strange, twisted forms bowing to the north by the consistent breeze that could blow up to a full gale from the sea. As they progressed down the valley, the breadth of the welcoming sea widened.

Shortly, they reached the cliff's edge, to find a ledge of rock eighty or so feet further down, where the gentle waves of the December morning lapped over the limestone. There were three men and a horse, with a wooden crane that the captain informed Lady Bankes was called a 'whim' and was being used to lower a large slab of limestone into a twenty-five-foot, flat-bottomed wooden boat, with two men aboard, that bobbed gently in the sea. The boat was moored by two ropes to two boulders on the ledge, but jagged rocks on either side of it were peeking out from beneath the water. Lady Bankes marvelled at the seamanship that had enabled the boat to be steered to where it was tethered, as well as the skill, even audacity, to stand on the boat being gently rocked, whilst the limestone was loaded. The captain explained that the limestone was being quarried in caves behind them, and when Lady Bankes turned, she could see a series of man-made caves behind some hawthorn bushes. The quarrymen had left pillars of stone just three feet wide, which held up over a hundred feet of limestone, arching above them.

As she looked, a quarryman emerged from one of the caves with a horse that was dragging another limestone slab, presumably destined to join the other slabs beneath them and to be loaded onto the boat. The captain explained that the boat would take the slabs to Poole, where they could be loaded onto a larger vessel and taken to London to be sculpted and polished for the palaces, churches and mansions that were being constructed in the booming city. The blood, sweat and toil that it took to unearth this stone and get it to London intrigued Lady Bankes, even more so when the captain pointed out that this was all part of the estate that she was considering purchasing. On the opposite side of the valley to where the captain and Lady Bankes watched, there were four little stone cottages, all just comprising a single room, which was where the quarrymen lived.

The captain then reined his horse away from the cliff, and towards the man dragging the slab of stone with his horse. He nodded to the quarryman, who saluted him back, and then guided the horse to the left of the caves, up a very steep path that went back up the cliffs on the east side of the valley. Lady Bankes followed behind, and after a steep and somewhat precarious ride to the top, the couple let their horses gallop the four miles along the cliff of the limestone ridge and down into the bay of Swanage, at the eastern end of the Purbeck Isle.

Swanage comprised a small hamlet of ten fishermen cottages, fronting a glorious bay of sand with the sea lazily lapping onto the shore.

A half-dozen small fishing boats bobbed gently in the bay, whilst children and wives repaired nets and salted catch on the shore. The couple rode their horses right onto the sand and continued their gallop along the waterline, with the wide-open beach and golden sand spread out in front of them, the sea horizon to their right, the splashing and spray of water beneath them. It was exhilarating, but in no time at all they had reached the far end of the bay, and the captain led them to a small stream that was flowing into the sea. He jumped down from his horse and let the panting Thunder recover from the gallop and drink from the steam, while the captain walked to Lady Bankes, who had just caught up. She was laughing with joy, her cheeks blossoming in the sea breeze. The captain helped her dismount.

"That was wonderful — thank you, Captain. I feel ecstatic and at peace at the same time. This place has so much beauty but a natural ruggedness that is exciting and energising. There is even something spiritual about it. No wonder Agnes has foresight living here. You can breathe it in the air," Lady Bankes said, as she took off her cape, pulled up her dress to mid-calf height and danced in the sand, her movement extenuating the outline of her body beneath her holy green, velvet dress.

"I am so glad you like it. I would have hated to drag you down from London and disappoint you," the captain replied, with a smile that disclosed the joy he felt from seeing Lady Bankes so happy.

"Like it? I love it. This is just the type of place where I wanted to bring up my family. I just have to persuade Lord Bankes now. But I assure you this will not be a problem. What a woman wants, God wants, and man must oblige."

The captain laughed. The couple traced the hoof prints in the sand back to the water's edge and walked along the shoreline, talking as if they were old friends. They certainly felt very comfortable in each other's company. Before they knew it, they had walked across the entire bay.

"We appear to have run out of beach, Captain!" Lady Bankes exclaimed.

"This is true, and before long we will run out of daylight. We had better be heading back to the Castell," he replied.

Their eyes met and remained in contact for a second longer than expected and he was sure he spotted a flicker of attraction, or had he imagined it? What was he hoping for or even thinking? He was a gentleman and she was a married woman, and not just any married woman: she was married to a very powerful man. But he had enjoyed the day and certainly her company, and he was reluctant to let the day end.

"Thank you, Captain, for such a delightful day. You were right in Oxford. Dorsetshire is an enchanting place and I am so grateful for you acquainting me with it. I am so looking forward to living here."

In the bay, nets were being drawn as the fishing boats prepared to return, and the couple turned and headed back to their horses. As they rode back to the Castell, Lady Bankes was drawing up plans in her mind; what to bring from Middlesex to Corffe, when and how she would do this, alterations to the Castell, arrangements for the children and an endless list of things to be done.

It was not until April of the following year that the Castell was finally owned by the Bankes and Mary could put her plans to convert it from a Norman Castell into a seventeenth-century home that reflected the status of her husband and family and the tastes of the time. She enjoyed the flare and elegance of good design, largely influenced by the French, which could be seen in many modern houses being developed in the west of London, and what Puritans frowned on as opulent. She sent word out for designers and artisans, as well as merchants who could source furniture from France, and tapestries from even further afield. She brought with her drapes and velvets from her home in Middlesex that instantly started to transform the place. In the village, the talk was of her velvet cover to the toilet seat in her bed chamber, the silver cutlery and the leather-bound books in the library. Pride of place in the grand hall was a portrait of King Charles' queen, Henrietta Maria, painted by the acclaimed Dutch artist Van Dyke, which had been given to her husband by the king. Lady Bankes had met the queen on many occasions and admired her in many ways, despite what many said about her. The French queen's self-sacrifice to marry as a duty to state, rather than love, at such a young age in a male-dominated world and so far from home; her devotion to her faith in such an obviously hostile environment; and the calming influence she had on the king were just some of her attributes. Whilst many guests at her home in Middlesex had been surprised to see the portrait and made comment to the queen's faith, Lady Bankes saw her as a person in her own right and she could draw strength from the portrait.

John spent much of his time away at boarding school, but when he returned, he and his older siblings, Alice and Mary, would spend time with Tom, Francis and often Joseph, as well. John and Tom became very close friends, wildly competitive, whether it was running, swimming or climbing, but also both inquisitive, and John would teach Tom history, geography and classics, whilst Tom taught John about nature, agriculture and estate management. Both boys were approaching fifteen now and were starting to notice the girls as more than just less-adventurous playmates. They could not understand them but they did talk about them to each other — the prospect of courting, and the merits of different girls in the village — but would soon find it too daunting and get back to more boyish subjects.

Back at the Castell, the other siblings could frequently be found running around the ramparts in a pack led by the eldest, Elizabeth, who was ten, and followed by Jane, who was seven, and Ralph, aged five. They were dressed as princesses or knights with wooden swords. The youngest, Jerome, was only two and stayed mainly inside whilst Mary was also expecting another child in September; a fact that would certainly not hold her back from the nesting instinct but just added more urgency to transform the Castell.

Lady Bankes' quest for the best artisans and merchants of French finery brought a trail of people from across the Channel, and a couple of French families ended up residing in the village. The first to arrive had a profound effect on Tom Harvey. He had been helping Thomas Moreton, at the Fox Tavern in the newer street in the village, to arrange some barrels at the rear when, Beth, his wife, called from the front to say that she needed some help as some travellers had arrived looking for lodgings. Tom followed the publican back inside where there was a man with Beth who was obviously not from these parts. He was not much taller than the publican's wife, with dark features, weathered skin and a nose with a prominent bridge. His general demeanour was of a tired traveller, with bedraggled hair and dusty but stylish, quality garments.

"Thomas, this gentleman is from France and requires a room for a few nights," Beth said to her husband.

"For myself and my family — my wife and my daughter are outside, Monsieur," the man said.

"Muss who? You have come to the right place, sir," Thomas replied, reaching out to shake the man's hand with a warm smile. "We have the best rooms in the village, that is for sure." And with a warm laugh he added, "They are the only ones. Let me take you up and show you."

Tom listened into the conversation from the foot of the stairs as Thomas escorted the Frenchman to the room upstairs, designated for travellers. It was quite rare for travellers to pass through Corffe and when they did so, they stayed just for the night. The prospect of a whole family staying a few nights or more was manna from heaven for the publican. Tom learnt that the Frenchman was from Rouen, the capital city of Normandy, and his name was Jacques Duchêne. He was a master craftsman and had learnt his skills in the Compagnons du Tour de France, travelling and working on palaces and cathedrals around the country. He had heard that Lady Bankes was looking for good craftsmen and had been sent by the Compagnons to determine what skills were required so he could bring the right craftsmen to her service. He was a Master of the Masters. The two men came down the stairs after a brief haggle over the appropriate rate for a week's stay.

"Can you help our guests with their luggage, please Tom?" the publican asked.

Tom nodded and followed the Frenchman outside through the front door of the pub. Outside was a small carriage, not of the ornate finery of the aristocracy, but still of a quality that showed that the Frenchman was doing well. It was covered but with open windows and a Fleur-de-Lys painted on the door. A man, who Tom took to be the driver, had already started to unpack some of the bags from the back. Alongside the carriage stood a woman, presumably his wife, and a girl, who instantly caught Tom's attention. She was about his age, a little shorter and with long dark hair that contained some strands of lighter shades, an olive skin and shimmering green eyes. Dressed in a simple dress that matched her eyes and flowed all the way down to her ankles, she smiled, revealing perfect teeth as her lips parted and Tom's stomach filled with giant butterflies. He had not seen a girl of such beauty before and he did not know how to respond. He kept his head down and focused on the task in hand. The girl's mother said hello and asked if he could help with a leather bag. She was also attractive for a lady of her age, with remarkably good teeth and the same green eyes. Her hair was hidden behind a laced brown bonnet, matching her dress.

Tom picked up the bag. It was heavier than it looked, but he was determined to show that he was effortlessly up to the task, despite the tingles that seemed to be running down his spine. He glanced again at the girl as he took the bag inside and up the stairs. He started to feel claustrophobic in the room. He needed air. He needed to escape as he did not know how to handle this situation. He put the bag on a chair, and then headed back to the door and down the stair, but the girl was now part-way up. He stopped and backed up, looking down on her, her eyes looking up at him above the breast line of her dress. His mouth had dried up, and he took a further step back, but tripped on the top step and found himself falling back onto the landing. He hit the ground with a thump, but his pride was wounded far more than his behind, as the girl looked down on him with a mixture of laughter and pity.

"Monsieur." She held out a dainty hand to help Tom up.

"I do not need any help," Tom said, brashly, annoyed with himself, and regretted his manner as quickly as the words left his mouth. He got up and for a fleeting moment stood staring into the depths of her eyes. The tingles in his spine spread to both arms and down to his fingers. He started to feel hot, and even breathless.

"I must go," he said, and after allowing the driver to complete his ascent of the stair, he bounded down.

"Merci. Au revoir," the girl called after him, but he had only one thought, to get out of there as quickly as possible. He almost knocked over the Frenchman leading his wife into the tavern as he hurried through the door and out into the spring air. He looked up to see Nine Barrow Down — that was where he needed to go, to be safe and alone and off he ran.

He reached the top where he could look down on the village, a haven from what he had just experienced and what he did not understand, induced by his own feelings and his own bodily reaction. He lay down on the grass and looked up at the blue sky with its wispy white clouds. What had just happened? His heart pulsated: a combination of the exertion but also the emotion. He had to calm down and apply his logic to the events that had occurred, the new arrivals, the girl — yes, the girl. He had not seen a girl like that before; one of such beauty and with those eyes, her hair and skin, her breasts, her everything. And that smile. But what had he done? Behaved like an imbecile. Fallen over the stairs. What would she think of him? The village idiot, no doubt. He thumped the ground with frustration. What was he to do now? How could he face her again? But he had to. Even if he had not made such a fool of himself, he would have no idea how to approach such a beauty — a girl, or young lady, who had travelled, who was no doubt courted by men all over France. Aren't the French supposed to be the romantics? Who was he? Maybe he could hold his own in the village of Corffe, but he knew nothing of French ways, French romance or even the language. Yes, she had spoken to him in their tongue but he was ignorant of the words. Was this not the language of aristocrats? How could he learn it? Maybe John Bankes could have helped but he was away at school. What about Alice or her governess? They knew French. But how could he talk about this to another girl or woman? Francis was at the quarry and Joseph at the mill, but he felt neither could be of any help on either dealing with girls, nor the French. What about Captain Cleall? He was a wise man and was sure to know some French. Why, he had led armies in that country. He also knew about women. He had wooed Lady Bankes all the way to Corffe and there was gossip in the village about the two of them, but Tom did not listen to it. Captain Cleall was too honourable a gentleman to court another man's wife. But what could he learn in a few days? There was one way to find out.

Tom headed back from the Down in the direction of the Castell, in search of the captain. He found him as quickly as he could hope for as he was just returning his horse to the stable near the gate.

"How are you, young Tom?" the captain greeted him as he approached. He was wiping his brow with a handkerchief as the stable boy removed his saddle to take it into the tack room.

"Fine, Captain, sir. Ah, would it be possible to have a chat with you, Captain? I need some advice. Urgently." Tom replied.

"Yes, of course. Let's have an ale at the Fox. There is still plenty of sun left in the day and I could do with a drink."

The captain's suggestion made Tom's heart sink. He could not go back there. She might see him. He needed to come up with an alternative suggestion — quickly.

"Ahhh, what about by the Wicken?" Tom hesitantly suggested.

"The river? Are you going soft as you grow up? That is where you should be taking young maidens, not a cavalry captain. No, the Fox it is. I need ale to quench my thirst from the ride. Let's go."

Captain Cleall patted his trusted destrier and off he marched in the direction of the gate and village beyond. Tom had no option but to follow and feared he was risking making the whole situation worse, but he had no other plan. He caught up with the captain.

"Captain, sir — when you were in France fighting, did you learn French?"

"Well, I learnt a lot of French as a boy but was able to brush up on it over there, although the dialect in Bretagne is very difficult; it's a bit like talking English to anybody from Cornwall or Wales," he responded.

They were approaching the tavern, which had some seats outside to one side, and the captain sat himself down, ordering two mugs of ale from Beth, who had just cleared the table.

"So, Tom. What is on your mind? How can I help you?" the captain asked.

"French is on my mind. I thought if I was to make my way in the world it would be good to have a language like French. I was wondering if you would have any time to teach me the letters and words?" Tom replied.

"Quelle bonne idée," the captain retorted.

"Pardon?" Tom answered.

"There, you are already speaking it," the captain exclaimed, slamming the table in delight.

"Pardon, sir? I do not understand," the boy said, in bemusement.

"Non. Pardon, je ne comprends pas," the captain continued to correct the perplexed boy.

Just then Beth returned with the two ales, and behind her followed three people. Tom's head dropped as he recognised the French guests.

"Here are your ales, and Captain, I have brought down our new guests, all the way from France. They would like an audience with Lady Bankes, and as you were here, I thought I would introduce you to them. The Monsieur is a Master of the Master Craftsmen in France and understands Lady Bankes is interested in French workmanship." She turned around. "Monsieur, may I introduce you to Captain Cleall."

The captain stood up. "Bonjour, Monsieur," he volunteered, and then continued the conversation in French, to Tom's bewilderment. He was not sure what to do or where to look but was frustrated not to understand the conversation. He looked up from his ale and caught the eye of the girl standing behind her father, with her mother, listening to the conversation between the two men. She smiled back. Tom felt himself blushing. He had to think fast and pull himself together. Suddenly, he was struck by a thought, which he knew he had to act upon, before his fears and self-doubt stopped him. He jumped up, grabbed two stools from a neighbouring table and positioned them at his table.

"Please. Please, take a seat," he said, beckoning to the wife and daughter. He then grabbed another stool. "Please, sir — a seat."

Captain Cleall smiled. "Good idea, Tom. We should host our visitors." Then, again in French, he asked if they would like a drink. "Tom, can you go and ask Beth for a bottle of wine and three cups."

Tom felt pleased with himself. He had acted decisively and could now gather his thoughts whilst he went inside to find Beth. Actually, he had now positioned himself well: he was with the captain, who was seen as an influential person for the visitors, especially as he spoke their language. But what next? What could he say to the girl? He had to find out her name, but how?

He returned with the wine and cups and handed them to the three, new table companions. The captain was still conversing in their tongue, then he paused and turned to Tom.

"I have had a brilliant idea, young Tom. Camille wants to learn English, and you told me you wanted to learn French. I suggest the two of you teach other. What do you think?" the captain asked.

Tom did not know what to say. It was too much to take in. Firstly, he had learnt her name: Camille, Camille. What a wonderful name — so sweet. But the suggestion made by the captain was too good to be true.

"Eh, eh… I do not know, Captain, sir," was all he could come up with. But the captain would have none of it.

"Tom, meet Camille. Camille, enchantez Tom. Tom, teach Camille English. Camille, enseigne le Français à Tom. Take your drinks and start talking. Prenez votre gobelet et commencez à parler," he commanded and raised his glass, an action shared by Camille's parents.

Tom and Camille looked a little sheepish, but glanced at each other, and Tom started to stand up. She followed his lead, and they both gathered their cups and started to walk. But where should he take her, Tom thought. Then it came to him — the Wicken would be perfect. Captain Cleall had jested that the small river was the place to take maidens, a short while ago. Well, now he had the chance. He led the way and in no time at all they were by the riverbank, and Tom had found a limestone rock for them to sit down. The walk had revived the butterflies in his stomach. He daren't look at her. Instead, he picked up a stone and threw it into the water, focusing on the ripple.

"Je m'appelle Camille," she suddenly said, touching her chest. "Je m'appelle Camille," she repeated.

Tom picked up the thread. "Je m'appelle, Tom. My name is Tom."

"My name is Camille," she responded. They both laughed. Slowly but surely, they started to communicate, and share understanding of each other's respective languages. Camille had an advantage as she knew quite a few English words already, whereas Tom was starting from scratch. But this did not bother Tom: he was on cloud nine and pure happiness was pumping from his heart through every vein in his body. He was not sure how long he could stay with her without being overcome with joy. He was mesmerised by Camille's smile, the sparkle in her eyes, the outline of her body. Everything about her was just perfect and here she was talking to him, by the Wicken. This was what dreams were made of. Time disappeared without trace as they talked and the sun was already low in the sky before Camille suggested she had better return to her parents.

They returned to the Fox and said goodbye in both languages before Tom set off to find Francis Trew. He needed to tell his friend about his day — the most perfect day of his life.

Chapter V
Local Rivalry

September 1637

John Bingham, the alderman of the Borough of Poole, was riding with his trusted clerk, Mellendrew, to meet the Bankes at Corffe Castell. He had a well-trimmed dark beard, which disguised a weather-beaten face from many years, in his youth, on board ships between Poole and Newfoundland. He had removed his hat as it was a warm afternoon, revealing that he was losing some of his hair on top, which was also turning grey, but this added to his distinction; a Puritan and man of authority. He was eager to meet the Bankes, who had acquired the estate earlier in the year and had finally moved in after commencing alterations to the Norman building. Bingham wanted to welcome the new neighbours, as well as discuss a few matters of commerce. It would be a pleasant day's ride, with the first colours of autumn sprinkling the trees that lined the road, and the sun playing hide-and-seek behind the clouds. He liked to ride and think about his life and the world, for in both matters there was much to reflect upon, now he was a man of such influence.

It was three years earlier that he had been made the alderman, something for which he had worked hard and achieved on his own merit. It was not a hereditary appointment or that he was in favour with any influential person, but due to his own toil and graft. As a Puritan, toil was a means to sacrament with God although his work ethic was something he had inherited from his father before he discovered his new faith. The Puritan doctrine had just been a natural extension of this and he was grateful to God for the opportunity that this position provided. Yet he had bigger ambitions to fulfil, in enhancing his own position and, more importantly, the service of God through the Puritan movement. He was a radical Puritan who wanted to purify the Church of England from the trappings of the Catholic faith — the Book of Common Prayer, the pomp and ceremony, and the hierarchy. Yes; especially the elitist hierarchy that meant priests were from the noble classes and supported religious privileges for their peers.

Yet the actions and morals of many of the nobles, even those who were priests, were as far away from the teachings of Christ as John Bingham could imagine. Their opulence in dress and comfort, their lust, gambling, drinking and over-indulgence, when most of England was living in poverty, made Bingham cringe. As Christ said, "I tell you the truth, it is hard for a rich man to enter the kingdom of heaven. Again, I tell you, it is easier for a camel to go through the eye of a needle than for a rich man to enter the kingdom of God." Bingham understood exactly why. In contrast, in this small part of Dorsetshire, he was leading a whole new movement for the glory of God, where values and morals were at the forefront and where people could be rewarded for good living and hard work, both in this world and the next. And yes — if he profited on the way, that was all right too, and thanks be to God.

John Bingham had been brought up in the borough, which was an up-and-coming port within its harbour on the Dorsetshire coast. Traditionally, trade had by-passed Poole, and ventured up the River Frome, at the back end of the harbour, to Wareham. However, over the last hundred years, larger ships were trading to Newfoundland and were unable to navigate the Frome River. A quayside was developed in Poole to service these ships, and gradually Poole grew from a village to a borough, eclipsing Wareham, and now competing to be the largest town in the county, with Dorchester and Sherborne. John Bingham was determined to ensure it achieved this goal.

His father had worked his way up to be the first mate on Captain's Boyd's twenty-man Newfoundland trading vessel and he knew everything there was to know about the ship and navigation. The trade was a three-cornered route, as ships went out to Newfoundland loaded with salt and provisions, then caught, dried, and salted fish in the best stocked waters in the North Atlantic, before bringing it back to ports in Spain, Portugal and Italy and finally returning to Poole with wine, olive oil and dried fruits in their holds. As first mate, Bingham's father had a small share in the bounty of each three-month voyage and had put this away to ensure that John would have more opportunity than he had during his life. From the age of ten, John had joined him on the voyages, and he had not protected him from the inevitable hard work of a cabin boy on board an ocean-going vessel, with its three, square-rigged masts. He was often sent into the rigging and along the yards to unleash the sails. However, Captain Boyd had taken a liking to the boy and had helped him read, write and do his numbers, as well as learn navigation. Six years on, John Bingham knew almost as much about shipping as his father.

One night, mid-Atlantic, on a calm sea on the way to Portugal, as the two of them sat on deck looking up at a clear sky of abundant stars, John's father revealed his plan to his son. He wanted to send his son to a school that taught the commercial side of shipping, such as accounting, ledgers, and contracts, because he did not want his son risking his life battling the sails and rigging against storms and gales for the rest of his life; not to mention the risks of piracy, which had resulted in the loss of twenty ships from Poole in just the last few years. The real money was on-shore and with those who owned the ships and the cargo. John's knowledge of shipping, with the education that could be offered by this school in Portsmouth, would give him opportunities that his father could only dream of and he had hoped this would enable John to support his mother and father in their old age. So John went to the school and worked studiously, recognising the sacrifice his father had made.

Two years later, he did return to Poole and found employment as a Ledger Clerk, working for the town's alderman. He was eighteen years of age and already earning a shilling a day, the same wage his father made as first mate after twenty years of voyages, but with prospects to quickly advance. He could not wait to welcome his father back from his current voyage and tell him his news, as he was sure he would be very proud. But his father did not return. Nobody did. After months of waiting, with no word of the ship, it was declared lost, having battled one too many storms. John's father, Captain Boyd, and his old shipmates were all lost without trace: no news of their fate, no goodbyes, no bodies to bury, but just a slow realisation and coming to terms with the loss.

John took solace in religion and he found it in the energy of the new Puritan movement. A young Puritan minister had come to Poole: Francis Eaton, with his wife Sarah and new-born son, Samuel. He was the grandson of one of the founders of the Puritan movement in Bristol, but had much more radical ideas. With bible in hand, dressed in grey, the twenty-year-old man stood on a crate on the quayside and preached the word of God outside the Guildhall, where John Bingham worked on his ledgers. He could hear the call to faith and ministry from his desk, and the directness of the message started to resonate.

Outside on the quayside, most people were too busy to pay much attention to the young minister but at midday, John made an excuse to leave his desk and made his acquaintance with Francis Eaton. John said he was interested to learn more about his message and invited the minister and his family to meet up at John's house that evening. Supper was potage, a ham and mushroom pie, bread and ale, but for John it was Francis's words that provided the nourishment. He was surprised that his guest did not drink ale and preferred apple juice, but he soon discovered that this was part of his new Puritan message.

His grandfather had wanted to purify the Church of England from within — stripping back the ornate trappings and hangovers from Catholicism. Francis wanted to purify it much further: purify the message to make it simple and understandable to every man and woman in England, and his pulpit was the streets or a barn in which people could listen, rather than be intimidated into absolution. He wanted to inspire people to sing and praise God in everyday language. He preached not absolution, but education, understanding and enlightenment. Through prayer and discipline, a light shone along a path of devotion, rather than preaching fear and faction. Everyday life, including the method of working and the exertion itself, would be for the glory of God, rather than the show of sacramentalism found in the church.

Furthermore, John wanted to purify body and soul by the method of living. This meant pledging to live a life for the glory of God and not drink, gamble or frequent the playhouse, and dress in simple, unadorned ways that did not symbolise status or position, but made people feel and look equal as they are before the eyes of God. The overarching philosophy was to enter the kingdom of heaven in the afterlife through hard, honest toil, living a pure life and with prayer. And it was through the grace of God alone that one could be saved, and this grace was the direct gift of God, unmediated by any earthly institution. This message was for all, for in God's eyes all men were equal and the spirit flowed to every man, woman or child who would listen, and people of all social grades could have their hearts lifted by its breath; from aristocrats and country gentlemen to farm labourers and ships' crews. But, according to Francis, it was in the cities, towns and ports that there was much work to do, for the needs of men were greatest, yet the temptations away from this path were more plentiful: that is why he had come to Poole.

Francis had a sparkle in his eye and a warmth in his smile that made his message sincere and honest. He was humble but fired by a passion that burnt inside him, and he preached in an intoxicating way. John was won over and converted to Puritanism there and then, throwing the remains of his ale glass out of the window. It all made sense to the young clerk and echoed many of the values his father had imparted to him on the voyages across the Atlantic — education and working hard. He plotted with the young minister on how to spread the word in Poole.

The next day, Bingham had agreed that he could use the upper floor of a quayside granary, one evening a week, with one of the merchants with whom he had regular dealings, free of charge. His mother and his sister produced thirty leaflets on some old ledger paper for distribution around the borough. On the front side was the notice of the 'Word of God Service and Sermon for you by Minister Francis Eaton' and with the information of when and where. On the reverse was a hymn, a song that praised God in a simple and easily understood language. People were always cagey about new things and even John, at this stage, was careful with whom he spoke about it, but he was excited every time he talked to and listened to his new friend, the minister.

The first service was held in the grain-stall loft on a Wednesday night, so as not to conflict with the Sunday services at St. James' church. Eleven people turned up, including John, his sister and his mother. John was disappointed by the turnout but was heartened by the sermon and the singing. They sang the hymn on the pamphlet three times and learnt another hymn by heart, as a congregation, and agreed to have another service on Saturday night. A new pamphlet was produced with a new hymn, and this time twenty-one attendees turned up. By the end of the month, the congregation had swelled to more than fifty and services were being held two evenings a week.

John had changed his attire and adopted the more sombre style of the Puritan, which made him stand out in the Guildhall. There had been some whispering amongst the senior citizens in the borough about this new movement and the alderman himself asked John about it. He played it down, just saying it provided another outlet for his gratitude to God for the opportunity he had been given in servicing the alderman. Many of the Puritan congregation still attended St. James' to ensure they kept up appearances with the merchants of the borough.

However, six months after the founding of the new religion, the priest of St. James' died suddenly and it took several months for the church to find a replacement, whilst his assistant and acolyte, a sixty-year-old man, tried to conduct the services in the meantime. People started to complain and talk, wondering whether it was a sign from God that they had lost their priest at a time when Francis Eaton's sermons were resonating with so many of the town folk. As weeks went by, more and more voted with their feet and came to the granary services, although most still maintained their attendance at St. James' on a Sunday evening.

In May 1620, John and Francis decided that now was the time to really test people's faith and the borough's acceptance of the new faith. They decided to put on a Sunday service under a canvas awning that one of their congregation owned, and was used for the market on rainy days. Indeed, it was proposed that they should make use of the market square, so Bingham approached James Pellet, the alderman, to seek his agreement. He timed the conversation just after Bingham had presented a set of ledgers which showed a healthy profit for the alderman, a man who liked Bingham. He agreed, as a one-off occasion, but as soon as the pamphlets hit the streets, several senior citizens of the St. James' congregation complained and the alderman had to renege on his agreement. However, he offered the use of the field at the end of the quay, which he owned, instead.

Sunday brought a bright May morning, and it seemed like every songbird alive heralded the day and the prospect of this new service. John was concerned that most people would stay loyal to St. James' and all the effort of publicity and erection of the awning, the previous night, would be in vain. He deliberately commenced his service half an hour before the normal start time of the church service: indeed, it would begin as the bells would alert people to start their way to church. But as people broke their fast and put on their Sunday best, many did decide to pass by St. James' and wandered down the quay to the Puritan awning.

Francis Eaton heartily welcomed everybody and before long, the sound of one of their favourite hymns hallowed God from under the canvas. The singing could be heard down the quay, filling the streets of the borough, encouraging more worshippers, who were on their way to St. James, to divert and join the congregation. The atmosphere under the canvas was filled with excitement and anticipation, in stark contrast to the poor old acolyte's attempts at inspiring his flock. Bingham had a huge smile on his face as he made quick glimpses around to his left and right from his front pew position, counting in his head the numbers in the congregation. He knew there were benches, chairs and stools for about eighty and all of these were taken, but he counted double this number standing on the sides and to the rear. What a success and better than he could have dreamt. Furthermore, one of the latecomers who arrived at the back but was being given a seat by the blacksmith's apprentice, was James Pellet, the alderman.

At the end of the service, almost as many people came up to thank John Bingham as Francis Eaton, for he was recognised as a driving force behind the new movement. The alderman himself sought out his ledger man and said he had enjoyed the service and could understand what Bingham was doing. Bingham saw the opportunity again. There was a seed of an idea that had been planted in the back of his mind for a few months, but it had suddenly taken shoot and it was now time to provide the nourishment it needed to ensure it flourished. He asked James Pellet if he could purchase part of the field. When the alderman asked why, he was taken aback when Bingham said he wanted to build a church.

"You have ambition, my son. I would like to help you. Let me sleep on it and we will talk in the morning."

"Yes, sir. Thank you, sir. And one more thing: could we please keep the tent up for the summer season?" John replied, his mind already racing to how he could build the church. He was delighted to hear the alderman's response.

"I think God would indeed want that and who am I to stop what our Lord would decree?"

After most people had departed, Francis Eaton, John Bingham and two of the early converts, Josh Smith and Samuel King, sat down at the front of the tent and discussed what next. Bingham shared with them his idea about building a permanent church and the conversation with the alderman. The others were in awe at his ambition, as they were still comprehending the success of a single Sunday under an awning. The prospect of continuing the services for the foreseeable future was a big enough challenge and they did not understand how building a church could be funded. John could see their concern but knew in his heart this was the right thing to do: he just needed to work out how and he did not have the answer, currently. They decided to revisit the topic at a later date but it was agreed that the success of the movement required better organisation and allocation of roles and responsibilities. Francis Eaton should focus on spiritual leadership, supported by Samuel King in organising services and the broader mission of the movement, whilst John Bingham would be secretary and treasurer, including premises, and Josh Smith would be responsible for promotion.

The next day, John Bingham arrived at the Guildhall with great expectation as he had barely slept that night following the elation of the first Sunday service and the plans for the new church that were forming in his mind. He had already been to see John Burns, who was the master builder in the borough, and asked how much it would cost to build a hall. John Burns was a regular member of the Puritan services and was excited to hear Bingham's ideas.

"Well, if you want to build a hall the size of that tent, you will need an oak frame, and that would be — let me think — twenty-four uprights, four trans and forty-eight cross members. We can get those from the oak dale just north of here."

"Stop! Stop — let me take this down." John Bingham got out a sheet of paper, a quill and ink bottle from his satchel and started to capture the ledger of requirements. As Burns specified, Bingham asked him to cost each item: a farthing for each cross member and so on.

"And how much labour time and cost?" Bingham asked, as Burn finished itemising the components.

"Well, I would supervise at a shilling a day and we would need two craftsmen at fourpence a day and two labourers at tuppence a day. And it would take twenty weeks."

Bingham's quill itemised the expenses and he added up all the rows.

"So, four guineas in total if we include a one-fifth extra contingency," Bingham declared.

"Sounds about right to me," Burns said, with a smile. "But where will you get that from?"

"That is my problem, for which I am sure God will provide guidance," Bingham responded, and thanked Burns for his time.

The total did not include the land cost and would certainly be difficult to fund, but at least he knew the amount he had to find.

The alderman arrived mid-morning and Bingham had to stop himself from approaching him straightaway about the land: he knew from experience that his master was always more affable after lunch. So he kept his head down and concentrated on the ledger of a cargo that was being loaded onto a Dutch trading vessel and the borough mooring fees and trading tax. He could now do these calculations very quickly, having a year's experience, but always ensured they were presented in an exemplary way and padded out the work to make sure he could manage the expectations of the workload. However, with the knowledge and expertise of his six years at sea, he was starting to advise the alderman in new innovative ways. Most notably, he had developed what he called a planning ledger. Rather than just keeping the books as ships came and went, he made a forecast over a twelve-month period, which anticipated the typical voyage time of each ship, its outgoings on the voyage, and the revenue it would bring when it returned. He mapped each of these sheets onto a single page, which had revenue and outgoings for each ship over the year and showed the total income and outgoings. James Pellet, the alderman, had been delighted by this.

The alderman returned from lunch with two other merchants. The meal had clearly included a fair quantity of wine, for his face glowed and there was no doubt that he was in a fairer temperament. John could wait no longer, so approached him and asked about the land.

"John, my son. I did enjoy the service yesterday and I do want to help you. But I also need to consider my position as Alderman. Many people in the borough are against your new church under canvas, let alone anything more permanent. At lunch, Hobbard and Drake were very concerned about what was going on. I am happy for you to carry on services under canvas for the next couple of months. This is my decision and I will defend this, as I have already offered it to you. But I cannot be seen to be selling land to the Puritan movement, as well."

Bingham's heart sank. His plans would come to nothing.

"But I have a suggestion," the alderman continued. "Whilst I cannot sell land to the Puritan movement, I would be prepared to sell land to my ledger clerk. I would be prepared to sell half an acre for two pounds. I believe I pay you two shillings a day. If you worked one day a week for free, you would be able to pay this sum in—"

"Five months, sir," Bingham butted in, enthusiastically.

"Yes — five months. That is correct. How does that sound, Bingham? What you do with the land would be clearly up to you and outside my control and influence."

"It sounds perfect, sir, if we could have use of the land straightaway," enthused Bingham.

"There is nothing stopping you, is there? I think God has plans for you, Bingham, and your talent and determination will fare well for this borough."

And so Bingham left that evening and started to put his plan into place. He now could finance the land. His commercial head could see some added benefit to him, personally owning the land for the new church, but he still had four guineas of construction costs to find. The offerings to date had just funded the minister and the pamphlets, but the offering on Sunday had amounted to a total of four shillings and two pennies. If this level of donation continued, he could put two shillings from the Sunday service and another one from the mid-week one each week for construction. There were twenty-one shillings in a guinea and so he would have the money in twenty-eight weeks. Construction would take seven to eight months, according to John Burns, so it would all work out, as long as donations were maintained.

The following week, the sun shone again on the Poole Puritans. Even more people turned up to the Sunday service. Eaton was on fire from his makeshift pulpit, and the offering produced almost five shillings. This gave Bingham the confidence to commission John Burns to commence the building, and as the weeks passed, firstly the oak frame and then the walls started to take form. The congregational numbers were maintained and the collection each week was entered into Bingham's ledger, and matched the outgoings needed to pay John Burns for his materials and labour.

But then disaster struck. James Pellet asked Bingham to stay behind after work and when they were alone in the Guildhall told him that he could not continue to let him host the Sunday services on his field.

"I said I would let you use my field for two months and I have kept my word. But despite my joy in attending the services, I have been put in an impossible position and so have no option but request that you seek alternative arrangements next week."

Bingham was devastated. He pleaded for more time but the alderman could not be moved. Behind the scenes, Hobbard and Drake had been squeezing Pellet, both threatening to not only remove their cargos from the three ships that the alderman owned, but said that they also spoke for Sir Edward Coke and Lord Cranbourne. Bingham recognised the implications of this threat. These four merchants represented nearly three-quarters of his business. He went back home for supper that night, and told his mother, Francis and Sarah Eaton the news. The meal was very sombre, and John's mother excused herself so she could retire early for bed, as she had not been sleeping well in the midsummer heat, whilst Sarah nursed baby Samuel. This left the two Puritans looking at each other over the table.

"What are we going to do? Without a place to worship, what chance do we have in attracting a congregation of sufficient size to fund the building works?"

"I am afraid that is not the only challenge. I have some news of my own. I have received a letter from London. There are two ships that will soon be sailing from Southampton to start a new life in the new territories across the Atlantic. A new life in a new continent based on Puritan methods and ways. We have been offered a place on one of the ships and

105

I have discussed it with Sarah. We feel it is God's will that we go," Francis stated.

Bingham stared at him. He did not know what to say. He believed in the new movement in Poole and had been working so hard over the last year to make it happen, and indeed up until a few hours ago everything seemed to be developing at a pace. The silence between the two young men was deafening before John stood up suddenly, pushed over the table between them and stormed out. He did not know where he was going but had to go. He saddled his horse and rode.

The late July sun was starting its descent over the Purbecks on the far side of the harbour and John rode out to meet it, along the eastern shore and along a sandbank that took him to the harbour entrance. He dismounted but the thoughts continued to race around his head. He felt betrayed by Francis, by his own faith, and he felt stupid. How did he get into this mess? He was only twenty and why was he taking on so much? How could he continue building the hall and for what aim anyway, if there was no one to preach? He wanted to wash all this away, so stripped and ran into the sea. Would this cleanse him of this nightmare? He swam and swam, at one stage thinking that he could end it all by just swimming into oblivion, but something inside told him to swim back. He heard a voice, a familiar voice, saying, "A sailor does not learn to master the sea in calm waters". It was his father; something he often said and now it started to make sense. He had to face the challenge and navigate his way through the storm until he found calmer waters.

So John turned back to shore, where Nutmeg, his father's old horse, was loyally and expectantly waiting. He had to swim hard against the current, and fatigue was setting into his arms. He rested and floated but the current took him out further. He dug deeper to fight the fatigue that drained his muscles, and kicked and clawed his way back to shore, a sense of panic and doom growing inside him. But slowly he cut down the distance, halving it and halving it again. He did not think he was going to make it, as his legs drained and dropped into what he thought was going to be his watery grave, but he stretched out his toes, found a sandbank and his face was just above water, between the rolling waves. He stood and caught his breath, resting his aching arms.

The sun had now fallen behind the Purbecks and the sky had turned into a night blue, with the first stars glimmering above him through watery and salty eyes. His arms were in agony and his legs barely able to hold his weight. He had used all his energy to get to his resting place. But the tide was going out and so, with time, he knew the distance to swim would be getting shorter, and his head would be able to emerge from the water. But as he rested, he was getting cold in the water which would sap his strength further, so after a while he decided he had to make a last effort for shore.

He kicked off, and gritted his teeth to fight the pain, urging himself on. Sluggishly, the metres between him and Nutmeg disappeared and he staggered out of the waves, where his horse greeted him. He grabbed the rein and Nutmeg dragged him the last few metres out of the water, through the damp sand and up to the dry shore. He lay there and entered a sleep-like trance as the warm summer breeze dried him out. He dreamt about his father on board a ship in a storm, battling the wind and the waves but coming through safely. As he returned to consciousness, he concluded the dream was a sign not to give up and keep fighting for what he wanted; what God wanted.

Time passed and some strength returned. He dressed, mounted Nutmeg and allowed him to slowly find his way home, where Eaton was still up, waiting for him. "Where have you been? I was worried," the minister asked.

"Looking for meaning and finding inspiration," Bingham responded.

The two young men discussed the situation and between them managed to hatch the bones of a plan. The next day they awoke and set off together to Southampton. On the journey, Francis and Sarah told John more about the vision for a new world based upon Puritan values and beliefs. He was starting to understand and was even a little jealous not to be embarking on the adventure himself. But John was convinced God had a reason for him to be in Poole and was determined to see that through.

When they reached Southampton, they found the Mayflower moored to the bustling wharf with other cargo ships, readying itself for sail the following week. The ship was not much larger than those John had sailed across the Atlantic, in his childhood, but with castle-like structures at both fore and aft. Bingham knew that these were designed to protect those on board but also had heard that they made sailing close to the wind difficult, so they would find it challenging in the Atlantic westerlies. The Mayflower was awaiting the arrival of another vessel, the Speedwell, which was due to arrive in the next few days from Defthaven in the Netherlands. The two ships would make the voyage together, but with no cargo of olives or fish in their holds; instead, as Francis declared, the hopes of the Puritan church and the dream of a Puritan nation. That was, indeed, precious cargo.

John, Francis and Sarah, with young Samuel, who was now starting to crawl, met Thomas Weston on board the Mayflower. Weston was orchestrating the expedition and was bringing people from all across England to join the voyage. Weston was a man in his mid-thirties, dressed in Puritan charcoal grey, but his manner and voice intimated he was somebody of substance, who was well connected. It turned out that Thomas had been converted to Puritanism by Francis' father, and so held the young minister in high regard. He was eager to hear about his ministry in Poole, and over supper, Francis, Sarah and John told him of the momentum behind the movement, and the struggles they had faced, as well as the current predicament. Francis and Sarah opened up their hearts, sharing how they had been torn between the prospect of this new adventure and their commitment to the people of Poole, but they believed that God was guiding them to join the Mayflower and would equally support John in continuing the mission in Dorsetshire, but they had no idea how.

Bingham was at ease with Weston, who had a calming influence and listened to all that had been said, probing with a question here and there. He said he had two things to settle before he could retire to bed for the night; the first being Francis and Sarah's commitment to the Mayflower, and the second was a plan for Poole. All three listened intently, whilst Samuel slept.

Weston first addressed Francis and Sarah, and told them that the journey ahead would be very tough and that they must be certain that this was the call of God. They had to think of Samuel, who was so young and would be at even greater risk. The couple confirmed that they understood all of that and John Bingham had been trying to persuade them not to go, ever since they left Poole, with vivid descriptions of life at sea from his experience in the North Atlantic. They were adamant that God would protect them and had called them for this mission. Thomas Weston acknowledged their commitment and led the table in prayer to thank God for the opportunity, his guidance and safeguarding.

He then turned his attention to the situation in Poole. He enthused about the success of the mission in Poole to date and said that he could not allow this good work to be undone. His understanding of the situation that some money was needed to complete the church, as well as a minister with passion and conviction. He had a proposal to make which would address both. He was a man of some substance, but much of his wealth could not be taken on the voyage, and what better use for it than God's work. He would provide the five guineas it would take to complete the work, and a further two guineas to be invested in promoting the ministry. Bingham could not believe his ears, but the good news continued. Weston said that there was a minister who had travelled with him on the Mayflower from London and had been sick all the way. He was now sure that it was God's will for him to be in Poole, not the new territories. Perhaps his destiny was to continue Francis Eaton's work in Poole. Bingham felt as though all his Christmases had come at once.

The next day, Thomas Weston confirmed that Jacob Winter, the minister, had agreed to continue the ministry in Poole. It was an emotional goodbye with Francis and Sarah, all saying that they would meet again, but all knowing that this was really a goodbye forever. The Mayflower and Speedwell set off together to whatever future God had planned and by the end of the week, Bingham was introducing Jacob Winter to his new congregation, and showing him around the partially completed church.

Bingham smiled to himself as he and Mellendrew continued the journey to Corffe. There had been many other challenges and many milestones along the way between saying goodbye to the Mayflower, and his position now on the road to Corffe as alderman of the Borough, seventeen years later, but his happiest day was the opening of the new church in Poole and Jacob Winter's first service there. The congregation was so numerous that day and the hymns sung with so much vigour that

Bingham would not have been surprised if Francis Eaton could not hear the rejoicing on the winds across the Atlantic, as they carried the Mayflower on to its destiny.

With the success of the church, Bingham's position and status increased. Thomas Weston had introduced him, by letter, to traders in Leiden and London and he was able to exploit these with some wise investments, initially in cargo, and then a quarter share in a trading boat, the Silver Ghost, that voyaged to Newfoundland. The death of James Pellet, in 1626, meant that he no longer had a job, but nor did he need one. The alderman had left Bingham a small dowry in his will that enabled him not only to buy out the remaining stake in the Silver Ghost, but also acquire minority stakes in three other ships. The following year brought a significant return on this investment, as the Duke of Buckingham's expedition to assist the Huguenots at the siege of La Rochelle resulted in an undeclared war with France. This meant no cross-channel trade with the French, so the cargoes that Bingham had secured from the Netherlands and Newfoundland were doubling in value. By the end of the year, he had five ships and had been elected an alderman.

He had visited Corffe Castel once before, when it was home to Sir Edward Coke, with whom he had found common ground when the new King, Charles I, issued an edict compelling every county in England to pay ship tax, but did not seek Parliament's consent. This was contrary to Sir Edward Cokes' Petition of Rights, which stated that the king's subjects 'should not be compelled to contribute to any tax, tallage, aid, or other like charge not set by common consent, in Parliament.' The king's outright flagrance of Parliament's position, within months of granting him consent, riled Bingham. He became very active, not only in Poole, but rallying sheriffs throughout Dorset to reject the king's tax and found an influential champion in Coke. Other counties followed suit and a few months later, Charles withdrew the proposed tax.

Bingham's enterprises and reputation prospered into the 1630s and by 1633 he had been elected leader of the aldermen. Yes, he had much to reflect upon, as he approached the Castell for his second visit, and as he rode through the Outer Gate, he saw the hive of activity of master craftsmen, busy transforming the ancient building into a modern home for the Bankes. Temporary lodgings had been erected in the grounds of the Castell, three dwelling places made from timber and straw, and an open craft shelter from where the chink of iron on metal and saws easing through timber could be heard throughout the day.

As the men from Poole walked to the inner gate, they passed the inner embankment beneath the Castell gloriette that Bingham recalled had provided a firing vantage for cannons over the outer walls, which was well on its way to being converted to gardens for leisurely walks. But it was inside the inner bailey that most of the noise and activity could be heard, where the grand hall had been at the heart of the renovation in Lady Bankes' plans. The three-storey room was a harsh medieval relic of the past. The Bankes had no need for such a large austere place — no need for medieval banquets or presiding over judgement of their tenants and serfs. They would like to entertain, but in a more intimate setting, and she had devised a plan with Jacques Duchêne to put a staircase up to new bedrooms, whilst the main room would be divided into a reception room to greet guests, a dining room and a library, all with their own distinct style and décor.

It was Ralph Povington who greeted Bingham and Mellendrew at the inner gate to the Castell. He informed the visitors that Sir John Bankes had been called away the day before, but Lady Bankes was looking forward to greeting them in the newly completed reception room, although she had recently become a mother again so would soon tire. Povington had warned Lady Bankes about Bingham's reputation and was secretly looking forward to the encounter. Bingham was conscious that the head of the household appeared to be giving him the once-over before he invited them in. Who did he think he was? He was just a servant but appeared as stuck up as his masters. Bingham was not only leader of the aldermen, but he had also set up his own bank, and he was funding many of the neighbouring land-owning gentry. He had position and status and was doing God's work at the same time. Or was Povington looking down on his attire? Yes, it was Puritan style, but of the highest quality cloth with a very modest lace ruff around his collar and a simple, unadorned, dark-blue felt doublet. He was accustomed to being received by aristocracy and gave Povington an impatient look, which signalled that he was not going to be messed around.

Povington led the guests into the reception room of the gloriette; a room that had been renovated with tapestries and painting on the newly plastered walls, a large candelabra hanging from the ceiling and welcoming fireplace. Lady Bankes sat with a book, in a large upholstered chair. John Bingham walked over and removed his dark-blue felt hat, bowing his head to Lady Bankes as she stood up.

"I am honoured to make your acquaintance, Lady Bankes, and congratulations on the new addition to your family. I trust you and the baby are well."

"Thank you, Mr Bingham, and please forgive the noise. We have some wonderful French craftsman currently working in the library and dining room next door, but they are noisy. We are so looking forward to the end of the work, especially the library for our children to have some peace and freedom to read and be educated by their governess. Please take a seat."

Bingham looked around the room at the ornate ceiling with cornices and the new window that had been created adorned with red satin window seats, overlooking the inner bailey garden, which was being redesigned with a water feature. The furniture was ornate and elaborate in the French, highly polished ebony style with elaborate fabrics and exquisitely carved and gilded features. As he admired the room, Bingham caught a glimpse of the portrait behind Lady Bankes.

"Queen Henrietta Maria, if I am not mistaken, my Lady. The Catholic Queen," he said, barely able to quash the venom in his voice. The look of disgust on Mellendrew's face reinforced the two men's loathing of Catholics.

Lady Bankes was not in any way intimidated. This was her Castell, and she knew how to deal with these two upstarts.

"You are correct, Mr Bingham. The beauty of your Queen has been captured in all its radiance by the celebrated artist, van Dyke, do you not agree? The painting is a gift from your King." She emphasised the 'your' on both occasions in her response.

"Alas, I have not had the pleasure of an audience with King Charles's wife, but I bow to your acquaintance with her."

"Yes, I am acquainted with her and I assure you, Mr Bingham, she is a remarkable woman of very good temperament."

Lady Bankes landed another punch, and Povington smiled as he recognised the brinkmanship as his mistress conversed with men from Poole.

"Sir John has been called away by the king. He has arrested John Hampden for his opposition to the Ship Tax. I believe you know Mr Hampden."

"I do, my Lady. I met him in Oxford recently as I am co-ordinating the opposition to the same tax in Dorsetshire. I have written to Sir John on this matter and it was something I wanted to discuss. When I met Mr Hampden, I believe he did say he was acquainted with you and Sir John."

"That is true. We met him in Oxford, as well, last year. He is a man who is perhaps a little too passionate about what he believes in and less considerate to the sensitivities of others. Clearly, he is upsetting the king now. Nobody likes tax but somebody needs to pay for the protection of the ships that sail from Poole, would you not agree, Mr Bingham?" Lady Bankes asked, knowing he would not.

"It is not the need for the tax, but the fact that it has not been ratified by Parliament that is in dispute. I am sure your Lady is familiar with the Petition of Rights which was masterminded by Sir Edward Cokes, the previous owner of this very Castell," he replied, as Povington kept between the two.

"Of course, you are right, Mr Bingham. Sir John believes the king will find it difficult to make a case against Mr Hampden this time, for it is unclear that the Ship Tax is legal without the endorsement of Parliament. It will be for the judges to decide. But perhaps you should be careful in the meantime. We would not want you arrested," Lady Bankes smiled, as she reminded Bingham of her husband's power.

Bingham changed the subject and enquired about the wellbeing of her family and how she was settling into the Castell. Having been offered a glass of apple juice, he talked about the Borough of Poole and that Lord and Lady Bankes would be welcome to visit at their convenience. Bingham stirred the conversation to the alterations to the Castell.

"I can see you are in the progress of making significant alterations to the Castell."

"Indeed, Mr Bingham. I want to make a home in the latest style and fashion of British and French society."

"I would not know about that, my Lady. As a Puritan, I believe in the augmentation of God, not our human bodies or houses."

"But did God not make man in the form of God, and so why should we not dress and live in style?"

"I fear we will not agree on such matters, my Lady."

"And so what can we discuss, Mr Bingham? We do not appear to share the same views on style, politics, royalty or religion."

"I would like to see how we can promote more trade between Corffe and the Borough of Poole, but I assume that would be something I would discuss with Sir John. May I enquire when you next anticipate his return?"

The assumption Bingham made about Lady Bankes' inability to discuss trade and business further annoyed her. She had already taken a dislike to this man and was now eager to see the back of him.

"You are mistaken, sir. I am very capable of discussing matters of trade and business, both when my husband is at home or away. What is it that you have in mind?" she retorted.

"Well, there is the matter of the shipments of limestone from your estate quarries that are going through Poole."

"What of it?" Lady Bankes fixed her eyes on him.

Purbeck limestone was well known across England, particular one vein known as 'Purbeck marble'; not a true metamorphic marble found in Italy but it could be polished to look as good, and was certainly cheaper, and so was used to dress columns and provide the floors in cathedrals all across England, including Westminster Abbey itself. It could be found in many of the new houses being built by the gentry in London and was being shipped there via Poole.

"The alders of the port are reviewing the loading and carriage costs. Currently you pay a shilling a ton, but we are able to get much higher fees for our shipments from Newfoundland. Business is business, my Lady, and so we would propose an uplift in levy or maybe you should refer your trade to Melcombe."

"This is a business I have some knowledge of, Mr Bingham. The attraction of Poole is your berthing capacity, and it is very close to our quarries, in an easterly direction on the way to London, the primary market for the stone. It would make us much less competitive if we were to incur the additional carriage cost and time in going west to Melcombe. A significant increase in cost could put our quarry out of business. I am sure you also know that, Mr Bingham. What are you and your Alders proposing?"

"You are well informed, my Lady. I will ask Mr Mellendrew to outline our proposal."

"As Mr Bingham said, my Lady, business is business. It is for God to decide, through the natural forces of the market, what should and should not go through our port in Poole. If God wanted limestone to go through the port I am sure he would ensure a price in London to justify it. We are proposing two shillings a ton from the autumn," Mellendrew replied, with an inept smile on his face.

"You know that is an outrageous figure, Mr Bingham," Lady Bankes retorted. "We could not justify it. I think God would not like to see the decline of quarrying in the Purbeck, and the loss of work to people in this shire, neighbours of the Borough of Poole, and I would urge your alders to reconsider. If that is all the business you would like to discuss, I bid you and Mr Mellendrew a good day and farewell."

Lady Bankes got up from her chair and asked Povington to show them out.

Mellendrew and Bingham felt put out at how she had dismissed them so promptly, but both raised their hats and followed Povington out. On the road back to Poole, Bingham felt pleased with the meeting. Lady Bankes had been condescending and was an obvious Catholic sympathiser but he would get the upper hand in the end. He had no desire to be friendly to the Bankes, but did want to ensure that they were aware of him and his commercial and political strength in the area. In shipping terms, he had just fired a shot across the Bankes' bow. And frankly, he did not mind how they responded. If they went to Melcombe, he would use the quay capacity for other more profitable trade. If they agreed to the increase rate, well — he had doubled the revenue. What did he have to lose? He did regret that Sir John was not there to discuss the matter and no doubt no action would be taken until he returned, which could be months away, by which time they would have no option but to pay the increased levy.

Back at the Castell, Lady Bankes had no intention of waiting for Sir John's return. Indeed, before the men from Poole had left the Castell, she had sent for William Harvey so that they could discuss the quarry. It was a serious situation requiring urgent attention. She did not want to lose that income from the quarry; nor did she want to see any loss in livelihood amongst the local villagers. She suspected she could negotiate with Bingham but would prefer to develop a plan that would give her independence and show that Corffe and the Bankes should not be held to ransom. Within the hour she was discussing and developing just such a scheme with her estates manager. They debated the merits of Melcombe as an option. Lady Bankes did not like it as she feared that the alders of that borough could hold her to ransom, as well, and it was far less convenient.

"Why can we not build our own small quay at Swanage? The bay is a safe harbour and it would make us self-sufficient as it is on the estate. Would it be possible? Would it be expensive?" she asked.

William Harvey fingered his beard in contemplation. "You might have something there, my Lady. The western side of the bay has sufficient depth for the fishing boats, except at low tide. We could build a small platform on a wharf with a gantry and winch on top. The quarry boats could berth one side, and the cargo ship the other side. Poole quay has the benefit of not being tidal, whereas we would have to load from mid-tide to mid-tide. Hmm... That may mean building another quarry boat to ensure sufficient stone can be loaded on board in that time. It would mean changing some of the operations and some inconvenience, but we save the shilling per ton, as well as the sailing time it takes to get into Poole Harbour. Why, my Lady — I think you have hit on something."

"Can you design it and cost it, Mr Harvey? But keep it a secret. If this plan is viable, we need to put it into operation before the Poole aldermen get wind of it."

William Harvey left the Castell, his mind already buzzing with the plan. First, he found Jacques Duchêne, the French master craftsman. He explained the idea before they both mounted horses and set off to Swanage Bay to think it through further and start to work out how they could build it. When they reached the bay, the tide was out, enabling them to identify the best spot. The challenge would be how to embed the wooden pilling that would be required in the wet sand. Jacques Duchêne had some knowledge of how this could be done, for he had worked on a château in France with a bridge over a lake and had watched how the master masons had created the pillars. While at Swanage the tide would go out, the sand would still be saturated, and Monsieur Duchêne explained how, by using water-tight barrels, they were able to create a water-tight space to construct the pillars that would support the bridge. He started to draw on the sand how it would work.

A large barrel, as tall as a man, would be set in as deep a hole in the sand as could be created before water caved in the sides. Then a man would be lowered inside the barrel to continue to dig out the sand and water, allowing the barrel to gradually sink further into the sand. When it was fully immersed the man would be pulled out. The Frenchman drew a slightly narrower but equally high barrel, being lowered inside the first one. In his pigeon English, he explained that at the bottom of the inner barrel would be laid a large, limestone base stone, which would have been carved to exactly the same shape as the inner barrel, and so would both plug any water trying to come in, and also be the foundation for the wharf pile. An oak pile could be now loaded down onto the limestone plinth and secured with a scaffold wooden frame. Once secure, stone blocks could be constructed and set in place around the base of the pile, and gravel padded into any gaps. The mortar binding the stones would have until the next day to set, when, at low tide, both the barrel casings would be removed and a new pile could start.

William Harvey soon grasped what needed to be done and started sketching out a design for the whole pier. They estimated that they would need twelve piles to support a platform of sufficient size to be able to transfer the stones from the quarry boats to the cargo ships. Harvey knew where, on the estate, to get twelve oak piles that would be sufficiently large and strong. Sizing and costing the limestone plinths and stones, as well as the barrels, would require estimates from craftsmen on the estate. They jumped back on their horses and headed off, first to the quarry and then to the cooper in Corffe village to discuss the barrels.

Lady Bankes was delighted to hear the result of William Harvey and Jacques Duchêne's investigations. The verdict was that a wharf could be constructed and it would take no more than three months at an estimated cost of four guineas. Lady Bankes quickly calculated that she would be able to recover this investment within six months from not paying the fees to Poole borough. It made the decision easy, although she was already committed in her mind to doing whatever it took to save the livelihood of the quarrymen, whilst not bowing to the demands of John Bingham and his fellow aldermen. She commissioned the work and asked the two of them to manage the project. She stressed that the project should be kept secret for as long as possible, using the pretence that the piles, barrels and limestone were for work at the Castell. She did not want the men of Poole to hear of her plans.

Two weeks later, on the last day of September, Lady Bankes received a letter from the aldermen of Poole saying that they could not accept less than two shillings per ton if her limestone was to continue to be shipped through Poole, and that the fee would be introduced from the first day of November. Most of the preparations for the Swanage wharf were complete; the oaks had been felled and prepared and shaped as piles; the two giant barrels were made and most of the limestone was ready. They had not wanted to start any work until all the materials were ready and could be moved to Swanage so as to ensure the plan did not leak out to the men of Poole.

"So can we do it, William? Can we do it by the first of November?" Lady Bankes demanded.

"We need good weather and good tides. It may be possible, but it is also harvest time and it will mean taking people out of the fields," he replied.

"I do not want to hear 'maybe'. We must make it, and it must take priority over the harvest. Please can you start tomorrow."

"It is the Sabbath tomorrow, my Lady."

"I am aware of that, William, but I am sure this work would be favoured by God, given the jobs it will preserve. I will make sure that prayers are made for you and your men."

The next day, at church, Lady Bankes did more than just say a few prayers for the men. After the sermon, she stepped up to the front of the church and requested that she could say a few words. Nearly all the villagers and folk on the estate were at the church as always but there were a few noticeable absentees, including William Harvey. Lady Bankes addressed the congregation and told them that the quarry was at risk due to action by the Poole alderman, but there was a plan to address this. However, it required everybody here to keep this a secret from anybody outside of the Estate for a whole month. She told the congregation about her plan and she asked them for their prayers for good weather, and the safe working of the men involved in the venture.

While William Harvey and Jacques Duchêne had been busy on the wharf design and planning, their offspring continued to get to know each other. Tom and Camille had been meeting regularly to help each other develop their respective language skills, but for Tom this was just a façade. He just wanted to be with the most beautiful girl he had seen in his life, and although he genuinely wanted to learn French to be able to communicate and express himself to Camille, he found it very difficult to focus in her company. He often found himself totally spellbound as she spoke to him, developing her English skills much faster than his French. He started to worry about his lack of progress. Maybe she would start to think that he was a dummy or just could not be bothered to learn her language, yet his was far from the case. He agreed with Captain Cleall that he would give him a couple of hours of supplementary lessons each week. This seemed to help, and Camille seemed to take a little more interest in their lessons now Tom was keeping pace. They had now reached a level where they were conversing well and as their language skills progressed, they became less reserved and started exploring each other's past, as well as likes and dislikes. Tom was starting to discover that Camille's beauty was not just skin deep: she was a person with strength of character and views on many different things. The more he got to know her, the more his attraction was amplified.

He talked about her incessantly when he was not with her, and it was driving Francis Trew and Joseph Cobb mad. John Bankes was far more helpful and suggested poetry and literature to further charm Camille. This meant more private lessons, and when Tom did start quoting Shakespeare's Hamlet — "To be or not to be" — Camille did raise an eyebrow. But she asked why Tom should question his 'être' when he was such a lovely person. Nobody had said such a nice thing to Tom before and he gave John Bankes a grateful embrace when he saw him, to tell him how successful his advice had been.

William and Jacques put their plan into operation each day the tide withdrew from Swanage Bay. By the end of the first week, after getting everything in place and a production process organised, two piles were in place, but the builders' joy was soon washed away when the start of the second week resulted in three days of storms when no progress could be made. Time was running against them with ten more piles required in just fourteen days, assuming the weather held. William commissioned two more barrels to double the production capacity. William, Jacques, Tom and Francis, as well as four other villagers and two Compagnons, joined the original four labourers to help meet the deadline. It was hard, wet and cold work, but with the benefit of some ale, some hearty songs, in both French and English, one by one the piles were completed. Jacques and the two French Compagnons set to work on constructing the platform on top of the piles. With every plank that was nailed into the emerging structure, William Harvey felt the pressure release, and even allowed a smile to his co-workers, while he continued to pray for consistent good weather and offered thanks for the progress they had made.

The last day of the month arrived and Lady Bankes was invited to inspect and open the new wharf. A toast was made to all who sailed from it, and the patron of the wharf was delighted. She thanked everybody for their hard work and was determined to convey the good news to the aldermen of Poole herself. So, escorted by Captain Cleall and William Harvey, she set off.

It was just passed midday when they arrived at the gate to the town, where two carts carrying entertainers and players were struggling to make their way through the entrance and into the town. The Corffe contingent bypassed them and made their way straight to the Customs House to seek out John Bingham. His henchmen, the oversized Dutchman, von Gauul, was at the door, but was too taken aback to make a move, as Lady Bankes marched straight into the large hall, with its vaulted, oak-framed roof. A huge oak trestle table, at the far end, had eight chairs and hosted Bingham and three other aldermen of the Borough, all cloaked in the greys and blacks of the Puritan style. They were accompanied by a more traditionally dressed craftsman, who, apparently, was a shipwright. They were so immersed in their conversation and focused on a large drawing of a ship that had been presented to them by the shipwright that they did not notice the approaching Lady Bankes. She paused a few yards from the table, and the other people who were milling around the hall had all stopped talking to turn around to watch the woman, obviously one of status in her crimson dress and black cloak, as she stood ready to confront the aldermen. The quiet in the room amplified the conversation the aldermen were having, making them self-conscious, until they all looked up in turn to see Lady Bankes awaiting to address them.

"My dear Aldermen, I believe today is when you intend to double the duty on my limestone going through this port. Mr Bingham, you suggested I go elsewhere when I told you that the increase you were proposing was extortionate, and so I have. I am informing you that I will no longer require the services of your quay, as I have erected my own wharf in Swanage. Good day to you all."

The tone of her voice was definitive and authoritative, deploying the strength of her aristocratic upbringing. And with that, Lady Bankes turned and headed straight back out of the Customs House before anybody could utter a word; not that many could have done as they were awestruck by what they had witnessed. On the way out of the town, she saw the players again and stopped to address them. She suggested that they would not be welcome in this Puritan town, but would be more than welcome in her village and that she would make it worth their while. The players agreed and followed the Corffe contingent west.

The players drove their carts right into the Castell grounds and in consultation with Povington, began to set out their stalls. It was soon announced that they would take a day to set up a makeshift theatre but in the eve after the morrow, they would stage a rendition of Romeo and Juliet, a popular play in London from the quill of William Shakespeare. Barrels were arranged to create the foundation of a temporary stage, over which planks were hastily nailed together for the platform. The players had drapes and pre-painted boards for their scenes in their cart, and these were erected onto a scaffold, over which was draped a large canopy that would protect the audience from any inclement weather. It was rare for players to stop at a small village like Corffe, and all the villagers from miles around arrived to join in the festivities, as well as celebrate the saving of the quarry and the victory over the commercial exploitation of Poole.

Nobody enjoyed it more than Tom and Camille, who sat centre stage, and absorbed every word of the tragedy, Camille seeking comfort in Tom's shoulder as the final scene unfolded. After the play, Camille was bubbling with enthusiasm.

"Such passion; such devotion; such love… How do you say — transcendante? Spirituelle?" She paused. "And such tragedy. How does it make you feel, Tom?"

Tom was in a state of bliss and could just listen to her all night. John Bankes had been so right about the power of literature.

The next day his happiness was shattered when Camille told him she would be leaving to return to France with her mother and some of the Compagnons. He father would be staying and she would return in three to four months' time, but her mother needed to spend some time in her native country and to see her grandmother and sisters.

"There are things about France I also miss, Tom, but I will be back. I will miss spending time with you, of course," and with that she gave him a peck on the check and waved goodbye, leaving Tom by the Bankes of the Wicken in total disarray. She had kissed him. It was just a peck but he could still feel the sensation of her tender lips on his cheek and tingling throughout his body. But she was going. How would he cope without her? Would she come back? Would she not meet a Frenchman who would woo her with charm beyond Tom's know-how?

He picked up a stone from the riverbank to throw into the water. But then he had a better idea. He ran after her.

"Camille! Wait — Camille!" He caught up with her.

"Take this with you. It is a small piece of Corffe to remind you of this place and the people here." He handed her the rounded chalk stone. She smiled.

"Tom, thank you. That is very sweet. I will cherish it and I will think of you and Corffe every time I touch it."

Chapter VII
Mistletoe and Misery

1638

Tom was with Camille, in the twilight, on the eve of Christmas, walking across the snow-covered village square, as the stars emerged in the darkening clear sky. The air was cold and crisp, and the village looked festive with holly leaves on the doors and candlelight glowing through snow-lined windows. The freshly laid snow was soft and cushioned their feet as they walked. Everything was quiet and peaceful. They spoke in whispers and were reflecting on the year. Camille had been away longer than anticipated because her grandmother had been ill and eventually passed away in the summer. She had finally returned in September, two hundred and eighty-seven days after departing. Tom counted every day. The emptiness in his stomach seemed to stretch to his whole soul through those months. He had not got into the spirit of last Christmas and had tried to keep himself busy working for his father to stem the yearning he felt. But it would not go away. He had hoped for her return in the spring but as every day that passed with no sign of her, he assumed the worst. She was not coming back and had found love elsewhere. He tried to forget about her, but it seemed like nature itself was a constant reminder of everything about her — her voice, her grace, her beauty, and her spirit. Then, in May, two French Compagnons returned, and with them a letter for Monsieur Duchêne. When Tom heard about their arrival, he rushed to the Castell and found the Master Compagnon. He spoke to him in French and asked him if he was well and had he news of his family.

"Yes, Tom. I do have news. Alas, my mother-in-law is not well, so my wife and Camille will be staying with her for a while longer."

"I am sorry, Monsieur. Do you know how long?"

"No, but I also have a letter for you, Tom. I believe it is from Camille."

Tom could barely disguise his excitement as the Frenchman handed him the letter.

"Thank you, sir," he enthused, but then, as he took it, he was flooded with doubt and despair. She could be writing to tell him that she was about to marry a French craftsman and would not be returning to Corffe, after all.

Tom took the letter and ran to the Wicken where he could read it alone.

"Dear Tom,

I hope you are well. Pardon for my English poor. With no talking to you it is more bad. I have liked France again. I have seen my family and many of friends. The food is good. I do miss Corffe and I look at your stone every day.

My grand-mère is ill very bad. My mother and me will stay to take care of her until the end. Then we return to England.

I miss you my friend
Camille x"

He read that letter over and over and then every day until the end of September, when she finally returned; a day he would always remember. Tom had been pushing a barrow across the market square, when three travellers on horses came into the market square; a Compagnon, Camille, and her mother, with another horse carrying baggage. He immediately dropped the barrow's handles and ran to Camille's horse. Her smile beamed down at him, and he helped her down and they embraced.

"You are back! It is so great to see you again, Camille. I had almost lost hope that you would return," he said, feeling the warmth of her embrace. He was conscious of Madame Duchêne still in her saddle, looking down at them.

"Pardon, Madame. J'aide," and he helped her down from her horse. As he did so, he realised their arrival must mean that Camille's grandmother had died.

"Your grandmother?" he asked Camille. She nodded. "I am sorry," Tom said.

"At least we were there to help her during her last few months and say goodbye. But now you must tell us all the things that have happened here."

"Of course. Unpack and tidy up and then we can go to the Wicken, like old times."

And within the hour, the couple were sitting by the riverbank, catching up and talking until the sun went down. Since then, they had revisited all the places Camille loved — Green Island in the harbour; Swanage Bay where the large ships would dock amongst the fishing vessels every other day to pick up the Purbeck stone; Worth Matravers to see Agnes and the cliffs where the stone was quarried; and of course, Nine Barrow Down, overlooking the Castell. Camille was amazed at the changes to the building that her father and fellow countrymen had made. Her father had taken her on a tour and showed her the new library, full of leather-bound books, and a dining room with the most exquisite table she had ever seen, all the way from Paris. All the individual bedrooms had fireplaces and had also been plastered and decorated with curtains and tapestries. Even the kitchen and staff quarters were given new décor and made to be more functional and comfortable for the new era. The changes had been the talk of Corffe. The design feature which provided most cause for gossip around the village was the separate bed chamber with a velvet seat cover. Camille thought her father had excelled and she was overjoyed when Lady Bankes offered her to become her lady-in-waiting to her. She would spend time in the wonderful rooms her father had created, making sure they were clean and tidy, as well as helping Lady Bankes dress and make up every day, which would give her access to all her finery and clothes closet. She could not have dreamt of a better way to earn a living.

The end of 1638 brought a severe cold spell, which resulted in some hardship in Corffe Village and the wider estate. At first, it was just a severe frost with temperatures close to freezing for several days, but then the snow came and lasted a week. At night, temperatures plummeted to below-freezing levels, and everybody was struggling to stay warm at this time of fasting, which made it more difficult. For twenty-four days in

December, people would not eat meat, as part of the Advent period before the twelve days of Christmas festivities. Fires in the grand new rooms seemed to do little to warm the interior of the Castell, and the brassieres in front of the guardroom were eating wood with little benefit to the men manning the gate. The snow even settled on the roof of the blacksmith's, despite the heat coming from the furnace. Lady Bankes order a cartload of logs and a barrel of brandy to be dispersed amongst villagers and estate tenants in the battle against the beastly chill. The gesture was warmly received as people counted down the days to the festivities that Christmas would bring.

As Tom and Camille continued to walk through the snow, the smell of wood smoke softened the air. Tom was telling her about the festivities that would come over the next twelve days. First there was Christmas day, where everybody feasted with their families, followed by St. Stephen's Day, where the Castell hosted a big feast for the village, which would include a roasted goose, a wild boar, wassail and plum pudding. Tom had only that day been out with Capitan Cleall and a company of village men to hunt the boar and had played a much more active role than on his first occasion, the snow and cold making the hunt more atmospheric. He told Camille all about it; the fear and the exhilaration before Ned Parfitt speared the beast and seeing the life disappear from the boar's eyes. The festivities would continue throughout the twelve days in a variety of ways, culminating in another celebration for Epiphany at the Castell, when a Lord of Misrule was elected for the night. The Lord of Misrule was a peasant who had the power to make anybody do anything he demanded.

The two of them rested in the porch of the church where Camille reflected that traditions in France, were similar, although the big feast was on Christmas Eve, with another feast on the last day of the year to celebrate Réveillon de la Saint-Sylvestre, followed by a very festive Epiphany to celebrate the kings on the Twelfth night. Tom was totally in love with her, infatuated by everything about her. They had spent much time together over the last few months, on the pretence of continuing to teach each other their respective native languages. But now, Camille was a fluent as she would ever need to be, and Tom's conversational French was also passable. They were both seventeen, and he was determined that something should happen this Christmas to take their friendship to the next level. Indeed, time was running out, as the work at the Castell was almost complete and Camille's family would be moving on. But could he pluck up the courage to ask for her hand in marriage? And would she stay with him or would she return with her family? He was sure she had some feelings for him but he was not convinced his love was reciprocated. She never seemed to speak about settling down and homely things; just adventures and philosophical questions and concepts. These were both areas of conversation that Tom enjoyed. They had a lot in common, but how to talk about feelings and love was something Tom had no idea about. He remembered the warmth of her embrace when she had returned, but nothing more had happened since and the more time passed the more difficult it seemed to be to make that move.

He had discussed it with John Bankes, who confessed that he had little knowledge of these things but suggested that there would be a time when it would happen. Francis Trew told him just to kiss her and get on with it, which had been based upon his experience with a maiden in Kingston in the summer. But the fact that Francis' relationship had been short-lived just made Tom more concerned and determined that he had to get this right.

Saint Stephen's day, or Epiphany, were Tom's best hopes. Camille would certainly be at both celebrations, and there would be enough alcohol and good spirit to make it easier for Tom to pluck up the courage. Christmas Day brought a warmer air into Dorsetshire, which started to melt the snow and was welcomed by all, given the cold period the village had suffered. Much of Christmas Day was spent thinking about what he should say and how he should say it. He watched his parents over Christmas lunch. He was sure they loved each other but how did they express this? Rarely did he even spot them share a kiss. Yet they seemed to be natural in each other's company, even communicating without talking, knowing what the other was thinking or wanted. Was this love? It seemed strangely at odds with the passion roaring inside Tom for Camille. He longed to be with her, to talk and listen to her, and to explore her body. In his mind, he had already done this a thousand times, but so much of this was fed by his imagination. He had never been with a girl before, and his knowledge of their bodies was limited to seeing his stepmother or sister Beth in the tub, something he had avoided over the last three years or more, since he felt conscious of his own maleness and growing manhood.

The Castell alterations had resulted in a significantly smaller hall now that a dining room and library had been calved out of the original room, but it was still large enough to host many in the village once the furniture had been removed. And so, on Saint Stephen's day, the villagers were crowded into the Hall, the boar roasting on a spit in the fire at the end of the room. It had been mainly cooked in the kitchen but brought in to ensure the scent of the cooking meat could provide a festive backdrop to the occasion. A whole array of other food had been cooked, prepared and laid out on trellis tables around the hall, along with wooden plates. This was not a sit-down banquet that Lady Bankes would have arranged for her gentry friends, but a late-afternoon gathering for all to freely feed from the buffet provided and make merry, and that included the Castell staff. Villagers would carve the meat and serve themselves ale and cider, pies and stews, bread and cheeses, puddings and cakes. The Bankes mingled amongst the village folk, as did the rest of the Castell household. This was a day when all men were equal; privilege and status were set aside.

Tom and Francis gathered in one corner with the Bankes boys and talked about the boar hunt, which Ralph and John had also joined for the first time. They were proud to be part of that hunt and see their kill above the fire, for all to see. They all could not wait to taste it, and it was not long before the spit was moved to the side of the fire and an orderly queue started to form and villagers carved their share of the hunt. The taste of the boar for the boys surpassed their expectations. It was their boar and more succulent than any before.

Tom caught Camille's eye on the other side of the Hall and decided to ensure she got her share of the kill, making his excuses from his friends. He had made a small gift for Camille; a necklace made from shells he found at Swanage. He had taken many months making it, carefully selecting the right ones. He had been wanting to give it to her for some while, and now was the time. His greeting was welcomed and reciprocated by a warm, welcoming smile from her enticing lips.

"Camille, I have been wanting to give you something for some time, and what better time than Christmas," Tom said, slightly louder than he had intended, and his voice caught the ear of a couple of village folk. However, he was determined to see it through, and pulled out a small woollen pouch he had used for years to house his precious clay marbles, as a lad. He passed the pouch to Camille.

"It is for you. I made it myself," he said, as he handed over the gift.

She remained quiet, as her delicate fingers pulled the drawstring of the pouch and furrowed inside, retrieving the necklace that contained a full array of shells and several beads.

Camille's smile widened with approval. "It is beautiful, Tom. Merci, mon ami," and she fastened the string around her neck. Tom breathed a sigh of relief, as he had little knowledge of female fashion and jewellery and so had rested his faith in nature.

They enjoyed the festive offerings of the feast before Tom plucked up the courage to ask Camille to take some air and walk with him. He led her out of the Castell gloriette and on to the terrace that Lady Bankes and the Compagnons had fashioned below its ramparts. The terrace was still within the boundaries of the outer walls but was double their height and so provided a great vantage point, overlooking the village nestled below. The terrace had at one time provided the perfect position for cannons to protect the Castell, but now, although three cannons remained, the terrace had been fashioned into a garden, and they were there for decorative purposes. The garden was still immature, and the plants winterised, yet only a few patches of snow remained and it still made a good spot for what Tom had in mind. It was a clear, still evening, with the face of the night sky freckled with sparkling stars, like diamonds. The quarter-crest moon provided enough light to highlight Corffe's rooftops below, already adorned with a frosted sheen. The couple wrapped themselves up in their coats to keep warm and admired the beauty of the scene, beneath flaming torches that marked the way back to the Castell gloriette.

"It is a wonderful view. I feel blessed to live in such a place. It feels safe, protected by this magnificent Castell, and Sir John and Lady Bankes are good people, building the estate and protecting the community. We have good land for crops and grazing, as well as stone to quarry and the sea to fish. What more can a man wish for? One thing of course. A beautiful woman to share it with."

He turned to Camille, taking both her hands in his own, partially kneeling, looking up into her eyes.
"Camille, I love you with all my heart. Could you possibly consider sharing this life in Corffe with me? I will work hard and will do everything I can to provide a good life and — God willing — a righteous and healthy one. The truth is I loved you from the moment I saw you. I have treasured all our time together, getting to know you and learning French, and seeing your smile just makes me so happy."

Camille was smiling, but a tear seeped out from one of her eyes. It was a tear of joy, but Tom could not understand it and the butterflies in his stomach were, by now, in full flight. He pulled himself up.

"Why do you cry, Camille? I am sorry. I do not know what I was saying, but the last thing I wanted to do was upset you."

"No, do not stop. You have not upset me. The tear was for joy — if not cold — but certainly my heart is warm with the words you were saying. Please continue."

Camille's words gave Tom renewed hope, but before he could collect his thoughts and think what to say, she pulled him closer to her and kissed him gently on the lips. She pulled back and they stared into each other's eyes. Tom felt as though his heart was going to explode. The kiss was so sweet, he was overwhelmed with emotion. He asked with a trembling voice,

"Camille, will you marry me?"

"Yes," she responded and they both kissed; this time intensely, with passion.

The rest of the evening became a euphoric blur as they both struggled to keep their emotions intact, as they kissed, cuddled and giggled, before they returned to the hall, to share their news with their parents, family and friends. On the way back, Tom stopped under the mistletoe that was hanging outside the hall door. This time, he was going to take the lead and his arms were around her, drawing her closer, lowering his head to meet hers, kissing her softly at first but then with gradually increasing intensity. They clung to each other in a world that had been transformed into a dream, where everything seemed distorted, giddy in their bliss. Tom felt omnipotent as the kiss sent wild tremors throughout his body, evoking sensations he had never known before. He did not want the moment to end, but at the same time felt he could suffocate with all the emotion.

Inside, everybody was overjoyed and told them that they did not understand why they had taken so long and that they were a perfect match. Monsieur and Madame Duchene saw the happiness in their daughter and had secretly been bracing themselves for this news, knowing that it would mean leaving Camille behind, but they made Tom vow to come and see them often in France. The best day of Tom's life came to an end with much singing, dancing and joy amongst the Corffe villagers.

The next day, there were plenty of sore heads in the village. The Castell Hall was being cleared up by the Bankes' staff, under Povington's direction, as he set out to restore order and cleanliness. But by midday came news of two villagers being ill with a fever. By nightfall, several more villagers were ill, and people started to worry. People were concerned that the gathering on Saint Stephen's day could have resulted in spreading the illness.

Word of the sickness came to Lady Bankes. There was no doctor in Corffe, but Dr Phelps was called from Wareham to see a few of the villagers at Lady Bankes' expense, with the hope of understanding what the illness was and how to mitigate its spread. Phelps could do little. He suspected it was putrid throat, an illness that was very dangerous for children and weaker adults. He advocated keeping the patients as warm as possible, brandy and hot vegetable soup, but no apothecary. All of the Christmas festivities were cancelled and villagers started to pray as word spread of more people falling ill. The day after Doctor Phelps left, there was the first fatality: a two-year-old boy, the son of Alfred Smith.

Lady Bankes received word of this tragedy while having breakfast with her eldest daughter Alice and eldest son John, as the other children were still upstairs being washed and dressed by Camille and another maid. Sir John had left the previous day to travel to Winchester, where the king was staying for a few days, but he would rendezvous with Captain Cleall at Lord Cranborne's hunt later in the week and then be back in Corffe for Epiphany. It was Captain Cleall who arrived at breakfast bearing the sad news. He had been down to the village to discuss the crisis with William Harvey and the vicar.

"Oh, how sad, James. What can we do for Alfred and his wife? I guess this will not be the last. What is to be done?" Lady Bankes asked.

"I am not a physician, my Lady, but when I was fighting in Saxony, a battalion suffered from a sickness very similar and it was taking the lives of many men before they were taken into a nearby monastery and given beds and warmth and hot soup, just as the doctor has said."

"James, what if we convert the hall into a temporary hospice, with straw bales as beds, and provide blankets? We could keep the fire going, fully stoked, and women in the village could hold a day and night vigil, providing care: water, broth, brandy, whatever it takes. Would it work, James? Would it save lives?"

"My Lady, it is a plan, which is a good thing. When facing all the odds against you at battle, a plan provides hope and gives people focus and helps them fight the enemy, even if the plan is not that good. I believe it is worth a try, although one thing is certain: Povington will not be happy," he replied, smiling at Lady Bankes' generosity, as well as the thought of Povington's anticipated reaction.

"Let me deal with him. So let's do it, James. Can you organise getting the sick to the Castell using wagons draped in skins and I will work with Camille and Povington to make the hall ready. Come on, John and Alice — you two can help, as well," Lady Bankes commanded, and left her breakfast table to be followed by her two eldest children.

"My Lady, I would also suggest sending for Agnes, up in Worth. She may be able to help with some draught that will help with recovery."

"Good idea, Captain. We have to try everything."

The plan came together with a combination of military precision and female determination. Povington was appalled by the idea, but when

Lady Bankes threatened to use his quarters as lodgings for the sick, as an alternative, he came around. Hay bales were brought up from the barn adjoining the stables and four were placed together each to create one of sixteen beds that were spread out through the hall, with all the existing furniture moved to the dining room and library. A skin was found to cover each bale, and then on top of that a woollen blanket from the Castell laundry. Soon the patients started to arrive; firstly, the four-year-old daughter of Alfred and Annie Smith. Lady Bankes expressed her condolences for the loss of their son, and both were clearly distraught but overwhelmingly grateful for what she was doing and prepared to do anything they could do to help. Alfred was sent with John Bankes on wood-carrying duty: they would need a lot to keep the fire going at full stoke, day and night, while Annie became the first nurse in the hall, attending her daughter with Alice Bankes.

The beds soon started to fill up: Elizabeth Trew, Francis Trew's mother, who had been the first to catch it and was looking in bad shape; Jed Parfitt's mother, who was one of the oldest in the village, but also his ten-year-old son; Josh Miller's wife and daughter; two of the Compagnons, and Elspeth Duchêne, Camille's mother.

Lady Bankes, Alice, Camille and Annie Smith created a shift for nursing, while the captain and William Harvey travelled to the surrounding hamlets to ensure the message was clear — ill family members should be brought to the castle and isolated. While the captain was at Worth Matravers, he saw Agnes, who looked rather pale herself. He enquired after her health but she said it was not a physical ailment that troubled her, but the cloud in her dreams was getting darker and more oppressive. She said she feared that the omens were bad for England and it would mean many deaths. The captain feared it related to this current illness that was spreading across the Purbeck and maybe it would spread across the country. But she was adamant that this cloud represented something much worse and much more sinister that was still some way off.

The next day, Jed Parfitt's mother became the second victim and by then, most of the beds were filled. One was taken by Camille after she had woken up with a sore throat but within hours had developed a fever and malaise. Tom heard about her illness from his father and rushed to the Castell to see how she was and what he could do to help. By now there were half-a-dozen women caring for the sick, and Monsieur Duchêne was by Camille's bedside. It was Lady Bankes who had taken charge of the situation, organising fresh linen and towels for the sick, ensuring the fire was maintained and organising the distribution of a hot broth, made of lentils and potatoes. She spotted Tom.

"What are you doing here, Tom?" she asked.

"How is Camille? Is there was anything I could do to help?" he replied.

"All I can say is that she is in a good place but should not be disturbed. Her father is at her bedside. If you want to help, fetch more wood. We need to keep the Castell warm," Lady Bankes requested.

Tom ran off, and in no time at all had two baskets of logs which he distributed to fires at either end of the Hall. At the furthest end was Camille's bed. She was asleep, but feverish and very restless, as Alice mopped her brow. Her father looked on and came over to Tom.

"She is not in a good way. We all need to pray," he said, in French, with an arm around Tom's shoulder.

Tom relieved Alice and sat with Camille, while her father went to see his wife. He held her hand, which was deathly cold, and prayed with all his might. He could not imagine a world without her. Many hours later, he was asked to leave, along with the other men in the room. More beds and more room were required, as two more victims came in. He left the Castell feeling numb, and found his friend, Francis Trew, waiting at the gates, pacing around. Seeing Tom, he ran to him.

"Tom, it is my mother. She has the fever and has been taken inside."

Tom took his friend's hand and gave him an expression of sorrow.

"Camille is also inside, burning up. There is little we can do, my friend. We must leave them to the care of Lady Bankes and the womenfolk."

The boys turned in silence and headed back to the village, each deep in thought. They returned the next day and sought word of Francis' mother and Camille. There was no change in Camille's condition, but Francis' mother had taken a step for the worse. Francis was invited in and stayed with his mother as she gradually declined over the course of the morning, before taking her last breaths before noon.

Francis was distraught and there was not much Tom could do to console his friend, as he sobbed, sitting on a horse-mounting block by the blacksmiths in the outer bailey. What would Francis do now, aged sixteen and with no kin? Tom assured him that he was certain that he would be able to stay with his family, which temporarily eased his friend's sobbing, but then Francis jumped up, pushed his friend away and ran in the direction of the village. Tom turned to follow but stumbled to the floor, before picking himself up and starting after him. Francis was already through the Castell gate. By the time Tom reached it, a cart was blocking the way as it trundled through the gate, holding him up for a moment too long. He managed to squeeze himself passed and continued the chase. He ran into the market square but had lost sight of his friend.

Tom first headed to the pub, where Thomas Moreton was rolling a barrel of beer in through the front door. But Thomas had not seen Francis. He must have taken another route out of the square, so Tom doubled back. He then decided to go along the upper street out of the square, but enquiries in that direction also proved unproductive. Back in the square he had two more options: up Nine Barrow Down or the road to Wareham. He thought if he were Francis, he would climb the Down, and so he started the ascent, but soon realised that he had again made the wrong choice, for by the time he had reached halfway up the Down, he could see in the distance a figure that he was sure was Francis, along the road to Wareham. He was nearly halfway there but was still running after two miles. Tom cursed. He would have to catch him but would need a horse to make up the ground. He headed back down the hill and ran back home to fetch his father's horse.

Francis ran and ran. The grief was like a treacle through which he had to track to free himself. But it was pulling him down and sucking the life out of him. He stumbled into Wareham and passed people attending their daily chores and trades. He continued through the quay fronting the river and down Church Street. The feeling of the grief catching up and bearing down on him was all encompassing and suffocating. He just had to escape it and a mad idea came to him. There were two horses tethered to a post outside a house a few yards ahead. He would take one and ride away from here, leaving behind the pain and the grief. He looked around and could see nobody watching, so he dashed for the nearest horse, freed its rein and with one mighty jump pulled himself onto the saddle. The horse reared up and Francis struggled to rein him in, which stirred the other horse. People from down the street started to look and then the door to the house opened and a stern-looking man came rushing out.

"Stop! That's my horse. Stop!"

He tried to grab the horse's rein, but Francis had just kicked the horse into action and it galloped away to more cries from its owner.

Moments later, Tom arrived on his father's horse to find a commotion. Such a short time can change a life and so it was. In that time, Francis had got away but the horse had reared again at the crossroads when the blacksmith, seeing something was astray and recognising the horse, bravely stepped out in its path, waving frantically for the horse to stop. This gave enough time for John Pollock, the town's watchman, to catch up. He happened to be the second person to come out of the house and had mounted the second horse in pursuit and now, daringly, jumped from his horse onto Francis and brought him down to earth.

Tom found the town mob encircling his friend, dismayed at what many had witnessed and declaring his friend a thief. He dismounted and ran into the crowd, pleading for his friend, and explaining the circumstances, but all to no avail. It appeared Francis had not only stolen a horse, but it had belonged to the newly appointed magistrate, Robert Bacon. Within minutes, poor Francis was bundled off to the town jail, a small, rancid, single-room stone building, which was cold and damp. Tom followed him and then persuaded the jailer to let Francis have his coat, without which he feared his friend would freeze. He had heard that there would be a trial the day after Epiphany in Poole.

Tom rode back to Corffe was determined to raise as much help for his friend as possible. He picked up Joseph Cobb and they decided that Will's father would be the best person to know what to do. They found him at home: over the Twelve Days of Christmas, nobody was to work except for essential livestock maintenance and feeding. Will Harvey listened to his son's story and put his head in his hands.

"Oh dear — what a mess. Poor Francis. You did well to give him your coat, my son. The first priority for him will be staying alive until the trial. You and Joseph should take it in turns to take him a hot broth, twice a day. Then the next priority will be to avoid hanging — stealing a horse is a capital offence."

"What can we do, Pa?"

"The likes of us must focus on feeding and keeping him warm, and alive. I will ask the captain what else can be done," he replied.

John Bingham was riding into Wareham that same day to see Robert Bacon. John was now senior magistrate, covering the Purbeck, Poole and Wimborne area, and he had to discuss protocol and future proceedings with his new bench colleague. He arrived to find the town buzzing with news of the earlier incident, and Bingham was made fully familiar with events before he had time to knock on Bacon's door.

"I hear there is business in Wareham that needs our attention, Robert. It is good that I am here. Tell me all about it."

On hearing the full rendition of the incident and that the villain was from Corffe, John Bingham realised that this was an opportunity to demonstrate his power and send a message to the villagers and especially the Bankes. What could be more of a water-tight case — stealing the horse of a magistrate right in front of his eyes? The boy must be made an example of: firstly, for the crime, but also to show how Bingham was upholding justice. He may also be able to paint a picture of Corffe as the old world, with villains with low morals protected by the Bankes, in contrast to the righteous, hard-working people of Poole and Wareham, following the new way of Puritanism.

"We should try him in Poole, where he will be isolated from Corffe. We also need to emphasise the boy's moral shortcomings, of which I am sure there are many. Send people to Corffe to find them out. We can paint a picture of a morally corrupt individual who goes around stealing horses, in contrast to the Puritans of Wareham and Poole," Bingham told Bacon. The two men continued to scheme and developed a plan to progress their political and religious influence on the back of the boy's trial, which could not be held until the day after Epiphany. But that was then just four days away.

The next day, Captain Cleall left Corffe for the traditional fox hunt held by Lord Cranborne, along the Cranborne Case, north of Wimborne, where he would meet up with Sir John. It meant staying overnight for two days, returning in time for Epiphany. Will Harvey had immediately briefed the captain of the situation concerning Francis, and the captain suggested the best hope Francis had, indeed his only hope, would be with Sir John Bankes. But he also knew that Sir John did not like getting involved in local justice issues. There was not time for discussion with Lady Bankes before their departure, so it would be up to Captain Cleall to convince the chief justice that it would be the right thing for him to intervene this time. He thought carefully about this on the way up to the hunt, which was half a day's ride in itself. He knew Lady Bankes well, but Sir John kept himself to himself and was more difficult to get to know. After two days together, hopefully he would have developed a better relationship and would be able to influence him in the right way.

The following day, the front of Cranborne House was an array of brightly coloured riding jackets, reds and blues, as well as magnificent horses and yelping dogs. This was a men-only hunt, with some challenging riding and jumps along the way. Bankes was apprehensive about the event as his riding skills were only just up to it, so he was pleased to have the benefit of Captain Cleall's horsemanship by his side. Cleall sensed it, and on the more challenging jumps and water courses, he sympathetically showed the way at close quarters to Bankes.

By the end of the afternoon, three foxes had met their end, and Bankes was very pleased with how he had maintained pace with the pack and fellow riders. He was all smiles as he enjoyed the thrill of the adrenaline flow and his own achievement. Cleall told him that he would make a good cavalry officer and Bankes welcomed the compliment. Back at the house, the men all washed and dressed for a night of dinner, tobacco and cards. Some women had accompanied their husbands and would join them with Lady Cranborne and her two daughters. Cleall and Bankes arrived in the ballroom, where drinks were being served, well before most of their co-huntsmen. After Bankes had recapped what he called the fight with that cunning second fox, Cleall thought that this was perhaps a good time to raise the matter of Francis's fate.

"I was wondering, Sir John, if you would be prepared for a fight with another cunning fox over the next few days? The fox in question is a local Puritan magistrate, who has his eyes on hanging a villager from Corffe. Whilst there is no doubt the villager did wrong, he had extenuating circumstances, and surely does not deserve the punishment. I am sure Lady Bankes has told you that she has already crossed paths with this man — John Bingham from Poole — and I fear he wants to dish out justice for his own political ends."

"I do not really like to meddle in local matters, Captain, but was this not the magistrate and banker from Poole who paid a visit to Lady Bankes in my absence, and took exception to our painting of Queen Henrietta Maria?"

"The very same fox, Sir John," Cleall replied.

"And he then tried some devious trick to increase shipping charges for our limestone for our quarries, but William Harvey and my wife got the better of him?"

"You are well informed, sir. The very man."

"And the accused — what of his character?" Bankes asked.

"I can confirm I have known him well for nearly ten years. He is the best friend of Tom Harvey, and although seventeen now, he is really merely a boy. He lost his mother to the illness infecting Corffe in the passed few days, and that caused him to run off. In a state of grief and madness, he tried to steal a horse in Wareham. He awaits trial the day after Epiphany in Poole."

"Hmm." Bankes was thoughtful, and nodded a few times before saying, "I think we should pay a visit to this fox and make sure the king's justice prevails over any cunning he has planned. Let's drink to keeping foxes in their place, Captain."

Back in the Purbecks, Bacon had made a visit to a couple of acquaintances in Corffe to determine what more he could find out about the accused. The first was Josh Miller at the water mill, Joseph Cobb's uncle. He informed him that Francis Trew was as good a boy as there was, and that the whole village was devastated by the loss of his mother and the predicament that the young lad found himself in. Bacon feared that would be the case. Villages were very close communities and he should avoid entering the market square for fear of a confrontation.

His second visit was more successful and was to the only Puritan family in the Corffe area, John and Jessie Coombs, who lived just west of the village. They had sympathy for Francis but confirmed that they had seen him drinking on many occasions with his friend Tom Harvey; they recalled, in particular, at harvest night, but more recently on St. Stephen's. This was the sort of information that Bacon and Bingham were after. They could link poor moral conduct with a crime. Bacon talked to them about the importance of the Puritan moral code, and how the Coombs were critically important in God's mission to spread the word. Bingham would invest in events and activities in the Corffe area, as soon as the Wareham stronghold had been established, and this would result in rewards for them in heaven, as well as influence on earth. The couple were clearly excited by this prospect, and it became quite easy for Bacon to persuade them to testify in writing and then agree to appear at the hearing, confirming what indeed they knew to be true and had witnessed: Francis had been drinking on the Saint Stephen's celebrations.

In Wareham jail, Francis was alone in a cold, damp cell. There was barely a shaft of light coming from a small opening at ceiling height, grated with iron bars, too high to see out of but open to the elements providing a freezing downdraft. As he shivered and mourned the loss of his mother, the prospects of being strung up until he choked to death seemed appealing. He found himself ravaged by the demons of despair, sending him into unconsciousness, where time had no meaning. His stupor was broken only by a vision of his mother telling him to drink and he would find a flask of warm broth, with bread. He knew not from where it came and assumed it was from the angels watching over him.

The trial day soon arrived. Francis Trew had been taken to Poole the day before. He was in poor health and despair, but the broth and bread Tom and Francis had provided had kept him alive. Bingham woke up with a good feeling about the coming day. A criminal was going to get the justice he deserved, whilst this would also send a strong signal on two counts: the power and influence of the Puritan base and the importance of a strong moral code.

After a hearty breakfast, he went over to the courthouse to make sure everything would be in order for the early morning hearing. Indeed, it was and some spectators had already arrived. The boy could be hanged by lunch time and they wanted to see the entire spectacle from beginning to end. Bacon soon arrived, along with the third magistrate, Joseph Joyce. They had a brief discussion about the order of the hearings. Trew would be first, followed by two minor hearings; one about a land infringement, and another an overdue shipping duty. The courtroom was starting to fill with locals, as well as Joseph, Tom and Will Harvey. With the cancellation of the Epiphany celebrations, due to the illness in the village, they had travelled over the day before and stayed in the Helmsman Tavern. There was a lot of talk in the town about the prospect of the hanging the next day, and it was clear what the verdict would be. It could not have been more clear-cut than stealing a magistrate's horse in front of his eyes. Why had Francis been so stupid?

In the courtroom, the three wigged magistrates sat at the far end, with Bingham in a slightly higher chair in the middle, behind a large oak bench table which was adorned by a large bible and a wooden cross. The clerk sat at a desk to their right, and in front of a door which led to a small adjoining room, where the accused were kept. The rest of the room consisted of a witness stand next to the clerk, and a bench for the jury on the opposite side. At the rear of the court were five pews packed with the 'spectators' or members of the public. There were fifty or so seated here, and a further twenty or so standing. There was no décor and it was really very small and functional; Puritan-style, as Bingham liked it. There was no fire, even, but with all those people crammed in, it was not cold. The buzz of anticipation fizzled out as Bingham brought the court to order with three strikes of his gavel.

"Order. Order. We will start with the trial of Francis Trew. Bring in the accused."

The clerk opened the door to the side of the bench and two men brought in Francis, ironed at both feet and hands, pale and drawn, stubble around his face and bedraggled hair. He looked like a petrified rabbit about to face the boiling pot. He scanned the courtroom and caught the eye of Tom Harvey. Apart from his two friends and Will Harvey, he found no other friendly faces in the packed room. All other eyes looked at him with disdain. Then the courtroom door opened and in came Sir John Bankes and Captain Cleall.

"Ah, Captain Cleall. What brings you here? I have just brought the court to order and strictly should not allow latecomers," Bingham asked.

"We have travelled from Corffe, sir, and the rain last night made the going heavier than we thought. I would trust you will be able to make an exception this time, especially as I would like to give evidence on behalf of the accused."

"You would? And what type of evidence would that be?"

"I would like to provide evidence of his good character. I have known him for nearly ten years. I would also like to introduce Sir John Bankes to the court; attorney general to the king."

There was an immediate hum around the courtroom and Bingham tried to maintain a dignified face, but his frown gave away his annoyance.

"You are, of course, welcome, my Lord and Captain Cleall. Mr Stark, would you be kind enough to see if you could find two chairs for our guests in the anti-room," Bingham asked his Clerk.

"Sir, I am here merely to champion the course of justice, on which side I am sure we both belong," Bankes said.

"Yes, of course, sir," Bingham responded, as the two guests were seated and the court was brought back to order.

"Our first case is that of Francis Trew, who is accused of stealing a horse from Robert Bacon on the 28 December. Is that correct, Robert?"

"As you say," the magistrate to Bingham's right responded.

"I apologise, sir, but may I intercept?" Sir John Bankes stood up.

"If you must, my Lord," Bingham responded.

"Am I correct in my understanding that the victim of this offence is the magistrate on your bench, seated to your right?"

"That is correct, my Lord"

"Well, in which case it is not possible for him to hear this case. He must stand down," Bankes insisted.

"He must?" Bingham pondered the situation. Sir John was right but it had not occurred to him in the rush to bring justice. "You are right, my Lord. Robert, would you mind taking your leave of the bench for this case? You can return for the following ones," Bingham asked his neighbour, who had already started to get up.

"Do you have another magistrate to take his place?" Bankes asked.

"Not in Poole today, my Lord."

"Well, we cannot delay justice on points of administration and order, so I will join your bench and the matter can proceed," Bankes said, moving around to the bench, as more muttering around the court could be heard.

Sir John stood behind Bingham, who was still trying to understand what was happening and how he had been outmanoeuvred, even before the hearing had started. He heard Bankes cough behind him, and then he realised that the Lord chief Justice meant not only to join the bench but take his natural place as its leader. Bingham slowly got up, bowed and offered his seat to Sir John. The humiliation in his own court, in his own town... The hate for aristocratic un-earnt privilege was burning inside him. He could not look up but sat down, frowning. Captain Cleall gave a wink to Francis Trew, a gesture that brought as much warmth to him as all the broth over the last few days. Was there hope?

"Clerk — Mr Stark, is it? Can you read out the crime of which the defendant is accused, please, for the benefit of the bench and the jury."

"Yes, sir. On the 29th December, shortly after noon, Francis Trew was seen stealing Robert Bacon's horse from outside his house in Wareham. He rode off but was intercepted almost immediately by John Pollock, the town's watchmen. He is now being tried for theft of a horse, which carries a capital punishment," the Clerk recapped.

"Thank you, sir. I would just like to clarify a technical point I believe is important. Mr Bacon, your horse was returned to you in good health, sir?"

"Indeed, it was, sir," Robert Bacon responded, from the chair previously assigned to Lord Bankes, next to Captain Cleall and the Clerk.

"And approximately how long was it stolen from you? Can you be precise?" asked Sir John.

"Well, not long at all. It was just a few moments before John Pollock managed to recover it, sir," Bacon replied.

"In which case, I must direct this court to consider this case a crime of attempted theft rather than actual theft. The victim has suffered no loss. And in which case, Mr Stark, I am sure this is not a capital offence and please remind the court of the penalties."

"You are correct, sir. Attempted theft of a horse has a penalty of between ten and one hundred lashes," the Clerk replied.

A murmur went around the court. The anticipated hanging was not going to happen after all. Bingham's day was getting worse as his whole plan was backfiring.

"I thought so. The court has now to decide whether or not the defendant is guilty of this lesser offence and if so, are there any extenuating circumstances that should be considered to determine the penalty. I would first like to ask the defendant how he pleads, given the charges we have heard. Mr Trew, do you plead guilty or not guilty to the charge of attempted theft of Mr Bacon's horse?" Sir John asked.

Francis looked up and then around at the court. He caught the captain's eye again and detected a nod.

"I plead guilty, sir," he said, quietly.

"Guilty, was that? That will make things easier and shorten proceedings. Mr Bacon, do you have any witnesses or evidence that may help inform the court as to sentencing?" Bankes asked.

"Ah, yes, my Lord. I would like to call John Coombs from the Parish of Corffe. He will give evidence of the boy's character," Bacon replied.

Coombs came to the stand and Mr Stark asked him to take the oath, which he did. He was dressed in his Sunday best; charcoal grey doublet and breeches. His matching hat was clasped in his hands as he stood in readiness to take the stand. He had been well briefed by Bacon and Bingham and so still felt confident, despite the turn of events that he had witnessed with Bankes taking over the bench. It was the chief justice who addressed him.

"Now, Mr Coombs, how well do you know the defendant?"

That was a question he had not been briefed on but he answered it as best he could.

"I know him by sight and by name. I am indeed acquainted with him but we live outside the village on the Lulworth road and he lives on the Swanage side, sir," he replied.

"So, other than his identity, Mr Coombs, what other evidence of the defendant's character can you bring?"

"Well, on several occasions I have seen him drinking, my Lord, and most recently at the festival of St Stephen. I believe drinking is the way of the devil and could have led him to conduct this crime," Coombs said, as he had been trained to do. What he said was received by a muttering of support around the largely Puritan courtroom. A bang of Bankes' gavel brought order again.

"Mr Coombs, on St Stephen's day, you may have found that I, too, had had a couple of drinks and maybe several others in this courtroom. That does not make us criminals. You are free in this country to view drinking in the way that you do, and may God preserve that freedom. But drinking is not a crime in this country. People are free to drink in the same way as you are free to practise your religion. Have you seen the defendant drinking to excess and acting as a drunkard, which can be a crime?"

"No, I have not, sir."

"In which case, have you anything else to add?"

"No, sir."

"Please stand down, then. Mr Bacon — any further evidence?"

Bacon was going to testify himself but having witnessed what Bankes had just done with Coombs, he decided against it.

"No, sir."

"Is there anybody here who has evidence to support the defendant?" Bankes asked.

"Yes. I would like to testify to his character, my Lord," Captain Cleall said, standing. He took the witness stand and made the oath.

"I am Captain Cleall, retired officer of the king's Household Cavalry. I have known Francis Trew for at least ten years. I have spent a lot of time with Francis and his friend, Tom Harvey, seated here at the front. They are both good boys. I have taught them to ride and hunt, as

146

well as helped them with their reading. In all that time, Francis has always been attentive, eager to learn and polite, and has never done anything wrong. Five years ago he lost his father, and over this recent Christmas period, as you know, Corffe was subject to an infection of putrid throat, which took the lives of several in the village, including Francis's mother. It was on hearing of the death of his mother that he fled the village, running to Wareham. God only knows what his state of mind was. This is when he stole the horse."

"Thank you, Captain. Your testimony has proved very useful. Finally, I would ask the defendant to make a statement."

After taking the oath, Francis made a short statement.

"I do not have much to say, my Lord. The captain is right. I was in a bad state of mind after witnessing my mother's death. I am deeply sorry for what I have done and would recompense Mr Bacon in whatever way I could. I am also sorry for all the fuss I have caused."

"Thank you. I will now take a short recess with my colleagues on the bench," Bankes said.

"All rise," the Clerk summoned, and Bingham led Bankes and Joseph Joyce out through the small door behind the Clerk's desk. They were gone barely two minutes before returning and taking their places behind the bench. The gavel again brought the muttering amongst the crowded courtroom to a halt in anticipation of the verdict and sentence.

"Francis Trew — you have committed a crime: one attempted theft of a horse. You have admitted to your guilt and we have also heard that such a crime is totally out of character and was due to extenuating circumstances. However, the seriousness of the crime cannot be overlooked. We cannot have people attempting to steal horses without fear of serious consequences, and that is why such theft is a capital offence. The magistrates on this bench have reviewed the evidence, and with the benefit of my authority as attorney general to the king, we have the ability to seek alternative punishment. In this case, you will be required to do one month's cleaning of Mr Bacon's stable. This punishment will provide Mr Bacon with some benefit, whilst preserving your back from the whip. You are otherwise free to leave the court and your custody today."

The spectators started to comment amongst themselves about the sentence but were quickly brought to order again, whilst Francis's face started to defrost into a smile, as he began to comprehend — through disbelief — what he had just heard.

"Mr Bingham, does the court have any other business which for any reason cannot be conducted by yourself and the resident magistrates? If not, I would like to discharge myself from your service and return to Corffe, where I have other business to attend to before returning to the king's court next week."

"No, my Lord. I am sure we can deal with the remaining cases. We thank you for your service today," Bingham said, bowing his head to Bankes.

Tom, Joseph and Will Harvey were already up, hugging Francis, who now had tears rolling down his cheeks, and kept saying how sorry he was. They were soon joined by Captain Cleall, and Francis continued to plead gratitude.

"It is not me you need to thank, but Sir John," Captain Cleall remarked, as the chief justice also joined them.

"I am eternally grateful, sir. I will learn from this incident and ensure that I will never see the inside of another courtroom again in my life," Francis said to him.

"Well, the most important thing is to get you home and well. I am sure the last few days have been hard," said Bankes. He then turned to Captain Cleall. "Hopefully, another fox who will be a little more cautious, in the future, in playing tricks with people's lives for the benefit of politics. It is ironic. I spend a lot of time as king's attorney general curtailing the abuse of power by the aristocracy, and this typically means sharing the positions of justice with a wider range of society, often the new wealth of merchants and puritans. But today, I had to impose myself, an aristocrat, to prevent the new wealth from abusing their power."

"Justice and mercy are not the domain of any class," Cleall responded. "They have to bridge all classes, all religion, all society, to ensure that the nation believes in them."

"Wise words, Captain. Now let's get back to Corffe."

They arrived back to more good news, as Camille had recovered from her sweat and was now conscious again, and hopefully passed the worst of it. Tom thanked God with all his might for the return of his fiancée and best friend, both of whom had almost been taken away from him at the same time.

Chapter VIII
Two Weddings and a Masquerade

Within a few weeks of Francis returning to the village, Corffe recovered from the outbreak of putrid throat and soon settled back into the new year of seasonal routine. For Tom and Camille, it would be a special year: the year of their wedding. They could not wait to be man and wife, but were enjoying courting, as well. Camille's parents were set to leave Corffe in the spring, the work at the Castell almost complete. And so, the wedding was planned for late March before they would be leaving. Camille said that people would be happier then as the trees would be blossoming and nature returning to life; a time of rebirth and reawakening.

When the day came, it was a fabulous occasion. The church was packed, and Camille was dressed in a yellow skirt and bodice with white-laced chemise, adorned with violets in her hair and around her neck. She looked like sunshine and encapsulated all the beauty of nature in front of that altar, and Tom was happier than he could ever have imagined.

After the wedding festivities, which Lady Bankes kindly agreed to host in the Castell outer bailey, under a canvas, with a roasted boar that had been caught the day before and speared by Tom, the dancing and singing continued into the night, and everybody was so happy. Sharing their joy with all their friends and family left Tom and Camille with little time together, but this was made up when they retired to their room. Lady Bankes had arranged for Monsieur Duchêne to convert a room in the Castell especially for them. It was positioned under the library, but still high enough to have a view over the ramparts, to Wareham and Poole Harbour with Green Island, home to some of their best memories together. But now for the first time, alone, in the dark, the view from the window was of little consequence. This would be the first time together sharing their intimacy, when everything mattered but nothing at the same time, other than being together. Did they make love four, five or six times that night? It did not matter and neither could tell. But what the new couple could remember was their initial trepidation melting away in the natural tenderness of being together, and a spiritual atonement that was breath-taking and serene at the same time. They were together as the heavens had always intended, and nothing else mattered. Tom now understood Romeo and Juliet for the first time.

In contrast to the bliss of the newly wedded couple in Dorsetshire, elsewhere in the nation feelings and tensions were rising. There was increasing strain between king and Parliamentarians. John Hampden had been imprisoned over his resistance to paying the Ship Tax and that had stoked up more anger. London had become an increasingly uncomfortable place for the king. The Puritans and Parliamentarianism each had grievances, and so Sir John Bankes, and others in his counsel advised the king to spend more time away from the capital. This was not to avoid any confrontation but his mere presence seemed to exacerbate the situation. The Puritans were infuriated by Charles' extravagance, and others were still frustrated by not having a Parliament in session.

Oxford, on the other hand, was much more in line with the king's ideals, with few Puritans, and many wealthy scholars and professors who owed much to the investment of Charles and his father. It was agreed that Sir John would pave the way for the Royal household by establishing a safe haven of appropriate grandeur in the city. He knew Oxford well, and indeed had a small residence there himself. Lady Bankes was reluctant to go as she had only just completed adapting Corffe and wanted to enjoy living in their new home, with their children. Sir John understood, so it was agreed that their eldest daughter, Alice, who was now coming nineteen, would accompany him. Her brother, John, was already studying at Oxford and now Alice would help with the new house decoration, for which she had a particular eye. Sir John would also be accompanied by Jacques Duchêne, who would ensure the expectations of the king and queen would be met and would bring some of his Compagnons with him. This meant Camille parting from her father and mother for the first time, but she was glad that they were not too far away and felt happy and safe with Tom and Lady Bankes. They agreed to make regular visits to Oxford, with the backing of Lord and Lady Bankes, who could see the benefit of having willing messengers between Oxford and Corffe.

Alice was overjoyed by the prospect of mingling with Oxford society. She had matured into a pretty, tall, dark-haired and well-composed young lady, with a reserved but thoughtful personality, taking after her father. She was very much Sir John's special one, and so he was more than happy to have her company in Oxford. Girls of her class typically had limited education, relying mainly on the lessons of a governess, who had little education herself other than being familiar with the etiquette of the aristocracy, largely directed at keeping women in their place. Indeed, gentlewomen with intellect were often spurned by society and so those who did emerge, like Lady Bankes, were the results of accidental circumstances. But that is what had attracted Sir John Bankes to his wife, whilst other women seemed dull and uninteresting because they could only talk about the weather, social events and fashion. Sir John had been determined that Alice would follow in her mother's footsteps, and so she had been educated at a seminary near High Wycombe from the age of twelve, then for the last two years a governess was hired to provide her with the necessary social etiquette skills to ensure she could capture a suitor.

During this time, she had been allowed to accompany her parents on some minor social events amongst the Dorsetshire aristocracy — garden parties and recitals — although she was kept on a short lead by her mother. Meanwhile, the Bankes' boys had schools such as Eton, Harrow and Winchester, followed by universities at Oxford, Cambridge and London to provide them with the opportunities to enter professions, such as law or medicine, or enter parliament. In addition, they had hunting, shooting and other sporting past-times to socialise and broaden their horizons.

A lady of Alice's status had a very short shelf-life and would typically be expected to be married between the ages of seventeen and twenty-two. Both father and daughter recognised that the chance of her meeting the right man in Oxford was significantly higher than in Dorsetshire. So whilst the Bankes and their entourage made preparations for the king's court in Oxford by day, dinners, balls and social visits were conducted by night. At the same time, these social events were opportunities for Sir John to gauge the political sentiment in Oxford: after London, it was the second most influential city in England.

Two months after arriving in Oxford, the Bankes were invited to a dinner hosted by Sir Francis Windebank, who had significant influence over the king, via the queen, due to his French and Catholic sympathies. Bankes regarded Windebank as a man of influence who needed to be controlled.

Sir Francis' estate was a thirty-mile ride south of Oxford, and so Alice and Sir John set off early. It was a wonderful summer's day. Their carriage took them along a road that mainly followed the Thames until they arrived at the estate. It was one of the most beautiful houses they had seen, overlooking the river in a setting of nature at its best, with honeysuckle and a carpet of wildflowers winding between an assortment of willows and ash trees down to the water. Sir Francis had built the house twenty years earlier, and the sand-coloured stone still looked new and fresh, in contrast to many of the more common brick constructions of the Elizabethan era. But what made it particularly stunning were the windows that formed towering screens of glass. The surrounding gardens were laid to lawn with beds of flowers landscaped in majestic style. The carriage was greeted by a footman who helped them down, and then the head of the household, a Mr Grieves, showed them into the house and to their rooms, after informing them that Sir Francis would be free to receive them for tea at four o'clock and would like to walk them around the grounds.

Their host greeted them in the drawing room, where the polished teak furniture and elaborate décor was rendered even more magnificent by the sunlight filling the room through the full-height windows. Sir Francis was silhouetted by the glare, but as he stepped forward to receive his guests, Alice could see he had dark but greying hair that flowed down to his shoulders, and a pointed beard, with rich, dark-brown eyes that twinkled as he took her hand and graciously kissed it, on her father's introduction. He was a man who was well groomed and looked very healthy for his age, for Alice understood he was in his late fifties. Sir Francis and Sir John started to discuss the architecture of the house, when Grieves returned to the room.

"Sir William and Lady Borlase, and Sir John Borlase," announced the servant, and in followed the three guests. Alice caught the eye of Sir John immediately; a young man who was immaculately dressed with an extravagant white ruff and she guessed a similar age to herself. She could barely stop herself blushing when she was introduced to the Borlases and Sir John took her hand and delicately kissed it.

"I am honoured to meet you, Alice,' he said, graciously.

The young aristocrat had wavy, light-brown hair, an angelic face and intense hazel eyes, with a warm, becoming smile. The party was soon joined by Lady Windebank, and they set out for a tour of the grounds. Alice was delighted to find herself being chaperoned by the young Sir John.

"Is this your first time to Marlow, Alice?" he asked.

She could feel flutters in her stomach as they exchanged small talk between each other. She discovered he was a man not only of charm but of wit, and scholarly in his recital of poetry. The tour of the gardens passed by in no time, and then they lounged in the drawing room, before retiring to their rooms to prepare for dinner.

Alice wished her mother had been with her to help prepare for the meal. She had a crimson dress to wear but wondered about what would go best with it: the necklace her father had given her for her eighteenth birthday, or a more ornate one that she had recently received from her aunt. Just getting into the bodice of the dress was a task, but ensuring it was worn in the most appropriate way, not too much bust but enough to entice Sir John. She reprimanded herself for thinking such thoughts, but it was true she did want to entice him. But what if he just found her a bore from the country? Did she have the conversation to interest him? But this needed to be balanced with the risk of sounding too intellectual for a woman. He mother had always frowned on such notions: be yourself and learn to speak up as you wish, irrespective of your sex, she would say and certainly practised. But Alice knew some gentlemen did not like this in a woman. What type of gentleman was Sir John? He had certainly engaged with her in lively and stimulating conversation, but was he just being polite and underneath the façade, begging to be free of the questioning and opinionated female?

Alice decided she had to be herself but was disappointed to find that she had been placed at the far end of the table from Sir John. Indeed, she found herself seated between his mother, Lady Borlase, and Sir Francis, their host. She looked over at Sir John, who nodded and smiled back, before Lady Borlase asked her what she thought about the garden and in particular, the camellias. This was the start of a tiresome, small-talk conversation which would lead Alice to despair, not only in its content, but her fear that Lady Borlase was exactly that type of woman, who had no opinions or conversation other than that which was deemed appropriate for women. But then a thought occurred to her. As she was Sir John's mother, would that not be the type of woman he would be looking for? Alice did as best as she could to stay within the margins of small talk but was thankfully saved by Sir Francis.

"Now Alice, as the daughter of Sir John Bankes, the attorney general and chief justice to the king, you must have some views on the state of things in London and the king's move to Oxford?" Sir Francis asked her. Alice was astonished. What an opening question, and how should she respond? Her mind was still tip toeing around Lady Borlase's small talk, and now to be elevated into a discussion on politics with somebody her father had declared a potential risk was fraught with danger. Perhaps this was a trap. She tried to sidestep the question.

"I'm sorry, Sir Francis, I am not acquainted with the state of politics, although I do know Oxford is a very vibrant place to live and I am sure the king will be happy there."

"And the queen? Perhaps a Catholic will be more welcome in Oxford?"

"I am sure the queen of England will be welcome in any town in the land, Sir Francis, and I can see no reason why Oxford will be an exception," Alice responded, again trying not to be drawn. She then decided to go more on the offensive. "Tell me, Sir Francis, what is the state of affairs in London, as my father shares little with me?"

"Ah, I fear for London. The Puritans are strengthening their position as more and more merchants — and increasingly gentry — convert to their ways. They are attracted by the success of the merchant classes of Amsterdam and their desire to match their success and wealth as much as any real theological drive. Personally, I cannot understand them or see the appeal. They are closing down taverns and playhouses and making it difficult to sell wine or ale. Why, they would frown on this evening's dinner. They want to control us and our natural way of life. Sunday should be for spiritual reflection, with which I agree, but why can it not be combined with some sport or hunting? Why should people not enjoy the better things in life: fine food and drink, good company, music, dance and song? And the finer the food and the company the better. Those who say different, like William Pryne and his followers, should be locked up for good."

Alice was interested to hear more and wanted to maintain the conversation for fear of being dragged back into Lady Borlase's world, who was now discussing the camellias with her father, who knew absolutely nothing about flowers but was smiling sweetly. She had heard her father talk about William Pryne before. He was a Puritan lawyer who had written a book about what was morally wrong with plays. He had been tried and locked up in the Tower of London, after his ears had been removed, because people like Sir Francis had seen his book as an attack on Queen Henrietta Maria, who very much enjoyed plays. Alice had heard her father say that some Parliamentarians were of the view that he should be released because the basis of the sentence was illegal.

"Tell me more about William Pryne."

"Why, that troublemaker has been locked up and should stay in the Tower for the rest of his life, so that his venomous poison cannot be spread any further. He is radicalising Puritans into becoming miserable anti-everything revolutionaries who will suck every ounce of joy from life."

"But do the Puritans not provide the working classes with more opportunity to better themselves, with education, morale guides, and access to the scriptures?" Alice asked.

"My dear, why on earth would we want to give the working classes any of that? They would not know what to do with it, and if they did, it would risk undermining your family and my family's position in society. God appointed kings across Europe, and the nobility are here to service them, whether English, Spanish or French. And that means managing the lower classes, whether as servants, labourers or infantry. This is God's will and it is wrong to question it. It is why the marriage of the king to

Isabella is important, as it strengthens the monarchy and natural hierarchy."

Sir Francis obviously saw this statement as a defining moment and so he excused himself before proposing to his guests a toast to the king and queen. Alice reflected on her conversation with Sir Francis. Her father and mother had always advocated a much more progressive view and had encouraged a positive engagement with the people who worked within their households and estates. Self-improvement through hard work, enterprise and education had always been encouraged. But Alice had never considered where this could end. Could this inevitably mean undermining their position, with wealth and power being shared amongst a greater number of people? People like John Bingham in Poole came to mind. Would this power now be abused and threaten society? But then she thought of Camille, Tom Harvey and even Ralph Povington; good honest people who craved to better themselves.

Sir Francis used the calm that followed the toast to announce that he had spent the previous two days with the king and that he and the queen had planned a masquerade to be staged in the new Whitehall Palace Banqueting Hall. The king was determined to set up a show of extravagance for the benefit of his queen but also to counter the growing influence of the Puritans. He would invite all the gentry and was looking to find out who would accept, irrespective of their politics.

"Sir John, he is definitely hoping to see you and Lady Bankes," Sir Francis reinforced.

"Of course." Sir John nodded a response, but behind his facial façade he was working out how he could avoid an event he knew would be the manifestation of all the things he detested about the Royal court and indeed his gentry class. His passion and motivation to serve the king was to guide him in matters of justice and he avoided as much as possible the extravagances and festivities that surrounded the monarch.

Dinner came to an end and Alice feared that she would be segregated with the female guests to drink tea, whilst the male guests would retire to a separate room for brandy. But fortunately, Sir Francis announced he had organised a harpist to play to them, and so this gave Sir John Borlase the opportunity to chaperone her once again to the ballroom.

"I hope you have had an enjoyable evening,' Sir John enquired.

"I seemed to be lost between forced conversations on florae and the politics of nations, neither of which could compare with our dialogue in the gardens this afternoon," Alice responded, but as she did, she was worried she had been a little bit too forward.

"I, indeed, would share the same sentiment," Sir John replied, failing to hide his obvious delight over Alice's comments. "I was wondering, Alice, would you mind if I called upon you, when we return to Oxford?"

Sir John did call on Alice two days later and escorted her through the streets of the city, showing her Magdalen Hall, the college where he had studied, and then taking her along the river. Two days later, he called again, this time to take her riding to the woods north of the city. They enjoyed a picnic together and were enchanted with each other's company. He talked of his plans to become a lawyer and a Member of Parliament, if it were ever to sit again. Alice suggested that he should discuss both matters with her father. He thought that was a wonderful idea but countered that he would also like to discuss with him the hand of marriage to his daughter. Alice could not believe her ears and was overcome with joy. The next day, Sir John did request an audience with Sir John Bankes.

September 1639

Sir John and Lady Bankes' found themselves in London with Alice to prepare for the wedding in the following spring. Alice's brother, John, who was now training as an officer, had time off and had joined them. The Bankes had also brought Camille to aid Lady Bankes, as well as Tom and Francis, who drove the carriage and were there to conduct some repairs and redecorations to their London house. But the other reason for being in the city was the king's insistence that Sir John and his wife attend the Masquerade at the Banqueting House. Queen Henrietta Maria had brought with her from France the idea of a masquerade ball and there had been several over the king's reign, but Sir John, who was not a society man, had always managed to avoid them. He tried to separate the official duties of the court from the more social ones: concerning the former, he was very much at ease and the latter he escaped from as much as he could, often appalled by the stories of the opulence of events and festivities that circulated around the court. But the king had been planning the masquerade for months and was determined to make it the best yet, themed on the Legend of King Arthur. Sir John was horrified at the cost, which amounted to several thousands of pounds — an imaginary amount of money even in aristocratic circles, but sinful given the pains in the country, the plague outbreak in Southwark, the talk of war and tension everywhere. And Sir John could not think of a better bellow to flame the fire of Puritan and Parliamentary discontent than an extravagant masquerade. But there were some areas where the king would not heed any advice and this was one: so much for bringing the country together.

Lady Bankes and Alice travelled passed St James's Palace, the king's residence, in their open carriage, enjoying the September sunshine of the late morning as they returned from an appointment with a seamstress who was going to make the wedding dress. Alice had also finally persuaded her reluctant mother to make some effort for the masquerade or she feared the king, if not the queen, would have her sent to the Tower. Alice had been through the options from Queen Guinevere to Morgan the Fairy Queen, but they all seemed to be too much in the spotlight for Mary, who finally settled on Igraine, Arthur's mother. The seamstress drafted out on paper a modest outfit she would make for the following week that nodded to the mythical charter.

Travelling through this ever-changing part of London, with its new squares and parks, mother and daughter had asked their driver to take a slight detour to see the new Banqueting House in Whitehall, which had been designed by Inigo Jones and would play the part of Camelot in the masquerade. As the carriage approached, it was clear that this was another symbol of monarchy extravagance, built on three floors, with Corinthian-style columns. The façade of the middle tier was dominated by seven double-height, large bay windows, reflecting the sun majestically. Preparations were already well in hand with decorations internally and outside.

"It looks wonderful. I am sure you will enjoy it, Mother," Alice said, secretly wishing she could attend.

"Corffe has more character, is more Arthurian and with real knights," replied Lady Bankes. She was thinking of Captain Cleall, rather than her husband, which gave her a feeling of guilt, but also a realisation of how much she missed his company, having left Corffe to his care two weeks ago. She reflected on this thought for the remaining journey home.

The carriage pulled up outside the Bankes' modern, three-storey brick house, overlooking Lincoln's fields, in the most fashionable part of the city, to the west of the old historic gates. As their driver opened the carriage door for the ladies to get down, John came out of the house, and Lady Bankes had to take a second look at her son, now a full-grown man and officer. What had happened to her little boy? He was followed by Tom and Francis, two more strapping young men.

"Good morning, Mother. Good morning, Alice. We are going to explore the city. I trust you had a fruitful trip to the seamstress. Will it be Guinevere or Morgan, Mother?"

"Neither, John, but you will have to wait to find out. Please take care in the city, all of you. Stick together and stay on the main streets."

"Yes, Mother. But I am now an officer — well, almost — trained to take on whatever the French or Spanish can throw at us. And look: I am fully prepared," said John, pulling back his coat to reveal his sabre.

"Just keep out of trouble."

The three young men set off, heading east to the historic part of the city. They were strictly forbidden from going south of the river, where a lot of the attractions for young men in London were clustered. However, what the Puritans had not closed down, including theatres, gaming houses, bear-baiting, brothels and the more raucous taverns, the Plague put firmly out of bounds. Southwark and south of the Thames had effectively been quarantined by forbidding passage across the five bridges with each bridge having guards at each end.

Therefore, John, who knew London well, took Tom and Francis east. In no time at all, they were walking along the Holborn road, comprising many of the new residences of aristocrats and the professional classes, including lawyers and physicians, and passed the Old Bailey, the courthouse and the prison just outside Newgate, the gateway into the thriving heart of the capital. Despite its name, it was not new but resembled the walls of Roman descent, with a portcullis gateway spanning a double road, with two square flanking towers. Behind it was a myriad of narrow and often twisting streets, wooden houses with a mixture of slate and thatch roofs overhanging the roadway at first-floor level so people could throw their waste into the gutter that flowed down the middle of the cobbled streets.

Most houses extended to three storeys, and every now and again there would be a more substantial brick-built building housing a wealthy merchant or a guild; the association for different artisans, such as butchers or ironmongers. There were crowds of hustling and bustling people going about their everyday lives in whichever direction the boys looked, with an incessant but changing blend of sounds of people talking, laughing or shouting their wares, of boots, horseshoes and wheels on cobbled stones, and of the banging and grating of cobblers and knife grinders. They would be bumping into people with strange faces and clothes from far-off places whilst the smells of humans and animals, of tanneries and taverns, would percolate all around them. The vibrancy and diversity, the energy and the pulse of over three-hundred thousand people living in a square mile was almost overwhelming for Tom and Francis.

As they ventured further into the city, they found many attractions and novelties; the magnificent Guildhall, the glorious St Paul's Cathedral and the enchanting Tower of London. But these were interspersed with familiar, everyday taverns and churches, shops and workshops, but on a scale and density that was awesome. Many of the wealthier populace had moved out of the city to find more space to live along the Strand, or Holborn, as the city's tentacles stretched out west. But they were still present on a daily basis for commerce or trade, and rubbed shoulders with the poor, the artisans, the apprentices, the traders, the sailors, the soldiers, children, and the elderly, as well as people from all across Europe and from further afield; every type of skin colour and creed. Nevertheless, it was in the back streets that they found themselves most in awe.

"Let's find a tavern. I need to get some ale," Tom said.

The three of them set off in search of a respite down Coleman Street, which appeared to be quieter, behind the Guildhall. But they found people grouped around a young man standing on an upturned wash tub talking to them. The three of them stopped to listen to the man, who was only a year or two older than they were. He was sporting the distinctive bowl-shaped haircut of an apprentice. He was talking about Puritanism and the importance of a strong work ethic for the glory of God, and he was articulate and passionate in his message. John suggested they move on, but Tom and Francis were intrigued and wanted to hear him out. His message seemed to be directed at them in a way that they had not heard before: the speaker was criticising the gentry for their extravagances and morals.

When he finished, they found a tavern and whilst John ordered some drinks, bread, ham and cheese, Tom and Francis reflected on what they had heard.

"I have never heard somebody talk in that way before. How can he be brave enough to do that and not fear being arrested?" Francis wondered.

"But he was right about many things. Why should God not reward those who work hard, and why should others be given the luxury of never having to work?" Tom replied.

John returned and explained the apprentice system to his two friends. Teenage boys and young men of their age were tied to a master, who would train them in a trade and provide them with food and lodgings while they learnt their craft, typically over five to seven years, whether as goldsmith, stationer, printer or solicitor. Once they had mastered their trade, they were free to join the livery companies that monopolised the service within the city.

"So until then, they worked hard for little pay?" Tom asked.

"I believe so," nodded John. "They are often made to have short, round-headed haircuts so people can easily distinguish between master and apprentice."

They diverted the conversation back to the city, its sights and the experience.

"Yes," John affirmed. "There is no place like this. I think it is the busiest place in the world now; well, much bigger than Paris or Rome, although Captain Cleall told me he had heard that Constantinople was bigger."

"It is not possible? How can there be such a place? Where is it?" asked Francis.

"It is the capital of the Ottoman Empire, Francis; a long way to the east," replied John.

They continued to chat, enjoying their company and the experience of being three young men in the heart of at least the second biggest city in the world. It was like the adventures they had as boys on Green Island, but the fantasies of danger and adventure were real. When they left the tavern, there was a much larger crowd surrounding another man, perhaps in his mid-twenties, who was speaking from a high stool with even more passion and vigour. Tom and Francis insisted that they listen, despite John's reluctance.

They learnt from one of the people at the back of the crowd that the speaker was 'Freeborn John' Lilburne, who had recently been released from prison. He was dressed in the Puritan style of shoulder-length hair and a distinguished moustache, his eyes blazing with conviction. He spoke with a deep, rugged northern accent but his voice resonated with his message and points in a captivating way. As they listened, they realised that this man was taking the debate to another level, more radical and more dangerous. He spoke about equality amongst Englishmen, something that John, Francis or Tom had never encountered before. From their respective positions in society, the natural order of people — gentry and the labourers — was set in stone. They learnt from the crowd that the speaker had been imprisoned and tortured on a number of occasions by the authorities but this made him more determined and his voice and following seemed to grow stronger. He was gesticulating to make his points, using his whole body to woo the crowd that was vocal in agreement. His voice became louder as it reached a crescendo for his final call for action at fever pitch. The crowd applauded and roared approval before dispersing on their ways, all in deep conversation or reflection.

Tom, Francis and John were dumbfounded because they had experienced nothing like that before and for different reasons — fear, hope, excitement — they all sensed the oratory was indeed a powder keg and highly dangerous, and that they should get away in case there was trouble.

"What do you think, John, about Freeborn John?" asked Tom.

"A harmless lunatic, although a very charismatic speaker. He will be back in the Tower before long," John replied, authoritatively.

But Tom was not so sure. He felt moved and he sensed the feeling of the crowd around him. There was something real and whether or not it was harmless was dependent upon one's opinion of his message. He suspected, for John and the gentry, this lunatic could cause some harm. But for now, the three young men returned to the safety and civility of their respective positions in Lincolns Field.

Francis and Tom did talk about what they had heard when they were alone that evening, and after John returned to his officer training, they ventured back to Coleman Street and heard Lilburne and others talk more. They meet apprentices in the taverns and found their desire and collective will to make change happen infectious and they started to question the status quo back in Dorsetshire. Why should the Bankes be the masters and everybody else toil, just like apprentices, for their welfare? Yes, the Bankes had been good to the people of Corffe, but that was just fortune and not right. They could sell the estate to a tyrant and the people of Corffe could suffer as a result. Camille had told the lads about the extravagance of the costumes and attire for the masquerade. Lady Bankes' dress alone could handsomely feed and house a whole family for a year. How could this be just, when so many people in London and Dorsetshire struggled to gather a meal each day?

There had been another man from Dorsetshire, deep in the crowd, listening to John Lilburne that day, unknown to Francis, Tom and John. He was a man who was from the lowest of backgrounds, who had worked hard and educated himself, guided by Puritan values, and God had rewarded him with status, influence and wealth; not for his own benefit, but to help him spread God's message and the Puritan values further. It was John Bingham, whose views on life resonated with Lilburne's message. He could see the power of the man, and how he had roused the crowd. What if he could channel the oratory to help him achieve God's work? He believed that it must have been God who had guided him to Coleman Street, for he had come to the Guildhall on business and by accident turned the wrong way when he had concluded his meeting. He waited for the crowd to disperse, and then made his acquaintance with the orator, before inviting him for dinner.

While the political voice for change grew in the city, beyond its walls to the west, the royal court and the gentry planned to celebrate kingship through the King Arthur Masquerade in the most elaborate style at the king's command. Sir John was not the only person who had counselled against such extravagance, but the king had no ears for such talk and kept his political head in the sand while his societal head soured through clouds of excitement and anticipation, as months of planning brought together the most indulgent of the French and Stuart traditions. The King Arthur Masquerade would be created by the brilliant partnership of playwright Ben Jonson, and set and costume designer, Inigo Jones, with the help of the queen who was interested in every detail of the arrangements.

Finally, the day arrived. As a safeguard, the king had stationed his guard along the whole length of Whitehall to secure the passage of the Royals and their guests. Sir John relied merely on a hand-held facial masque to denote one of the Knights of the Round Table, although he was not entirely clear which, while Mary Bankes' model purple dress depicted Igraine, Arthur's mother, befitting a woman of her own age and status. The extravagant costumes should be left to the younger generations. But she did wish she could give the king a motherly reprimand to show him the fallacy of this whole occasion.

As they entered the hall, the Bankes were amazed at the mass of people, all exquisitely dressed to impress with much flamboyance in Arthurian character. The stage was set at the centre of the hall where the masque would be performed; a heady combination of opera, theatre, and ballet. Around it was the dance floor where the guests would dance, and then there were the tables set for the courtiers and gentry, with the Royal seats at the very front. The room was only three-quarters full, but was already warm in the September evening, lit up by hundreds of torches surrounding the room and candles on every table. The noise was oppressive, as people were bubbling with excitement, calling out as they found friends. The Bankes were shocked by the outfits; in some cases, with little left to the imagination. One, who claimed to be the Lady of the Lake, had merely a thick veil over her breasts, there for all to see, and although her face was disguised by a silver masque, the cackle of her laugh was surely distinguishing and would betray her identity. Another, who claimed to be the enchantress Morgan, was also using her breasts to bewitch the young aristocratic gentlemen.

"What is happening to our world? This is like a scene from Nero's Rome…" Lady Bankes remarked to her husband.

"Yes, and we all know what happened to Rome," he replied.

The Bankes quickly found their seats before they could be confronted by any other Arthurian characters. They looked up at the hall's ceiling, painted by Rubens. It was the talk of all society after it had been commissioned by the king as a testament to the glory of the Stuart monarchs, showing his father, James, ascending to heaven, surrounded by angels. Charles was reinforcing his belief in his divine right to rule.

Just when they thought things could not get worse, Humphrey Weld came over to greet them. He was a renowned member of the social side of the royal court with suspected Catholic tendencies. He was flamboyantly — as ever — dressed as Sir Lancelot, pretentiously full of superlatives about the venue and the occasion and had obviously had a little too much alcohol already, as another glass of claret disappeared while he spoke to them. The Bankes were surprised he had sought them out but then the reason became clear. Lord Howard de Walden was selling Lulworth Castle, a short ride from Corffe. Humphrey was planning to purchase it and would use it for hunting and parties. He was hoping to welcome the Bankes and their family soon. It was a dreadful thought for Lady Bankes, but fortunately he then caught the eye — or perhaps some other part of the anatomy — of the Lady of the Lake, and made his excuses as he darted off like a dog chasing a bitch on heat.

A gong sounded the start of the performance and thankfully the noise gradually abated as people took their seats. The Bankes tried to follow the story as the actors performed in elaborate costumes and with stunning stage sets, but the smoke and the continued laughing and chatting of people around the hall made it difficult. The first set featured Arthur as a star, bestowing a shield on Meliadus, who was called forth by Merlin and the Lady of the Lake, to find the House of Chivalry in ruins. Meliadus was then treated to a brief sketch of British history by Merlin, which was supposed to teach the young prince how to be a good king.

Sir John was hoping the king was listening as Merlin talked about the importance of tolerance and sound governance for the people but as he looked over, Charles seemed to have been distracted by his queen. This was followed by the masque proper, portraying the idealistic world of peace and harmony under divine kingship. Charles' message to his subjects was clear, but to Sir John and others it was equally clear how far from reality this masquerade was. At the end of the masque, the king led the dancing and the courtiers enthusiastically joined in, to show off the steps that many had practised for weeks beforehand. Behind them, Humphrey Weld and his table guests started smashing glass platters with great glee. Other tables followed suit, and the Bankes saw this as the perfect opportunity to depart.

The September night air that welcomed them as they left the hall was refreshing, and it was a relief to leave the masquerade, with its smoke, noise and extravagance. A footman had been sent to summon their carriage as they waited underneath the star-speckled sky. It was not long before they were comfortably seated within it and ready to head back to their house but as they departed, something hit the window, and then a second and third missile. Half a dozen men had thrown rotten vegetables from a side street and were now running away with guards setting off after them. Sir John had expected some trouble, and he was sure it was not directed at them specifically; just guests departing from the hall. Sure enough, he heard the next day that several carriages had been bombarded in the same way, but he was just grateful it was nothing more serious as he sensed the potential for an uprising in London. He was glad that his wife would be escorted back to Corffe at the end of the week, while he and Alice would be on their way back to Oxford.

It was Scotland, not London, that brought Charles the trouble Sir John feared, which was ironic as the king was a Scot, although he had spent little time there and did not really understand the country. If he had, perhaps he would have better understood the reaction of the Scots when he sought to impose uniformed Church of England practises and the Common Book of Prayer on the Presbyterians of Scotland. The Scottish response was to draft a National Covenant, declaring resistance to Charles' new rules. Most Scots across the country signed it and the Scottish Parliament went even further by expelling Charles's bishops. The situation was escalating and Charles had to respond with force: this meant he had no option but to recall Parliament to fund an army.

For Alice Bankes, this was not good news. In December, the death of Lady Borlase, John's mother, had already delayed the wedding, but now her intended wanted to stand for Parliament, representing Corffe, at the suggestion of her father. She was furious with her father, for he just wanted somebody he could trust on the inside and had not considered Alice's feelings. The elections were called for March 1740 and Sir John was overjoyed at the prospect of first, fighting a seat and second, going to Parliament. Seeing his excitement and enthusiasm, Alice reluctantly conceded. The population of the borough was approximately nine hundred, but only male householders, rather than tenants, were eligible to vote and this amounted to just forty-eight voters. With his future father-in-law's backing, it was almost a certainty that he would be elected. However, the young candidate was not going to take anything for granted and he want to canvas all the voters, which was not an easy task as all but ten of the households were vacant, their owners living elsewhere.

So John spent a month riding around the country, making his case for people's backing, accompanied by Captain Cleall, who had taken an instant liking to the young man. He could see that he was wanting to go into politics for the right reasons; to make a difference to the country and society, which was a rare motivation. His efforts proved to be fruitful for he was elected in first place and in April, Sir John Borlase set off for London promising to return within six months to wed Alice.

However, three weeks later he found himself back in Dorsetshire after the king had once again dissolved Parliament. He had expected his request for funds to be approved straightaway, but after such a long period with no parliamentary voice, the members needed time to air their grievances and vent their frustrations. The last thing they wanted to do was to play poodle to the throne, but the king was impatient and despite the counselling of Sir John and other advisers, he dissolved the parliamentary session, which was to be known as the Short Parliament. Hence, wedding arrangements became the focus for the loving couple once again, before Alice had a riding accident and broke her arm. She refused to countenance walking up the aisle with a splint so the couple put the arrangements on hold once again. Meanwhile, Sir John Bankes was doing his best to persuade the king to reconvene Parliament and had finally got him to agree to do this in the autumn, as the situation in Scotland further deteriorated.

Back in Corffe, the betrothed couple agreed that they could not hold off the wedding purely for the parliamentary agenda and so decided that they would be married in December, in London, after Parliament reconvened in November. When the new Parliament met, it was determined to stand up to the king and also reflect its growing constitution of 'Puritanical' influence, reinforcing individuals' rights but also setting more controls on society. It was a Parliament that was dominated by a more radical wing that wanted to change the establishment, not simply its relationship with the monarch. One of the first things the government did was to release William Pryne, to the annoyance of the more noble members. There was an air of excitement amongst the members; a can-do attitude that caught the imagination of the young Parliamentarians, including Sir John Borlase, who was starting to sympathise with some of their radical views.

London St Giles in the Field Church, London December 14th 1640

Mary Bankes was welling up with emotion as she listened to Alice say "I do", in affirmation of her vows of marriage to Sir John Borlase. She could see the radiance of happiness on her daughter's face as she stood at the altar in a gold and blue silk dress, with sky-blue skirt and rose-pink puffed sleeves. She looked beautiful with the blue silk representing loyalty and pink for passion. She was marrying well, to an educated nobleman who was a barrister and Member of Parliament, but most important of all was that she was marrying for love, which was quite rare amongst the noble classes. Mary had always enjoyed Sir John Bankes' company: he was handsome in his own way, intelligent, charming and was always kind to her, and over time she had indeed grown to love him. She looked up at him, standing next to her, and he smiled back but his face gave away little emotion. He kept that buried deep within, but Mary knew that Alice was his favourite and he was more than happy. She knew her husband and his inner workings better than he did, himself. Mary saw that Alice's marriage to Sir John Borlase had all the ingredients of a perfect relationship: romance, adoration, passion, consideration, a sense of oneness and of course, love. When the couple first returned with her husband, from Oxford, in the summer of the previous year, she could see how well suited they were and never doubted for one minute that they were a match for each other.

Mary Bankes glimpsed down the pew to admire her eight offspring, dressed in their finery next to her. St Giles was a wealthy suburb just outside the city walls, which had built up around the church over the last couple of hundred years. A few years earlier, the church was rebuilt in the latest and most elaborate style, with contributions from the wealthy residents of the parish and that is why it was such a splendid place to be married. It was also close to the palace of Whitehall, which also made it convenient for many of the Parliamentarians, whom the groom was rapidly getting to know, and more than a dozen attended the ceremony. The church was indeed quite full with people dressed in diverse styles that reflected the tensions of the nation. Some of the most flamboyant dress could be found on the Borlase side of the church: bright scarlets and blues, and laced collars. Behind the Bankes' side of the church was Captain Cleall and a few friends and estates folk from Dorsetshire, in more rural, conservative attire, although all had new outfits funded by the Bankes; Ralph Povington, Tom and Camille Harvey and Francis Trew. Intermingled on each side of the church were many Puritans, dressed in greys and blacks, with much smaller, discreet collars. Their number reflected their growing power base in London and included many of Sir John Bankes' friends and acquaintances in the city, as well as those of the Borlase family. The groom was dressed in a dark-blue suit, only a few shades from black, and with a relatively modest collar. He was making a statement that he sympathised with the Parliamentary radicals, at least in political terms if not religious.

Following the ceremony, the guests were invited for a drinks' reception at the Banqueting Hall in the Palace of Whitehall. King Charles had granted his consent for the function while he remained in Oxford. The size of the hall meant that it could be an open invitation to the gentry of London, as far more could be accommodated than in the church.

London society responded to the opportunity with enthusiasm, for the Bankes and Borlase families were both well respected. It was seen as a welcome respite from the tensions with the king. Over the past few weeks, since the Parliamentary session had started, apart from the original opening ceremony, the king had not been seen in the capital. The MPs felt they were having endless debates and votes on changes they wanted to see, but the king was simply ignoring them. A more radical wing had started to emerge within their numbers that was advocating seizing more and more control with or without the king's sanction. Within this group, William Pryne was a provocateur with plenty to say to anyone who would listen, following his release from the Tower. But already, more respectable members were taking an active interest in this side of politics, including Oliver Cromwell, John Weston — the brother of Thomas who had sailed on the Mayflower — John Milton the poet, as well as a reformed Harry Coke.

Following the death of his father, Harry Coke had spent much of the remainder of his inheritance, after he had cleared his debts, in the whorehouses and taverns of Southwark. On several occasions, he had been locked up for drunkenness by the new London Puritan law enforcers. It was while in one of these gaols that Harry experienced an apparition and changed his ways. It was John Weston, who was the minister of the new church, built by the Puritans south of the river in the heart of the rowdy district of Southwark, to whom Harry Coke turned in an attempt to make sense of his vision and his calling. John Weston converted him from a person with no morals to one who became a zealot for the cause of Puritanism. Over the first year, the drying-out period and withdrawal from the yearning to sow his seed amongst the whores was almost unbearable, but he replaced these sinful thoughts with a fanatical retribution towards the purveyors of his erstwhile passion; — publicans, alcoholics, whores and theatrical players.

With John Weston's theological guidance, and the financial backing of some Puritan merchants, he built up a Puritan enforcement force that operated initially in Southwark and then across the entire capital. Parliament had passed The Act to Repress the Odious and Loathsome Sin of Drunkenness back in 1606 and three years later added punishments for the 'inordinate and extreme vice of excess drinking and drunkenness' to the statute. These laws were really aimed to curb the worst drunken behaviour in the streets and taverns, amongst the lower classes, but even then, were rarely enforced.

However, as the Puritan movement gained momentum, so did the application of these laws, and Harry Coke made it his personal mission to be at the forefront of the moral crusade. He was applauded by many of London's most influential figures as he was seen cleaning up the morality of the city, despite some of the harsh tactics he deployed. Funded by the wealthier Puritans and following his own example, he would recruit amongst his victims, turning poachers into gamekeepers. He organised the operation into a a militia, with two groups of men: the informers and the enforcers. His informers would frequent the taverns, acting merrily but with jugs full of water, rather than gin or ale. They would even provoke drunken behaviour before calling the enforcers in to lock up all the drunks.

Coke's militia became feared by many and not just the obvious lower classes in their original sights. As they gained authority, the focus was on the more cavalier amongst the gentry. For this was the age of alcohol discovery for those who could afford more than the gin and ale served in the taverns. Wines and brandies from France, whiskies from Scotland and Ireland, and rum from the Caribbean provided a new level of sophistication that enabled the gentry class to flaunt their status. For many cavalier members of society, it fuelled extravagant and brash behaviour, whether in hunting, sport, or at the card table. This enraged many Puritans in the upper echelons of society and provided the justification for a wider remit for the enforcers.

In only the past two weeks, the son of an earl and another of a 'Sir' had been arrested and imprisoned for gambling and debauchery. Harry Coke had finally found a position in society that he could call his own. He was respected and moved amongst the Puritan top echelons in his own right and not in the shadow of his father. Furthermore, he was taking a share of the fines imposed on publicans, theatre owners and especially the gentry, providing him with a very respectable income. He had been reconciled with his wife and family, who now lived with him in a new house constructed in the fashionable area of London, not far from St Giles' church.

When Harry Coke heard about the wedding reception, he decided to make sure he attended, partly out of curiosity to see the Bankes family, given the association with Corffe, but primarily to ensure compliance with the moral code and reinforcing his position in society. He was accompanied by John Milton, the poet, who had by now positioned himself as a strong advocate for the Puritan cause, and a new acquaintance from Dorsetshire, John Bingham. As he entered the hall, there was a very noticeable hushing of the chatter and many heads turned before resuming conversations. The person who was closest to the door, turning and making eye contact with Harry Coke, was Captain Cleall.

"Ah, Mr Coke. Good to see you again," he said, disingenuously, and bowed his head.

"Captain Cleall — of course. It has been many years since my father's funeral. I hope you fare well and protect Corffe as loyally as ever?"

"Indeed. The Castell has much changed from your family's time. The Bankes have modernised it and made it into a very nice home. You should visit it. I am sure the villagers would welcome back the son of Sir Edward Coke. He was a very respected landlord."

Coke cringed. He recognised the insincerity of the captain's comments and he felt the shadow of his father being thrown back at him. But he had learnt to control his temper and developed maturity regarding how to respond to taunts of this type. If he were dealing with a member of the lower class, he would strike hard and mercilessly, but with people like Cleall he needed to be more circumspect. He would get his revenge but the moment was not now, and so he savoured his anger for another day and instead introduced Cleall to John Milton.

"I believe we have met previously," Cleall remarked. "Sir, did we not travel down from Cambridge to London together a few years back? Indeed, it was after Sir Edward Coke's funeral. You were a journalist and wrote a feature about him."

Milton was not yet thirty but his hair was receding into a widow's peak which, together with his sharp nose and pointed beard, gave him a birdlike look.

"That is true. It is a pleasure to be reacquainted with you, sir. I am still a journalist but have also developed into a poet since that time."

"Well, we need some honest journalism and enlightening poetry in these troubled times. I was handed a pamphlet yesterday, written by somebody called Pryne. It was advocating all sorts of moral discipline. Does that man think we are all saints? As a soldier, I thought for this country's freedom and to enjoy the freedom of expression that surely must be the drive for great poetry. Would you not agree, Mr Milton?"

The two newcomers looked at each other. Captain Cleall had been living in the rural retreat of Dorsetshire and was obviously not in tune with London's progressive thinking and certainly not with John Milton's poetry, which was a flagbearer for the Puritans' progressive thinking in London, as well as the radical Parliamentarians.

"I beg to differ, Captain. God provides me with everything I need to express myself in poetic form whilst maintaining a Godly lifestyle. I wish you good day, sir."

With that, Coke and Milton left the captain and headed for a gathering that included John Pym, Oliver Cromwell and two other young parliamentarians.

The captain sought better company and joined a cohort of young Dorsetshire men in the corner. John Bankes, Tom and Camille Harvey, and Francis Trew were talking to the groom.

"You have made my sister so happy, Sir John. I thank you and wish you the happy life you both deserve," John said to the groom, who was overflowing with joy.

"Thank you so much, brother-in-law. I just hope Alice and I can spend time together for the last few months have been frantic. We are renting a house in London but will make our home in Oxford."

"Well, that is great news, as my father is hoping to use his influence to get me assigned to guard the king in Oxford, which would be perfect, as I will be able to visit you and Alice regularly. But I fear I could be sent to Scotland."

"Well, you do not want to be fighting the Scots. I have fought only alongside them, and braver soldiers I have not come across," Captain Cleall joined in the conversation.

"Nor did I enlist and train to fight my fellow countrymen. But father says he fears a major confrontation is almost inevitable."

"Are you ready to kill, John?" Tom asked

"What a question, Tom," Camille interjected.

"It is all right, Camille. I have had the training right enough but ask the same question of myself. I doubt if I know until I am on the battlefield," John responded.

Lady Bankes had just finished talking to a very flamboyantly dressed gentleman in a bright green satin tunic and extravagant lace collar when John Bingham, dressed in his contrasting Puritan style, approached her. He nodded respectfully.

"Lady Bankes. I do hope you do not mind me joining the party. I am newly acquainted with the groom, who invited me."

"Mr Bingham. Fortunately, Alice is marrying Sir John, and not his acquaintances."

"My Lady, I fear our relationship started on the wrong footing and I know I have played my part in that. I wish we could be neighbourly. How is the trade from Swanage?"

"Very good, Mr Bingham, in that your actions resulted in a positive outcome for our estate. We will no longer need the services of Poole Quay," Lady Bankes said, with a wry smile.

"Commerce is commerce, my Lady, and I am sure God was at the tiller of the market forces that set the course of that outcome, happily for us both. But you will be aware of my bank I have established in Poole. If I can be of any assistance, you know where to find me."

"I will certainly pray to God that our fortune does not fare so badly that we would have to stoop so low, Mr Bingham. Now, if you will excuse me, I need to have a word with the captain." With that, Lady Bankes headed off to Captain Cleall, who was a few yards away.

"Who was that? I think I recognise him," the captain asked Lady Bankes.

"John Bingham. You recall the magistrate and banker from Poole? Look, he is talking to Lord Windebank now. That will be an interesting conversation. My husband tells me he is a Catholic sympathiser but has the ear of the king and queen. He is the one pushing the king into the war with the Scots. I met him earlier and I can honestly say I cannot think of many people to whom I have taken such an instant dislike. Yes, he has charm but everything about him makes me shiver. But Bingham could be a match for him; another man I dislike. And he hates Catholics, so I would love to know what they are talking about," she replied.

"I think I would have a match for them both. Do you remember Sir John's Coke's eldest son, Harry? Well, that is him, over there, talking to Sir John Borlase, your son-in-law."

"Yes, I remember him from purchasing the Castell, but I had heard that he became some kind of Puritan enforcer in London. He has a reputation for locking up the gentry for having too much to drink."

"Well, last time I saw him he could have drunk for the whole of London, so that is a turn around. But his character, underneath, I am sure is the same."

"Let's just hope he does not make any trouble today," Lady Bankes replied, as the couple watched the guests from the corner of the room.

"London has changed. England may be changing but London has already changed. Our guests look like two factions, like two armies ready for war."

"What do you mean?" Lady Bankes asked.

"Well, I have been talking to people across the hall and it is clear that you have the Puritans, the younger Parliamentarians, and even a few of the older ones, in the charcoal-grey or black uniform, with their high morals, progressive poems and literature. Their message seems to be gaining traction amongst the lower classes attracted by messages of equality and equal opportunity. Then there are the traditional, more flamboyant gentlemen, more cavalier in their dress and attitudes and political supporters of the king, despite how badly he treats Parliament or the mad decisions he makes, such as antagonising the Scots. I have always fought for my King and country, which includes its people and Parliament, but looking before me I am not sure if that is a single cause or even one nation."

The captain paused but Lady Bankes did not respond. She seemed deep in thought.

"Did I tell you that Agnes, the gin lady at Worth Matravers, the one with foresight, has been predicting bad boding for this country for a couple of years now? Every time I see her, she tells me the shadow she can see coming is getting darker and bloodier and it is over only our realm. I first thought it could be a war with France or a plague, but now

I wonder whether, perhaps, the divisions over politics and religion in this country could start some kind of war. Perhaps starting with the Scots, but what if that spread?"

"Is that possible?" Lady Bankes asked, looking up.

"I fear, in these times, anything is possible," the captain replied.

With the captain's words, the unthinkable became possible. Harry Coke had briefly left the hall but had now returned with four men dressed in black leather, round helmets and heavily armed. They were his enforcer guards. He headed straight to Lord Windeback.

"Lord Windeback, I have a summons here from Parliament for you to answer a charge of conspiring with Catholic priests and Jesuits. You are to accompany me to the Tower and then will appear before Parliament tomorrow," Coke announced in a voice that would ensure the whole hall would hear and be attentive.

"Utter nonsense and how dare you interrupt a wedding of the nobility. I am not going anywhere and if you or your cronies touch me, the king will have you strung up," Windeback responded, with an air of defiance.

Coke hesitated briefly, turning towards Cromwell for reassurance, who gave him a nod.

"I answer to Parliament, my Lord, and you will come with me as instructed."

With that, Coke's four comrades pulled out their swords.

"The king will hear about this before the sun is down," Lord Windeback riposted and nodded to a nobleman, behind the arresting contingent, who slipped out of a back door. "I will come out of respect to Lord Bankes and Sir John Borlase as I would not want to spill blood on this day. But any other day I would teach you a lesson, Coke, and I will promise you that tomorrow will be another day."

The four guards marched him out, and the hush in the rooms turned to a new level of chatter, as the group departed.

The king did hear about the incident that evening in Oxford, and was angry that Parliament had targeted one of his closest advisors. However, he was weary of Windeback. He had urged him to fight the Scots and he was having doubts about the wisdom of this stance. He decided to sleep on matters and decide what to do in the morning. Maybe he would let

Parliament have its way and deal with Windeback or would this give them more belief and power that would haunt him later?

The next day, Windeback did appear before the House. The House presented evidence of letters, signed by Windeback, of grace to recusant priests and Jesuits, and more suspect evidence of a wider conspiracy. Oliver Cromwell and John Pym oversaw the proceedings and declared that Windeback would be returned to the Tower and face trial by judge and jury at the end of the week. Before the hearing, the king arranged for Windeback to be released and smuggled out to France. The monarch had decided he could not let Parliament win, but he was equally keen to see the back of his former advisor.

Chapter X
The Still before the Storm

16th June 1641 Worth Matravers, Dorset

Tom and Camille found themselves riding to Agnes tavern upon the limestone ridge in Worth Matravers. They rode up together from Corffe after their supper, at the request of Daniel Spear, Tom's step-brother, had asked them to come up that evening. Daniel Spear had been to Poole earlier in the day and picked up a news pamphlet, but his reading was not good, so on his way back through Corffe he found Tom, who agreed to read it over a mug of ale.

Daniel and four other locals sat outside in the summer evening sun, on stools round a barrel, with Daniel's spaniel lying next to him, attentively, on the ground. Amongst them was Francis Trew, who had recently moved to live with Daniel Spear and his family. Old George, who was said to be in his seventies, sat amongst them, smiling toothlessly and at peace with the world, as always. On seeing Tom and Camille, Daniel got up and made his way to the horse as Tom pulled its rein to a standstill.

"Good evening, brother. Thank you for coming. And the beautiful Camille…" Daniel took her hand and helped her off the back of the horse, and tied its rein to a ring on the wall. Tom followed.

"Agnes — a drink for our visitors from Corffe."

Francis greeted his friend and Camille with a hug. Drinks soon arrived and the banter continued amongst the six, but before long Tom asked Daniel about the newsletter. He pulled it out and started to read, first about how the king had arranged with the Irish Catholic gentry to raise an army to put down the rebellion in Scotland. It had been mobilised in Carrickfergus and was ready to invade, because the English Parliament had failed to provide him with the funds to raise his own army. The king had granted rights of more religious freedom to the Irish Catholics, which the article reinforced with a cartoon of the king as a puppet of his Catholic queen.

"There are people in Poole who say that the king is supporting the Irish and Popists," Daniel said. "They say he is battling against Parliament, which represents the People, and that people should support Parliament, not the king."

"The news here says similar but it sounds like treason to me," Tom replied.

"Maybe it does, but it was treason when the Popists tried to blow up Parliament. Now the king and his Popist queen are constantly closing it down. What is the difference?" Daniel asked.

Tom looked at Camille for support but simply received a raised eyebrow, implying that maybe he had a point.

"That is an interesting question, Daniel. There are many people in London questioning the king and even the structure of our society, and the rights we have, or do not have," Tom said.

Francis joined in. "Is the king our king any more? The queen has poisoned him against his people. We do not want to go back to Popist ways. Parliament may not represent the likes of us in Worth but it is more understanding of ordinary people. People like Sir John Borlase are people we know and they know us. We can trust them but not the king," Francis added, in an assertive voice that surprised all of his friends. He obviously had a lot of pent-up feeling on this subject.

"Why should the gentry own all the land? It is a question that people are asking. And if the money is raised for an army, who should it fight for, the king or Parliament? Captain Cleall often talks about La Rochelle and the disaster of the king's last military campaign. Why, that is the reason he retired as an officer, given the needless loss of life that resulted from his folly. If I was asked to fight, I would want to do it for Parliament," Francis continued.

There was a pause in the conversation. Tom had not realised how radical his friend was becoming, although he sympathised with much of what he said.

Old George broke the pause in a very matter of fact tone' "There are some men who are put on this earth to plough, and others to be preachers, some to be quarrymen and others to be kings. God gave us different skills and know-how for a reason. We should not meddle with what God have bestowed."

"The king would agree with you, George. He believes he has the divine right to do what he wants. My father holds the same view as you, and until I went to London so did I, George, but it is not as straightforward as that and I can see things differently now," Tom replied.

But George had not finished. "I hear a lot of calls for change, some be religious and some be other motivations. Whenever I hear such calls, they be followed by bad times. My eyes may be failing but as I grow older, I can see this as clear as day. Why can we not be grateful with what God gives us and thank him in our own way? Seventy years I have been on this earth and God has always provided for me. Sometimes it is difficult to get by but generally there has been food on my table. Why do I need more? I only have one arse."

That brought laughter all around and when it died down, Agnes, who was standing in the doorway listening in, entered into the conversation.

"You young'uns should listen to George. His years give him wisdom. I see darkness descending on this nation. It will be a darkness like no other before it; one that forces father against son, and brother against brother, friend against friend. It will bring blood and heartache and it will last for many years. And I see fire; so much fire that it devours me. These dreams mean something, I have no doubt."

"But how can there be such a darkness when we have the beauty of this summer's evening? And there is nothing stronger than family and friendship in places of such beauty, and I toast to that with your fine gin, Agnes." Old George held up his mug and the rest followed.

The pamphlet, their differing views and especially Agnes's predictions had made the company of friends all feel uncomfortable, and so they moved the conversation on to local gossip and the cricket match between Corffe and Worth that was scheduled for the coming Sunday, after church.

The following month, Mary Bankes was in her bedroom at her dressing table within the Castell at Corffe. The sun shone through the window, tempting her out into the summer's day, which was warm and full of the fresh sea air below a bright blue sky. But she felt the weight of the world heavy on her shoulders and was in a melancholy mood. Since the wedding she had not seen her daughter Alice, and only once her husband, who had remained in London for a while trying to appease the situation with Parliament as the king's representative and then returned to court in Oxford. In April, the king had summoned him to York. Mary missed him but the amount of time that they were apart was taking its toll on their relationship. There were three people in the relationship and she felt the poor relation, second to the king.

Her elder son, John, had finished his time at the Cavalry Academy and he had now gone north with his battalion to support the king, whilst his brother Ralph was at Oxford, studying medicine. Her youngest daughter, Katherine, was playing in the courtyard outside with a hobby horse. She was still only four and brought many smiles to her mother every day, keeping her young in spirit, but she yearned for the rest of her family and adult company. Camille Harvey and Ralph Povington were the only adults with whom she had regular conversation as Captain Cleall's mother had been taken ill in Devonshire shortly after the return from London and he had departed to comfort her. He had written to her regularly since his departure and it would seem that she was in a gradual, drawn-out decline to the inevitable end. Poor Captain Cleall. He was not the nursing type and would hate to be stuck in a house watching his mother's demise.

His absence made Lady Bankes realise how fond of him she had become, for he had spent much of his time over the last six years at the Castell and had become part of the family. It was just a friendship in her mind. They enjoyed each other's company, rode together often, and he became her main confidant in matters that involved running the estate when her husband' was away. But the captain's absence meant she realised that there was perhaps more to their friendship, and that the gaps left by her husband had been, at least, in part filled by the captain.

Her sanity was largely maintained through the letters she received from her family and the captain, and she occupied herself with speedy responses, keeping everybody informed of news in Dorsetshire, in the hope that a quick response would result in swift replies. But through these letters she was able to piece together what was happening in London and the rest of the country, and the struggle between Parliament and the king, and the growing tension across the nation. The tension was self-evident from the different perspectives across her own family, with Alice and Sir John closely associated with the Parliamentarians and her husband, John, and Ralph remaining Royalist in their outlook. John wrote about the tension in Oxford, where there had been support for the king, but within its colleges Ralph wrote of many who held more radical opposing views. Even Captain Cleall talked about a recent visit to Exeter, which he described as rebellious in nature.

From what Lady Bankes could piece together, the king had got the better of Parliament when it came to Windeback, but Cromwell, Pym and Hampden were committed to standing up against the monarchy. So the new Parliament proved even more hostile to Charles than its predecessor and took advantage of its strength, given that the king had lost face against the Scots and needed Parliament's financial support to strengthen his position. The Parliamentarians started to flex their muscles, first by reforming measures that the king and his anti-Puritan Archbishop Laud had introduced and then passing a law, which stated that a new Parliament should convene at least once every three years, without the king's summons, if necessary. Parliament resisted but then, every so often, there would be a concession or gesture that would play to the king and his Royalist view of the world, often following the counsel of Sir John Bankes. Seeing the power of the signing of the National Covenant in Scotland, Sir John had proposed a similar unifying action in England and Parliament, surprisingly agreeing to pass a law requiring all adults to sign The Protestation, an oath of allegiance to Charles.

Sir John had written to Mary, saying he had been hopeful of appeasing the king and his followers through this initiative. But the underlying tension continued to bubble and the pressure pot boiled between the opposing sides. Charles and his supporters continued to resent Parliament's demands, while Parliamentarians continued to suspect Charles of wanting to impose royal rule by military force. The letter from her husband this morning confirmed the worst and an escalation of matters. He wrote of an uprising by the Irish Catholics, fearing a resurgence of Protestant power, and this had resulted in all Ireland descending into chaos. But worse still, Cromwell and Hampden were spreading rumours that the king supported the Irish and he would soon be supporting uprisings in England to take back power from Parliament. John Milton through literature, John Weston from the pulpit and Harry Coke through his thugs on the streets of London fanned the flames of these rumours. In the meantime, pamphlets of lies, as her husband called them, were spreading across the country like a plague.

Alice's letters described her husband getting ever closer to the Puritan and Parliamentary powerhouse, but for every couple of steps he made, he would then distance himself again, as his upbringing had taught him to honour and obey the king. He was often distraught by the conflicting views he held; the attractiveness of the new way but the safety of the old. Alice, in her letters, detailed the impact this conundrum was having on her newlywed husband. She wrote of the fear they both had for the future and that the conflict in Ireland could come to England. Harry Coke's power was continuing to grow. For the rich and middle classes, it was becoming a choice between remaining in London and supporting Parliament and converting to Puritan ways or leaving, heading for the safety of the court at Oxford or their country estates in the shires. Parliament become less tolerant of cavalier behaviour and supported the penal approach of Coke and his henchmen.

One respite for Mary, in her isolation, had been a visit by Charlotte Coke, Harry's sister, who had written to her and said that she would love to visit Corffe again. She arrived from London the following month, and she and Mary got on very well. Charlotte was pleased to see the Castell in such good hands and delighted to observe the changes that the Bankes had made. The two of them went riding, visiting Swanage and Lulworth, and catching up with William and Tom Harvey and others who knew her well from her time at the Castell. As they rode, the two women talked about the national crisis, as well as local people and events. Charlotte had moved to London after the death of her mother the year before, whom she had nursed through a long illness, and she was now staying with Harry and his wife.

She was very candid with Mary about her fears for her brother and the strain that he had put on the family, almost bankrupting them through drinking and gambling, but equally as worrying now with his puritanical dogma and political manoeuvring. Charlotte confessed her worry for the nation and informed Mary that her brother had told her that a battle of some sort with the king was almost inevitable. Harry had been given the rank of colonel and Lord Essex was gathering a military force that was already numbered in the thousands. Pym, Essex, Cromwell and the other Parliamentary radicals were always meeting and scheming, often in her brother's house. Charlotte and Mary promised to spend more time together, as they really enjoyed each other's company, but as she left to return to London, Mary reflected that Charlotte was returning to the capital where dark clouds were gathering, as Agnes had predicted.

For Mary, it was like seeing her own family torn apart by issues that she did not really understand; not because of their complexity, but because of the strength of feeling that they evoked. King Charles was surely not the best king, but the country had had plenty worse — Bloody Mary, for example. Was it not possible for people just to live together? She felt helpless, stuck in the Castell and since Charlotte's departure a month ago, there was nobody with whom she could talk about this. She yearned for Captain Cleall, or her husband, to guide her through what she should do.

Her thoughts were interrupted by a knock at the door. It was Camille.

"Beggin' your pardon, my Lady. Captain Cleall is here. He is downstairs in the hall, my Lady," she said, with a twinkle in her eye. "Will you be wanting to change your dress, my Lady?"

Lady Bankes' heart pounded. Was this a dream or the end of her nightmare? She found herself uncharacteristically in a bit of a fluster. Should she just rush down and see him, or indeed change as Camille had suggested? No — she could not wait. She got up, whisked passed Camille, and down the stairs to the hall. And there he was, waiting. He turned as she entered the room, a big smile on his face, and she responded in kind as she skipped towards him, almost hugging him before she refrained herself at the last moment and held her hand out for him to kiss, as would be her normal greeting.

As he took it, she said, "I missed you, Captain, but how is your mother?"

He looked up at her, with his mouth still perched on her hand.

"I missed you also, my Lady," he said, raising his head and taking a deep breath. "More so than I should admit, but I also missed Corffe, and Dorsetshire. Indeed, I missed the world. I have been locked up for six months with my poor mother, seeing her decline gradually into more of a vegetable than a human, but she has now passed away and was buried yesterday."

"Oh, I am sorry, Captain."

"Do not be. It is for the best, I assure you. It is a relief to us all. But now, my Lady, will you go riding with me? It is a wonderful day and I should want nothing more than your company."

"Why, of course. I would be delighted. If you fetch my horse, I will meet you at the gate in a short while," she replied and turned to go back to her room where Camille had already prepared a dress.

The couple trotted through the village and then galloped up towards Kingston, on the top of the limestone ridge, where they could look down and see Corffe and its Castell, toy-sized in the distance. The vantage point the Castell enjoyed, on a rise in the gap in the chalk down, was plain to see from here and behind it was the turquoise blue of the harbour beyond, with its islands and a tall ship sailing in, sails being released and gathered into the rigging before it reached the Poole Quay. The couple admired the view whilst their horses refreshed themselves, drinking from a trough by the roadside, before setting off to the cliffs and the coast. Just passed Worth Matravers, they dismounted and rested in a shallow dip in the cliff line. The captain had a blanket rolled up at the back of his saddle, which he untethered and spread on the grass, inviting Lady Mary to sit. He then pulled out a flask of water from his saddlebag, which he also offered to his companion before sitting down next to her. They had stopped here before and knew it gave then a little shelter from the sea breeze but still a vantage point to admire the rugged cliff line that stretched out beneath them.

"James, I cannot tell you how much I have missed you over these past months. Sir John has been away all this time with the king, and now with Alice, John and Ralph away from home, I have felt alone in a world that seems to be entering into turmoil from all accounts. I have had nobody to share and allay my fears. Sitting here in beautiful and tranquil Dorsetshire, where the sun rises every day and sets over the sea, it is difficult to relate to what I hear in London, Oxford and from your own pen, in Exeter," Mary began to pour her heart out.

"Mary, I am deeply sorry that I could not be of some comfort to you. I agree, blessed with this beautiful place, it is difficult to understand the winds of change that are blowing through this land. Whilst in Devonshire, I visited Exeter each week. I found a city totally divided from top to bottom. The city's Chamber had half its members Puritan and others very traditionalist and strong King supporters. Both sides were most vociferous and similar to what we witnessed in London at Alice's wedding. And I fear there are many cities that are equally divided. The divisions would appear to be amplified by newsletters from London and Oxford on both sides, and from these it is difficult to fathom what is fact and what is fiction. I have seen articles about the same events that tell totally different stories. I fear truth is the first casualty in a struggle which has already shed blood in Ireland and Scotland and will inevitably follow in England."

"Where do you stand, James? King or Parliament?" Mary asked, tentatively.

"I would prefer not to have to choose. I would prefer to stay here in Dorsetshire and if you would allow me, at your side."

She smiled warmly. "That is sweet, James. I am truly glad you are back."

The two sat in silence for a moment. Where was this going? Neither knew. Lady Bankes had been a loving, dutiful wife and mother. But she needed security, reassurance and indeed love, yet her husband was hundreds of miles away, with the king. He was duty-bound to try and reconcile the warring factions in the country before it became too late and many lives were lost. Blood had already been spilled in Ireland and Scotland and from her husband's letters, he thought time was running out and he was doubtful if peace in England would hold much longer. The thought of war horrified her. She had heard of the terrors in France and elsewhere in Europe, where the horrors that people had inflicted on their own people in the name of religion were abhorrent. But as she looked down on the waves licking the rocks at the base of the cliffs below, the glistening sea and the herringbone-scattered clouds on a palette of glorious blue sky, she struggled to see how such a horror could manifest itself in such a wonderful peaceful place like Dorsetshire.

"Even if it does come to war, I cannot believe it could come to Dorsetshire. Surely it will be fought somewhere else and it will not reach this peaceful enclave," Lady Bankes said, as she emerged from her thoughts.

"Let's hope you are right, my Lady," the captain replied, reaching out and holding both her hands in a gesture of comfort and reassurance. He had seen the horrors of war on numerous occasions and had been thinking about what he should do for some time. He was retired yet was also duty-bound, but in many directions. Of course, he had fought for his king and country on many occasions, but he had been questioning that loyalty, given the actions of the king, and did not Parliament also represent the country? However, Parliament had been infiltrated by a radicalism that he felt was unwarranted and could turn his country into a dull and austere land.

But then there was Mary. He had admired her ever since he had met her for the first time in Oxford. She was intelligent and strong, something that was often frowned on by gentlemen, but he enjoyed her company and found her conversation fulfilling. But he had realised, only in his recent absence, that his admiration had turned into love over the last few years, something he was unfamiliar with. He had truly yearned to be back in Corffe and now found his love not only looking as beautiful as ever, but in such need of protection and reassurance. But he was a gentleman and how could he prey on such vulnerability, especially when her husband was a man of integrity and serving the nation so loyally? He was torn in all directions, wishing he had met her twenty years or more earlier.

"I fear for John in the cavalry, and Alice, often in London. I fear for all my children. And the men of Corffe, could they be called on to fight? Tom Harvey, so recently wed; Francis Trew, just recovering from the loss of his mother. If they are called up to fight, on which side? And what about you? Will you have to fight? James, take this nightmare away from us," Mary pleaded.

James sighed. "If only I could."

They sat in silence and let time pass, whilst their minds raced through the events surrounding them and the emotions between them. Mary leant her head against the captain's shoulder. He could smell her perfume and lowered his head so his chin brushed her hair. He felt butterflies in his stomach. It would be so easy to kiss her but he contented himself with her scent and warmth, and stroking her hair. Whilst the country sensed it was enjoying the quiet before the storm and not quite sure what to do, Mary and James were suspended in their relationship, equally paralysed and unsure what path to take.

The following day, an invitation arrived at the Castell from Humphrey Weld, who was now the owner of neighbouring Lulworth Castell. Lady Bankes was invited to a hunt in a week's time, and would have declined under normal circumstances, but the prospect of more adult company persuaded her to accept. She would have to be chaperoned by Captain Cleall, which was also an enticing prospect. The days soon passed, and the couple rode up to Lulworth.

"It is more of a lodge than a Castell," Lady Bankes remarked as they arrived to find many folk already preparing for the hunt. Humphrey Weld came over to greet the new arrivals.

"Lady Bankes, I am so pleased to see you. Alas, no Sir John?"

"He is on the king's duty in London, trying to reconcile the situation with Parliament. But may I introduce you to my chaperone and good friend, Captain Cleall?"

"Captain — Humphrey Weld at your service. Welcome to my new country retreat. I have just purchased it for a snip from Lord Howard de Walden. Thirty thousand pounds, can you believe it? Wait until you see the views and my plans for it. I understand, Lady Bankes, that you have been busy renovating Corffe. Please introduce me to your master craftsmen. But first, let us hunt some fox or maybe even a stag. Come this way."

The young aristocrat was clearly full of himself and Lady Bankes and Captain Cleall looked at each other with a knowing smile, for they had anticipated such a reception. Humphrey introduced the visitors to the other guests, a few with whom they were already acquainted, such as Lord Cranbourne, but most were from his wider circle of friends, including the royal court. Sir Humphrey was well connected in these circles. He held the title of Cup Bearer to the queen, an honorary title for the person who would historically have tasted and poured the wine, but now one bestowed upon people whom the Royals trusted and held in high esteem. Amongst the guests were two of the queen's ladies-in-waiting.

Before long, they were riding through the estate, which indeed had a glorious view of the sea and the coves below. It was a perfect day and backdrop for the hunt as ten horses and a similar number of hounds headed off in search of game. Nature seemed to be alert to the danger as rabbits bolted into warrens and birds soared into the sky in advance of the oncoming hoard. Weld had provided muskets for the men on the hunt who claimed the necessary horsemanship, which included Captain Cleall, in the event of them tracking a deer. It was not long before the hounds were tracking the scent of something, which a short while later revealed itself as a fox. The chase was intense, as their prey led them through woods, which made riding precarious, as riders had to watch out for low-hanging branches, as well as streams and ditches. Some of the women bowed out of the chase, but Lady Bankes kept the pace with vigour. But it was not long before the ruthless dogs caught up with the fox and savagely brought its life to an end. The hunt master salvaged what was left of the fox from the dogs as the day's first trophy.

"You ride well, my Lady," Humphrey commented.

"The captain keeps me well trained, but I do believe I will take a break and catch up with you shortly."

"I will stay with you. Look — there is a stream where we can water the horses," the captain said, and the two dismounted and wandered over to the fresh-flowing water.

"As we rode and as we hunted, I kept having flashes of John, riding into battle," sighed Lady Bankes. "I worry for him, James. I have had similar dreams over the last weeks. I see him falling off his horse, and cannon fire and slashing sabres. It is a recurring nightmare. Please tell me he will be safe, if fighting starts."

"My dear Lady, I wish I could. The truth is there is a high casualty rate for all novices in their first encounter with fighting, but in the next conflict they are already battle-hardy and no longer in awe of the firing and killing. That is why you get rogues like me, with many battles behind them."

"James, you are not helping. What can be done? I could not face losing John. They are all precious to me, but he is my special one."

Captain Cleall came up with a rash proposal, one from his heart rather than his head; one that was a response to Mary's pain and his love for her.

"Mary, if war comes, I will re-enlist, and with Sir John's influence, I am sure I could get into John's brigade, as his superior officer, and will do everything I can to guide him through his first battle," he declared.

"You would do that for me?"

"For you. Yes. And for John, of course."

"Oh, thank you. But I am unsure that I will not then start to have nightmares about you in battle…"

"Mary, there is no need to worry on my account. My new horse, Lightning, has just shown what he is capable of, and my sword arm is as agile as ever. Nobody will be a match for us. So let me protect John, just in his first battle. At least then I know who I will be fighting for and why."

"Thank you, James. You are so kind and considerate. I am sure I will sleep better now and will never forget this."

The couple soon caught up with the rest of the hunt, and enjoyed the rest of the day, mainly in each other's company as observers to the flamboyance of their host and his acquaintances.

In September, Sir John returned to Corffe for a couple of weeks before escorting Lady Bankes to London, so they could spend some more time together. Sir John was continuing to negotiate with Parliament on behalf of the king. He spent many hours with John Pym, their defacto leader, as well as John Hampden and Oliver Cromwell. Hampden was as quick-tempered as ever, with the same passion as he exerted at their first encounter in Oxford, all those years ago. Bankes' relationship with Hampden had further deteriorated during the Ship Tax crisis when, contrary to Bankes' advice, Hampden had been imprisoned. It was Bankes' actions behind the scenes that freed him, but Hampden painted him with the same Royalist brush and always held it against him.

In contrast, both Pym and Cromwell were intelligent politicians who thought through all eventualities before they responded to any proposal or offer. Pym was especially savvy and made a worthy opponent, especially given that the stakes were so high, both nationally and personally. In their negotiations, both sides recognised that the country was in danger of falling into war but the personal stakes were also high. Any criticism of the king could be construed as treason, being hung, drawn and quartered as the punishment. However, Sir John also recognised that making martyrs out of any of these men — even if tempting, in Hampden's case — would most probably be a shot in one's own foot, strengthening their position. Furthermore, the issues facing the monarchy and Parliament were complex and involved interrelated nation status, religious and political issues. But one thing was certain for Sir John: every time he met the Parliamentarians, their confidence and position appeared to strengthen.

Sir John had just had a frustrating and unproductive early-morning meeting with the three representatives and returned to his Lincoln Field's house to find some solace with Mary. He proposed they go for a walk, so he could take his mind off things, and she agreed. So the two of them set off in their carriage, travelling north of the non-resident palace, which was where many new homes had been built by wealthy merchants and aristocrats. Mary admired the new styles of architecture of the houses with larger glass windows. West of this area was a large park that had become a fashionable walking area, which was where they were heading. But as they travelled in that direction, a crowd crossed their path heading further north. Sir John enquired of his coachman what was the cause and found out that there was to be an execution of a Popist priest at Tyburn. There had been no priest executions during Charles's reign, which was a welcome relief after the blood bath that followed the failed gunpowder plot against his father. However, in April of that year, the Puritan-led Parliament had issued a proclamation banishing all Catholic priests under pain of death. They had a month to leave, but William Ward, a man in his eighties, had refused and had been found hiding in a priest hole and arrested by Harry Coke a week earlier. He had been sentenced at the Old Bailey the day before and since day break, had been making his way to the new place of execution for criminals at Tyburn, with the crowd coming from all directions to taunt him and see the spectacle. The coachman informed Sir John that the priest was to be hanged, drawn and quartered. Sir John was shocked.

"Nobody for decades had been hanged, drawn and quartered. It is a punishment reserved for treason. How could it be applied to a Catholic priest? I must do something,' Sir John said to Mary. "Driver, make haste to Tyburn."

Mary admired her husband for his passion to do the right thing, whomever it was for; Catholic, Puritan, Parliamentarian, or monarch. He was the true champion of justice but in the current climate, few backed his cause.

There were several hundred people already assembled for the spectacle when they arrived and an elderly man in a heavily spoilt shift was being pulled up from a cart onto the platform beneath the gallows. The cart had been pelted with rotten vegetables and horse shit along the route from Old Bailey, and the priest looked dazed and unsteady on his feet. The mid-morning sun was rising higher and the blue sky would be the last glory to God this priest would see on this earth. Sir John ordered the coachmen to get as close to the platform as possible, where he descended and strode through the crowd, his obvious status and dignity creating a pathway, but not without several insults and aggressive comments. He pulled himself up onto the platform, where the two executioners had forced the prisoner to stand on a small stool, with the gallows noose tightened around his neck.

"Who is in charge here?" Sir John demanded. A familiar face turned and faced him. It was Harry Coke.

'Ah, Sir John. Good to see you. You have come to witness the justice of sending this papist-scum to hell? I am sure I can arrange an appropriate seat for you, here at the front."

Harry pointed to a few chairs which were indeed positioned a few yards from the platform. Dignitaries were already seated in some of them. The crowd continued to taunt from beyond the chairs.

"What are you waiting for?"

"Get on with it!"

"Cut the goolies off the papist bastard!"

"Harry Coke," Sir John retorted. "I might have guessed you would be here. Are you in charge? I am sure there must be a mistake. I was the architect of the proclamation by Parliament to which the king agreed and called for Catholic priests to leave England. And yes, under extreme circumstances death was the ultimate penalty. But never hanging, drawing and quartering."

"Well, Sir John, I have the sentence here. Let me read it to the crowd."

Harry Coke turned and faced the crowd and the priest.

"William Ward, you have been found guilty of treason, practising and promoting Popist treachery to undermine Parliament and the king. You have been drawn on a hurdle to the Tyburn where you shall be hanged by the neck and being alive cut down, your privy members shall be cut off and your bowels taken out and burned before you, your head severed from your body and your body divided into four quarters to be disposed of at the king's pleasure. So, people of London, do you want to see justice and this sentence carried out?"

"Yes, yes, yes! Hang him! Quarter him!" was the overwhelming response.

Sir John knew his cause was lost but he tried once more.

"Give me until noon. I will be back, I am sure, with clemency from the king. He should die but a civil death by simple hanging," he pleaded to Harry.

"Listen, people of London. The king's attorney general, Sir John Bankes, is pleading with me on behalf of the king. On behalf of the queen, no doubt. He wants me to commute the papist's sentence to just hanging, when it says on this paper from the Old Bailey, that I have just read, that this papist has committed treason. What do you say, people of London?"

"Quarter him, quarter him, quarter him!" the crowd started chanting, no doubt led by Harry Coke's cronies.

"And there you have it, Sir John, attorney general to the king and Lord of Corffe Castell. You need to understand, my Lord, that the power has shifted. It rests with Parliament and the people. But I can still find a seat fit for somebody of your status, if you so desire," Harry sneered.

"No, thank you," Sir John replied. He walked over to the prisoner. "I am sorry. Have faith and may your soul rest in peace."

The prisoner looked down on him. "Thank you, my Lord. I am ready to see my maker now."

Sir John jumped off the platform and pushed his way through the crowd, back to Mary, and ordered his coachman to leave as quickly as possible before the execution started.

It was a subdued walk around the park for the couple. In contrast to the joy of the songbirds, the summer colours in the trees and hedges, and the blue sky's reflection in the lake, the Bankes were melancholy. The park would have been filled with the wealthier classes taking a stroll at this time of year, but plague and politics had kept most of them out of London. As they walked, Sir John explained to Mary what had happened, and his humiliation. She told him he had no choice but to try and do something. But both the Bankes realised the truth in what Harry Coke had said about the changing control of power in London.

"What is going to happen, my darling?" Mary asked.

"I do believe the future looks bleak, and I have tried to advise the king to the best of my abilities but have failed. As you know, my love, the desire for justice in this country, at all levels, has been my passion, but as chief justice and attorney to the king, I appear to be powerless. Justice can be served only if there is authority built on a foundation of common moral principles and laws. Today, I have learnt that this has dissolved into nothing as populist mob rule is taking over. Why? I must now admit it is difficult to defend the king, for he is the reason why we are in this situation. The king is a fool with his head buried in the sand. It was his foolhardy decision to suspend Parliament despite the counsel of most of his advisors. Every time he did this, it fuelled the opposition against him, and gave the Puritans more power. Parliament and the monarchy should work together for the benefit of the nation and its people. Instead, they are at loggerheads and the situation is getting worse, as both sides seek ways to undermine the other. If only the king had worked with Parliament, there would be a House of Commons of Royalist supporters. Now it is a viper's nest of Radicals, Populists and Puritans, and with many of the remaining Royalist supporters making excuses to leave the capital and not be represented in the House at all. It is difficult not to blame the king for much of this.

"On top of this, the situations in Scotland and Ireland. What a mess... A war with the Scots was unnecessary and driven purely by the king's dogmatic imposition of the Book of Common Law. Any fool could have told him that was like throwing fire into a hornets' nest. But no, he would not back down and the resulting war was a disaster. It cost a fortune, to no avail, and resulted in a humiliating defeat. At least he is going up to Scotland next month to make amends but all too late and to what end?"

"Now we have the Irish Catholics' uprising against the Protestant minorities all across the island of Ireland. The Book of Common Law imposition was fuel enough for the Populists and Puritans, but the fear of a Popist uprising that could spread to England is manna from heaven for them. And this is a genuinely difficult area for the king, as they will use the Catholic faith of his Queen to fuel that fear. So, my love, we are going through very difficult times, when one's own faith and principles are questioned."

Sir John paused and took a deep breath.

"But still, he is the king and I am duty-bound to defend him. That never changes. And the Bankes family and the Bankes estate will defend the monarchy, for God provided us with the king and if he is not the strongest nor the wisest, then that is a penance this country must live with. I fear at what cost. One thing I am certain about is the strength of my wife through these times. But I do worry about your safety as I am away from you so much. At least Dorsetshire is a much safer place than London," Sir John continued.

Mary stopped and held both of Sir John's hands. "You do not need to worry about me, my love. The king and the kingdom must be your priority, to help pilot a course to peace and unity. In any event, I have a Castell to protect me, as well as John, who will be returning home soon as a cavalry Lieutenant; not to mention Captain Cleall."

"Yes, Cleall is a good man and I know that he cares for you a lot, my dear."

She smiled back at her loving husband and the couple continued to walk, Mary with mixed emotions. She felt for her husband and loved his devotion to the cause of justice, as well as King and country. No man could have worked harder for these causes. But she needed more than that. She needed somebody by her side and it seemed as though her husband recognised that.

Chapter XI
The Nation Divides

London November 1641

The fate of nations is often determined on the narrowest of votes, as slender majorities take a country on a course with dramatic consequences for all. And so it was, in the early hours of the 22nd of November 1641, in St Stephen's Chapel, which had been the Commons Chamber since the Reformation. Through the candle smoke, the saints on the stained-glass windows witnessed history in the making.

"The Ayes, 159 votes, and the Noes, 148 votes. The Ayes have it," the Speaker declared.

His announcement was met by a loud cheer from the radicals and Puritans in the House. John Pym had pulled off his master stroke as he succeeded in passing the Grand Remonstrance, a list of two hundred and four separate points of objection to the king's action and calling for the expulsion of all bishops from Parliament, a purge of officials, with Parliament having a right of veto over such appointments. It had taken months of preparation and careful wording of text, and negotiations with the members. The opposition was strong, as Sir John Bankes had ensured a solid Royalist representation by arranging for the king to write to every Member he could rely on, ordering them back to London. They all obeyed, fearful of the king's wrath and so faced the turmoil and fear of plague in the capital. The final, long hours of debate were tense and passionate on both sides, and many feared the consequence of voting either way; if they supported Parliament and they lost, surely the king would be looking for revenge on the perpetrators, and the prospect of a charge of treason was high. Yet if they voted for the king and Parliament won, this would increase Parliament's power, which was already dominant in the capital, and the victors would be looking to strengthen their position even further at the expense of the Royalists. In the end, Sir

John's efforts had not been enough, for people finally declared their positions and the Remonstrance vote had succeeded.

The Grand Remonstrance was delivered to the king but to little avail, for His Majesty did not even read it and certainly would not contemplate engaging with Parliament on how to address any of the concerns. So Sir John Pym sought the power and backing of the people, publishing the text and circulating it nationwide. The situation in Ireland had further deteriorated, with a massacre of Protestant women and children, who were stripped and thrown off a bridge into a freezing cold river. This story added fuel to the public fear of a Catholic uprising and the king's sympathies towards that faith. But the monarch's response was to use the bishops to block any Parliamentary Act that came out of the Commons Chamber, rendering Parliament powerless.

Throughout London, posters were plastered on walls: 'No Bishops. No Popish Lords' and the populists and radicals in Coleman Street and beyond rallied the people to their cause, with riots across the city, aimed at the bishops. The apprentice 'Roundheads' were at the heart of many of the uprisings. Fearful of the mob, the bishops decided against turning up to vote, and declared any law passed without their presence would be illegal. But Sir John Pym, strengthened by the rebellion in the streets, turns this against them, for if they were preventing laws from being passed by the country's Parliament, it was treason. He locked the bishops up in in the Tower, and the church bells across the city rang in jubilation.

The king had been totally outmanoeuvred and was now feeling vulnerable. He moved his court permanently to Oxford, into the house that Sir John and Alice had prepared three years before, leaving in his wake a boiling pot of discontent that manifested itself in anti-Royalist petitions, impeachments, demonstrations, strikes, riots and Parliamentary declarations.

August 1642 Nottingham

Captain Cleall's horse trotted passed a field of tents where an army had been camped and on through the gates of the city of Nottingham. It had been a long ride: it was seven days since he left Corffe, sleeping rough to avoid any trouble in the towns, other than one night staying at Alice's house in Oxford. He proceeded along cobbled streets and passed a tavern nestled at the foot of the granite escarpment on top of which Nottingham Castell stood. A fortification overlooking the trade on the River Trent had been here since Viking times but it was William the Conqueror who had built the first stone Castell at the same time as he had Corffe constructed. Cleall reflected on the difference between the two in style. The French King must have been suffering from a hangover when he commissioned Nottingham, for the building lacked the elegance and interest of its Dorset cousin, with austere ramparts and a single tower. Nor did it have the Purbeck backdrop that made Corffe such a treasure in his heart. The streets were crowded with a mixture of townsfolk, soldiers, tinkers and traders, and animals of all types. He carried on up to the Castell gate where he was challenged by two sentries.

"I am Captain Cleall, here to see Sir John Bankes," he responded and dismounted his horse. He was left to wait a few moments while a runner was sent to verify his access. Captain Cleall was there at the request of Lady Bankes. Sir John had written to her, saying that the king was now committed to war following a series of events that had escalated matters further. The Parliamentarians had voted to raise an army of ten thousand volunteers and appointed the Earl of Essex as commander.

The king settled on Nottingham to plan his campaign. He had managed to conscript ten thousand men who were now camped around the city, but only four thousand of these, were professionally trained soldiers. The rest had been rounded up from rural communities in the shires around Nottingham. But amongst the tents and ranks of soldiers in Nottingham were two thousand cavalry, including Lieutenant John Bankes, and that was why Captain Cleall was here, to honour his pledge to Lady Bankes.

It was not long before a guard escorted him through the gate to the Castell bailey and then to the inner keep. Sir John was there to meet him.

He greeted Cleall warmly and showed him into the keep, a building as plain as he had seen anywhere on his travels in Europe, but its interior revealed at least some styling and elegance. Tapestries, portraits and armament on the walls of the entrance hall nodded to the importance of this fortification over its history. This was where the Crusaders assembled with King Richard for the first Crusade.

"Cleall, I am taking you to see the king," whispered Sir John. "He needs good fighting men and your experience, I fear, will be invaluable given the inevitability of war. He is so uncompromising in his attitude and has been for nearly ten years now, with the taxes he imposed, the suspension of Parliament, the war with the Scots and simply ignoring the Grand Remonstrance."

The two men walked quickly upstairs and along corridors, Sir John talking in a whisper as they went.

"He now wants to teach Parliament a lesson, and firmly establish his Divine Right to Rule. He says that his brother-in-law in France is not frustrated by a meddling Parliament, so why should he: the same God appointed him to rule. But this is not France. He has forgotten the Magna Carta. Even Henry VIII was not this cavalier. He is stretching my loyalty to the limit, but he is still our King."

Cleall had no chance to respond but was concerned to hear Sir John so anxious and talking so fast and frankly as he escorted him through the Castell. Sir John was always so calm and measured but here was a very different man; clearly one who was at the end of his tether. The flag of St George was draped above the entrance into the next room into which Sir John led the captain. It was the main hall in the keep and it was serving as the king's temporary court, for there, at the far end, was the monarch himself, seated on a throne next to his queen. Captain Cleall was not expecting this at all and was trying to take it all in. He paused to gather his composure but was ushered in by Sir John. Captain Cleall had always imagined the court of the king of England to be one of total splendour, with decorative art and nobles dressed to impress, and this court, even although it was temporary, could hardly be more austere.

The Royal Standard was draped over the wall above the thrones, but other than that and a few candle sconces, the walls were bare. There was an enormous fireplace opposite the thrones, with logs arranged ready to be lit, and a large lead-lined window to the captain's right, allowing the sunlight to flood into the otherwise grim room. Beside the queen were two ladies-in-waiting, one of whom was chatting to the queen: the captain thought he recognised her from Lulworth, and the hunt with Lady

Bankes. Elsewhere, there were three nobles in the far corner, including Humphrey Weld, in such deep conversation that they had not noticed the new entrants. The king was much shorter in stature than Cleall would have expected and was dressed in a black velvet doublet with lace collar and plenty of decorative embroidery, black knee-length pantaloons, and leather boots. His attire was of the finest quality but appropriate for travel and action, not the court lace and finery that the captain had imagined. The length of his face was amplified by a brown, pointed beard and matching curly hair that flowed to below his shoulders, and he was looking at Sir John as he entered, a frown above his eyebrow and a slight twitch from the moustache that was positioned above his lip.

"And who have you brought to me, Sir John?" the king enquired, with a voice that was firm and commanding, as one might expect.

The queen looked up from her chat and eyed the new entrant with her dark, shrewd and sparkling eyes, which made the captain almost blush. There was no doubt she was a queen and her beauty more than lived up to what the captain had heard. She was exquisitely dressed in a stunning red outfit that oozed passion, and displayed a well-endowed cleavage adorned with a sapphire stone that hung from a gold chain around her neck. Her hair was as black as the night and pinned up to expose her sumptuous neckline. There was no doubt that she was the most beautiful woman the captain had seen. He wondered what she could see in Charles, who was actually smaller than her, but he guessed power was an attraction, and Sir John had always said that they were a couple very much in love.

Sir John introduced his friend and stepped aside to allow the monarch to have line of sight.

"This is Captain Cleall, who has travelled up from my Castell in Dorsetshire, sire. He is a cavalry man." The captain bowed.

"Good. We need cavalry. What experience have you, Captain?" the king enquired.

"I hope I have served you well over many years and many campaigns, Sire: most recently, La Rochelle."

"La Rochelle was not the triumph we had hoped, Captain, but perhaps a venture that was mismanaged by Buckingham."

The king stammered on the name 'Buckingham', perhaps indicating a reflection of his dislike for the man, who had once been so close to him.

"But right now, I need experienced military officers to help me quell the revolting Parliamentarians, as well as the Celts in Scotland and Ireland. Are you prepared for it, Captain? Cavalry is good. I need cavalry and musketeers. Today I will raise the Royal Standard against the Parliamentary upstarts and I want to bring back order to this country under my reign as the monarch appointed by God to rule over these nations."

"I am retired, Sire, but I am at your service. I am also at Sir John and Lady Bankes' service, and seek the welfare of Sir John's son, a young Lieutenant and also a cavalryman in your service, on behalf of Lady Bankes."

"I am sure Sir John will be minding his welfare, but with you as his captain, surely he can come to no harm. Lady Bankes is a fine woman, and you should write to her to assure her of the king's victory, which will be to God's glory and the safety of her son.'

The king was interrupted by one of the nobles approaching from the corner.

"Sire, I suggest I gather the troops for you to inspect, address and then you can raise the Standard while the sun remains high."

"Yes, you are right. There is no need to wait any longer, and I have another captain for your cavalry — Prince Rupert," the king replied.

Cleall realised this was Prince Rupert of the Rhine, who was the king's German nephew with a reputation as an outstanding cavalry commander across Europe. The prince looked Cleall up and down.

"You had better join me, then," he said.

An hour later, Cleall found himself on his mount, Lightning, at the front of forty other cavalry soldiers and officers, and between twenty other groups of similar-sized units, in the field beneath the Castell rock. It was late afternoon but very blustery. To the left of the cavalry were the musketeers, their officers on horses, but the troops with their muskets and stands. Captain Cleall estimated there must have been three hundred in total. Beyond the musketeers, as well as to the right of the cavalry, were the infantrymen, flanking the Royal force. To the side were the artillery; Cleall counted twenty cannons, hardly an overwhelming force.

The infantry were more of a rabble than an army. In the centre was a group who looked the part, equipped with pikes that towered above them, but in contrast they were flanked by farm labourers with pitchforks, parading as infantry.

There was a sudden blast of horns as the heralds called the forces to attention, announcing the arrival of the monarch as he crossed the bridge over the River Trent, in the Castell's shadow, and into the field beyond with the awaiting army. His horse was a black charger, dressed with a turquoise coat with gold braiding. The size of the horse certainly gave the monarch extra stature and made him look more of a leader. The king was wearing a Cavalier hat with ostrich feathers, holding its brim to stop the wind stealing it. This was the king of England, Scotland, Ireland and Wales; the man appointed by God to be the leader of these nations, as well as the Protestant faith; a man who many believed sat just below God, amongst angels, in the celestial hierarchy; a man whose touch could heal, as many in Nottingham had come in hope to testify; a man who was about to take his country into war with itself, a prospect that was so dark, it was unimaginable. It was the manifestation of Agnes' dreams and foreboding back in Worth Matravers and now it was about to be realised, as the dark clouds would erupt into a stormy fury.

Behind the king was Prince Rupert and several other nobles, and then the Royal Standard-bearer. The king pulled up on his rein and then turned his horse to face his troop, the nobles filing in behind him and the Standard-bearer to his right. There was a hush amongst the assembled troop, as they waited to be addressed by their monarch. The quiet seemed to infect the whole countryside to the south of the Trent and rippled through the crowd who watched the proceedings from the north bank, or vantage points on boats and buildings nearby.

The king addressed his troop but Captain Cleall could not make out his first words, as the wind bellowed over them, before dropping to allow some of his speech to be heard.

"…and so I raise my Royal Standard here in Nottingham for you to follow, and make a stand in the name of God and your King, against the revolutionaries in Parliament and beyond."

The king stammered on the word 'Parliament' which meant his speech finished on a much lower note that he had hoped.

Prince Rupert raised an arm as the speech finished, which was a sign for an artillery of six cannons to fire. Simultaneously, the Royal Standard was raised on a large pole that had been positioned behind the king. As the giant flag was lifted, at least eight yards in length, it revealed the king's arms in blood red on a yellow background, but also with a hand pointing to a crown, and the words 'Give Caesar his due'. The flag flapped excitedly in the wind as Captain Cleall thought that this was indeed a declaration of war, but the king was hardly inspiring his troops with either words or symbolism. Then an even stronger gust of wind caught the Standard and the pole started to fall under its strength. It was a gradual fall which added to the drama but enabled the Standard-bearer to catch it before it hit the ground. That was certainly a bad omen, the captain thought, as the Standard-bearer and two other soldiers re-based the pole, the wind continuing to thrash the flag for being so disrespectful to God's chosen monarch.

August 1642 Poole

John Bingham was making preparations to protect Poole in the event of the war breaking out in southern England. He and most of the Council leaders supported the Parliamentary cause, still recalling the suffering the king's Ship Tax imposed on their livelihoods. But much of Dorsetshire was staunchly Royalist, including Blandford, Bridport, Dorchester and obviously Corffe, with the king's puppet, Sir John Bankes, owning the Castell. Only Melcombe had come out for the Parliamentary cause, west of Poole.

Bingham felt exposed: most of the land to the east, between Poole and London, favoured Parliament, with some notable exceptions, such as Arundel. Poole was on the front line. Bingham was worried about a pre-emptive attack on the town from the Royalists as a gesture of support for the king and to break the sense of anticipation that gripped the county.

Three days after the monarch had raised his Standard in Nottingham, Bingham was addressing the borough's aldermen. It was a warm summer's evening, with the threat of rain, or even storms, along the south coast hanging heavy in the air, making people apprehensive and irritable over and above the political anxiety that faced them all. Bingham held his position as head of the aldermen, seated in a large oak chair with a back that was a foot higher than his head. Around him sat his fellow councillors; most of them he had appointed or were known to be supporters of his views. He knew that three out of the ten would dispute what he was going to propose. The first was the vicar, who had a legal right to be on the Council as a representative of the Church of England, headed, of course, by King Charles, despite the borough being largely Puritan. The second was his own Puritan minister, Jacob Winter, but on the grounds that he held strong pacifist views and would not countenance anything that would lead to conflict. It was essential that he brought Jacob on board, somehow, as he was a force to be reckoned with and his views were well respected. Finally, there was Captain Smithers, a successful merchant who had settled in Poole three years previously but had been a captain in the Royal Navy and was instinctively Royalist.

"Gentlemen, you will all have seen the news pamphlet, which tells us that the king has raised his Standard in Nottingham and declared war on Parliament. We also know Lord Essex has assembled a Parliamentary army and intends to march it north from London in the next few days. Conflict, I fear, is inevitable, but we should all pray that a peaceful settlement can be found. However, as aldermen with the safeguarding of our citizens at heart, I propose three measures. Firstly, I propose we build a wall to protect the borough. Secondly, I propose we acquire more ordinances, again to protect our citizens, and finally, we train and equip a small defensive guard to be stationed on the walls, day and night."

"It sounds expensive and may make us more of a target for aggression than prevent it," Smithers was first to comment.

"I have costed the wall. As we only have the north of the borough to protect, given the harbour that surrounds us on the three other sides, it would cost about twenty guineas, which I agree is not a small sum. It would take six to nine months to build to its full height. The budget I propose for ordinances would be another twelve guineas. These are not small sums, but we are talking about the defence of our citizens, our commerce and indeed our own personal assets."

"I would agree with the captain," the vicar commented. "Such investment and construction would be a sign of intent that Poole is making a stand and will attract aggression. Otherwise, conflict could pass us by."

"I cannot support any aggression. The Lord advocates 'love thy neighbour'." Winter seemed to be supporting the vicar for the first time since he had arrived in Poole.

"If I may, I would like to invite Mary Bristow into our meeting. I believe she has received a message from God that we should regard in considering this matter," Bingham informed the aldermen and asked the secretary to invite Mary Bristow in. She was known to the Puritans amongst the Councillors for she would often go into trances during their services. Jacob Winter believed she was possessed by the Holy Spirit during these times. She was a widow in her early thirties, whose husband had died at sea, and she now lived a very pious and meek life alone, cleaning the church, salting fish and making nets. She was a plain-looking woman, who dressed humbly and was very timid, never making eye contact and barely saying anything to anybody. However, every three or four weeks she would enter into a trance during worship and her whole demeanour would be transformed. She would look bright and pure, her face glowing and she would talk in a language nobody could decipher, as she swayed her body with her hands reaching out to the heavens but with her eyes closed. This would last for about the length of two hymns before she would collapse with exhaustion, and she would not come round until the end of the service. Afterwards, she would say she had travelled at speed, flying out of her body, and had witnessed many different phenomena, snow-covered mountains, vast oceans, magnificent citadels built to the glory of God in far-off lands and a monastery on an island. But now she was before the aldermen, the most important men of the borough, without the power of the Holy Spirit, as just the nervous and shy church-cleaning woman.

"Mary, please take a seat and do not be afraid. We would all just like to hear what you told me this morning, about your vision. There is nothing to be worried about. I believe you may have received a message from God and as servants of the Lord, we need to know what He has said to you," Bingham reassured her.

Mary sat down and looked up at Bingham for further reassurance, before focusing back down onto the skirt of her dress, which she held tightly with both hands.

"I will tell you what I have seen. But I know not what it means, or if it means anything," she whispered, briefly raising her eyes to see the aldermen all eager to hear what she had to say.

"Mary, just repeat what you told me," Bingham said, in a comforting voice.

"Well, sometimes when I wake — well, just before I am fully awake — I am able to leave my body and I believe the Lord or His Spirit takes me to places. It is like in my trances. First, when this happened, I was scared and my fear prevented me going. But now I have faith and the Lord takes me. I know this sounds strange, but this is real and is not like a dream at all. I believe I do really travel."

"Please carry on, Mary." This time the reassurance came from Jacob Winter.

"Well, this morning I had one of those experiences and I was taken up, up, up... So high I could see the whole of England. It was as if I was sitting on the moon and I could look down and then dive into different parts of the country. I could see armies gathering in the heart of the country, armies preparing for battle. Around them, I could see families digging graves, endlessly digging graves, Castells being destroyed, towns being torn apart and country houses being ransacked. Hate, fear and blood were everywhere to be seen. But there were a few towns that maintained a purity and rose above it all. They had built walls to keep the evil at bay. They stayed true to God and were protected. Behind the walls they became stronger, until they were able to venture out and bring peace to their surrounding lands."

"Well, Mary — thank you. And so, gentlemen, I believe God, through Mary, has shown us the way. It is His will that we build a wall, to protect Poole, to maintain the purity and build the strength of the borough and then spread the word, the pure word, of peace and God, when the time is right."

The motion to build the wall was passed, with only the Reverend objecting, as even the sceptical Captain Smithers knew when to concede defeat. The next day, construction started on the wall.

Tom had picked up a leaflet, one of several that had been pinned onto the Corffe market square notice board, and had ridden over to Worth to discuss it with Francis, whom he found working on repairing the roof of Tom's step-brother's house.

"Francis, you remember in London we heard that Leveller, Freeborn John, talking about being a free-born Englishman and everybody being equal?"

"Why sure, Tom. It was something to behold; standing on his soap box, talking as if kings and aristocrats were to be overthrown."

"Well, next week he is coming to Poole and speaking. Look at this." Tom handed Francis the leaflet.

Francis read it and his face lit up.

"We should go, Tom."

The two of them discussed and planned how they would arrange to see the Leveller speak. They knew Tom's father would not be happy for them to go and so they decided to keep it a secret and make up a story about going fishing in the harbour and visiting Green Island, but instead they would row across the entire harbour to Poole.

The 6th of September was the scheduled date for the event and it soon came around; a cloudy day but with no wind and perfect for fishing, and so the boys set off shortly after dawn. They clambered up Nine Barrow Down and jogged along its ridge, before descending, harbour side, where just passed the Devil's Anvil they found a familiar path that meandered through the brambles, ferns, and gorse of the sandy heathland to the harbour shore. It took them no time at all to find their boat and Tom was soon rowing them across the still waters of the harbour, as the sun climbed higher in the morning sky. They rowed between Green Island, where they had so many adventures as children, and on the leeward side of Furzey and Brownsea Island, towards Poole. The quay had been constructed on an inlet to a backwater, and the masts of trading ships pierced the skyline, while the town's houses and warehouses were nestled behind. Francis had now taken over the rowing while Tom directed him to a small beach to the west of the quay, where they could tie up the boat.

The Corffe men found Poole to be abuzz with life. Along the quay, ships bobbed and creaked, tugging on their moorings to the wharf as they were being unloaded; barrels of olives, wine, and grain being stacked on to wagons, while new supplies of water and food were being loaded for return journeys. Traders and merchants watched the labourers hard at work as they sweated in the midday sun. But amongst these usual quayside activities were groups of artisans from across the shire, who had also journeyed to hear the talk of the famous Leveller. They were mainly men, but some had brought wives and even kinfolk, as elderly parents and young children were amongst the groupings. And of course, any large grouping of people also attracts peddlers of all types of goods; apples, berries, cider, fish, crabs, hats, knives, waistcoats. If it was wanted, there was somebody to sell it. St James' church bells struck midday, signalling an hour to go; an hour enough for a drink and a pie in one of the taverns on the quayside.

They chose the Helmsman but found many others had chosen likewise. It was jammed with more people from all walks of life; sailors spending their share of the trade profit from their most recent trip to Newfoundland; artisans from across the shires eagerly anticipating the afternoon's events; some of the tinkers and tailors who had already sold their wares, and the locals, including two whores eager for business. But there was something else Francis and Tom realised. There was an air of anticipation and expectation. Something that was about to happen. The country was on the brink of war, one that would be fought between its own people, but in the taverns and streets of Parliamentary Poole, there was a feeling that this was a necessary stage of transition into a world of more opportunity. As the men from Corffe listened in to discussions, they heard voices of hope, and even those who were like them, curious, but where curiosity was seeking new purpose.

A bell rang as they finished their pies, and this was presumably a sign that the first speech was about to start, for much of the tavern emptied out, leaving a few sailors and the two whores. The crowd was joined by others exiting from different taverns as Tom and Frances made their way through the backstreets to Market Square, where a great marquee had been positioned. By the time Francis and Tom had arrived, all the benches had been taken, so they joined many standing at the back.

Tom looked around. A platform had been erected at the front, and three chairs awaited whoever was going to host this session, along with John Lilburne. As Tom panned around the crowd, he estimated at least five hundred faces, the majority like him and Francis, twenty-year-old labourers, artisans, or apprentices. This was not a gathering of Puritans, for those dressed in their austere clothing were a small minority, but a collection of workers filled with hope and anticipation. In the audience they spotted a few from Corffe and the surrounding Purbeck villages. Were these the free-born Englishmen that Lilburne had talked about in London and to whom he would be appealing directly, but to what aim?

Three men then arose from the front bench and stepped up to the platform. The first was John Bingham, well known locally in his distinctive Puritan clothing, and of course the magistrate who had tried Francis. But then there was the Leveller himself, John Lilburne, looking as Tom had remembered him in Coleman Street, well-groomed but barely hiding the pent-up energy and passion Tom and Francis knew he was about to release. The third man was dressed in a military uniform with polished breastplate and was clearly an officer of some elevated rank but beyond that, Tom had no idea. Bingham soon unveiled his identity, for after welcoming everybody he said that the Lilburne address would be followed by a brief talk by Colonel Brook, and with that, the Leveller got up. He had a presence about him that was captivating, and it was hard to determine why. He was not physically distinctive: a neat, pointed moustache; short, well-cut hair; a white laced collar over a dark grey tunic. He could have been a merchant in the Poole Customs House. It was when he started talking that his presence was magnified; his voice resonating and arms gesticulating with the points he was making, while his eyes scanned the audience, seemingly resting on each individual, personalising his address.

His message was tailored to the audience but politically charged; one that questioned the notion of royalty, but advocated the notion of freeborn rights, which for each and every member of the audience was God-given. He justified this with repeated references to the bible in a way that made it obvious and common sense, quoting Christ, his Apostles, and all the way back to Jacob and Adam. The rights that all Englishmen are born with were different from privileges bestowed by a monarch or a government, and he made it sound like God, Jesus and everybody in the bible, known to the crowd, were behind his message.

Throughout his speech the audience responded with repeating acknowledging 'yeahs' and 'noes' supporting what he was saying in ever-increasing levels of enthusiasm. When he sat down, the whole marquee rose with a standing ovation. The fervour was infectious and there was a sense that everything was being made clearer and a real sense of change was apparent. Tom and Francis looked at each other as they applauded and started whooping with joy, with smiles on their faces and fire in their hearts.

The colonel now got up to speak but had to wait several minutes before the crowd would allow him to start his address.

"I was elected a Member of Parliament fourteen years ago, driven by a passion to make change for the better and not for any privilege or status. The king denied me that opportunity for many years by suspending Parliament and denying my voice and others with similar motives from being heard. But now Parliament is back, and it has started to fight for those rights articulated so forthrightly by John Lilburne; those rights that are God-given to each and every one of you. The king has received the Grand Remonstrance from Parliament, stating over two hundred misdemeanours and breaches of his royal prerogative. The king still has not sought to apologise or address a single one of them. Instead, he seeks to silence the voice of Parliament, your voice, the voice of the people, by running off to Nottingham and raising his Royal Standard against his own people, against each and every one of you. How can that be right? How can that be just? How can that be Royal? How can that be Christian? My message is simple, people of England, people of Dorsetshire, people of Poole — we must fight not only to preserve those rights but to enhance them."

He spoke in a tone that the audience could relate to and his message was clear and directed at them. He even sounded like one of them, rather than a member of the gentry.

"The king has waged war on us, and I am here to seek your support and ask you to join that fight back. I am here to sign up the men of Dorsetshire and the men of Poole to join the Parliamentary forces, which are already strong, but we need you, each one of you, to guarantee the victory for righteousness. This is a war where you will be fighting not for King and country but for your rights and to define your country in the future. We are building an army that will fight for the glory of God, which will be modelled on God's principles of discipline and moral righteousness, and within the ranks there will be opportunities for all. If you fight hard and show courage and leadership, I promise God will reward you. We all fight together for God's victory, and are equals in his sight. And so God will give us victory."

He held up a paper and waved it.

"The first step is to sign up here. The first step towards a country where your rights are guaranteed, and that will open the door to opportunity to all, not just those born to privilege. Opportunities to better oneself in the eyes of God and man through hard toil, as well as bravery and courage. So — who will be first?"

As he laid down the paper on the table, he was greeted with an enormous cheer and several men rushed forward to sign up.

Colonel' Brook's new conscripts, eighty-two in all, destined to join one of his foot regiments, left Poole the next day, and marched north. Tom Harvey and Francis Trew were amongst the ranks. They had been in no doubt that it was the right thing to do. It was simply so clear to them, they had no option. However, when they returned to Corffe, persuading others of this wisdom was altogether a different challenge. They first passed the mill as they entered the village, where Joseph Cobb was loading up a cart with flour sacks. Francis ran over to him and explained how they were going to change the world and give the king a lesson. Joseph looked at them as if they were mad. They had talked to him previously about the Levellers and apprentices in London and he had seemed to listen, expressing some interest, but not now.

"Why would you leave Corffe, going to God-knows-where and fight for people and causes that are not ours? You should be here with friends and family, and if there is any fighting to be done, it should be protecting them," he declared.

That first encounter did not go well, and now Tom had to face his family, whilst Francis returned to Corffe. Camille would be with his father, as they had arranged to have supper together. He walked into the house to find Camille, Beth and Elizabeth busy preparing the food and his father, lighting the fire. He stood in the doorway and announced his intentions. His speech could not have been received with less enthusiasm, as his explanation and motivations fell on deaf ears. His father was appalled at the idea of fighting the king and stormed out of his house, refusing to say goodbye. Camille could not believe her husband would leave her to go and play soldiers.

"Non! Non! Non!" she screamed.

"Camille, I will be back before Christmas, and the new year will be better for us all. I know it is the right thing to do and it is for us all," Tom pleaded.

"Non! Non! Non!" she screamed again, as her eyes welled up with tears.

It was not until midnight that she calmed down and finally her mood changed. She clung to Tom and they returned to the Castell not saying anything. In the early hours they made love, and then Camille wept until Tom got up at first light to make his way back to Poole, with Francis.

As Tom marched north, doubts about whether he was doing the right thing did start to filter through his mind, and the journey gave him plenty of time to worry over it. At one stage, he was toying with the idea of running back to his Camille. He already missed her and he was trying, in his own mind, to rationalise his motivations. For Francis it was clear: the dream of a new world appealed to him as, frankly, the world had dealt him a rotten hand thus far, with the loss of his family, and so he had far less at stake. Tom shared Francis's dream, but with far less passion, yet he was motivated by a sense of proving himself, and also by one of adventure. Of course, he had a beautiful wife and a future wherein he could follow in his father's footsteps to be the Corffe Estates Manager, but that all seemed too easy. He had listened to Captain Cleall's stories of travel on the Continent and throughout England and yearned to know more about different places. He also understood from the captain that battle was not glorious but indeed horrific, but it did make men out of boys and this was something Tom felt he needed. Yes, a real broth of motivations, and all in conflict with the love he had for Camille, as well as his home. But he would return soon; a better man in a better country. And then the regiment started to sing. It was a song had been crafted from the Psalms of the Bible by one of the Puritan recruits at the front and the words were picked up, line by line, throughout the regiment, until by the fourth rendition, they all were singing with their hearts as they marched.

Behold, how good and joyful a thing it is: brethren, to dwell together in unity!
It is like the precious ointment upon the head, that ran down unto the beard: even unto Aaron's beard, and went down to the skirts of his clothing.
Like as the dew of Hermon: which fell upon the hill of Sion.
For there the Lord promised his blessing and life for evermore.

The singing, the feeling of comradeship and purpose was the antidote Tom needed, and all his doubts were left behind as they marched down the hill into Salisbury later that day, the spire of the cathedral symbolising to him the righteousness of his mission. The colonel and John Lilburne had ridden ahead and obviously addressed similar gatherings elsewhere, for overnight their numbers were to swell by seventy more fathers, sons and brothers from across Wiltshire, marching to fight for their rights.

Another day's march and the Regiment found themselves in Hungerford, where they were allowed a day's rest, but were joined by not only more local conscripts but troops marching from Winchester, Bristol and Reading. There were now more than a thousand on foot and a hundred cavalry. As the numbers swelled, Francis and Tom conversed with fellow conscripts from across the south and west, and they were all convinced that they were on a mission to change the country; a belief that this was a defining moment in history to make a stand against the king, which would benefit them all. They would soon teach him a lesson and be back with their loved ones.

At Hungerford, Francis and Tom were made pikemen and each given a fourteen-foot pike and trained how to use this weapon against both horse and infantry. They were trained on how to charge the enemy and deploy their long weapons in battle in different situations, the upward thrust to unseat a cavalryman, the downward thrust on opposing foot soldiers, and then defensive lines or walls to create a barrier to protect musketeers and hold positions. Tom and Francis found the pikes not too dissimilar to a hay fork, just longer and heavier; too heavy to throw as a spear but strong enough to impale a horse. But with a hundred men waving them around in close proximity, the training was essential to give them discipline and stop them wounding each other, let alone provide a defence against the enemy.

Colonel Brooks' plan was to meet up with the Earl of Essex and his Parliamentary forces, who were marching north out of London. Essex had marched via Northampton, where he was joined by a detachment of Cambridgeshire cavalry raised and commanded by Oliver Cromwell. Colonel Brooks' regiment met them in Moreton-in-the-Marsh, five days after leaving Poole, by which time Essex's forces totalled twenty-one thousand infantry and four thousand two hundred cavalry and dragoons. Tom and Francis were amazed at the scale of the force. They were starting to realise the full extent of the conflict that was about to commence and felt some trepidation. However, with such purpose and passion, with such numbers and with God on their side, a quick and decisive victory was inevitable. They would all be back in Corffe in no time.

Chapter XIII
The War Begins

With only the county of Worcestershire separating Parliamentary troops, under the command of Lord Essex, and Royalist forces, led by Prince Rupert, it was inevitable that cavalry reconnaissance units would meet, sooner or later. Captain Cleall led several of such missions, and under his command was the young John Bankes, 'but the fledgling officer hardly knew his arse from his elbow when it came to fighting. Indeed, John was very grateful to have the experienced Captain as a commanding officer and even more grateful that they had not yet encountered the enemy. But the enemy was engaged in the first major skirmish when a cavalry troop of about one thousand Royalists, commanded by Prince Rupert, encountered a Parliamentary cavalry detachment at a bridge across the River Teme, close to Worcester, and came out the better. The Royalists presented it as a victory and this gave Lieutenant Bankes renewed confidence.

Prince Rupert withdrew to Shrewsbury, where he held a council-of-war, to which Captain Cleall was invited, with twenty or so other officers. The king was not present, as he was enjoying dinner with his family before they would be sent away to be smuggled out of the country. Rupert and Cleall were both pleased that the king was not at the Council, which was held in a large marquee, and those in attendance discussed two courses of action; whether to advance towards Essex's new position near Worcester, or to march towards London. It was considered important to get back to London and regain the capital before it was lost. Rupert wanted to be decisive and go on the attack, rather than wait to be attacked. Cleall agreed with this in principle but stressed that it was even more important to select the field of battle and ensure that the king's army was positioned with advantage on that field.

However, his counsel was lost, partly due to his relatively low rank, but mainly because the hunger for battle was strong following Prince

Rupert's recent success and a desire to fight Essex before his army strengthened yet further. They were hoping and expecting a single, decisive battle and victory, which Cleall felt was unlikely to be the case, given that half the country was prepared for war and tensions were at a fever pitch. The Council decided to head towards London but on a route that would make sure they encountered Essex along the way. The Royalist army left Shrewsbury the next day, which brought them two days' start on the enemy, and it had the desired effect as it forced Essex to move rapidly with little planning or preparation to intercept them.

It was at Edgehill, in southern Warwickshire, that the armies first met in earnest. The king and Prince Rupert had made camp on the hill and the dawn brought a bitter cold with a frost blanketing the fields. The sky was a metallic blue to the west, but from the east a grey, dirty cloud was approaching as if the heavens were dragging a blanket across the nation as it awoke to the commencement of a vicious civil war. The drama was accompanied by the thrashing and squawking of crows from the surrounding trees, heralding the woe to come. It was not long after daybreak when the church bells from the nearby village of Kineton, beneath Edgehill, started to chime, awakening any Royalists who were fighting the prospect of the new day. But the toll of the bells was soon joined by a growing sound of the bustle of Essex's army amassing on the road ahead in the direction of Kineton, having moved into position through the night. It was a Sunday morning on the 23rd of October 1642, with the king's army at the top of the hill, and the Parliamentarians about half a mile from the bottom. It was the first time that any two English forces had opposed each other since the Wars of the Roses, two hundred years before.

Captain Cleall and John Bankes looked down the slope through the fog of their own breath in the cold air. John tightened his ox-hide jacket to protect him from the cold. He had been told the thickness of the jacket would resist many sword strokes, as well as long-range shot but he had yet to put it to practise. Next to him, the captain was able to measure the quantity of the opposition, if not the quality of the fighting force that was assembling below; the foot soldiers comprising pikemen and musketeers, artillery and of course, the cavalry. To his eye it looked like the forces were fairly evenly matched.

"John, the key to victory is always the cavalry," Captain Cleall sought to reassure the lieutenant novice. "I believe we have the upper hand as our cavalry is mainly from gentry with better mounted skills. But we must take nothing for granted and must plan accordingly. I have always said that in the confusion of battle, it is a plan that gives you the edge, not a sword. So listen to me. I understand, from Prince Rupert, they are likely to be drilled in the Dutch tactic of firing pistols from the saddle. I have seen these tactics first-hand and they have an effect but nothing compared with the shock and horror that a cavalry charge with swords in hand can produce. The objective is to disable the enemy as quickly as possible, not kill. Dismembering, wounding, even just a severe cut will take scores of the enemy out in the time it takes to reload a pistol and make a pistol shot. Our job is to act like a sickle, cutting down as many as possible, and we must stick to the plan, John, in order to reap our victory. It will be tough but we will prevail."

John looked uneasily back at the captain, who even had a hint of a smile on his face, as part of him relished the prospect of action once again. Cleall turned back to his protégé and saw the fear in his eyes.

"Just stay with me, John. We will see this through together. As long as we avoid the artillery's firing range, the cavalry will reign supreme," the captain assured him.

Just then a horseman rode up to them, in a dashing red tunic and large black hat adorned with a feather plume. "Ah, Captain Cleall — I thought it was you."

"Humphrey Weld — a captain also now, I see." Cleall nodded to the sash around his shoulder and chest.

"Yes. Ready to give these rebels a good beating. It will be like a good hunt in Lulworth, I wager you. See you at the other side once we have mown through the bastards."

As he left, Cleall said, "That is exactly the cavalier attitude you do not want on a battlefield. Well, not on your side, anyway. I will not be surprised if we do not see him on the other side."

Cleall then thought he saw another familiar face organising some men behind the lines. He rode over and greeted him.

"Dr Coke, you have left the needy in London to serve your King?"

"Captain Cleall, good to see you. I fear there will be more need today here on this hill than all of London. I am just setting up a medical tent in the hope of being able to provide aid to the injured, but frankly provisions are dire."

"Alas, provisions and organisation generally are not anywhere near the standard of the armies I have fought for, but it is reassuring to have you here, Doctor. I will leave you to make preparations, and I hope not to be attending your services later," Captain Cleall replied and then returned to his command.

The Royalist army quickly awoke from its early morning stupor, and started to develop into a formation. The sun, obscured by the eastern blanket of cloud, every now and again found a break and lit up the battlefield ahead, taunting both sides. The Royalist right wing of cavalry and dragoons was led by Prince Rupert, with Captain Cleall and Lieutenant John Bankes among its ranks. The centre was made up by the infantry, including musketeers and several cannons, but largely unregimented troops with picks and staffs. The left wing was comprised of more cavalry and dragoons. There was a growing sense of apprehension along the ranks that also infected the horses, who were restless and difficult to control.

Cleall had been in this situation many times before, having fought in battles during the Thirty-Year War when the English were fighting alongside the Protestant forces of the Dutch, Danish and northern German states against the Habsburg States, Austrians, French and Spanish Catholic forces. He recalled his first battle at Dessau Bridge, back in 1626 in Saxony. He had trained in mock battles for two years before, but it was nothing like the real thing, and when he faced the enemy, he felt totally unprepared and was struggling to contain his bowels with the fear and trepidation. It had seemed like an eternity back then as the opposing forces were lined up against each other and eyed up each other's positions. He had been minded to turn his horse and gallop away, but instead he bowed his head and prayed in his saddle for courage and that he would see another day. Nearly twenty years later and after dozens of battles, the captain found the fear just as heavy; not only his own, but young John's and the entire Royalist army's fear was so thick that it could be tasted in the air with each breath he took. The captain's experience had given him the ability not to overcome the fear but channel it into strength and courage to see him through. But his experience also gave him the knowledge that battle was a lottery. Yes, there were overall winners and losers, but the dead were often plenty on both sides. How many close comrades had he lost when his side claimed victory? How many close shaves had he personally had with death, not to mention the wounds and scars from close battle? How often had he been locked into battle with an enemy combatant and seen fear swirling around the whites of their eyes and the stench of it on their breath, as they both knew that only one of them was going to survive?

Standing on Edgehill was completely different. This was English soil and those lined up in front of him were Englishmen. Amongst the mass of swords, pikes and shields, there could be people whom he had fought alongside before, maybe with whom he had drinks with, or even friends. It was the same King's Standard that he was fighting for but not the same enemy. Friends and foes divided battlefields of the past but this was a battle where family would fight family, friends would fight friends, Christian Protestants would fight Christian Protestants and the tribal divides of faith and country were torn apart. And for what course? The king's arrogance and Parliament's stubbornness. For Captain James Cleall there was no purpose to this madness, but he was there for one and only one reason and that was his love for Mary and because he had made an oath to protect her son. He was the man who was still furious with the king for La Rochelle and yet he found himself fighting for him again. If it were not for Mary, he could have been in the ranks of those lined up against him today. But he only had to look around at John, who had the same almond-shaped eyes as his mother, as well as mannerisms that occasionally would take the captain back to Dorsetshire, to the rides along the cliffs and along the beaches with Mary. Oh Mary, if only… So many ifs, but back to reality and back to keeping John alive through the forthcoming hell.

Amongst the Parliamentary foot soldiers, Francis and Tom looked up the hill to the Royalist forces. They were both trying to shake off the shackles of a sleepless night that had involved the Parliamentary forces moving into position, with minimal rest and no fires to keep the chill away. On top of that, a concoction of apprehension and the trepidation of their first engagement in battle. The hope and inspiration of John Lisburn's talk, back in Poole, now seemed a distant memory. Tom had to pinch himself as he wondered how he came to be standing in this line, with his ash pike towering sixteen feet over him, and wearing his steel helmet and rusty breastplate. Was he just in a nightmare and if he woke himself up he would be back in Corffe? He had never even punched another human being and here he was supposedly ready to thrust his pike into the guts of fellow Englishmen lined up before him; men with families and homes just like his from villages just like Corffe.

As Tom and Francis looked up at the mass of the Royalist troops and horses, their own force seemed to shrink in size and capability, and any confidence they had waned. The fear of death that haunted them during the night was now at play again, for in the open there was no protection from one's worst fears. They were facing the king's own guard; hardened soldiers who had seen action across Europe, and here were they, seasoned in the Dorsetshire fields of barley with just a few days training in how to use a pike. They saw cannons and musketeers amongst the Royalist ranks. Were they to be the fodder for the royal artillery and were they about to meet their maker at the bottom of a hill in Worcestershire, whilst the king looked down upon them, still unrepentant and unyielding to the voices of change from his people, as always? It would not be the king fighting today, but the knights and pawns on the Worcestershire chess board beneath him.

Tom looked down his line of troops. He was taller than most and so had a good view. There was Jacob Vaggs and Harry Mason, both from Corffe; Arthur and Jack Pitt from Wareham; and a dozen men from Poole, all with faces that betrayed their anxiety. They had been issued with metal breastplates to wear over their jackets, as well as lobster pot-shaped helmets. Arthur and Jack were musketeers and wrapped diagonally across their chests were belts called bandoliers, from which hung the apostles; twelve wooden bottles, each of which contained one shot, sufficient gun powder charge and a cord to light it. Behind them their brigade's Standard flew limply, a bottle-green with a St George cross in its corner. To his right was Jerome, a Devonshire man almost as tall at Tom, with whom he had made friends. He was looking very pale. Whether they were novices or hardened veterans, the soldiers each had their own way of managing the self-control to ensure they maintained their lines and did not simply turn and run for safety. Whilst honour, reputation, comradeship, or fear of the consequences of desertion bound them to the spot, the flames of the fear of mutilation or death fanned across the line, and each individual tried to manage this deathly brew of emotions and thoughts in different ways.

For Francis it was talking. Tom's friend would not stop wittering away, talking as much to himself as Tom, making endless observations about the opposing forces and asking the same questions repeatedly. When do you think we will start fighting? Will the cavalry lead the way? Do we outnumber them? Is that the king? Where is Essex? Will we eat today? Tom focused on his inner self, and the prayers he was making to God, Jesus, the saints and all the angels he could imagine for himself and Francis, asking for strength and courage for them both, but he also prayed for Camille and the people of Corffe. Francis's wittering just became a background noise, which was fine for he was not looking for answers, although a comrade bellowed from down the line to shut him up. The smell of shit and piss percolated through the ranks, as fellow soldiers struggled to maintain control of their bodily functions.

The morning developed into a stalemate, with the Parliamentarians not wanting to march up a hill to attack, but blocking the Royalist road to London, while the Royalists were keen to maintain their elevated advantage. But as the last wisps of mist cleared, King Charles and Prince Rupert realised that they could not stay at the top of the hill for long; not least because there was no water there, but also the men were restless for a fight. Essex showed no signs of wishing to attack, so the order was given for the Royalists to descend the slope of Edgehill shortly after midday. But the Parliamentarians did not move. Another hour passed as the forces eyed each other, now on the same level. Their respective leaders had pulled both armies together, as there was no standing army at the time. Armour and weapons were gathered from wherever they could be found and distributed without any consistency, and neither side had any uniformity of dress, other than a few groupings of green, red or blue tunics spread erratically amongst both lines. The opposing forces looked like two neighbouring villages coming together for a tug of war, just on a larger scale, rather than a battle between King and Parliament.

Only the officers on each side were well equipped, with polished armour and glinting steel swords, but most wore their own fine-quality civilian clothes under a buff coat, with a sash over the left shoulder, across the body, to indicate their rank.

Prince Rupert headed the cavalry with a line of colonels and captains behind him, each in front of fifty horses, comprised of lieutenants in charge of groups of ten horsemen. The prince had a pet hunting poodle in his arms, apparently called 'Boy', which made Cleall shake his head. What did he think this was — some kind of Royal Garden party? John Bankes was stationed immediately behind Captain Cleall, and he was assured by the experienced officer's presence. He had been trained but he felt totally unprepared for battle. Despite this, he was eager for it to start as he was already saddle-sore, and his bladder was once again calling upon him.

The king recognised the stalemate and rode with his entourage from regiment to regiment to encourage his soldiers for the fight ahead. It was this action that goaded the Parliamentarians into opening fire, with cannon directed at the king, but finding its home amongst infantry in the regiment he was addressing. The shrieks and cries that followed declared the death of three soldiers as the Parliamentarians claimed first blood, but there was bellowing from both sides as the battle started. The king's party withdrew out of range and an artillery duel took place. Smoke started to pour onto the field, and the smell of gunpowder filled the air.

On the right flank, Rupert passed his poodle to an aide before giving the order to advance, and the drummers started the marching rhythm for the foot soldiers. Captain Cleall led his cavalry forward with a scream of 'Attack!' pumped by his fear from deep within his stomach. The thunder of horseshoes on earth and the cries of men filled the air. Shock and horror. The Royalist swords were drawn and directed at the enemy en masse. It was an awesome sight and as the charge gathered momentum, the ground between the Royalist position and the Parliamentary ranks was swallowed up. A troop of Parliamentarian horses seemed to defect, riding off to the west in the direction of a wood. But there were many other cavalry to form a stand, but instead of meeting them in the field, a volley of pistol fire was heard from the saddled cavalry, as the captain predicted.

The rider next to John fell with a thud, and another on his other flank was wounded but carried on his charge with gritted determination. Seeing the limited impact their shots had made, the Parliamentarian cavalry started to disperse. This was the first defining moment of battle and the Royalist cavalry could sense it. Cleall cried out 'Kill them!", his spurs urging Lightning to gallop faster. The Royalist cavalry responded, slicing and hacking through the Parliamentary opponents. The captain set the example — first slashing at a roundhead to his right, smashing his helmet with one blow that dazed him, and following up with another that took a chunk out of his arm, leaving blood and tendons flooding out from his split tunic. Before his opponent could scream, the captain had charged on to the next, with his sword plunging through his ribs, and on to the next. John had followed him and saw the captain's first opponent dazed and clutching his wounded arm. He had no time to look up before John's sabre found his other arm and with a force that surprised him, dismounted the Parliamentarian. As he galloped passed, he looked back to see the man hit the ground, his battle coming to an early and abrupt end. He turned back to see the captain in combat with a fourth opponent, and a new wave of courage drove him forward, screaming, with his sabre showing the way.

John's cry turned the head of Cleall's opponent for a fleeting moment, enough for the captain to thrust his sabre forward, clashing with his enemy's, becoming locked between the two crazed adversaries. This meant that John had a free passage to drive his blade home through the leather of the man's tunic, into his rib cage and finding his inner organs. John was fixed on his opponent's eyes that conveyed the horror of what he had just experienced, before blood spewed from his mouth. His body fell towards the captain but he pushed him off and his adversary fell to the ground, taking John's sabre with him.

"Here — take this one, John!" The captain handed over the sabre that had previously belonged to his last victim. John grabbed it, the fear and trepidation on his face erased with his first kill. The rest of the cavalry had continued their charge and had severed a large gap through the ranks of the Parliamentarians. Several had fallen to the pistol fire, and their bodies laid abandoned in the mud while their horses cantered away from the battle and gunfire. However, their numbers were as nothing compared to the unmanned Roundhead horses galloping in the opposite direction, leaving corpses on the field or even dragging riders still attached to reins or stirrups, shrieking out their last cries before death.

Captain Cleall recognised the damage that had been done and the turmoil around him and sensed a victory in the making. Keeping his head in battle amongst the cannon blasts, gunshots, smoke, screams and sheer horror was something that his experience had taught him. In the confusion of battle, it is a plan that gives you the edge, not the sword. All that was required now was to regroup his troop, and charge back into them from the rear. He and John galloped on to catch up with his men, but to his dismay a large contingent of the Royalist cavalry had continued the charge, for they had seen the Parliamentary supply carriages lined up a few hundred yards away with virtually no guard. They could see rich pickings as the men at the front shouted 'Booty!' Captain Cleall cursed and shouted after them. A few tail-enders turned back but the rest charged on like men possessed and Humphrey Weld was amongst them. The captain surveyed the situation — just thirty cavalry left; less than half the number of the remaining Parliamentarians he had devastated. Battles are won and lost on split decisions and plans being executed effectively. He could see that although outnumbered by the parliamentarians, they were in total disarray and if he acted quickly, he could still get the upper hand. So he ordered the charge back and led the way, with John at his side.

What Captain Cleall was unable to do, given his numbers, was protect his infantry, for while the Royalist infantry advanced in the centre, they faced the foot soldiers of both Colonel Oliver Cromwell and Colonel John Hampden brigades, who stood their ground'. This was where Will Harvey, Francis Trew and the men of Corffe were to see their first action. They had charged forward with pikes and muskets held high, screaming at the Royalist lines, but as they came within fifty yards of the enemy, the musketeers amongst them fired a volley of shots, which resulted in a peppering of casualties along the royalist line. The pikemen did not stop, continuing their charge, amidst the smoke, until they were twenty-five yards from the enemy, when they were ordered to make gaps in their line, all pre-planned by Hampden and Cromwell, to allow the

Parliamentarian cavalry within the Brigade to charge through and to raise havoc amongst the Royalist infantry.

The Royalist foot soldiers had been prepared to fight the oncoming Parliamentary opposition, with pikes held under arm and horizontal, not grounded and facing up to defend against mounted cavalry. The men of Corffe cheered on the Parliamentary horses, with their sabres drawn, as they sliced their way through the confused and disorderly Royalist troops. With no Royalist cavalry to support them, the sabres started making meat out of the Royalist line. Arthur, Jack and the musketeers were lighting fuses and pummelling them with shot, before discharging another apostle of shot and powder into their barrels. The sizzling of fuses and gunpowder smoke ignited the adrenaline flow amongst the Roundhead foot soldiers who piled into the furrows of death and injury ploughed by the cavalry.

Tom Harvey was the first of the Corffe men to engage with the enemy through the cannon smoke. A foot soldier was recovering his pike after the charge of a horse had pushed him off balance, and Tom saw his opportunity. He lunged his pike at the man's groin and pushed him over, the spearhead buried deep in his tunic beneath his breastplate. He pushed it down further as his opponent screamed, and a pool of blood flooded his torso. Adrenalin pumping inside, he realised he had killed his first man, but at the same time he realised he was very exposed. The pike was a lethal but very sluggish weapon. He yanked at it once but the steel end seemed stuck as it caught between the dead man's belt and breastplate, while he realised that a Royalist foot soldier was about to lunge at him with his pike from the right of the fallen colleague. Francis Trew anticipated the attack and parried the lunging pike with his own. Both pikes ended up in the ground, and there was a moment when the three men — Tom, Francis and the Royalist foot soldier — just looked at each other, all with their weapons astray, amidst mayhem all around. Action in these moments separate the dead and the survivors. Tom seized the initiative and jumped on the man, his height advantage and strength forcing him to the ground. This gave Francis sufficient time to recover his pike and he followed up the flying Tom with a lunge into the opponent's thigh, impaling him to the ground.

"Tom, get up! He is done for!" Francis cried, and pulled up his friend, who had lost his helmet in his tussle. By this time, many of the Royalist troops around them had made flight in disarray from the cavalry charge, and the Parliamentary forces were making significant ground. As the fighting advanced to the Royalist central ranks, there was a moment of panic, whilst the king ordered his sons, Charles and James, to be moved to safety. The Parliamentary troop had made so much progress they were menacing the princes' escort as they left, and at that moment a Roundhead captured the king's Standard, before turning back with his trophy to the Parliamentary ranks.

Captain Cleall saw what had happened as, at last, a Lieutenant Colonel Robert Welch, a man in his late twenties on a white charger splattered with blood, returned with thirty or so cavalry from the direction of Kineton.

'Sir, the Royal Standard: we must recover it!" Captain Cleall said.

"Right, Captain. How many cavalry do we have?

"Sixty now, sir. If we charge on two flanks, sir, I think we will cause enough mayhem for at least one of us to recover it."

"Good idea, Captain. I will take the western side and you take the eastern. Thirty horses each. May God be with you."

The captain could see the flag being taken back through the central ranks of the Parliamentary foot soldiers, a band of men dressed in distinctive green coats. Cleall had been informed, in his briefing, that this was the colour of John Hampden's men, whom he recalled from Oxford and his first meeting with Lady Bankes. The Greencoats were about to give the Parliamentary cause a symbolic trophy that would provide them with a rallying call and could be a defining moment in the battle. Cleall led his horse into the mayhem and was facing foot soldiers with pikes; a different proposition to the cavalry. The power and might of the horse charge was critical, to send fear into the lines of the troops they faced. Once the line was broken, the unwieldiness of the pike was a foot soldier's downfall — a cavalry man's sabre could easily cut through running or disorientated troops, especially from the rear without the protection of their breast plates. But a brave foot soldier with the strength to hold a pike could take his horse down, let alone its rider.

He charged with horses fifteen-abreast and two-deep, so if the front horse was taken down, the rider behind would be able to cut through the line. John rode behind him, which provided him with some protection, but for now he had to focus on the charge. The front horses gathered momentum across the field that had already been churned to mud, adorned with corpses, helmets, and pikes, and he could see the line of infantry in front of him. They were spread out, two-deep, all with pikes. Behind them the land rose up slightly and there was a line of cannons, beyond which Cleall could see that the Royal Standard was being carried off by thirty or forty jubilant Greencoats to the west, where Essex's command was stationed. If he could come up behind it, and Welch intercept it from the side, they would have a chance. But the success all depended on breaching the line of foot soldiers, and driving through the raised pikes with enough momentum, force and horse to get to the Royal Standard and recover it. He knew he must not hesitate in his charge and dug his spurs into Lightning to urge him on. He also needed to select his spot to pierce the line, for he could now see the faces of his foe and the strength and resilience in how they held their pikes. He was looking for any wavering, any hesitancy. It took a brave man to kneel in front of a charging horse, holding a pike up, anchored into the ground behind and angled to impale the horse. He knew most of the foot soldiers ahead would have been recruited from the barley fields of England over the last few weeks and would not have had training or experience in standing up to a cavalry charge. But amongst them would be some hardened warriors, some of whom he had fought alongside in the past. His life would be dependent on recognising them and avoiding them.

As the charge intensified, Lightning's speed increased, the distance between the horses and foot soldiers narrowed and Cleall spotted a group of soldiers he was sure were weak — they were looking along their lines for support and instruction, not with a determined face forward, and their pikes were waving around, rather than being grounded to take the force of a charging horse. He would set his course just to their left and at the last-minute swing into them. This would have the added benefit of surprise and they were likely to train their pikes to the left and be unable to straighten them in time.

And so, the distance narrowed to a few feet, and he could see the foot soldiers straight ahead, facing him, were holding fast, shouting insults. They were obviously hardened, experienced troops. He would not give them the pleasure and reined Lightning to the right, where the novices had even started to stand up and lower their pikes in anticipation of the charge going to their left. Pikes were dropped and the foot soldiers ran for cover, creating a gap for Cleall to charge through. But to his left, he could hear a horse rear up with a pike impaled in its neck, throwing its rider. And at the same time, he felt a cut on his left arm.

Looking around, he saw that one of the experienced warrior foot soldiers had come across with his pike and lunged at him. The force of his charge had resulted in the spearhead being pushed off, rather than penetrating his flesh, but he felt the pain of the steel and immediately took his left arm from his rein to stem the flow of blood. It was his sword arm that had been injured but he knew that it was not too deep and, grabbing the rein again, continued his charge with most of the other horses that had made it through the line, including John, who had now drawn up beside him. There was work to be done, and they set about hacking through the foot soldiers positioned between them and the Standard, many of whom had their backs to them, as they were running towards the Standard to join the triumph, unaware of the danger of the rampaging cavalry behind them.

Cleall's blade was crimson with blood, as another Parliamentarian's shoulder was sliced through before he could turn and know what had struck him. The captain slashed left and then right, finding flesh with each swing of his sabre. He grimaced with the pain in his shoulder as the sabre was swung, but the adrenalin was dampening the pain. He could now see Welch had broken through the line as well, coming in perpendicular to his route, but they would cross, as planned, roughly where the Royal Standard was. He was now going through a line of artillery; four cannons lined up and two still being deployed with their gunners positioning the weapons with a pair of horses. The artillerymen had no hand weapons, so they scattered when they saw Cleall and his men. One of them tried to use his cannon rammer, a long pole with wadding on the end, as a weapon to dismount John, but his sabre was too fast, and sliced through the man's forearm.

Cleall was leading the charge and had now reached the back end of the forty or so foot soldiers who were carrying the Royal Standard towards where Essex was positioned. He realised that Welch would get to the Standard first because his angle of arrival avoided the ranks of foot soldiers. What he needed to do was to cause panic amongst these troops, giving Welch a freer run to get the Standard, so he screamed as he charged. He screamed "For the king!" to ensure the foot soldiers turned and were concentrating on his charge, rather than Welch. It was these tactics in these defining moments of battle, conceived from the experiences of many battles before, that separated the victorious from the defeated, the survivors and the dead.

Cleall's cry was joined by John and the other remaining twenty or so horsemen, and it turned the heads of the Parliamentary foot soldiers they were pursuing. Cleall could see the shock and dismay in their faces, as their mood changed from the joy of running after the Standard to the despair of seeing the charging cavalry behind them. Some made attempts to turn and reposition their long pikes, but they were unwieldy. Turning a sixteen-foot pole around in an instant without becoming entangled with another pike, or indeed colleague, was difficult. The horses trampled on some as they surged through the troop, accompanied by the slicing sabres and ensuing screams, savaging the Greencoats. Cleall's men were unscathed as they reached the end of the Parliamentarian troop, by which time Welch had ploughed through the advance group and secured the Standard.

Cleall nodded to the colonel who was about to turn back to his position with the flag, and Cleall was about to join him, when he had a better idea. He ordered his men to turn about and charge back through the troop they had just encountered. Those who were standing put up no resistance and fled when they saw the returning horses. Cleall had his sights on something else, and within a minute, he and his men had reached the cannon and artillery again, where chaos prevailed, and it was the men with a plan who would have the edge. The captain ordered John and another cavalryman to grab the rein of the two horses that were attached to one cannon, and another two young cavalrymen to grab the other. He lined up the remaining fourteen men on either side of the two cannons and ordered the charge. Eighteen cavalry and two, gun carriages, with their two horses, stormed forward towards the waiting Parliamentary infantrymen, who had seen what had been happening and turned their pikes and defences around, separating Cleall's cavalry from returning to their Royalist positions beyond. Cleall's tactic was to concentrate the force of the charge, guns and horses into the smallest area possible along the line of the foot soldiers and see who dared to make a stand.

"Keep it tight!' he cried to his men. "No gaps for the pikemen!" and the horses came closer together as a single killing unit.

Will Harvey and Francis Trew were amongst the Parliamentary foot soldiers and had been lined up in four ranks; two facing the main Royalist force, and two others facing their rear to confront the returning Royalist cavalry. Will and Francis were in the second rear-facing row and could now see the cavalry returning, still about a hundred yards away, as the afternoon light started to fade. The men of Corffe watched as the distance narrowed, and the intensity of the screaming, mounted soldiers increased. The horses themselves looked wild, and were bunched up into a tight line, and now they could make out the cannon battery being pulled behind. Francis and Will looked at each other with trepidation. They were positioned at the centre of the charge, and the tightness of the charging horses would mean there would be no gap to step into whilst their pikes attacked the cavalry. They had not covered this in training. There was apprehension along the line. A musketeer fired from their line, and then another, but both failed to hit their target.

The pikeman beside Will cried, "We are going to be mowed down!" and with that, he dropped his pike and ran to the left, and he was followed by two, then three and then a rout of pikemen, as the cavalry were now just thirty yards away. Will looked at Francis.

"Let's get out of here!" he shouted and they both dropped their pikes and ran; Tom first and Francis behind him. Francis caught his foot on a fallen pike and fell. He cried out to Tom, but as Tom turned to see his fallen friend, the cavalry came through with the trailing cannons, right over Francis.

"No! No!" Tom cried, as he turned back into the wake of the cavalry charge to see dozens of mangled bodies from the two front rows of foot soldiers who had been much slower to react, but also his friend, Francis.

His face was buried into the mud, his back had been crushed by the wheel of a cannon.

"Francis. Francis…" He knelt down to his friend, whose head turned but his face was laced in pain. Tom just looked at the body of his friend, and tears started to well up in his eyes. He tried to recall what happened — images flickered through his mind. He could not join them up as he looked down at his friend, but there was something that was not right. He was joined by Jacob Vaggs and Arthur Pitt, the men from Corffe, and Jerome, who all stood back, knowing there was little that could be done.

He knelt down and turned his friend over. He was still alive but life was fading fast. His chest was crushed.

"Why did we leave Corffe, Francis? This is my fault. We should have stayed with our folk. But that bastard King… He is killing good, honest Englishmen because he is so pig-headed."

Francis's mouth opened and with his dying words, he murmured, "Do not give up, Tom. The new world must be worth dying for."

Long shadows stretched across the killing field at the base of Edgehill, and the crows were preparing to feast. In the twilight of the battle, there was a fire fight of cannon from either side of a dividing ditch, before nightfall eventually brought a natural close to hostilities. The Royalists had been forced back to the position from which they had originally advanced but had regrouped. There were too many dead to count, let alone bury, and many corpses were either too mutilated or just could not be distinguished regarding on what side they had fought, as they had all joined the same ranks of dead Englishmen.

Tom and the men of Corffe carted Francis and as many of the other dead as they could manage back to a field towards Kineton, where they were buried. As they buried Francis, the last seconds of Tom's life continued to flicker through his mind. Could he have done something? It all happened so quickly. The horse that was leading the charge, there was something about it. When the final shovel of earth was tipped on the ground beneath which Francis lay, Tom created a makeshift cross on the grave and prayed for his friend. With the amen of the prayer came the revelation. The horse. He knew the horse. It was Lightning. He had known it since it was a foal and reared from Thunder. The realisation that Captain Cleall had killed Francis suddenly struck Tom.

He stood for some moments by that grave, thinking about Francis and his life, and his final words. Was the dream worth fighting for? Was it worth dying for? Was it worth the heartbreak and sacrifice?

He took the shovel and threw it in the direction of the Royalists.

"You son-of-a-bitch for a King! Go to hell!"

After burying many other soldiers in the dark — unknown victims of conflict buried by unknown colleagues of war — the men of Corffe returned to Kineton with heavy hearts, in the bitterly cold night, with the rest of Essex's army.

On the escarpment, the Royalists regrouped. Captain Cleall had been taken to a medical tent, where his shoulder was stitched under the supervision of Dr Coke.

"I told you, Captain, I did not want to see you again today."

"Sorry — I could not keep away. But there are plenty more who need your attention more urgently than me."

But the captain had lost a lot of blood and was very weak and tired. He was given the luxury of a blanket on the floor of the tent where he slept, avoiding the cold endured by most of the army that night.

The following day was greeted by a drizzle blowing from the east, which dampened the fires as well as the spirits of both armies yet further. Neither side was willing to resume the battle and Essex withdrew his army to Warwick Castell to replenish and regroup. The battle of Edgehill had been indecisive, but Essex knew it was just one battle in a war of attrition. The weather was deteriorating and there could not be much fighting over the winter months, but it was essential to have a strong army. Supplies of food, drink and warmth would be essential over the next few weeks, and the most important goal would be to preserve and protect London to the Parliamentary course.

The king was shaken by his first experience of battle and was in a tantrum, possessed by the rage of a man who finds that the world does not work in the way he had taken for granted as his divine right. He had expected an emphatic victory and Edgehill was anything but. Indeed, at times, it seemed as though the Parliamentarians had the upper hand, with the loss of the Royal Standard, while he and his Princes were placed at risk. He decided to take his army south, heading for London, and the safety of Oxford en route, but not before sending Prince Rupert, with a strong detachment of horse and dragoons, to launch a surprise attack upon what remained of the Parliamentarian baggage train at Kineton. The prince had killed many of the battle's wounded survivors, discovered within the village, much to Captain Cleall's dismay, when he heard of the feat. He was at a loss to understand the king's tactics, for surely winning the hearts and minds of the people must be key to his success in battle, as well as remaining the monarch, but such mindless cruelty was just feeding ammunition to the Parliamentary cause. He would be portrayed as a heartless monarch, not only at odds with his people's wishes but mercilessly at war with his own subjects. It was the wounded husbands, fathers and brothers of England he had just killed; men who would have posed no threat in future battles but now whose memories would be recruitment sergeants for many more pike-wielding foot soldiers in the roundhead lines.

As King Charles' army travelled south, they had success, capturing Banbury. Captain Cleall was amongst the wounded who travelled by wagons directly to Oxford; a two-day journey. When he arrived, he found Sir John Bankes, who was staying at his daughter Alice's house. They immediately welcomed him in, and attended to his recuperation, with Dr Cole also visiting to attend his wound, and reinforce the hastily applied battlefield stiches to his shoulder. Cleall relayed to Bankes the events over the last few weeks since they were last together in Nottingham. Sir John shared the captain's concern about the king and Prince Rupert's tactics, and the danger of further alienation of the people. Bankes promised to speak to the king when he arrived. It was the end of October when Charles reached Oxford and he was greeted by cheering crowds. Here the king felt safe and was content to let Prince Rupert continue the campaign along the Thames Valley, capturing Abingdon and Maidenhead.

It was three days later when Bankes could speak to the king in private. He was staying at Christ Church College and seemed to be more preoccupied with his personal arrangements than the war that raged in his kingdom, but he finally received Bankes in the Deanery, which was now to be his palace. Sir John found the king on the first floor, standing by the window and looking out into the garden. His stature looked even smaller than usual against the backdrop of the large window that dominated the room. Was he physically shrinking as his power gradually waned, wondered Bankes.

"Ah, Bankes," the king said, as he was announced.

"Sire," Bankes bowed.

"Look here — what a wonderful garden."

Bankes walked to the king's side.

"I am building a new gate at the far end, so I can access Merton College, where Queen Henrietta Maria will be residing. It is all in hand."

"Yes, Sire," Bankes replied, thinking it would have been more sensible had the king prioritised the city's fortifications.

"You asked to see me, Bankes."

"I did, Sire. I wanted to discuss the tactics of the War."

"Since when have you become a master tactician of warfare, Bankes?" The king raised an eyebrow.

"I was referring to the wider tactics, beyond the battlefield. I have been your representative in London and travelled the country extensively on your behalf, sire. This is not just a war of cannons and pikes but winning the hearts and minds of the people."

"The people, Bankes, are my people. I am their King appointed by God, and so I am in all their hearts. Englishmen and the king of England cannot be separated," the king declared, forthrightly.

"Of course, Sire. That cannot be questioned, but as your advisor, I have to make you aware of the powerful workings of Parliamentary communication, which we have experienced before. It has the ability to spread lies and misinformation as news stories throughout the kingdom, and we have seen how this has turned people against their King. Remember the Grand Remonstrance news stories, Sire?"

"That bunch of lies... It is why we are at war now. A Parliament so fragrantly spinning stories based on half-truths and falsehoods cannot serve the best interest of its country. I should have acted sooner, when I first saw that document, and imprisoned Pym, Hampden and the whole conspiring lot of them."

"Perhaps Sire, but we must recognise their ability to take — as you say — a 'half-truth' and blow it up, to make their case across the land before we have got our boots on to defend the accusation. And this is my concern, Sire. Nobody could possibly question Prince Rupert's battlefield skills, and his reputation spans the whole of Europe. But this war is different. He is not fighting for one state against another along the Rhine. This is a war within England, amongst Englishmen. Needlessly attacking and killing the injured in Kineton could be described perhaps as a shot in our own foot. They were Englishmen who would never pose a threat to us again, as their fighting days had ended, but their deaths and how they have been killed, exaggerated by Parliamentarian merchants of false news, will recruit brothers, sons and friends of those who lost their lives needlessly to the opposing side. My King, I do believe that this war will not be won just by the heroics and tactics on the battlefield, but by the power of the printing presses. Have you read the rhetoric of people like John Milton? He seems to appeal to all classes in world and his words are fanning the flames of the parliamentarian cause. We must not give the opposition ammunition to attack us, and we need to counter-act with our own pamphlets and to propagate our cause with news to show Your Majesty as the people's King."

There was a knock at the door and a servant entered with a sealed message for the king in an envelope on a silver tray. Charles took the message, broke the seal and read it.

"It is from Prince Rupert. He says he has not yet captured Windsor, and instead attacked the town of Brentford to vent his frustration. The town has been, in his words, 'sacked.'"

As they were reading this message, the Parliamentarian printing presses were already in action. Pamphlets recording the loss of life and burning of property encouraged Londoners who were undecided but feared for their property, to side with the Parliamentarians. By this time, Essex's army, reinforced and refreshed, had reached the capital. London would remain in Parliament's control, at least for this winter. And how could the Royalists win the war without the capital?

Chapter X1V
Dorsetshire Prepares for War

1643

Poole was staunchly Puritan and a Parliamentary stronghold within a mostly Royalist Dorset. Nearby, Wimborne and the Bankes family in nearby Corffe Castell had sided with King Charles. John Bingham was determined to ensure the walled town of Poole would not only be a vanguard of Parliamentarianism but also Puritanism, and he would infiltrate the rest of the county from here. His Puritan values almost overwhelmed him with this sense of duty and he could not rest until he had achieved what he believed was God's will. He believed totally that his mission was to glorify God in his work and commitment, whether as a merchant, a magistrate and now as militia leader, for he had formed a small defence force to protect the town, but he had greater aims than this. He would glorify God by overcoming the powers of darkness that dwelt in the county's castles and country homes.

His first act of defiance had occurred at the end of the previous year when he was finishing the wall, which had been made from stone that was quarried from the Bankes' estate in the Purbeck; something he always found ironic. The wall had been quickly erected around the town to a height of eight feet, with the aim of increasing its height further in the new year. Two gatehouses were positioned on the road east, out of the town, and another west. It was the latter that was visited by a corps of twenty troops from Lord Hereford's royalist forces stationed in Dorchester. The troop was commanded by a young lieutenant who was met by a closed gate and John Bingham on the rampart above. The lieutenant said that he had orders to confiscate any ordinance and required John Bingham to yield command to him in the king's name, and in return he would protect the town.

"As you can see, Lieutenant, I have built these walls and as a town we are well prepared to protect ourselves. We therefore do not need your services and our weapons will remain on these walls to protect the citizens of Poole. Good day to you, sir," Bingham responded defiantly, to which the Royalists turned their horses around and headed back to Dorchester.

Essex recognised that no fighting in the field would occur, after Turnham Green, until the spring. He dispersed his forces to protect the towns that had been captured or declared themselves Parliamentarian. This also reduced the cost of feeding the army, with just one large contingent remaining in Windsor to protect the capital. Seventy-five soldiers were sent to Poole but Tom Harvey found himself preparing for Christmas in Salisbury, enjoying the comradery of the 'Roundheads', which was their new name. This had been adopted as there were many apprentices amongst their ranks at Edgehill from London, Bristol, and other larger towns, and they typically had very short haircuts. Tom had followed suit and had adopted a shorter style. He did miss Camille and regularly wrote to her, assuring her that the conflict should finish before summer. In the meantime, he would follow the dream that he and Francis had shared, as well as avenge the death of his friend. Next Christmas would be celebrated in a freer, peaceful country.

The Roundheads in Salisbury would certainly not be bored because the Parliamentarians had devised a new training regime for their forces. They had a belief that they could win this war by applying many of the principles that their men were fighting for. The concept of a 'New Model Army' had been developed by Oliver Cromwell, based upon a philosophy that military leadership and capability would be based on a person's ability rather than position within society. It would be piloted in a few locations, including Salisbury, and if successful, deployed across the entire Parliamentary force over the next few years. Will Harvey and his friend Jerome were excited by the prospect as it was applied through training in the winter of 1643.

A lieutenant, who was originally a butcher, had come down from London and started it all off. His message was two-fold. First, he wanted to learn from all those who had fought in Edgehill and elsewhere, from their experiences and how they thought they could be better provisioned, equipped, trained or deployed. Secondly, he was looking for people with ambition and with leadership skills. If you were good enough, you could be an officer in the New Model Army as it developed, irrespective of your upbringing. He took recruits through training drills which were all simple but could have saved many lives at Edgehill. It gave the army discipline and confidence to face different circumstances on the battlefield, although the training was strict and hard work. At the end of each day, the lieutenant was joined by the local minister who would confirm that God was on their side and teach them psalms that would give them strength as they went into battle.

Jerome and William Harvey spent much time telling one another about the merits of their respective homes, Devonshire and Dorsetshire, and the things that they would get up to in normal times. Both lived near the sea and shared a joy for boats and fishing, and agreed that when the war was over, each would host the other to share the joys of their respective homelands. Jerome had two younger siblings to return to, both boys and eager to fight, but now working hard on the land to support their father and mother. They were a Puritan family, but Jerome had seemed to leave those beliefs behind, for he was drinking and enjoying life as much as any man in the brigade. Indeed, his wit was something that kept Tom sane while they waited to be mobilised again.

Although there had been little activity in the south over the winter months, it had been a different picture in the north, and it was the Royalist forces who had the upper hand. Bankes had persuaded the king of the merits of creating a newsletter to counteract the Parliamentary propaganda. He commissioned a printing press in Oxford and proclaimed the Royalist victories in the north, admittedly in his accurate and precise legal commentary, without the spin and fiction of the opposition. He then recruited a dozen messengers to spread the pamphlets throughout the nation. Bankes felt that he was finally making an impact on the war and was not even disheartened when he heard that two of the messengers had been attacked and their pamphlets destroyed. He did realise that even in Oxford there was a strong Parliamentary following, and so beefed-up security around the press. Meanwhile, in London, it was not going all the Parliamentarians' way. There was unrest about the taxes being raised to fund the Parliamentary forces. The faction needed some good news to feed its propaganda campaign.

With the first signs of spring, Sir William Waller was determined to give them the news they wanted. He sent for the troops who had been stationed in towns in Hampshire and Sussex, and with the men from Salisbury moved north-west through Wiltshire. Tom Harvey was amongst them, equipped with a new jacket and boots, a better-fitting helmet and a promotion to sergeant. By mid-March, the force of over a thousand had entered Gloucestershire. It was at Higham that they found their first real Royalist opposition, although there had been plenty of small scuffles on the way. This was the first time they could put their new training into action, and the smaller Royalist force was destroyed in no time. In the spring, Waller and his men went on to secure both Gloucester and Bristol for the Parliamentary cause, and now the Parliamentarians certainly had something to shout about.

Back in Poole, Bingham had been assigned more troops, not just to host but to lead. In recognition of his recruitment campaign and the stance he had already made in Poole, he had been made a colonel. He did not want to admit it, not even to himself, but he was proud of this appointment and was sure his father would be looking down on him, glad of what his son had achieved. But he constantly reminded himself that he was a colonel in God's army doing God's work. The appointment did come with a condition.

Whilst his organisational skills and ability to get things done were recognised, Lord Essex had insisted somebody with some military background would jointly lead the forces in Poole. However, with a shortage of true military experience amongst their ranks, it was Harry Coke, also recently made a colonel, who was assigned to co-lead the Poole and Dorset Parliamentary forces. Coke, whilst enjoying his status in London, wanted to see some of the action, and made the case to Essex of driving along the coast from Poole, through more localised, underhand tactics, to take the smaller towns and villages in Dorsetshire, whilst Sir William Waller captured the larger towns to the north. His case was made easier as Sir John Bankes, as chief justice to the king, had just declared

Essex, amongst other Parliamentary leaders, guilty of high treason. In retaliation, Parliament declared Sir John Bankes and his family 'malignants' whose land should be forfeited, including Corffe. However, Coke was motivated by another agenda: revenge on Corffe. Deep in his psyche, the pain of the humiliation visited upon him by the villagers of Corffe had festered over the years, and he was now in a position to deliver retribution. He would join Bingham in mid-May but was already planning how to bring the downfall of the Castell.

In the meantime, Bingham had devised a plan of his own that he would put into action before Coke arrived. May Day was a traditional stag hunt for the gentry at Corffe and he had intelligence that Lady Bankes was inviting aristocrats from across the shire and was determined that the tradition would continue. Bingham's plan was that he would ambush the hunt and then take the Castell. The hunt traditionally took place in the woods between Swanage and Corffe, and he had a plan to sail across the harbour, wait for the hunt and then launch an attack, capturing the aristocratic Royalists and Popists who had been the bane of his life. He particularly liked the irony of setting a trap to capture the hunters.

In Corffe, in the week leading up to May Day, there was a debate amongst the resident Bankes concerning whether or not the hunt should go ahead. It was the start of the celebrations that were enjoyed across the country and culminated with the crowning of the May Queen, and dancing around the birchwood pole decorated with ribbons and flowers in the Castell's outer bailey. It was one of the highlights of the year and the entire village looked forward to it. There was only Lady Bankes, her seventeen-year-old son, Ralph Bankes, and daughters Mary, twenty, and Joanna, sixteen, but all were excited and looking forward to the hunt. But should they be having festivities and hunts whilst the eldest son, John, was fighting with many other English sons in battles across the country? In the end, Lady Bankes had decided it was a matter of principle. War or no war, the Royalist and English traditions should continue. Captain Cleall would be by her side, having returned from Oxford to recuperate and, at Sir John Bankes' request, to offer protection to his family.

Thus, the members of the neighbouring gentry were invited; the Cranbornes, the Welds, and the Digbys. They all had family members away, fighting for the king, but there were still enough to make up the numbers. So the invitations were sent out and Povington started preparing the reception for breakfast and lunch, as was the tradition.

A Dutch schooner, packed with forty men and six horses, sailed across the harbour's serene waters in the twilight of the evening. On board, Bingham went over the plans in his head: it must have been for the hundredth time. He desperately wanted to succeed and make a first and decisive mark on the war, and the campaign to take over Dorsetshire, before Harry Coke arrived. Had he thought of everything? So far, all was well and it was a perfect calm to make his move. By this time tomorrow, he should have the Castell in his control and several aristocrats safely locked up in its dungeons, including as many Bankes as he could find.

The ship docked at the old clay work's jetty on Green Island, and gang planks were put in position to take the horses and crew off, and they made their camp for the night while the schooner set sail again, back to Poole, having repaid its Captain's debt to Bingham. Blankets, bread and cheese were all the defence the men had against the cold and wisps of sea mist, partially obscuring the clear twinkling sky, for Bingham feared fires could be seen from the Purbeck in the night. As dawn broke, the low tide had expanded the island's reach, and the shoreline of Studland was nearer. A rowing boat, which had been towed over on the back of the ship the previous night, was used to ferry the men across, and each time a horse followed, swimming the twenty or thirty yards where it was out of its depth. That had been O'Kelly's idea: he was the man Bingham appointed as lieutenant of his forty-strong militia. Bingham had no idea horses could swim, and made the Irishman prove it in the waters off the quay before he built it into the plan. It turned out he was a master with horses, and so the nose, eyes and ears of a horse trailed the amused men throughout each boat journey.

"Well done, O'Kelly. Stage two of the plan executed perfectly. Now for the real challenge," Bingham said to his number two, as the final horse was dried down with its blanket, before being loaded with some of the equipment that was required for the planned ambush.

The sun was barely above the horizon, when the trail of men, and horses, led by Bingham and O'Kelly, mounted at the front, headed for Nine Barrow Down. Within an hour, they had climbed the chalk ridge and were in the woods on the other side, setting up their trap along the route of the hunt. The challenge would be to ensure the hunt funnelled into a place where they could wait and pounce, and this was where O'Kelly had again come up with the solution.

"We need bait for the dogs. The hunt will follow the dogs and the dogs will follow the scent of meat. The scent will lead to our trap," he said, as they planned the operation back in Poole.

Men were organised to create the trap, using ship rope tied to a ring of trees at three levels to form the skeleton of a trap, and then making a fenced perimeter from branches, entwined through the rope, but leaving the Corffe end open. Then, rabbit meat was positioned as a bait, after the flesh had been trailed through the wood from various routes into the trap. Behind the branches, men covered themselves with more branches and then prepared their weapons, muskets, pikes and swords, ready for their prey.

A couple of miles west, where the cut of the chalk ridge created the vantage point for the Castell, the Bankes' guests, who had stayed the night before, were awaking to the smell of the hunt breakfast, permeating through its Norman corridors. Bread, eggs, ham and fish had been prepared for them as they came down to eat, eagerly discussing the prospect of the mid-morning hunt, the sun taunting them to come outside as it shone through the windows of the main hall. As they were eating, Lady Bankes rose from her seat and addressed her guests.

"I just wanted to say how pleased I am to see you all. We live in deeply troubled times, and all with loved ones far away, fighting for our King and country. Many of the things we enjoy, such as visits to London, have been taken away from us and replaced with fear and anxiety. But that is why it is important to keep up the traditions of what we can do and be grateful for them, whilst Dorsetshire remains conflict free. The Corffe hunt and the following May Day festivities is one of them, and no Parliament or Puritan will stop us from enjoying this day. I thank God for this, along with the prayers I send for a Royalist victory that will bring all our loved ones back swiftly and safely. Thank you." As she spoke, there was the hint of a tear in her eye but her resolve was strong.

"Well said, Mary," Lord Cranbourne, the senior member of the guests, responded.

Following her words, Lady Bankes' guests readied for the hunt. In the outer bailey, horses were saddled up and awaiting their riders, as the dogs yelped in anticipation of the hunt. An impatient Captain Cleall was already mounted, his sabre gleaming by his side. Despite Lady Bankes' words, he would be happier when they were back inside the Castell walls, as he felt the burden of protecting Mary and her guest on his shoulders. Lord Cranbourne and Lord Digby were both in the autumn of their lives, and young Ralph Bankes and James Digby were each too young to be of help should there be an incident. The captain was normally never happier than when mounted ready for a ride or a hunt in the Dorsetshire landscape, but this morning he felt far from easy. His intuition sensed something, but logically what could be the danger? They were going hunting on the Isle of Purbeck, land owned by the Bankes, the entrance to which was protected by the Castell. No danger could possibly await them unless it had passed the Castell, or arrived by sea, both of which were not possible. But still he worried.

There was a commotion at the gate, and into the outer bailey ran Ned Parfitt.

"My Lady, My Lady! Captain Cleall! I have just come from the woods in the valley at the base of Nine Barrow. There are men hiding there. They are armed and they are making some kind of ambush," Ned panted.

"How many, Ned?"

"Difficult to say, Captain. From what I sees, at least thirty but I could not get too close for fear of being spotted. They had horses, as well."

"How could they have got there? In our own back yard. My Lady — that means the hunt must be cancelled and the guests must return to the safety of their estates as soon as possible. At least, if they are hiding east of the Castell, they cannot be of any danger to our guests travelling west," the captain informed Mary.

"You are right, Captain. We have no choice. But what if they come here?"

"We must barricade ourselves inside. But if Ned is correct, we have no need to worry. It would take ten, even twenty times that number to take this Castell. Let's see if we can arrange a surprise for them."

And so the Dorsetshire gentry set off home, the Castell gates were closed, and the Bankes waited.

By mid-morning, Colonel Bingham realised that their trap had failed. He was fuming and could not understand what had gone wrong. But he was not going to all this effort without some confrontation and decided to go to Corffe, anyway.

"What are we going to do when we get to Corffe, Colonel? We can hardly lay siege to a Castell with forty men," O'Kelly commented.

"I do not know yet, Lieutenant, but I will be damned if I have come all this way for nothing."

They packed up the horses and Bingham led his militia west. They marched through the village, which had locked down. There was not a soul on the main street, with the doors and shutters of houses firmly closed. An occasional head could be seen, peeking through a window or over a hedge, as the soldiers filed passed, their marching steps echoing amongst the stone cottages, accompanied by four gulls yelping behind them in the sky, as if they were a fishing boat, and awaiting their catch. Yet it was not fish these men of Poole were after, but Royalists. Bingham had no plan other than to confront the Bankes and make his presence known.

It was noon before they made their way up to the Castell gate. Bingham demanded to see the Lord of the Castell and was taken aback when Lady Bankes appeared at the gate tower.

"It is Mr Bingham, is it not? What is your business?" she demanded, in a condescending voice.

"We have a warrant, signed by a Parliamentary Commissioner, to take over battlements and fortifications across Dorsetshire for Parliament's protection," Bingham replied.

"This Castell answers to the king and does not recognise the powers that Parliament had granted itself unconstitutionally," Mary replied. "I can speak with authority as my husband is the chief justice to the king. And who are you? An alderman of Poole?"

Lady Bankes' defiance was like a tinderbox to Bingham. He rarely got angry but this woman had all the arrogance of the gentry he despised, and treated him as if he were nobody. He guessed she had just a few servants and villagers inside the Castell with her. Why, with forty men it must be possible to get in and teach her a lesson she would not forget.

"Lieutenant, get the men prepared. We will use the rope to scale the walls, and then she can see what authority this Colonel of the Parliamentary forces holds," he said, in a voice that ensured Lady Bankes could hear him.

O'Kelly reined his horse closer to the colonel and whispered to him.

"I cannot see how we can scale the walls without grappling hooks, Colonel."

But before Bingham could respond, there was a roar from the ramparts of the Castell, and a ball flew through the air over their heads, pounding into the market square behind them, smattering stones and mud. Bingham cowered as he and O' Kelly realised that they had been fired on by a cannon.

Lady Bankes could see their reaction below and was starting to enjoy herself.

"I stand before you a woman defending our King, and there is plenty more where that came from if you want to test my resolve. Mr Bingham, I give you this advice. If you want to play soldiers, go and find Essex and his rebels, and bring his army to Corffe, but you will find these walls are as strong as my steadfastness to defend the Royal cause."

Neither Bingham nor O'Kelly had faced cannon fire before and they realised they were out of their depth. They had no option but to march their men passed the Castell and back to Poole. As they turned about, in silence, Mary rushed down from the gate and along the ramparts to the second tower, where Captain Cleall had stationed himself with Ned Parfitt, and the small culverin cannon that had worked so effectively. She embraced the captain, much to Ned's blushes and embarrassment.

"Thank you, James. Thank you, Ned. One victory for the king."

"You were wonderful, Mary. Queen Boadicea would have been proud of you."

"Bingham just annoys me. But I must confess I am tired. It is exhausting defending a Castell, but hopefully if we can be assured, they have left, we can open the gates, let the villagers in, and then behind closed gates celebrate this victory as well as May Day. All is not lost, after all."

After the celebrations, Mary wrote to her husband that night, and told how she, her son and daughter, Povington, Captain Cleall, Camille, Ned Parfitt and just five menservants had held off the Parliamentarians. This gave her husband something to write about and the following day, a Royalist newsletter was spreading itself across the land telling of Lady Mary's courage and defiance.

At breakfast the following day, after allowing the villagers and Mary the joy of the celebrations, Captain Cleall confessed the precariousness of their situation.

"Mary, they will be back. You know that, don't you? And next time, a single cannon shot will not frighten them away," the captain told her.

"What can we do, Captain?"

"We need to turn your home back into a Castell, back to what it was designed for. We need to reinforce it, find men and weapons, and stock up in preparation for a siege. The Castell is strong and any attacker will have to most probably starve us out. The walls are solid, and it would take a large battery of guns to break them down, and they are thirty-feet tall, which is not easy to scale."

"Well, let's get prepared. Let's draw up an action plan here and now. I am so glad that you are here, Captain," stated Lady Bankes.

With that, she sat down with quill and paper and started making a list of supplies that would be required, weapons that could be sourced, and men in the village, who had not gone to fight, who she could trust and she felt would fight her cause.

"They will need to be trained, Captain. Can I leave that to you?" she asked, as she completed the list.

William Harvey was given the task of assembling the supplies and amassing weapons and munitions. Sheep and cattle were brought into the keep to graze on the grass, and a large coop for thirty chickens was created. Barrels of flour, salted fish, mead and beer were stocked up, along with oats and hay for the animals and cart-loads of wood for fires in the winter The gardens that Mary had so loved would have the flower beds replaced with vegetables and herbs. Weapons were gathered from across the Purbeck and ranged from pistols, crossbows, long bows, picks and axes, as well as buckets of tar, large stones and boulders to throw on besiegers. Regarding water, the Castell was self-sufficient through two wells that tapped into the ground supply beneath the limestone; one in the inner and one in the outer bailey. The captain had also advised medical supplies, beds, tools, timber and masonry blocks in case of urgent repairs. He was also reviewing the Castell's artillery, which consisted of six cannons, one of which he had managed to fire at the men from Poole. Two others looked in good order, but three of them needed attention. Alfred Smith, the blacksmith, was commissioned to make the necessary repairs, although one was beyond his capability.

The Castell itself had a mighty outer oak gate within a heavily fortified gatehouse and portcullis, and the inner gatehouse was even stronger with two portcullises. The baileys had a perimeter wall at least thirty feet high and towers evenly spread along its length, providing defensive vantage points for any attackers along the wall to be shot down. Around the outer tower, the River Wicken acted as a moat. Within the inner bailey was a raised bank which had been the location for many of the cannons but had been converted to a garden. Projecting from the gloriette was the bastion, a platform that was ideally suited for a cannon that could be fired well beyond the surrounding Castell walls.

The Castell was humming with activity as preparations were being made. While directing all of it, Lady Bankes received a letter from what was called the Parliamentary Committee of Dorsetshire, Bingham's new self-promoted position. The Committee demanded the surrender of the Castell's cannons. Captain Cleall advised Mary to adopt a conciliatory approach, recognising they needed to play for time, and she despatched a message back to Poole, offering to remove them from their carriages but without surrendering them. She even addressed it to 'Colonel Bingham.'

Lady Bankes decided to recruit a force of defenders, individually. The captain had advised a minimum of forty men would be required and they would need to be paid. She knew that people would have conflicting considerations. Some would be supporters of the Parliamentary cause, even though they had not gone to fight with Tom Harvey, Francis Trew and the others. Some would just want to avoid conflict or be with their loved ones during these troubled times. She drew up a list, with those most likely to answer her call at the top and sent for them, one by one.

She received each individual in the remains of her flower garden beneath the walls of the Castell's gloriette, which was already well on its way to becoming a vegetable plot. She had positioned two benches there, and a trellis fence provided some privacy, but she felt it was best to have a conversation in the relative open, and certainly not inside the ornate rooms of the Castell, because she wanted to appeal to them as an individual, not as the Lady of the Castell. Ned Parfitt was at the top of the list, followed by his brother, and both agreed immediately. Then came William Harvey, the man who had been loyal to both the Bankes and the Cokes, as estate manager, for over twenty years and had enjoyed a level of status and privilege within the community as a result. While she could take nobody's support for granted, she would have put her estates manager at the top of the list, were it not for his age.

"Thank you for coming to see me, William. You have been a loyal servant to me for ten years now, and to this estate for far longer. I fear that this estate and this Castell is in peril. It is only a matter of time before we are attacked, and I need to recruit loyal defenders; men who could defend the Castell in a state of siege. They will be trained and paid in addition to their usual wages, and I wanted to know if I could ask for your continued loyalty and support, William?' Lady Bankes asked, but she realised that William was not making eye contact and indeed looked sheepish. Was he not going to accept? He cleared his throat twice before he responded.

"My Lady, I will always be loyal and service the estate, but this war does not make any sense to me. Tom has run off, fighting against the king, and fighting Englishmen across the country for what he says is a better life. But all I hear about is needless bloodshed on both sides. My world has been Corffe, this Castell and the estate, and while it would break my heart to see any destruction come to any part of it in the name of any cause, I also have to think of Elizabeth and the rest of my family and I will be needed to protect them. In truth, I am not a fighting man and fear I am too old to help you. I am sorry, my Lady."

"But surely, William, by defending the Castell you will be preserving all that work that you have done…"

He looked up and there were tears in his eyes.

"Aye, I see that. But I also see that I would be at arms against my son. This war is just pointless to me, and I would prefer to die than be any part of it. How can men on both sides, educated men, be so stupid as to cause so much death and destruction on their own people and land? I am sorry, my Lady," and with that he got up and left.

Lady Bankes took a deep breath. This was going to be much more difficult than she thought, and she had anticipated it was going to be hard. As she worked her way through the list, the divisions and diverse views amongst the men of Corffe were laid open to her. Each individual had a different view on the war, how it related to them as individuals, their family, the Corffe community, their relationship with the Castell and the Bankes, their beliefs in God and religion, their view on the king and Parliament, their hopes and aspirations for change in society, their fear of change, their moral view on war and fighting, their fear of dying. This was not a simple black and white issue, and people, like William Harvey, declined her request for help for many different reasons, whilst others accepted for equally diverse reasons. On top of this, the deaths and brutality that the conflict created on the battlefields was creating even more divisions and a desire for vengeance, but again on each side. The realisation that this mosaic of views that spread across Corffe was, in turn, magnified across the nation made her despair at how this mess could be resolved and the nation healed and rebuilt.

By the end of the day, Lady Bankes had twenty-eight men confirmed on her list. Joseph Cobb, Tom Harvey's friend, was amongst them, enthusiastically wanting to join in the fight having decided not to join Francis and Tom when they signed up. Lady Bankes was worried that he was joining for the wrong reasons, attracted by the prospect of the excitement of a battle, and still young and naïve. However, Lady Bankes was not in a position to be choosey, and was her own son, John, not similarly misguided? Captain Cleall suggested that they had to look further afield; in Wareham and Dorchester and villages along the way.

He would ride out to all of them over the next few days and visit the taverns in a recruitment drive, but by next week they would need to start training. An attack could be imminent, although the captain expected the Parliamentarians would have the same recruitment challenge. From the news that Camille relayed, they knew that Tom Harvey and the men of Dorsetshire were in Bristol, and so suspected that the forty men from Poole comprised the extent of their garrison currently, and that was far too small a force to lay siege to a Castell. But who knew how quickly the Parliamentarians could reinforce the men of Poole?

That evening, Camille was brushing and arranging Lady Bankes' hair.

"Camille, you know we are likely to be attacked soon. We have a strong Castell but few to defend it. The odds will not be favourable but I will not lose my home and will fight for it, as well as my King. However, this is not your country, my dear, and nor is it your battle. And your husband is fighting on the opposing side. You are free to leave. Perhaps spend some time back in France until this madness is over."

"My Lady, my family have written to me from Rennes in France. Times are difficult there, as well, although we have a new king whom they hope will provide a better future. It seems strange that at the same time England is up in arms against its own king. But I have made my home here. I will await Tom's return. It vexes me that my husband and my Lady are on different sides; the rights and wrongs I do not understand. He is so sure that a new, better world awaits us, if Parliament is given its say, whilst you, my Lady, are equally sure that you stand for righteousness and the will of God. I just pray for peace and I am sure that is what God really wants. My Lady, I will stay by your side until my husband returns. If he returns."

There was a lot of emotion in that last 'if' and Lady Bankes looked up at her maid, taking her hand, and could see she was holding back tears.

"It is we women who have to do the praying and hoping for our menfolk, husbands and sons, to return. Thank you for staying, Camille, but if at any time you change your mind, I will not hold it against you, whatsoever. You have been a good maid and this is not your battle."

The next day, Captain Cleall found himself sitting in a small room within the Wareham Customs House, opposite the alderman of the town, with the Parfitt brothers standing behind him. The alderman was Joseph Baxter, a Royalist at heart. He had deployed a small militia of a dozen men guarding its Saxon earth walls and quay, where four ships were moored. The captain pitied the town's meagre defences as he had ridden passed them, for they would be overwhelmed in no time at all by any attack worthy of its name. The earth walls could easily be climbed as the wooden palisade that was originally mounted on them had rotted away many years ago. At least one of the ships was a naval frigate and it was flying the Royal Standard which gave the town some hope.

"What can I do for you, Captain?" the alderman asked.

"I would like to discuss how we could co-operate in defending our respective communities against Parliamentary forces. No doubt you heard that Corffe was visited by forty men from Poole and we expect, next time they come, there will be ten times that number, and no doubt marching through Wareham on route."

"I share your fears, Captain. The same men marched by Wareham eyeing up our walls. I am sure you observed our defences on the way in. It would not even stop those forty. But what can be done? I am struggling to fund the meagre defences we have."

"My proposal is that firstly we agree to come to each other's aid, and secondly, I can train combined forces. A well-trained defender of his home town is worth five poorly trained hired hands."

"Tell me more, Captain."

"We both have a core defence force, but perhaps we could double or even triple those numbers with volunteers, who will only be called upon in the event of an attack, but we train both groups to be defenders of your walls or our Castell. I will train them and Lady Bankes has agreed to pay for their time being trained. We then need to develop a warning system, such as in the days of the Armada. If you are under threat of attack, you light a brazier positioned above this Customs House, and if we are threatened, then we will light a brazier on the top of the Castell's gloriette. Our respective guards must be watching each other's brazier day and night."

"Your plan sounds better than anything I have come up with, Captain. Indeed, what have we to lose?"

"We have everything to lose if we do not act and work together. I would also advise you to consider constructing a palisade on your walls. Maybe the Corffe carpenters could help, but they would need paying."

The alderman and the captain visited the two taverns to raise the volunteers. The alderman announced the proposition to the locals, but in each place received a mixed response. It would appear that sentiment and views were divided as much in Wareham as Lady Bankes had discovered in Corffe. The captain returned to the Castell with a promise of the support of the twelve men who guarded the town around the clock, and fifteen more volunteers.

By the following week, after visiting Dorchester and a few other surrounding villages, Lady Bankes and Captain Cleall had a force of thirty-two men to train, in addition to the twenty-eight originally from Corffe. This was hardly adequate given that it would be very unlikely that, in the event of an attack, all thirty-two would answer the call, with the alert to Dorchester being reliant on a two-hour horse journey. Given this significant risk, it was decided that all the men and women within the Castell would also be trained in some form of conflict and siege defence, even if that meant just throwing rocks from the ramparts. This included Lady Bankes herself, as well as Ralph Povington, Camille Harvey, and the elder resident Bankes children.

Thus, throughout the rest of May and into June, daily training sessions were conducted by Captain Cleall, ten cadets at a time, covering everything from cannon-rigging and fire, musket-shooting, cross and long bow-firing, mixing boiling tar, throwing rocks and boulders, and close combat. It was never going to be straightforward, and not least when a dozen wives came to petition Lady Bankes at the Castell gate for their husbands' sake, weeping and pleading for the safety of their men. And so even husbands and wives were divided on what was the right thing to do.

In the summer heat, the suspense of endless waiting and the tedium of the repetitive training that threatened to became the enemy, rather than the Parliamentarians. But successes for Royalist forces throughout the country made this the Royalist summer, and this gave the Castell defenders hope and optimism. Mary started to better understand what the siege and fight would entail, so she decided that she had no option but to send her children away to Royalist Oxford to stay with her daughter, Alice, and son-in-law, Sir John Borlase. It was a decision she had tried to avoid as the thought of being away from her children for potentially months on end was something she felt she could not cope with, but nor could she put them through the Castell being under attack.

Mary and Elizabeth, both young ladies now, took responsibility for their younger siblings and they were packed into two carriages, with three trunks of clothing, toys and books attached to each. In the first carriage was Mary and the youngsters Edward, Bridget, Ann and finally Arabella, who was just one. In the second was Elizabeth, fourteen-year-old Jane and eight-year-old Jerome. Mary's heart was heavy to see her children leaving. She had already seen the departure of John, Alice and Ralph, but now the other eight in one go... What world had she brought them into? She just prayed that they would be safe until this madness ended. She hugged and kissed each one individually and then waved goodbye to the departing carriages, each with an armed guard sitting beside the driver. The younger ones had tears in their eyes as they said goodbye, while the older children were excited by the adventure of the trip to Oxford and seeing the king.

As they departed, William Harvey arrived at the Castell gate. He and Lady Bankes had not spoken since their discussion, the previous month.

"My Lady, I thought you should know that I have heard that Royalist forces are advancing towards Blandford under the command of Lieutenant General William Seymour."

Blandford was just eighteen miles to the north. This was Mary's last hope. She thanked the estates manager and returned to the gloriette to write to them. Her letter pleaded for help and stressed the importance of Corffe and Dorsetshire in their position between the Royalist strongholds of Exeter and Oxford, as well as the coastline, where the Royalist navy could land troops.

That night, Mary felt very lonely and full of self-doubt. Dinner with Captain Cleall was quiet and there was a heavy atmosphere. She had made an excuse to retire from the table and found herself on the bastion, which gave her a bird's eye view of the village in the twilight. She sensed the anxiety in each of the little cottages mapped out in front of her, the discussions between families about what was going to happen, mirroring her own concerns. Was she doing the right thing making a stand for the king and at what cost to the village and villagers? Would her children be safe? Where was her husband, when she needed him? She had been having more nightmares about losing her son, John, despite Captain's Cleall's assurance that he was as prepared as he could be for battle, but in her dreams, she could see him falling off his horse amidst musket fire. A bat darted through the air, devouring midges in flight, against the backdrop of the setting sun. Her foreboding seemed to heighten her senses, alive to nature, the heavens above and her own feminine sensuality within. She turned to find Captain Cleall behind her.

He smiled. "It's a beautiful evening," he said.

She could smell his manliness as she nodded and returned the smile, taking his hands and drawing him closer. She buried her head into his neck.

"Oh, James... I need you. Come to my room tonight," she said, the words coming out without any forethought. But she felt lonely and frightened and needed comfort.

They held each other in silence, woven together in a gentle embrace, as the velvet blanket of darkness quelled the orange and red passion of the setting sun. As the last rays of light were surrendered, Mary gave James a kiss on the cheek and quietly left for her room. The captain could feel a fire of anticipation and desire raging within him, and it was not long before he took his leave from the bastion and the woes of the impending battle to find comfort in Mary's room.

Mary awoke as the birds were twittering their daybreak songs and the world was perfect. She was naked and still embracing her lover's body. His chest gently resonated as he breathed peacefully. She studied the contour of his male form, his chest, his shoulders with the Edgehill scar, his biceps... So much power and strength, yet all dormant in its slumber. She recalled the passion of the night before as they had revelled in their intimacy, desire blazing as they kissed and explored each other's bodies. They had made love several times, fulfilling a desire that had been building up ever since they had met, ten years ago. The feelings of tenderness, warmth and wellbeing were mixed with others of passion and raw drive. The memory was arousing her, but then the captain stirred and was awake. He turned and smiled.

"Good morning, Mary."

They kissed and embraced, enjoying each other's company as the morning came alive before James left, worried that the servants would soon be awake.

That morning, as Camille was attending Mary's hair, she remarked, "You are blooming, my Lady."

"It must be the summer air, Camille," Lady Bankes responded.

"Ah yes, I am sure there is something in the air. Even in these times of anxiety, nature is alive, and I can sense love. Yes — despite all this war and hatred, love is supreme."

"What do you mean, Camille?" Mary asked, blushing.

"My love for Tom grows stronger every day. I can see families in Corffe getting closer as they prepare for what is to come. And as for my Lady, I am sure love is reaching out to you."

"Yes, you are right, Camille. I am sure it is. I hope I will hear news from Sir John soon," Mary said, trying to cover her guilt but inside, she was still full of joy from the night before.

Captain Cleall was pleased with the supplies he had gathered for the siege, which included six barrels of salted meat and a similar quantity of fish, twenty sacks of flour, two barrels of apples, ten barrels of potatoes and a cartload of grain for the chickens. The Castell also had five pigs, four cows and four sheep, which he anticipated would find themselves on a menu at some point, but he would send away the horses with William Harvey for safekeeping. Horses needed exercise and would consume a lot of food that could not be stored. He had discussed with the cook how long these supplies would last and developed a ration of meat, eggs and fish that would be rotated every three days, supplemented with fruit, vegetables and ale. They estimated that they had supplies for eight to nine months, as long as they were careful.

Seymour responded positively to Lady Bankes' letter and sent Captain Robert Lawrence with forty troops three days later. Mary was overjoyed with relief and new hope, and so was Captain Cleall, but he realised it would have a significant impact on food supplies, as well. He urgently sent for more supplies, and managed to secure six more chickens, another pig, two more barrels of ale and six bags of flour, but it meant that food supplies were now only likely to last six months. But at least Captain Robert Lawrence and his men provided some trained and experienced men, who would help to secure the Castell over those six months.

On the same day as the reinforcements arrived, there was also another pleasant surprise, for Sir John Bankes returned from Oxford. Mary was shocked at how her husband had aged and he looked extremely tired.

"I have requested leave of the court until this war is over. The king agreed I had served him well for many years, and there was not much need for a chief justice in a world when justice would appear to be something that has been lost. It is good to see you, my dear."

"And what a relief to see you. I have just sent the children to Alice and feel very alone. I am surprised you did not cross paths with them."

"Alas, I travelled on minor roads. But you have been a marvel, my dear; the talk of the Royalist forces nationwide. I am in the twilight of my years, but hope to shoulder the burden of defending the Castell with you, and indeed sharing my last years with you here."

"I have Captain Cleall and now Captain Lawrence," stated Mary.

A sense of guilt came over her as she said his name, having shared the last three nights together. She continued quickly, in an attempt to disguise it.

"We have forces and supplies, as well as the courage of heart, to stand against a Parliamentary force from Poole which we anticipate attacking us at any time. This Castell has stood firm against attacks in the past, and it will do so again, for king, country and Dorsetshire. "

"You sound like a Royalist general, my dear. Perhaps you should take on Essex for the king rather than Prince Rupert. Maybe you do not need me, after all?"

"Of course I do, my darling. I can only be strong for our family and our Castell. And it is you who has shaped this family with so much wisdom and moral fibre. We are the Bankes because of you, my darling."

She gave him a kiss and led him into the outer bailey.

"You have been busy, my dear. It is not quite as homely as I remember, but it certainly looks prepared," Sir John said, as he observed the animals and vegetable patches, as well as the cannons and stockpiles of stones and timber.

The Bankes dined together alone that night. There was much to talk about and catch up on; John and the battles, the king, the preparations for the siege, Alice and life in Oxford and all the children.

"Why don't we both just go to Oxford with the king? If the Castell is unmanned, it may not attract the attention of the Parliamentarians," Sir John suggested.

"What has got into you, John? Where is the fight left in you? Where have your principles gone? This is our home, and we are responsible for the welfare of our tenants. We have stood up for them in the past, for their rights and justice. We are not going to give them up. The Castell will stand any onslaught or siege, and when the king's forces win this war, our family can return to Corffe and enjoy the Purbecks again, heads held high."

"Well, perhaps you should go to Oxford. I can hold the fort. I am close to the end of my time, anyway."

"Are you sure you have not banged your head? My husband, you have always talked sense and I have always listened to you, but now you are talking nonsense. We have spent far too much time apart for this country. Now is a time to be together. I am sure you have many more years inside you, as long as it is spent in healthy Dorsetshire air and that you are cared for by your loving wife."

He smiled. He had missed her optimism and passion for life, which was in total contrast to the court, where the atmosphere was downcast. Even the king's closest aides were questioning, amongst themselves, the king's decisions and character. He should have made his stand in London, shown some grace and humility in accepting that he had made mistakes, and shown willingness to change, but dealt firmly with the leaders of the Parliamentary insurgents. Raising the Standard on his own people was a big mistake. How could the people forgive him? He had created a poison that spread throughout the nation and infected so many loyal citizens against him, and Sir John felt that he himself had been infected. When he had been negotiating in London with the Parliamentarians, he felt there was hope of a compromise, where both sides could find a solution that preserved the monarchy and the rights of Parliament were upheld. But now he doubted even whether the nation could survive.

The situation in Ireland was apocalyptic, with children and women being killed en masse by Catholics, and Protestant retribution equally as dire. He feared England was going the same way, and there was nothing he could do to stop it. This realisation weighed on him and had totally disheartened him. He had found it difficult to sleep, and when he had, he was haunted with dreams of the poison infecting people like a plague, and he would wake up in a sweat believing that he was himself disease-ridden. Was he to blame? Could he have managed negotiations differently on both sides? As his demeanour declined, he felt a pain in his stomach, like a continuous guilt sensation, which gradually became more intense. He had seen George Coke, the physician who was now resident in Oxford, having spent time attached to the Royalist forces as a medic. He diagnosed a growth in his stomach, which he said he could not treat and that it was likely to be terminal. He diagnosed some tonics for the pain but apologised for his inability to do more. That was three days ago, and he had come straight to Corffe, for at that moment he realised how much he had missed Mary, and how much he regretted being apart. He would not waste another moment, and rode in disguise and alone, which itself was a dangerous thing to do but what could the Parliamentarians do to him that the king's infection was not already doing? But now he had to tell Mary.

"Mary, I have to tell you something. It is not good, I am afraid, but I know you are strong. I have an illness in my stomach and I have been told it is terminal. I do not know how long I have, but inside me I am sure it is not long."

Mary's demeanour changed instantly, and she got up and rushed to her husband. She wrapped her arms around his head and buried it in her breast.

"My darling husband. Please do not let this be true. There must be something we can do?"

But her words were without conviction, for the moment she had seen her husband, she knew there was something wrong. His physical demeanour was one thing, but since their time together she realised the spark inside him had dimmed.

That night, she lay with him. They left the window of Mary's room open so that they could see the stars in the summer's night, and Mary held her husband while he fell asleep; something that evaded her. She lay in a trance for hour upon hour, watching the stars, comforted by the rhythm of her husband's breathing in her arms. Her thoughts oscillated from what she could do to comfort him, to the heavens and how life would be better away from the current hell on this earth; how she would cope on her own with all the children, with a Castell and estate to look after; then to the memories and happy times she had with Sir John, but then to Captain Cleall and her guilty love for him, and not forgetting the imminent threat to the Castell. She could have remained there all night, immersed in her thoughts, but the bell rang.

It was the warning. The bell meant that the Wareham brazier was alight or the Castell was under attack or both. She jumped out of bed and reached for her robe. He husband came round but she told him to rest whilst she investigated the cause. As she came down the stairs into the great hall, she found Captain Cleall already there.

"It is Wareham. It is under attack. I have seen it from my room. The brazier is alight. I will take a troop of men on horses to find out what is happening. If something can be done, I will stay there and give assistance, and send word back. But I fear that it may be too late. The defences are too feeble to stand much."

"Be careful," Mary said, as he turned and headed out the door. He was met immediately by Captain Robert Lawrence. They conferred and both set off to the stables. Shortly after, forty horses had been saddled and rode off into the night in the direction of Wareham.

Mary saw them disappear from the bastion, and then ran to the northern ramparts to watch them on their journey. It had been such a peaceful night, and a wonderful few days, but now the flames of war were creeping ever closer. She could see Wareham in the distance and there were buildings alight. She imagined the terror of the families who resided there and she feared Captain Cleall's prediction was correct. It was not long before she could hear the galloping horses returning and he himself was able to confirm that the town had been totally over run by what looked like hundreds of Parliamentarians. They were causing havoc, with the customs house and two ships in the quay ablaze. Wareham, just four miles away, would give the Roundheads a base to launch an attack on Corffe. He was sure they would not have to wait too much longer.

Chapter XV
The Siege

June 1643

Wareham would be the first town Colonel Bingham would capture —
not Corffe — to re-establish his credentials and power for the
Parliamentarian cause. But he would have to share the credit for this first
victory. Harry Coke had arrived in Poole a few weeks before, also
bearing the rank of colonel, but with a direct line back to the
Parliamentary headquarters. Bingham had taken a dislike to Coke when
they had met previously in London, recognising him as a man who was
motivated by personal interest, primarily, and that many of his
enforcement techniques in the capital were questionable at best.
Furthermore, Coke had heard about Bingham's recent confrontation with
Lady Bankes and came armed with one of the Royalist pamphlets that
made a mockery of Bingham's escapade into the Purbecks.

"Well, Colonel — it seems as though you need my help. Essex sent
me here because of my knowledge of the Castell and because he felt the
Poole battalion would benefit from a more — shall we say — direct
approach," Coke explained with a smile, as he arrived, his dark eyes full
of contempt.

Bingham was trying to quell the anger inside him. Since that fateful
day in May, he knew he had made a mistake, he had been driven by the
wrong motives and lacked the experience of battle and warfare. He had
been naive to think that he could take forty men into the Purbecks to set
up a trap without being seen. But now he knew that he had to work with
Coke, despite his reputation and methods. So together they worked out a
plan to conquer Dorsetshire for the Parliamentary cause, with Coke
repeatedly reminding Bingham of his failed mission to take Corffe. There
was one thing, at least, they soon agreed upon: it was essential for them
to gain control of Wareham, as the gateway to the Purbecks, before

taking Corffe and progressing further west into the shire. They soon devised a plan: a pincer movement on the town.

The first arm took the form of two Parliamentary ships sailing from Poole up the River Frome, each with forty men aboard. At the same time, the second arm, a force of twenty cavalry and eighty, foot soldiers, would attack the town through its eastern gate. Within a week, they had put the plan into action in the early hours of a Saturday night. The result was an overwhelming success: they captured the town in half an hour without the loss of a single man, and only four were injured. They had also captured three Royalist vessels that were moored at the quay, although two had been burnt out, and had twenty militia, and fifty sailors, prisoner, with a dozen of the town's defence dead and a similar number wounded.

As the dawn broke, the destruction of Wareham became evident. The Customs House had caught fire, as had a tavern and a dwelling, and were all still smouldering. The church bells sounded matins and the sun peeked over the horizon to provide some warmth to the town, the Parliamentarian troops rounded up all the inhabitants and herded them into the market place adjoining the quay. The prisoners were lined up on one side and the inhabitants, over five hundred people, half of whom were children, lined up on the other. They all looked very sullen and frightened, and there were cries from babies and younger children. The entire perimeter of the square was guarded by Roundhead foot soldiers, and in front of the smoking Customs House was a line of twenty mounted cavalry. In front of them, ready to address the crowd, was Colonel Bingham with Colonel Coke and Jacob Winter next to him.

"People of Wareham — I am deeply saddened to address you under these circumstances. But alas, this country is at war with itself, after King Charles raised the Royal Standard against his people and your Parliament. Your aldermen decided to declare their support for the king and harbour his troops and vessels. I am sure that was contrary to the views of many of you. In the short term, I will ensure that the damage incurred this night will be repaired. We will not be taking prisoners, other than the aldermen who made the declaration. We will provide as much care as we can to the wounded and we will ensure the dead have the respect of a full Christian burial. I want to offer you the opportunity of a new start as the Parliamentary cause is heralded across England and this shire. I am talking about a path that will reward people for their effort rather than their birth right; a life where rights of the individual are upheld and the people's Parliament has authority and most importantly, one where God is accessible to all through his written word, available to all in English. I want to hand over to Minister Jacob Winter to lead us in prayer."

The minister led them in prayer, praying for the dead and injured, and for peace following a quick victory to the Parliamentary cause. The crowd was allowed to disperse while the troops fell back to the walls of the town. Colonel Coke and Colonel Bingham, with their officers quietly celebrated their victory and started to put in place the plans for the next steps. It had already been agreed that Bingham would focus on ensuring Wareham was rebuilt and loyal to the Parliamentary cause before taking the campaign to Dorchester with the anticipated reinforcements, while Coke would lead the next stage in the campaign: the attack on Corffe. This was going to be far more difficult and potentially end up in a drawn-out siege, so having Wareham as a solid platform from which to launch and sustain the attack was critical.

Coke could not wait to launch that attack and get his revenge on Corffe village, and he had the force and power to inflict it. He was confident of victory but realised it would not be easy. He had been informed by people in Wareham that the men of Corffe had been training with men from Wareham, Dorchester and other villages, and the plan had been for these men to be paid as hired hands to defend the Castell in the event of an attack. He would ensure this would not happen. He also knew a lot about the supplies and defences that had been deployed over the last few weeks, as well as the recent reinforcements by the Royalists. But it was not just the Castell, his old home, that was his target but the village itself, which lay defenceless. He now had the benefit of ten cannons from the ships he had captured and had commissioned carpenters to modify the carriages so they could be taken to Corffe. He wanted to launch an initial attack at night; not that this would lead to a quick victory but it would strike fear amongst the inhabitants.

One thing Colonel Coke realised was that victory would not be through the might of the cannons alone but by also winning the battle of the minds. The Castell occupiers had the benefit of ramparts and thick battlements for protection but their main weakness was their lack of numbers to man these walls. His plan was to wear them down and keep them on edge, while they watched helplessly as he executed the plans he had for their precious village.

It was in the early hours of the morning on the 23rd of June 1643, when the first cannon was fired from Nine Barrow Down into the Castell. It was a dark, cloudy night with no moon or stars. The roar of the cannon fire echoed off the hills, and the reverberation was met instantly by the crash of the ball as it pounded into the wall of the inner bailey, sending masonry flying, and the animals penned in below into a frenzy. A few moments later the Castell bell was pealing but it was hardly necessary: the whole place was alive with men scurrying to their positions. Captains Cleall and Lawrence were bellowing out orders, and Sir John and Lady Bankes joined Cleall on the bastion, which provided the best vantage point.

As they arrived, the second explosion blasted the inner bailey wall, just twenty yards to their left, sending a shockwave to where they stood and more masonry flying into both the inner and outer bailey. Lady Mary clung to her husband, who held her tight. The explosive flash pin pointed exactly the presence of the Parliamentary cannon, as well as the presence of the one hundred parliamentary troops on the slopes of Nine Barrow Down. They were in range of the saker cannon positioned on the bastion.

Captain Cleall called for assistance, and five men repositioned the cannon to face the direction of the attackers. It was tied down to iron rings in the bastion wall, to ensure the recall on firing was controlled. The gunner eyed up the cannon, increasing its pivot by a few degrees, while another took a six-foot-long ladle to insert the powder into the depths of the barrel, and a third man set the fuse. Before he could finish, a third shot roared from the opposing hill, this time bombarding the wall directly below the bastion. The bastion was showered with masonry chippings, and the gun crew standing closest to the edge all instinctively dropped to the floor. Cleall ordered them back to action, and the powder in the bore of the cannon was now being pushed back to the end of the barrel with a long rammer, and a cannon ball was rolled into the nozzle and rammed into place. The first gunner re-checked the projection, using a quadrant this time, and then nodded to the captain. Cleall ordered everybody to stand back and put their hands over their ears, as one of the gunners lit the fuse with a torch. The taper hissed excitedly, and the flame travelled along its length before disappearing into the depths of the iron barrel. The onlookers held their breath, as well as their ears, before there was a roaring boom, and the machine recoiled two yards before the ropes tethered it into place. The bastion became immersed in smoke billowing from the barrel, obscuring the visibility of those on the bastion. Everybody was eager to see whether they had found their target but with the smoke and the darkness, it was impossible to tell.

Cleall shouted down to Lawrence asking how close they had come. Lawrence was stationed on the outer bailey wall turret, closest to the enemy, and the cannon smoke did not obscure his line of sight. He replied that they had most probably been twenty yards below where he thought the cannon was, and just to confirm his view, the Parliamentary cannon burst into life again. Cleall ordered the barrel to be cleaned, ready for another shot, and the men rammed a sponge dipped in a bucket of water attached to another six-foot-long plunger down the barrel, in order to remove all sparks, filth and dirt. By the time this was done, the smoke from the first round had cleared to reveal the moving shadows amongst the enemy on the opposite hillside.

Coke had positioned the cannon on the north-west wing of the Down. Two horses had pulled it up the slope, out of visibility of the Castell, almost to the top of its three hundred-feet ridge. Finally, a dozen men pulled it into position so it would have sight of the Castell, but it would only require the cannon to be pulled back twenty yards or so and it would again be hidden by the mass of the chalk escarpment. He knew this location was too exposed to hold a sustainable attack, and indeed he had lost two men with a further two injuries from the Castell's initial response. So after the fourth shot, Coke ordered the withdrawal as planned. The second round from the Castell may well have found its mark, but by the time it hit the chalk, the Roundheads had disappeared. They had achieved their objective of waking up and planting fear into the hearts of the Royalists, as well as some damage to the Castell. Tomorrow he would give them something much more to be afraid about.

It was a misty morning, not long after daybreak, when Colonel Coke led his troops out of Wareham, five hundred men in total, along that familiar road to Corffe and the Castell, which could be seen nestled on the hill in the gap between Nine Barrow Down and West Hill ahead. Behind his mount rode Captain William Sydenham, who was Colonel Bingham's right-hand man from the Poole Garrison, as well as two men of the same rank who had accompanied him from London, and another two captains who had brought nearly two hundred troops with them from Hampshire. The reinforcements also came with additional artillery, including a demi-cannon which could hurl balls weighing up to thirty-six pounds, two sakers similar to the one that Cleall had mounted on the bastion of Corffe, and two smaller but more accurate culverins. Coke marched his force passed the Castell to intimidate the occupants, with nearly ten times their number. He made camp in a field just to the south of the Castell but made no attempt to attack it. That could wait until when he was ready: in the meantime, he had plans. It was time to take out his revenge on the village of Corffe.

He assigned his captains to the various tasks with appropriate resources for each one. Sydenham was to make the camp ready, the men from Hampshire were to set up the artillery on the earth mounds of the Rings, south-west of the Castell, to give the inhabitants a clear indication of their intent and their strength, while he and his captains from London, both former members of his militia, returned to the village. There was not a soul to be seen as he led twenty horses and fifty, foot soldiers into the market square. Bingham had been conciliatory in Wareham but Coke would do it his way here. He would justify his actions to the other captains as necessary to ensure he could prolong a siege, but the real motivation was revenge, as he addressed his two captains.

"I want all the villagers out of their homes and out of Corffe. We need to establish an exclusion zone, as there must be no opportunity for sabotage by the locals or collusion with the Castell. Keep ten women back. They will stay in one of the houses near the camp."

"As entertainment for the men?" Captain Bulldock asked, with an eager grin. He was a man Coke had recruited from the pool in London and was his main enforcer.

"An interesting idea, Bulldock. But no, I had in mind being our cooks, at least for now. And do not show any compassion when kicking these people out; not a trait either of you is known for. But once that is done, we need to gather the resources for the siege; for example, lead to make cannon balls. Where could we find lead?" He looked at both captains inquisitively.

"The church roof, of course. And we would need wood for our fires at night. Why not the church pews?"

"The men will need ale, sir," Bulldock said, for although he had been a Puritan enforcer, he was not a convert.

"Well, take it, Captain. Confiscate it from the tavern, as well as flour from the mill, and anything of any use from the houses. The best houses will become officers' barracks and the others for the men as we do not have enough tents, and we need one to become the cook house. The houses closest to the Castell will provide protection for musketeers."

Lady and Sir John Bankes watched the assembled Roundheads beneath them, in the market square, from the bastion. They could make out the commanding officer by his actions, mounted on a black stallion, sending men this way and that, but not his identity. Beneath them, the outer bailey wall was manned by most of the Royalist defenders, with a clearer view of what was happening.

"I wish we could have encouraged more villagers inside the Castell now. Everything and everyone, looks so vulnerable outside our walls," Lady Bankes confessed to her husband.

"Time will tell. Our two captains feel confident that we can hold out for months, by which time perhaps the king will have come to his senses. I still pray for an end to this madness, but every day we seem to move further away from it. The kings of the past, who have stayed within these very walls, will be turning in their graves at the prospect of this Castell being besieged by Englishmen of the realm; the very people it was built to protect and defend," Sir John replied.

They watched as families were turfed out of their homes with just a few possessions and a trail of villagers started a march out of the village south in the direction of Kingston, Worth Matravers and Swanage. They heard screams as wives were torn from husbands and forced to stand in a line, surrounded by armed guards. Lady Bankes could feel the distress and fear of these women.

"What are they going to do with those women?" Mary asked, but her husband did not respond as the couple witnessed them being marched towards the camp, to a fate of worst nightmares.

As the villagers vacated their homes, soldiers ransacked them, looking for anything of practical use. Pots and pans, chairs and tables were taken to the camp to create the army's mess.

"What are those men doing down there? They are raising ladders on to the church roof," Mary cried.

The couple watched in despair as men at the top of four ladders began hacking off the lead, passing it down to colleagues in a pail attached to a rope. They were even more shocked when they spotted two men carrying a pew from the church to the field where the Roundheads were camped.

"This is sacrilege! The village and church are being plundered. It must be stopped," Mary declared to her husband.

"I am so sorry, my dear. But there is nothing that can be done. And I fear there is worse to come," her husband replied, sombrely.

A short while later, Harry Coke inspected his troops' progress and he was very satisfied. The church of St Edward the Martyr stood proudly and defiantly in the centre of the village, but already its demeanour was changing as men were on its roof stripping the slate, which could be rolled into balls to serve as shot for muskets. Inside, Coke found the columns dressed with the local Purbeck marble and the stained-glass windows paid homage to the church's namesake, Edward, who was the king of Wessex. It was another king he was at war with today, and the church would suffer for it. Inside the church, prayer books had been destroyed and the organ was in tatters. Coke smiled at the ingenuity of his troops using the organ pipes to hold powder and shot, and the font for drinking water for the horses.

"Take down the doors,' he ordered. "They will make a good siege canopy. And find some straw. We will stable the horses in here tonight."

He then trotted down the street where an altercation was taking place. A man was trying to cling to possessions he had loaded onto a horse. He recognised the man from somewhere and watched as one of his men smashed him on the head with the butt of a musket. His wife screamed, but three soldiers then held her husband as the colonel approached.

"We will need that horse. You can take what you can walk with," Coke intervened. The man looked up, blood flowing down his forehead.

"Mr Coke, is it not? We met at your father's funeral," William Harvey said, holding his head.

"Colonel Coke. And perhaps we had met before that time if my recollection is correct. In the back of the Ship Inn, when I wanted some fun with a village maiden. I have not forgotten and I am here to seek my vengeance. Is this your wife and daughter? Soldiers — escort them with the other women to Captain Sydenham. He will know what to do with them. And that will mean you will need fewer possessions after all and no need for a horse. I think I will also make this house my barracks. The other officers can have the adjoining ones."

And with that, Coke reined his horse round, leaving the three soldiers holding down William Harvey, who was struggling with all his might and shouting obscenities but all in vain, as another four soldiers grabbed Elizabeth and Beth and dragged them away.

A smug-looking Coke trotted back to the square to join his two captains. The three officers, with five other cavalrymen, then hurried up from the square to the Castell gate. Captain Cleall was stationed there.

"We would like to speak to Sir John Bankes."

"It's Coke, is it not?" Cleall replied. "I recognise you from your father's funeral. Captain Cleall, you may recall. I was fighting alongside your brother at Edgehill not long ago. What a gentleman. He did me the honour of patching me up. I was well acquainted with your father, as you know. A just and righteous man. A man who loved this Castell and village. He would be turning in his grave to see the destruction you have caused."

"He would be dismayed at the injustices of the king that have been served on his people," Coke snapped. "And if you want destruction, I will show you what that is when I turn our artillery on these old walls. Where is Sir John? He is wanted for treason. Let me address him."

"I recall a time when all the bells in the land tolled to proclaim the Petition of Rights, of which your very own father was the architect and one of the fundamental rights is a prohibition on soldiers being billeted in houses without the owner's will. It would appear that his own son, so many years later, will be the first person to break that law, in his very own village."

This actually amused Harry Coke. He had not thought of that but the captain was right and it felt good to him. He had returned to Corffe and exercised absolute power, taking revenge on the locals but also his father's legacy. Yes — what would his father think of that? He hoped he was turning in his grave, for Harry Coke was his own man and had the power to do what he wanted.

He began to laugh, but then replied to Cleall. "I have no time for this, Captain. We are in a war and you are harbouring a man who has been convicted of treason."

"Sir John left yesterday evening. You must have just missed him," Captain Cleall lied.

Sir John had arrived secretly and in disguise but it did not surprise Cleall that Coke knew he had been in the Castell and so should not deny his presence. He suspected that Sir John was the big fish that the Roundheads were after, for why else would they be worried about a Castell in Dorset to such an extent as to deploy five hundred men? Taking their prize catch away could weaken their resolve, and he instantly sensed from Coke's demeanour that this news was a setback.

"Then who is in charge? Surely not a lowly, retired captain?"

"This captain has most probably seen more battles than all your conscripts put together and was only recently at the king's side at Edgehill. It will take more than the turd I see before me, or should I say Little Lord Harry, and a bunch of hired thugs to take this Castell. Your father always said you were a failure, Coke. But he could never have imagined that you could plan your biggest failure with all of the nation watching on his home soil. But I will ask our commander to see you."

Cleall could see Coke fuming beneath him but started to descend the steps of the gatehouse behind him before Coke could respond. He jogged up the path from the gatehouse to the outer bailey gatehouse, where he found Sir John and Mary Bankes on their way down. They had seen the entourage approach the gate from their vantage point on the bastion and anticipated a confrontation.

"Sir John, I have told them that you have already departed. You are the one they are after, and if they believe you are not here, then perhaps they will think twice about a long siege. May I suggest that Lady Bankes addresses them and — another thing — their commander is Harry Coke, son of Sir John from whom you acquired the Castell."

"Coke — that thug, he has a reputation for brutality in London but as a commander of a puritanical militia, not a well-trained army. Mary, what do you think?"

"Captain Cleall has a point. Let's hide you, my dear, and I can address him. A female foe may further weaken his resolve."

"Very good, my dear," Sir John replied, and let Captain Cleall lead his wife down to the gatehouse. She was wearing a defiant, royal-blue dress, her hair pinned at the back with ringlets at the side, and Captain Cleall thought that she was definitely the most beautiful commanding officer he could ever serve under. They took their time as they knew that the Roundheads would now be feeling a little uncomfortable. Cleall helped Lady Bankes climb the steps up to the gatehouse tower, where Captain Lawrence was waiting and there, below, were the Roundheads.

"Mr Coke, I understand," Lady Bankes said. "What business do you have in Corffe? I will demand full recompense for the damage you have caused today. My husband will ensure your name is added to the list to be tried for treason."

"Colonel Coke, my Lady, and the business I have here is to requisition your Castell and estate, by order of Parliament, peacefully or by force."

"No doubt it was your peaceful means that woke me from my sleep last night. And which army academy did you train with to obtain your rank, Mr Coke?" she taunted him.

"I was commissioned by the Parliamentary forces, Lady Bankes."

"You mean self-appointed: no training and no education, Mr Coke. I think I will appoint myself a colonel as well. Why not? And this colonel and my two captains who, by the way, are genuine soldiers, do not acknowledge your title any more than that upstart Bingham, who from memory also called himself a colonel. But I sent him away with a flea in his ear and I am sure we will see the better of you, Mr Coke. I do not acknowledge a Parliamentary order that has not been approved by the king and my husband, as Lord Chief Justice. I believe your father held the same position, Mr Coke, and so I would have thought you would appreciate the correct procedures in this respect."

"My Lady, I do not care what you acknowledge or do not. Neither you, nor your stuck-up husband, and not even Charles Stuart, that midget you serve, have any authority any more. I have cannons and five hundred men who will bring you to justice, whether you like it or not. We have already taken Wareham and by the summer's end the whole of Dorsetshire will be mine."

"So you would declare battle on a woman defending her home. Very brave, Mr Coke. Could you not face any of the big boy battles?"

That was the final straw. Coke's face was flushed with rage, and he turned his horse to gallop away.

"We are going to give that bitch hell," he said to Captain Bulldock, as he rode to the newly formed camp.

Corffe and the people continued to torment him, even although he was a respected authority in London. In the camp, he started to prepare for the attack and to teach the bitch a lesson, along with the rest of Corffe; one that would be remembered forever. But he would decide when to attack, and in the meantime, he would keep the Castell on edge, because he could. Yes — he was in control and he would dictate proceedings.

Lady Bankes was indeed on edge and had been ever since the attack in the early hours. She had found solitude in her garden in the inner bailey. It had been her pride and joy with red and white roses, pink and gold camellias, and a base of lavenders in many shades of blue. A Mr Thomas Etty from Kent had been commissioned to design and plant it. But all those beautiful plants have been replaced with carrots, potatoes, lettuce, tomatoes, beans and peas in the last six weeks. She still took delight in seeing the plants grow but as she walked now her chest was tight, her stomach felt sick, and she could not focus on anything. Her poor villagers. Those women being sent into the Roundhead camp... She could not imagine what awaited them. Her beloved church... Her emotions and nerves were being stretched beyond what she envisaged was possible. Was she doing the right thing, supporting the king, but putting her family at risk and the lives of so many good men who had volunteered to defend the Castell? Her husband had lost faith in the Royal cause, but she put that down to his illness. Her resolve was stronger, especially when her home and Castell were at stake. She had led this community in times of trouble before, when there had been illness or economic threat from the Borough of Poole. Her strength of character has ensured that they had come through those times, but with the devastation of the village she realised that the stakes were higher now.

Her husband's news was devastating to her. Even though he had spent so much time away, he had been such a loving and devoted husband and was, after all, father to her eleven children. She had respected him as soon as they had met, and had grown to love him, for he had been her guiding star ever since. So wise, so committed to making this country a better place, but despite all his efforts, he was being overcome by the tides that were tearing the nation apart. And now he was half the man he was, and it was clear he would not be with her for much longer; nor would he be leading the defence of the Castell.

Then there was Captain Cleall. God had provided another guiding star, as the other one waned. Yes, she had the capacity to love two men, and her love for James had gradually grown, shielded by the devotion to her husband, before it revealed itself undeniably on the cliffs of the Dorsetshire coast last summer, and once again only a few days ago in her bed. The guilt she now carried, with the return of her husband, was immense. How could she endure a siege of her own Castell, trapped with both men she loved? But equally, she was certain that she could not have endured it without either of them. She yearned for James ever since she had slept with him. Not that she had not yearned for him before, but having made love, the passion for him was rampaging through her body and it took all her might to control it. Moments together, alone, had been few and far between since Sir John had returned, and James always behaved impeccably, but sometimes she wished he did not. She had to content herself with a glance here and there or, at best, an arm brushing passed her, which would once again ignite the explosive emotions within.

Joseph Cobb walked past with two pails of water for the kitchen. He looked out of sorts and Mary felt that she should have been less willing to let him join their ranks. He was still young, although not much younger than her own son, who had already seen his share of battles. The thought of John confirmed that, above all, it was her role as a mother she found most challenging. She was isolated from her children and she prayed every hour without fail that they were safe in Oxford. But was anywhere safe now? She missed them far more than she had anticipated and it would be, most probably, months before she saw them again, and with no means of communication in the meantime. It had been the letters that kept the departure of Alice and John just about bearable, but the siege had ended that. The war had brought mixed news for the Royalist cause, with the Parliamentarians taking Bristol, recently. There were deaths amongst her friends and acquaintances. Lord Cranborne's son had died at Edge Hill, as did Francis Trew from the village. Her own son, John, was stationed at Oxford and last time she had heard from him he was anticipating action again, imminently. Captain Cleall had been so good to protect him at Edgehill but now he was alone and for all she knew, facing death on a battlefield somewhere. It was the not knowing that was hardest to deal with.

Her train of thought was broken by Ned Parfitt bringing some wood up to the kitchen, which had a door off the garden. He looked around at the garden with a smile.

"More change here than the shoreline at Swanage. One minute it is flowers and now it is abundant with vegetables."

Ned always had a way that made things simple and expressions that cheered Mary.

He continued, "But I guess this is nothing compared with the changes that are afoot across Corffe, the shire and all of England. Why, the winds of change are blowing stronger than those off the cliffs of Worth in the winter. Who would have thought that Sir John's son would be camped outside this here Castell and ready to launch an attack on the very walls that nurtured him as a boy? Boggles the mind; well least mine."

Later that evening, Lady Bankes watched the sun go down in a blazing glory, reflecting blacksmiths' hearths across the nation, bellowing their embers as they hammered weapons and munitions for the forthcoming battles. Sir John, who was very tired and would sleep alone tonight, had already retired. And so she stood by herself on the bastion as the fire in the night sky slowly died and the same thoughts were bombarding her mind from all directions. She felt as though she was already under attack, with wave upon wave of anxiety. It was a very still night, with an owl hooting from within the wood to the north of the Castell, and a bat darting through the air in search of midges. The natural world carried on, with its beauty and grace, oblivious to the pain and suffering of humankind. She heard a step behind her and turned to find Captain Cleall. She smiled and he asked if she was all right.

"Yes, of course, James," she said but as she spoke her mask dropped and she revealed her anxiety. "No, to be honest. I am frightened," she confessed, and she reached out and grabbed both of his hands, pulling him closer to her, and burying her head in his neck.

Neither said anything. There was nothing more to say. They just held their breath and waited for the nightmare that they had anticipated for so long to unfold and consume their lives, for however long it would last. Cleall was so pleased just to be with Lady Bankes and feel her body. Since they made love, he had an insatiable desire to be with her, and it was only by using all his military experience to focus on preparations to defend against the forthcoming attack that he could keep it at bay and that was only because he knew that her safety and indeed life depended upon it. He asked himself, so many times, why they had not been able to find each other in any other circumstances, especially with Sir John's return and his terminal illness. Reluctantly, he came to the view that it was their destiny to be here, in Corffe, under siege, for they needed each other more now, in these extreme circumstances, than before.

Coke had much to consider before he could make his move. He was not a military man and gained his rank through connections and his militia tactics in London. A siege of a Castell was a different matter altogether. Two of his captains had military training but no real battle experience, and certainly were none the wiser when it came to a siege. The one advantage he had was that he knew the Castell inside out, its strengths and weaknesses. However, the strengths were many and the weaknesses few. The Castell was well resourced with two water sources, and plenty of areas to grow crops and keep animals. His enquiries amongst the villagers had confirmed that Lady Bankes had stocked it with meat, fish and produce over the past few weeks. His sources were contradictory regarding the number of defenders within the Castell, ranging from fifty to a hundred. When he first marched five hundred men to Corffe, a five-to-one advantage seemed to be undefeatable, but doubt grew in his mind the more he studied the Castell's walls and towers. Even a ten-to-one ratio seemed barely enough now. Furthermore, he had the challenge of feeding five hundred men and keeping them occupied, which itself was a task. He had sent men out to gather food, others to find resources, such as wood to make ladders, and more armaments. The clear summer nights became cold and there seemed to be never enough wood to make all the necessary camp fires, so Coke ordered the men to use the timber and thatch from the village houses closest to the Castell, which were being transformed into battlements for musketeers, rather than dwellings. At night it was quite a picture to see all the camp fires, almost a reflection of the stars in the clear skies in contrast to the darkness and lifelessness of the village. One thing that Coke did know was that discipline had to be maintained. On the second night, a fight had broken out amongst men gambling and Coke acted quickly. The sight of a man dancing on a rope, choking to death, would be a controlling influence to maintain order. And so it was.

With his captains, Coke concocted a plan. The Roundhead leaders were convinced that the resources in the Castell were such that they had to make an early and decisive move. A long siege would just play into the defenders' hands. Cannons were now in place, and ladders and siege canopies constructed, He had positioned his artillery on The Rings, a large mound to the south-west of the Castell, which had been constructed by King Stephen, when he had sieged the fortress four hundred years earlier, in his civil war against Matilda, after she claimed the throne. On this occasion, he would bow to Royalty's knowledge of warfare and follow suit, but the Roundhead commanders could see the benefit of this approach. From here, the cannons could be positioned to bombard two towers, and the wall between. All the walls of the Castell were approached by a steep, and in some instances, almost vertical incline, which made the fortress so strong. The defenders would look down on any attacking force from all directions. The steepness of the slopes was less severe along the elevation that fronted the Rings and so it made sense that the main force could be focused on this area. It did mean crossing the Wicken, which served as a kind of moat from this direction as it snaked around the Castell, but it was only a few feet deep and easily bridged by planks of wood. Coke and his captains also agreed that two smaller forces could attack from other directions to stretch the defenders' resources.

Five days after Coke's confrontation with Lady Bankes, they put their plans into operation. It was shortly after sunrise, when the first of the cannons broke the harmony of the early morning songbirds, with a roar from the Rings. But the ball fell short of the Castell walls, and the defenders of the walls jeered. Coke was furious, for his plan was to make a first impressive devastating blow, before addressing his men and commencing the full attack. He addressed his men, anyway.

"We will attack this Castell, in the name of God, who will provide us with the victory we deserve, as righteousness is on our side. We will bring the Castell to its knees for England and the freedom of its men. It stands before us, a symbol of the old order and is owned by Sir John Bankes, the king's chief justice; a man who is wanted by Parliament for treason. It is defended by just forty men and Lady Bankes, who is in league with the Irish Catholics. I want every man, woman and child killed to rid the country of these vermin. We have all heard what the Catholics did in Ireland to our Protestant compatriots. Well, now is the time to make amends. There will be twenty shillings for the first man over the wall, and nineteen shillings for the second, eighteen for the third and so on and so forth until the twentieth man gets a shilling. Our victory will enhance and preserve our rights as Englishmen. It is ours for the taking, and so with God's will, let us take this victory in his name."

And so the cannons started to roar and the Roundheads marched on the Castell to the beat of their drums.

Just to the north of Dorsetshire, the war continued to rage. The Parliamentary forces were gaining the upper hand, having taken Bristol. But both sides were desperately short of both money and men and were forced to resort to local conscription, whilst desertion was also rife. After a series of skirmishes across Wiltshire, with the Royalist troops from Oxford, Tom Harvey found himself under the command of Colonel Waller, starting a siege of his own on the town of Devizes, which had been the focal point for the retreat of a Royalist force they had confronted. He and his comrades had little to do for the first few days, as Waller had ordered the town to be pummelled with cannon fire, not realising that it was only lightly defended by infantry, as the cavalry had escaped just before the siege started and headed to Oxford to get reinforcements.

Tom, his Devonshire friend, Jerome, and the rest of the Dorsetshire troops were positioned behind the artillery, anticipating storming the town once the cannon had done the damage and breached the walls. This was Harvey's first siege and he quickly learnt that sieges were mainly a waiting game. The infantry prepared and waited for the entire first two days, manufacturing makeshift ladders from tree branches. At least the forces had been better supplied and provisioned since the winter, with tents, helmets and breastplates that fitted, medical and cooking equipment. It was already a 'new' army compared to the Edgehill one, and everybody felt more as though they were a trained and equipped fighting force. As a fighting force they were feeling confident from a string of victories across the south west and had many stories of heroics and gallantry to recount amongst the ranks. As they made themselves busy, Tom and Jerome told each other jokes, as well as making up songs and rhymes often making which made fun of the cavalier Royalists. Jerome shared Tom's hopes for a new and better world, and this is one of the reasons that they got on.

On the third day, expectations were high, and the foot soldiers were eager to engage with the enemy and end the waiting game. As the midday sun blazed down on the Roundheads, Waller organised them ready to make a charge. But as the final preparations were being made, and the foot soldiers had begun saying their prayers, news came of the Royalist relief force arriving behind their positions on Roundway Down. Waller abandoned the siege and decided to retreat back to the Down, hoping to confront and defeat the new arrivals before they could join the remaining

Royalists in Devizes. But now Tom was to learn what battle was like without a plan.

As they arrived on the Down, they could see the Royalist cavalry prepared and waiting. They were nearly two thousand-strong, nearly twice the strength of Waller's dragoons and cavalry but without any foot soldiers or artillery. Waller had over two thousand, foot soldiers, pikemen and musketeers, and thirty cannons. As he arrived, he decided to take the higher ground, which for some reason the Royalists had not occupied, despite being in position first. Waller ordered his infantry and artillery in the centre of his line, with cavalry on each flank, another classic formation which he hoped, combined with the higher ground, would ensure his forces would prevail. But Waller was going to be taught a lesson today: that it was foolish to accept the enemy's choice of battle positions. Alas, he would not have the opportunity to take this knowledge to his next battle, for today would be his last.

Within half an hour, the world turned upside down for the Parliamentarians. Since that time, Tom tried to pull together in his mind the series of events that would result in the biggest Royalist victory in the south of England during the Civil War. It all happened so quickly and all he could recollect afterwards was a series of flashbacks as he thanked God that he had escaped with his life, for so few did.

It started as they struggled to get their artillery to the higher ground. Tom and Jerome were amongst many foot soldiers who were deployed to help push the cannons back behind their lines to the top of the Down so they could fire over the heads of the infantry into the enemy lines. But as they were pushing the demi-culverin into place, with four other men, they could hear what sounded like thunder rumbling from the valley below and the ground trembling. The Royalist cavalry had started their attack. Tom recalled thinking that this was not fair as they were clearly not ready. In all the other battles he had fought, both sides had waited for each other to get in line and eyed each other up for an hour or more before commencing battle. In hindsight, Tom realised there were no rules and certainly no fairness in war. The Royalists had launched their attack when there was maximum disorder in the Roundheads' line, as foot soldiers and artillery were heaving the cannons into place. Nor did the Royalists attack the Roundhead cavalry, as had been the case in most of the other battles, but instead went straight for the foot soldiers and artillery.

A thousand horses charged up the Down at breakneck speed, thundering towards the troops who were still in disarray, barely a pike positioned amongst them, and certainly a vacuum of orders. Tom and Jerome watched as the inevitable carnage unfolded with the Parliamentary cavalry simply waiting on the flanks before somebody finally gave an order for them to engage. But they were vastly outnumbered and the delay meant that they were attacking from the side, with little impact to the central might of Royalist horses that was charging onto the foot soldiers. Every third man along the Parliamentary line was a musketeer but few had actually loaded their weapons. Those that did started to shoot and several found their mark, with Royalists falling in their saddles, clutching wounds, or some falling off their rides, but the peppering impact was slight on the mass of beasts and sabre-wielding men that was closing down on the lines of Tom's comrades. He was mesmerised by the shock of what was about to happen, before being bawled at by the lieutenant to put in place the chocks that would stop the cannons rolling down the hill. They could hear the cries and shrieks of men behind them as they readied the cannon, and released it from the gun carriages.

Tom's next recollection was looking up to see that a Royalist had made his way through the line, and was now just twenty feet away, pausing to determine his next course of action, with a sabre that was dripping with blood, matching the colour of his leather tunic. At that moment he caught Tom's eye, and there was a sickening feeling in Tom's stomach as he realised that the cavalryman had decided he was to be his next victim, and he pulled the rein towards him. The next few seconds were all replayed in slow motion, like a nightmare, when you can see what is going to happen but your legs appear to be running through mud for no apparent reason.

He heard Jerome scream at him, but the words seemed to vibrate in his head without meaning. He could see the intent in the Cavalier's eyes, the plume of the feathers in his hat bent back in the flow of air as he gathered pace, the sweat on the shoulders of the chestnut destrier he was riding and the vibration of the ground as its hooves pounded and the distance between them shortened. Tom's pike was on the ground to his right, but he had no chance to recover it in time. All he could do would be to back away and run for it. But his legs appeared to be weighed down, and just twenty feet behind was the top of the Down and a large precipice of two hundred feet. He heard a shot and in the corner of his vision, saw musket smoke. The Royalist was pushed to his right as the left side of his face simply disappeared, revealing his skull. There was no blood; just bone. Simultaneously, his hat was blown off from the rear. He tried to raise his hand to his face but the momentum of the shot continued and his body crashed to the ground almost at Tom's feet as the horse drew up. Tom was frozen as he looked down at the twisted body and deformed head, realising the musket ball had gone right through it. He just had time to take a deep breath before Jerome was yanking his arm and directing him back down towards the line but to the right of where his command was. As he started to run, Tom looked back and cried "Thank you!" to the musketeer who had fired the shot that had saved his life.

The Royalist charge was now retreating to their lines, leaving great holes in the Roundhead defences. Finally, a cannon from behind them fired into the retreating cavalry, and a horse went down, but this was a small compensation compared with the devastation that the Royalists had inflicted. Before the Roundheads could consider any respite, there was the realisation that a second wave of cavalry was advancing through the Royalist retreat, and on its way to spread more butchery.

Tom's mind could not comprehend it or think what to do, but Jerome kept pulling him further to the right, along the line of foot soldiers but to the flank and to the lower ground of the Down. They each found an abandoned pike and joined the line to face the charge. The speed of events made recollection difficult but in no time at all, the whole Parliamentary line was pushed back and up the Down by the second charge, almost in line with the cannons between them.

This was making most of the Parliamentary artillery redundant as they could no longer fire over the heads of their own infantry; only into their backs. Tom and Jerome had managed to bring down a Royalist before regrouping with their line. It was the third wave of attack that was to deal the devastating blow. Bodies, pikes and guts were spread out in front of them. The officers were clearing lines in front of some of the

Parliamentary cannons, which were now starting to come to life and having some impact as their smoke added more mayhem to the battlefield. But it was the disarray of the Parliamentary line from the very start that was to be their undoing, as well as deciding to take the enemy's choice of ground, even though instinctively the higher ground would be preferred. For it was the precipice behind the Parliamentary line that would take more lives than even the cavalry's sabres, as the third wave of attack pushed much of the remaining Roundhead defence over it.

Men fell backwards at the drop and landed on rocks below, breaking bones and bodies and limbs before another line of foot soldiers fell on top of them, in what became known as Bloody Ditch. Only on the flanks could men have any chance to escape, where the height of the drop was merely thirty feet. Even here, many broke ankles or fell awkwardly. It was Jerome's foresight of what could happen, having seen the lie of the land whilst manoeuvring the cannon, that saved Tom and his friend. Jerome had led them down the slope and they were now at the lowest end of the drop.

As the third wave of attack came, Roundheads along the line were surrendering, while many others became the victims of Bloody Ditch. Tom and Jerome both turned and jumped, and landed well.

"Get out of here — that way!" yelled Tom, pointing to the right, away from the Down. He was just in time, as musket shots were already being fired down from the ridge, as some Royalists had dismounted and were now shooting survivors. Tom was hit in the thigh by a shard of rock, when a musketeer just missed him and the ball ricocheted off limestone behind him. But he blocked out the pain, and the two of them ran to escape the carnage, leaving the deafening cries of dying and injured colleagues behind. Only a few would escape this massacre with their lives and it was every man for himself.

It was a warm afternoon to run and their heavy breastplates made the going hard. It was more than a mile before the two of them stopped running, soaked in sweat and breathless. They realised that they were alone and sought refuge in a thicket of trees, just to gather their senses. Behind them, the sounds of the battle could still be heard. Cannons, guns, shrieks and cries. What a disaster and what a close shave with death.

Roundway Down was the greatest cavalry victory of the English Civil War. The Royalists christened the battle 'Runaway Down'. The defeat of an army arrayed in proper battle order on high ground by a column of cavalry that had just ridden down from Oxford was regarded as remarkable, especially given Waller's 'recent victories and reputation. About a thousand Parliamentarian troops were killed and a further thousand were captured, with only the cavalry and dragoons escaping in any significant numbers.

"How is your leg?" Jerome asked, as he fought to recover his breath.

Tom looked down. His breeches were stained with blood. He took off his jacket, cut a strip off the back with his knife, and tied it around his thigh.

"I am sure it will be fine. Looks like this is the extent of our weapons now," he said, holding up his knife.

"That was hell. Even worse than hell. We were devastated. We had no plan, no orders, no chance. I am starting to wonder why we are doing this, Tom? What are we fighting for? Who are we fighting for? A Parliament that we do not even vote for? We should go back to our homes. There are the harvests to gather and our families need us."

"Jerome, we do not have time to discuss that now. The Royalists will be after us, I am sure. We should get as far away as possible before nightfall. There will be no regrouping of the Roundhead forces here. As you say, we were totally routed. I think we should head south. We can hunt for food but stay well-hidden and off the main roads," Tom said and they set off again at pace, leaving the distant battle cries behind them.

It was not long before Tom and Jerome ran into four other Roundhead foot soldiers, who were also making their way south. They joined forces for added protection, although they had only one pike and a couple of knives between them. As the day stretched into evening, they found a river which had fish and thought it would be a good place to camp. The water level was low in the summer, revealing banks of pebbles either side. Beyond the pebble beach was a hundred yards of grass, some quite long, with the occasional gorse thicket. The edge of the river valley was marked by the treeline of a wood. They agreed that they would see what fish they could catch, eat it and then seek protection and shelter in the trees to sleep. Some willow sticks were found and quickly whittled into spears and they set about catching their supper. Before long, half a dozen fish had been caught and were ready on the riverbank. Whilst Jerome and one of the others set about making a fire, Tom went to relieve himself in a thicket bush not far away. As he hummed to himself and reflected on how lucky he had been, he heard a rumbling sound and some shouts from the river. He turned his head, peered over the bush and to his dismay, the rumble was the sound of horses, Royalist horses, charging along the river towards his comrades. There were at least ten of them, with sabres drawn. There was little he could do, so he stayed hidden in the thicket. Jerome and the man making the fire had no chance and were cut down into pieces. Tom wanted to scream and charge out to seek revenge for the loss of yet another friend, but he just about managed to restrain himself.

The riders pulled up and confronted the remaining men as they came out of the river, dropping their fish and stakes with hands up, pleading for mercy. Jerome was lying face down in a pool of blood, never to see the new world he was fighting for. If it had not been for Jerome leading Tom to the lower flank of the Down earlier, he would have had no chance of seeing it, either. But there was nothing Tom could do with just his knife against fully armed cavalry, so he kept his head down and prayed silently for his friend Jerome but also an opportunity for revenge.

He watched the Royalists discuss what to do, dismount and then set their captors to work. Two were assigned to cooking and the rest to burying their comrades. There was something about the leader of the group that seemed familiar to Tom but he could not make sense of it from one hundred yards away in the thicket. While the other Royalists oversaw the work, the leader scouted the area on his horse, and after riding along the tree line turned and was now heading directly for Tom's hiding point. Was this the moment Tom had prayed for? He could jump him and then, using him as a captive, negotiate the freedom of his comrades, and then kill them all in revenge for Jerome's death, not to mention all the others on that bloody Down, earlier in the day. He curled up and made himself small, creeping further into the thicket. He would have to run from behind, jump and knock the cavalier off his horse, and then follow up with his knife as he hit the ground. He could hear the horse approaching, its gentle trot echoed in his own heart palpitations. The rider was level, and Tom looked up through the thicket.

"Shit," he said to himself. It was John Bankes. What the hell was he doing here? Tom did not know what to do. He certainly was not going to jump his friend and as he hesitated, the moment passed and the rider turned to the campfire.

While the fish was cooking, Tom thought through his options, but few seemed to make any sense. He could just turn himself in, for he would be well treated by John, although as a Royalist officer he would have to hand him over to be imprisoned with the other Roundheads. He could wait until dark, and then just leave. But it was some form of revenge for Jerome's death which he wanted and he sensed, if he waited, he might get an opportunity.

It was twilight by the time the Royalists had consumed the fish supper, leaving a few scraps for the captives before herding them to the tree line and making camp for the night. The four prisoners were placed around the trunk of an oak and then a rope was tied around them, as well as the tree, to secure them for the night. Tom could see that two of the Royalists were assigned to guard duty, while the other four made beds out of their saddles and bundles of fern they cut from the undergrowth. It was a clear night and would quickly become quite cool.

Time passed as the Royalists chatted around the fire before getting up, one by one, and going to rest. Tom could easily escape now. He was fifty yards from his comrades and their guards and they were a further twenty-five from the campfire and the other Royalists. There was grass over a foot high between them, which he could easily crawl through and make his getaway. He hardly knew the captive Roundheads but a combination of his desire to seek revenge for Jerome's death, the disaster of Roundway Down and Roundhead camaraderie meant he had decided to see if he could have an opportunity to set the prisoners free. And he would have to do that by killing the guards and not waking John Bankes or any other Royalist. It was madness, with a slim chance of success, even if an opportunity did arise, but for the moment he was staying put. The figures were just silhouettes now, in the moonless night, and the only movement was from the two guards who produced a whisper of indecipherable conversation, distilled by the chirping of the crickets in the grass.

The night deepened and the sky darkened when there was a laugh and one of the guards got up and patted his colleague on the back before wandering to a nearby tree and lying down next to it, to rest. It seemed like he was going to sleep, as well. Was this the chance Tom had waited for? Could he crawl over, kill the guard who was still on duty and then the other without waking the rest of the Royalists, and free the captives? For the next hour, as the dead of the night intensified, he developed a plan in his mind and then made a move, hoping by now that the second guard had fallen asleep.

His own breath reverberated in his ears as he crawled through the grass, inch by inch, to position himself to approach the guard from the rear, as he was seated with his back to a tree. His heart pounded and adrenaline was pumping through his veins. He had lost count of the men he had killed in battle but he had never killed anybody in cold blood before and with such high stakes. He knew his execution had to be perfect, a single decisive cut to the throat. He pulled his knife from his belt and was now at the edge of the grass cover, a few yards from the tree shielding the guard. He gradually rose from his hiding and made the first tentative steps towards his target. An owl hooted from within the wood, which almost made Tom shriek he was so tense but a following hoot gave him the opportunity he needed to make his second step. He had visions of the guard looking around the tree, sword drawn, and that would be the end of his mission. Tom held his breath and took another step which took him within reach of the tree. He was now positioned directly opposite his target on the other side. He had a pebble in his left hand which he now threw to his right into a clump of fern. The sound of the stone made the guard jump up and make an enquiring step towards where the sound had arisen, giving Tom his chance.

He stepped behind him, his left hand quickly covering the man's mouth while his right hand cut the Royalist's throat, a warm trickle of blood flowing down his tunic. The guard's hands tried, in vain, to release Tom's clutch and Tom also received an elbow in his chest but it was too late. A moment later, the life drained out of the guard's body and Tom slowly lowered the limp torso down to the ground, all the time watching to see if the other guard had stirred as he slept, just ten yards away. There was a snort but it came from one of the captive Roundheads tied to the tree.

Tom took a deep breath and very slowly released the air from his lungs to reduce the tension. He was tempted to leave the second guard, who was sleeping soundly, but he knew he could not risk this as the escaping prisoners would no doubt rouse him. Very slowly, he made his way towards his next victim but not directly, as he was sure his presence shadowing over the guard would risk waking him, so he set out to approach him from the side, doubling the length of time for the painfully slow journey. The campfire behind him, where the other Royalist slept, provided him with sufficient light to guide him, but also created flickering shadows amongst the surrounding trees that reached into the deep darkness beyond.

"Stop!" a voice yelled from behind him, and he looked around to see a body getting up, already holding a sword, reflecting the fire's light.

Tom ran into the shadows and darkness. He could hear a commotion behind him and somebody running, not far behind. A branch scraped his head, and then he ran straight into the trunk of a tree. He was dazed for a second but recovered to the sound of closing footsteps. He ducked left; a mistake, as he was running through thick, hand-like ferns coming up from the earth and holding him back. Darkness all around. He could not make out a better way, and his pursuer was getting closer. He dared to look around, but as he did so his foot caught on a root and he fell into the bracken, his face buried in the undergrowth. As he rose to his knees, he felt a sharp point pressed into his back.

"Drop your weapon," a voice whispered behind him. Tom dropped the knife and turned slowly. Yes — it was a voice he recognised. It was John Bankes. He did not know what to feel or how to express himself as he looked into the eyes of his old friend.

"John — it is me. Tom. Tom Harvey."

"Tom? You have just killed one of my men. I should drive this sabre through your heart."

"Your men killed my friend yesterday. I had the opportunity to kill you yesterday, as well. I'm here to free my comrades."

"What a mess, my friend. How did we get into this situation? I'm sorry about your friend but this is war. But we must act fast. You must leave straightaway," John replied, helping his friend up.

The sound of the other Royalists, spreading out in the darkness behind them, could be heard, yelling and struggling through the blackness of the forest.

"Francis is dead. He died at Edge Hill. I saw Captain Cleall amongst the Royalists who killed him. How vile is that?"

"Oh no, Tom," John lowered his head and took a deep breath. "Tom, I was with Captain Cleall at Edge Hill. I'm so sorry."

Tom was shocked again, as his emotions were given another twist.

"What are we fighting for, John? What is this madness? All purpose and hope appear to have vanished."

"I do not know, my friend, but I do know my men will be here in seconds. Go, my friend. Go that way. I will send my men over there."

The two friends hugged. There was warmth, sorrow and despair all wrapped up in that hug, but then Tom turned and left, with tear-filled eyes.

"Over here!" John shouted to his men, as he headed in the opposite direction to Tom.

Tom made his way more carefully through the forest and it was not long before the voices were lost amongst the trees behind him. He tracked through the night, his leg pounding from his battle injury but nothing compared with the pain in his heart.

It was not long before the sun was creeping over the horizon to his left as he headed south. By mid-morning, he had reached Salisbury, where he had trained. It was a Parliamentary stronghold. He reported to the commander and told him of the defeat at Roundway Down and his subsequent exploits and how he had tried to rescue his comrades, but had woken up a guard who had chased after him, although he managed to escape in the dark. He also told him of his experience at Edge Hill and subsequent battles. The colonel was impressed by the level of experience that he had, and assigned the sergeant to a new lieutenant who was departing with fifty newly trained recruits the next day to Wareham, to reinforce the forces led by Colonel Bingham. Tom was going back to his home shire, at last.

Captain Cleall was positioned on the first tower, one of two fronting the Rings, where the Roundheads had positioned their artillery, with Captain Lawrence on the second tower, as the Castell soaked up the morning sun. Their hope lay in the Castell walls, but their doom lay in the numbers of encircling Roundheads streaming from their camp along the contour of the valley, to the beat of drums. The flag of Oliver Cromwell flew before them, a mustard-coloured backdrop with St George's cross in the top corner, and five silver stars spread diagonally across it. The Roundheads appeared disciplined and well-equipped, many in red and others in blue tunics that had been supplied to them by the New Model Army provisioning organisation, along with breast plates and tortoiseshell helmets. The two captains and Lady Bankes had done their best to maintain morale and order in the Castell over the last five days, but the defenders were mainly just men who were simple farm folk and despite the training that Cleall had provided, their anxiety was growing by the day. They would gather and share their fears and worries in corners of the Castell before going to the walls to watch the encamped Roundheads. The men were restless, joking nervously one moment but then snapping at the slightest annoyance, the next. Cleall made the same prayer that he always made before battle commenced, looking for omens of hope in the sky and surrounds but he found none.

Now the moment of truth had come. How would his trainees respond in a real battle? The perimeter of the Castell seemed to be spaciously lacking in defenders, but Cleall suspected that the Roundheads would concentrate their efforts on one section of the wall, given the deployment of their cannons, and it was between these two towers. The captain estimated that there were three hundred or more of the Roundheads positioned between the Rings and himself, while two much smaller contingents had marched their way around the Castell. The slope to the wall was less steep in front of him, and he had arranged for all the bushes and shrubs to be removed as part of his siege preparations, ensuring there was nowhere for the Roundheads to seek cover. They would have to cross the Wicken, and then scurry up the steep slope before tacking the walls in clear sight of the defending force. He had also constructed an additional wooden barricade on the side of the tower that fronted the market square, for he knew the Roundheads had positioned musketeers there and he did not want to be caught in crossfire while his men focused on the main attack. Cleall had prepared as best he could, but now it was down to how the battle would unfold.

Then it started. The boom of cannons and the thumps and crashes of balls on stone became as steady and resonant as the drumbeats, echoing throughout Corffe valley, one after another, like giant rolls of thunder. The first balls that smashed into Cleall's tower shook its foundations and sent razor shards of rock flying in the air, but without any casualties or serious damage. Volleys of musket fire joined the crescendo of blasts and clamour as slate balls ricocheted off stone, above and below the defenders. There was a cry from the adjacent tower and Cleall saw one of the defenders go down, wounded by the lethal debris of a cannon ball smashing into the wall below him.

The hordes of Roundhead foot soldiers started to advance with charged cries of defiance and weapons abreast against a backdrop of cannon smoke. Most marched behind four advance parties, protected by siege canopies above their heads, manufactured from the main and two side doors of the church. Beneath them, they carried long planks to bridge the moat of the Wicken and ladders to scale the walls between the two towers. As they started to bridge the river, the two defending captains ordered volleys of musket shot and crossbow fire from the towers on either side through the arrow slits that gave the defenders visibility of the attack, but plenty of protection. Several of the infantry on the periphery of the protection from the siege canopy fell as the defenders found their targets, but Roundheads quickly replaced them from behind. Musketeers from the Roundheads' lines fanned out along the far side of the river, seeking the limited cover there was from the rock formations of the slope before emptying one of their apostles from their chest, loading their guns and taking aim at whoever popped a head out on the Castell walls. Their cover was limited, and as they reloaded, they became sitting ducks for the better-positioned and protected musketeers on the Castell walls, and one by one they started falling.

It was now time to implement Cleall's plan that he had been practising with his troop in the inner bailey throughout the preceding weeks. He had mounted two of the smaller cannons on the two towers that were being attacked. He had constructed a gantry on which the guns could be loaded, and then raised to above parapet-level by four men through a series of ratchets. A wooden shield protected the front of the cannon, and ropes secured the gun carriages to limit their recoil. Cleall knew he had to be very careful with cannon fire as he had only ninety-eight balls after using some for training, and two on the night attack a week ago. The siege could involve many attacks and he would need to preserve supplies, while his attackers could be re-supplied at any time. He also had a limited number of people who could be deployed to fire them, given the need to man the walls. Each cannon required four men, a significant proportion of his total fighting force. The saker on the bastion had the range to fire on the enemy artillery but the two on the towers could be directed on the Parliamentary foot soldiers directly beneath the walls.

Cleall carefully peered over the parapet, while the four men manning the cannon, Joseph Cobb amongst them, nervously awaited orders, as the smell of sulphur from the gunpowder filled the air. As the attackers reached the Castell side of the moat, Cleall ordered the firing of the cannon on his tower. The gun crew had already loaded the gun, and now ratchetted the cannon up the gantry until it was parapet height. It instantly attracted a lobby of musket fire, not only from the direction of Rooks Hill but also from the market square on the tower's flank, pummelling the wooden barricade. The defenders were showered with slivers of musket ball slate, as well as shards of stone and wood, causing cuts and bruises. But then the cannon fuse found its powder and blasted its shot, rocking the gantry, and recoiling until strained by the ropes. At that exact moment, a musket ball sliced through one of the restraining ropes, and the cannon spun round, toppling off its platform and crashing on to the tower below. One of the armourers screamed in pain, as the carriage trapped his leg. The gunner went to his aid but as he did so, a musket ball went straight through his skull, leaving a splattering of blood across the limestone walls. Cleall screamed at the other two to help shift the cannon carriage from the man who had been trapped and was crying out in pain, and not to worry about the dead man. One came to his aid, but Joseph Cobb was curled up in the corner, with his arms around his head, as muskets continued to pelt the wall above him. A musket was used to lever the carriage free, but the gunner's leg was in a bad way.

"Cobb, help take this man to the hall for medical attention," Cleall ordered, kicking Joseph into action. He had seen it many times before; the onset of real battle causing young men to turn into panicked, terrified wrecks. He could see the terror in Cobb's eyes as he dragged him to the aid of his colleague, while the captain and two other musketeers held the tower. As he regained control of the situation, the captain peered once again over the parapet and sighed in relief as the smoke had cleared and it was clear that the cannon had done its job. The siege canopy had been smashed and several of the troop beneath lay dead or injured on the moat edge, and a few other bodies could be seen in the water. Then there was a boom from the other tower, as its cannon sent a ball aimed at another troop who were bridging the moat closer to them. This time the ball missed the siege canopy, but smashed the makeshift bridge and dispatched it into the moat and a dozen Roundheads followed, many injured from the splinters of timber that pierced men like arrows. This time, the cannon remained tied on its platform, and there were cheers from the tower before the armourers ratcheted the platform down again and started to reload.

The other two advance parties had bridged the moat and were now heading for the Castell walls, which were still being pounded by cannon fire from the Rings, three hundred yards away. Most balls fired low into the walls, which were ten feet thick at this point, causing barely any damage. Others were fired high and landed harmlessly into the open bailey of the Castell, disturbing no more than the sheep or cattle that roamed there. However, one shot had caused some real damage as it had hit the parapet wall, killing a defender instantly and leaving a gaping hole. It was this hole that one of the advancing parties was heading for on and was starting to raise a ladder towards it, partially protected by a siege canopy that was being battered by musket shot and arrows from the nearest tower, and boulders being thrown from the walls above. Every third or fourth shot found a Roundhead and took him out of the action. But scores of foot soldiers were now crossing the make-shift bridges and taking the place of their comrades as they fell.

There was an almighty roar from the bastion as the saker came to life and sent a shot in the direction of the Rings. It found its target with a direct hit on one of the cannons stationed there. The sight of the cannon being sent twenty feet backwards, and several of the artillery men tending it being injured by flying debris or the retreating gun carriage was received with a cheer from the Castell ramparts.

The gunner returned from the sick bay but without Joseph Cobb, who was nowhere to be seen. Cleall handed him a musket and commanded him to do what he could, before turning and dashing down the steps of the tower and onto the wall, where the Roundheads' cannons had damaged the battlements. The Roundhead foot soldiers were now congregating below in an attempt to raise a ladder and assail the Castell walls. As he arrived, the end of the ladder appeared in the gaping hole in the wall. Cleall looked at two of Captain Lawrence's men, who were on the other side of the gap, throwing missiles down on the attackers. One of them was a half-head taller than Cleall, with a barrel-shaped chest.

"Grab it and pull it up!" ordered Cleall, pointing to the ladder. Musket shot was being fired at the gap, but the three men knelt as low as possible before grabbing the ladder, and between them, applying all their strength, they were able to leverage it against the stone wall, throwing an ascending Roundhead off and down to the ground. Musket shot continued to pepper the ladder, splinters flying off it, as they brought it up onto the wall, before discarding it into the bailey behind them. The remaining Roundheads, who had been waiting to scale the ladder, had received a barrage of musket fire from Captain Lawrence's men on the second tower, and they were all now dead or injured.

"That should delay them a while but help me fill the gap with the wood and stone stored over there!" Cleall commanded, putting another element of his preparation into action. The three men scurried along the parapet with their heads low and each brought back a large, limestone block, placed it in the gap, and then returned for another. The six blocks were then supported with a plank of wood and three buttresses that had been pre-cut to parapet height.

"At night we can mortar the blocks, but this will hold them back for a while. Keep bombarding them. I am going to check the other defences," the captain ordered.

He dashed along the wall and down the stairs from the ramparts as a cannon ball hit the parapet right behind him, and the force almost made him lose his balance. Very little damage was done, thanks to the strength of the Castell walls, other than a dust cloud descending into the Castell sanctuary. He raced across the outer bailey and through the inner gate to the northern wall, the stage for one of the secondary assaults. He found one of Captain Lawrence's sergeants there, a man by the name of Cox, who was in charge of ten men defending that wall, four of whom, including himself, were in the north tower, and the rest spread along the ramparts.

Cleall viewed the attackers from an arrow-slit in the wall as he requested an update and was pleased to hear that the sergeant had incurred no injuries and had inflicted hell on the Roundheads, who appeared to be in disarray below. They had two ladders but no canopy, as the hill approaching the walls was much steeper. Cox had deployed two musketeers on the tower, and for them it was like shooting practice. The defenders here had no cannon fire to worry about and with the advantage of the much higher elevation it was difficult to see how they could be troubled. So Cleall re-deployed two of the men to the towers, where the main attack was concentrated, and then raced on to the inner ward that protected the gloriette, where Lady Mary waited.

He found her on the wall overlooking the outer bailey on the eastern side of the inner ward. The Roundheads were attacking just below, on a section of the outer bailey between Plunket Tower and the wall where she was standing. She was with Sir John, Camille, Povington, a maid and one of the cooks. They were safe, as no ladder could stretch to this height; fifty feet higher than the wall the attackers were targeting. The defenders were using their height advantage to attack the Roundheads to their south by dropping stones and hot embers onto them. Even Povington seemed to be enjoying this, and the Roundheads had badly positioned their assault. The steep slope leading to the walls made the attackers sitting ducks for the musketeers positioned on Plunket Tower, as well as the eclectic group of defenders looking down from the inner ward.

"Captain Cleall, are our defences holding?" Lady Mary asked.

"I believe they are, my Lady. The main assault is between the first and second towers, and we are holding firm. I see you are keeping them at bay here, as well."

"Yes, we are. The Castell will not fall today with Sir John, Camille and Povington to get passed, that is for sure."

The final stop was within the gloriette, where the hall had been turned into a makeshift sanatorium for the wounded, reminiscent of when disease had struck the village nearly ten years before. Mary Hardy, the cook, was in charge, but fortunately she was not busy. Only one of the straw beds was occupied, with the soldier who had been injured when the cannon was displaced on the tower.

Cleall returned to his post on the first tower to find the Roundheads preparing for a third wave of attack, but in front of them the grass and river were littered with bodies, helmets, pikes and muskets. The attack came with a roar, but it was half-hearted compared with the previous assaults. The prospect of the twenty-shilling reward offered by Coke seemed very remote, if not forgotten, and the Roundheads' charge was much more tentative, with fewer men under the siege shield. They were again met by musket and crossbow fire, and then the cannon from the second tower burst into life again. It exploded less than a yard in front of the first advancing group, sending out shards of rock and stone, injuring the men at the front. This was the last straw, and the rest of the men turned back and retreated to their line, as hope and courage abandoned them.

Colonel Coke had seen enough and ordered a general retreat. Under the white flag of truce, the dead and wounded Roundheads were brought back to camp. Over ninety of their men had been lost, either dead or severely injured, and they had achieved nothing. The defenders had lost two and had a single series injury. Coke was furious and decided to resort to different tactics; strategies that would play on their minds, weakening the resolve of the defendants and be more effective than all his cannons. He was far more experienced in these tactics of war.

Chapter XVI
Summer in Siege

The siege in Corffe continued throughout the summer with daily shots from cannons and muskets to keep the defendants on their toes and entertaining the Roundheads but without any major assault. Elsewhere in Dorsetshire, the Royalist resolve was strong and Bingham's plan for a sweeping Parliamentary campaign was far from being realised when he understood the strength of the Royalist opposition in the Shire. Melcombe, which had declared for the Parliamentary cause, had just fallen to the Royalists under the Earl of Carnarvon, who had a force of two thousand. Bingham had also heard that a further three hundred Irish troops had landed at Melcombe. Would Carnarvon come east, or would he support the battles ranging north in Gloucestershire? Bingham did not know.

The other threat was to Bingham's north, where Lieutenant General William Seymour, the Marquis of Hertford, was stationed at Blandford and threatening to lead a Royalist force south towards Wareham and possibly then on to Poole or Corffe. It was essential that Seymour did not connect with Carnarvon's forces or else Dorsetshire would be lost and the Royalists would be able to create a front that could drive east towards London. Bingham wrote to the Earl of Essex to explain the situation and the imminent threat along the south coast. In turn, he received orders to hold Seymour back and consolidate the Parliamentary forces along the current holdings of Poole, Wareham and hopefully Corffe. Essex was planning an assault in the following year, but it was dependent on Bingham holding the line in the meantime, and he was ordered to be cautious, not to take any risks and play for time. Bingham had commissioned the building of the palisade along the earth walls of Wareham, thereby protecting this town which could also call on the support of some of Colonel Coke's men, camped at Corffe, if required, and then in mid-August launch a pre-emptive attack on Seymour to the north. Coincidentally, the day Bingham started marching was the same day that Seymour had started his move south, so the two forces met five miles south of Blandford.

Bingham's force was evenly matched to Seymour's with about five hundred men each, including eighty cavalry and a dozen or so cannons. Neither man had fought an open field-battle before and had little experience amongst their officers. Captain Francis Sydenham was Bingham's most experienced officer, the son of Colonel Sydenham who had first claimed Melcombe for the Parliamentary cause and had served with the Earl of Essex at Edgehill. Together with the Irish cunning of O'Kelly, they developed a plan to set out their forces in the field, but their main objective was to preserve life and not to lose. The aim was to halt Seymour, not for a victory with significant casualties, for they had to consider the longer-term perspective. So Bingham and his officers deployed defensive tactics with the musketeers and pikeman formed in the middle, and they split the cavalry on each flank, but to protect the musketeers and pikeman from the attacks of the opposing cavalry, rather than launching their own attack. The Roundheads had the benefit of a slightly elevated position, which allowed Colonel Bingham to watch the battle play out from his horse, behind the lines.

His men had been supplied with red jackets from Bristol, which made them distinctive and he could much more easily make out what was happening, with their opponents in no distinctive attire. The Royalist cavalry did charge at his lines and were met by musket fire followed by the foot soldiers closing ranks with their pikes. On the flanks of the charge, the Roundhead cavalry intervened and took the momentum out of the charge, taking out Royalists from the side, but could not reach the central thrust of the riders. But the Parliamentary infantry at the centre held their ground without flinching, bringing down a dozen horses, and causing the following mounts to rear up in fright. The Royalists regrouped and mounted a second and then a third charge, but each time the musketeers and then the defiance of the foot soldiers in the centre was steadfast. The few Roundhead victims were quickly replaced by the foot soldiers on the flanks, who had yet to see action. There was one soldier, a tall sergeant, right at the heart of the Roundhead defence, who was directing operations and ensuring the line held, keeping his fellow foot soldiers and the musketeers to their training drill.

After the third attack, Seymour had seen enough for the day, with the loss of over half his cavalry. He had lost his appetite for the fight and turned his forces back to Blandford, leaving Bingham's men cheering on the field. Amongst them was Tom Harvey. He was sitting on the ground managing his emotions. On one level, the aftermath of a victorious battle was like the moments that followed making love: the climax of passion, adrenaline and physical exertion, followed by a quiet, peace and immense gratitude shared with comrades. He missed Camille and those intimate moments of serenity and yearned to be with her and to escape this mad world. He said a prayer, thanking God for protecting him and asking to be reunited with his wife soon and for her safeguarding. As he said amen, he would look around at the carnage and realise, at another level, that his situation could not be further from his marriage bed. There were men crying out in agony from both sides of the battle, and even more men, as well as horses, who lay silent forever as their blood and guts soaked the earth beneath them. Amongst the bodies and clods of mud were scattered helmets, pikes, sabres and muskets, all soiled with blood and muck.

Bingham was tempted to ride after Seymour and his men, finish the job and take Blandford, but they were not his orders. He had learnt his lesson from his failed assault on Corffe and decided to return to Poole and Wareham, with very little loss of life, and dispatch a mission-accomplished letter to Essex. And that is what he did, after ensuring all injured on both sides were attended to, whilst the dead received a Christian burial.

Back in Poole, the troops refreshed and were given good food and drink as they recounted various stages of the battle to one another. Bingham summoned the sergeant at the centre of the assault who had clearly made such a difference: Tom Harvey.

"Sergeant, you were very impressive on the field of battle today," he said to Tom, when he arrived at the Customs House that served as his headquarters. "It is a wonderful evening, and I would like to know more about you. Would you care for a walk?"

The two of them wandered down the quay, passing the wagons offloading the cargo from the ships moored alongside.

"What would you like to know, Colonel?" Tom asked, looking down at Bingham, who was a head shorter.

"Well — plenty. What is your battle experience, to start with?" Bingham asked.

"I was there at the start: Edgehill. I was lucky to survive, in that I was so inexperienced, but I had to bury my best friend there. He was not so lucky and died next to me. Since then, I have fought all across the West Country, in sieges and field battles, and have learnt a thing or two. I was also trained in the new model army ways in Salisbury, but perhaps learnt the most at Roundway Down. Yes, our biggest defeat, but coming out alive from that teaches you more about yourself than any training, not to mention all the mistakes we made on the battlefield."

"This is very impressive, Sergeant. Sorry, I did not get your name?"

"Tom Harvey, sir."

"Yes, Tom. And what drives you? Why are you fighting for the Parliamentary cause?"

"Well, I think you are partly to blame, sir, or at least John Freeborn Lilburne is, and you arranged for me to hear him not one hundred yards from where we are standing."

"You are one of the Poole recruits? You are a local man?"

"Yes, sir. Born and bred in Corffe."

"You fight for Parliament against the Bankes?"

"I fight for the rights, opportunities and freedoms that Lilburne spoke about. I am not fighting the Bankes, who are good people. I heard Lilburne and other Levellers talking in London before the war and they had opened my mind. Why do you fight, Colonel?"

"To be honest, son, I have similar drives and motivations. I spent much of my childhood as a cabin boy with my father on similar ships to these, sailing to the Newfoundland. There are few harsher upbringings, but my father granted me an education before he was lost at sea, and I have spent most of my life trying to pay him back by helping to create a world where people like you, people who work hard for a good cause, are rewarded, whether in this life or the next. Puritanism was like a spark to my powder keg. It drove me to fight for the cause for people with similar values to come together and work for a better world, one where God will reward you for the effort you put in and the morals you live by, day by day. For me, this war is against everything that is a barrier to that crusade, and especially monarchs and aristocrats who rule or have power through privilege, or Catholics who put the church and rituals between everyday people and God."

"Colonel, a few years back, you were the magistrate who would have, no doubt, seen my friend, Francis Trew, hanged for attempting to steal a horse, whilst distraught with grief after the death of his mother not an hour before. How does that marry up with those values you speak of?"

"You are direct and speak from the heart. I like that, Tom. I recall the incident. Sir John Bankes intervened. Whilst I resented the intervention at the time, I looked back on it as God teaching me a lesson; the lesson of humility. I had been motivated more by my own personal ambition at the time, although I disguised it as spreading the Puritanism cause, rather than thinking what is God's will. I have learnt from this and other mistakes in my life, I will apologise to your friend."

"He was the one who died at Edge Hill."

"I am truly sorry, Tom."

The two men sat on the trunk of a fallen tree, now a few hundred yards from the quay, where the masts of ships clattered in the light breeze. To the east, the rest of the harbour was lined by sand and trees, broken by an occasional fishermen's hut. They were looking out over the harbour, water glistening in the sunlight; a ship coming in with more trade for the town, most of its sails already sheaved as it slowly made its way around the islands and to the quay.

"Francis, my friend, and I used to spend much time out there on Green Island as boys. We would play pirates and cavalrymen, with little expectation of any real-life adventure. And here I am, barely twenty years old, having fought on battlefields across the country, having learnt the horrors of conflict, and Francis lies buried in one of them. I sometimes wish I could turn the clock back, and be on that island again, with wooden swords and pretend horses, but Francis's dying words were to continue to fight for the dream of a better and fairer life, and so I continue to fight."

"I spent a night on that island, as well, recently, Tom. I had planned an attack on the Bankes' hunting party and we used Green Island to launch it. Somehow, Lady Bankes got word of it, and my plan failed. I rode to the Castell with forty men, but she stood firm and sent me away with my tail between my legs. Another lesson, for I fear I was again motivated by personal ambition as well as a personal vendetta with Lady Bankes. I believe she has Catholic sympathies, supports the queen and her arrogance is an affront."

Tom laughed.

"I heard about that, Colonel. She is a strong character but I can assure you she is no Catholic, and is also a very good person. My wife is her personal maid, my father is her estates manager and I am friends with her children. Sir John is away most of the time, and she is left to look after the estate and village, along with all her children and the Castell. She is as good a landlord as one could wish to have. When the village went down with putrid throat, she opened up the hall of her Castell to nurse and keep the sick warm, and she attended them as much as anybody. Francis and myself were converted to the Freeborn vision of John Lilburne, and the only thing that made us have second thoughts was the kindness, and indeed friendship, of the Bankes family. But there are many landowners who treat their tenants badly and if the Bankes decided to sell their estate, we could be at the mercy of some noble who would only be interested in the money he could make from our sweat and toil, and why should that be? Even with the Bankes, there is limited opportunity to make your way in the world as you have done, Colonel."

"Well, I would like to give you an opportunity, Tom. I see a lot of me in you. I see determination and drive, as well as clear thinking and a desire to make the world a better place. On the battlefield today, I saw courage and leadership. I would like to make you an officer, Tom: Lieutenant Tom Harvey."

Tom could not believe his ears. There had been other officers appointed amongst the Parliamentary ranks who were not from the educated and gentry but they were still exceptional, and now he was going to join this elite. Once an officer, always an officer, like Captain Cleall. This was certainly an honour.

"Thank you, sir. I pray I can reward you with the victories we need in return for providing me with this opportunity. From what I hear, we may have the upper hand since the Battle of Naseby, but there is still much work to be done."

"That is right and one of the first victories will be Corffe Castell and breaking the stalemate of the siege that seems to be occurring there. The Bankes would appear to be more than a match for Coke."

Corffe Castell

After the initial siege, the Castell had been bombarded with cannon fire, intermittently, for seven days. The gunners were directing shots mainly at the parapets on top of the thick walls: this was where Coke's cannons were having most impact. In several places, the parapet had been blasted away, but Lawrence's men had devised rapid repairs, having built replacement wall pieces out of timber from the Castell stable walls, and these were rapidly hammered into place. At night, more permanent repairs were made as Captain Cleall had stocked a large hoard of quarry stone. Elsewhere, the attackers' blasts left little more than scars on the mighty Castell walls, although one ball did blast through the window of one of the bedrooms in the gloriette, shattering glass and lead. Now it was time for the Royalists to go on the offensive, as Captain Cleall was not a man to sit back and be attacked. He had watched the attackers' routine and knew now that they would congregate in the large tent, in two shifts, for food in the early evening, and decided he would give them something to chew on.

Captain Lawrence lined up his two sakers on the rampart in the outer bailey, where they had a sightline to Rook's Hill, while Captain Cleall commanded the one on the bastion. The cannons were loaded and readied and then Cleall gave the order.

"Give it to them!" he yelled and the three fuses were simultaneously lit. A moment later, three blasts erupted from the mouths of each weapon and the booms echoed around the Castell walls. There was an almighty cheer from the ramparts as the besieged watched one of the balls make a direct hit on the mess tent, the other two going astray but still creating damage in the heart of the Roundhead camp.

"Twenty yards shorter!" Cleall cried down to the gunners below, as the guns were being reloaded. By now, men were streaming out of the tent, which had its roof ripped to pieces at one end. The Royalist cannons erupted again, first from the bastion and then the outer bailey. This time, all three guns found their targets and cries could be heard from Rooks Hill. The Roundheads were running to their own guns and readying them for fire, when the Castell's guns let roar for a third time. By then, Coke and his officers, who had been eating in the Ship Inn, were riding back into the mayhem of the camp to find many dead and wounded men. They ordered a counter-attack with several rounds of cannon fire on to the Castell but by this time, the defenders had returned to their defensive positions where they could observe the fireballs bombarding the Castel walls with little damage.

The next day, Coke was plotting his revenge and had gathered his captains together in the Fox Tavern to devise a plan. He wanted a quick victory but clearly this was not in his grasp and he would have to be patient. But he had lost a further fifteen men the day before, with another thirty injured. He could not suffer such high casualties and make no progress. He had time on his side, although he was worried that Colonel Bingham could take Dorchester, or some other quick and easy victory, and put his lack of progress in a bad light with the generals, Essex and Cromwell, and others in London would see Bingham's successes and be frustrated by his own exploits. He had already put in place a plan to stop attacks on his own camp and he was proud of its ingenuity. He had rounded up fifty men, women and children from the surrounding areas and marched them passed the Castell walls and into the camp. He then ordered that they were to be dispersed across the camp and staked to the ground: a human shield. Each day he would replace the shield with another fifty and so ensure his men were protected.

He also had some good news. The miller had told him that he believed Sir John was in the Castell, for he was sure he had seen him on the ramparts. This made his potential prize greater: the head of the king's chief of justice would certainly result in praise from London. So patience was required and he and his captains developed a plan to tunnel under the walls, as well as build siege engines. They had a rough plan of the Castell mapped out before them, partly developed from Coke's own knowledge of the fortifications, but also from the miller and a few other locals, sympathetic to the Roundhead course. At the same time as tunnelling, he would launch ad-hoc attacks at night, where a ladder or two would be deployed in a concentrated area of the wall, seeking to catch the defendants napping. If he could get just a few men onto the ramparts, they could protect a route in for the rest. And every day they would fire on the Castell with cannon and musket to wear the defenders down.

While they were discussing different options, a sergeant interrupted them saying there was a man to see Colonel Coke and that he claimed to be a general. In walked a tall man, clearly of some authority, followed by a stout man.

The colonel and his captains stood, and the man was clearly pleased at his reception, but then it was he who bowed his head and said, "John Hopkins, Witchfinder General Hopkins, and my colleague John Sterne at your service."

"Witchfinder General, you are not a military man, then, sir?" Coke asked.

"No. My battle is with the darker forces at work here. Parliament is convinced that where the war may not be going our way, or there is a stalemate, then Satan may be at work and that is why I am here. I have the authority and experience to track down witchcraft of all types and to sentence directly. It is all detailed in this document with Parliament's seal." He handed a scroll to the colonel, who untied it.

"There is certainly a witch by the name of Lady Bankes, who defends this Castell," Coke said but as he read the scroll a spark of an idea was already bringing a smile to his face before he could read the document in full. Coke ordered the sergeant who had brought the witchfinder general in to go and fetch Josh Miller. Moments later, the miller was being ushered into the room and Coke quizzed him.

"I recollect a woman who lived around here who was said to have foresight and healing powers. I think she was from Langton or Worth. Is that right?"

"That would be Agnes, Colonel. She has foresight right enough. I do understand that she was telling of this war coming, many years ago. She talked of a black cloud or something of the sort. Folk ignored her but sure enough she was right. Yes, and healing. She is a midwife and delivered my own sons and daughters and most of Corffe's children, including Lady Bankes'. But she has healing powers beyond that. When my Molly was almost taken from me with the putrid throat, along with many a villager, some years back, she provided a draught that healed her and many others."

"Thank you, Mr Miller. That is very helpful," smiled Coke. Then turning to the witchfinder general, added, "So what do you think — witch or saint?"

"The devil is very devious in the faces he wears. It is difficult for me to say now but certainly it sounds worthy of investigation."

"Well, let's find out. We cannot have a witch in our midst, no doubt making spells supporting that other witch, Lady Bankes, in her godforsaken Castell. Captain Bulldock — go to Worth Matravers in the morning and bring Agnes back with you."

The next day the captain set off with nine other soldiers to fetch her. It was midday before they returned to Corffe. Agnes had built up a sweat walking back along the limestone ridge and then down to Corffe in the late August heat. The captain had just told her that the colonel wanted to talk to her as he needed some advice about some injured men, but still she was anxious and sensed something was not right. She was shown to the Ship Inn where the colonel, the witchfinder general and John Sterne were having lunch. A large ham pie with lettuce and tomatoes was being shared between them on the table.

"Thank you for coming to see us, Agnes," the colonel addressed her in a welcoming manner as she entered the room. "Take a seat."

He pointed with his knife to a chair next to a barrel that served as a table, in the corner. She gingerly did as instructed, wiping her brow.

"I hear that you possess certain healing powers that could help my injured men," the colonel continued. Agnes looked at him and the other two men, in turn, but she said nothing. She sensed all was not well.

"Well, is this true or are you a Royalist?" the colonel demanded. "Will you help my men?"

"I am but a midwife and have delivered many of the babes in the village and I'm licensed to do so," she replied.

"But I hear that you have administered healing when putrid throat plagued the village; a draught made from some plants of yours."

"Yes. I have some knowledge of the healing power of plants and I did help people during that terrible time. It was the least I could do."

It was the witchfinder general who took over the questioning. "And what plants would those be?" he asked.

"Lavender, jasmine, thyme… The scent can help calm people when they have fever," she responded, dismissively.

"Hardly cures for such a sickness, but the miller has told me that you administered sage," he enquired, further.

"Only as a purifier for the air," she replied.

The witchfinder general raised an eyebrow. "But the miller tells me you administered a draught of it to the sick."

"I cannot recall that but if I did, I am sure it would only have been scented water." She detected that this was not about healing the colonels' men but some kind of inquisition and she would have to be careful.

"Where do you find these herbs and plants?" the inquisitor continued.

"I grow some in my patch of land at the back of my cottage. Others, I find in the woods."

The witchfinder general decided to change tack. "Tell me about the foresight you have."

This took Agnes aback, as it was a statement, not a question and she did not know how to respond. He had obviously been speaking to the villagers.

"Tell me, woman. I know you predict the future. How do you do this?" the Witchfinder demanded, raising his voice with authority.

"Oh," she mumbled a response. "They are no more than silly dreams, sir."

"That predicted this war?"

"I just saw dark clouds, sir. I did not predict a war," she quickly responded but then wished she had not, as the response seem to please the inquisitor.

"Colonel, I suggest you detain Agnes while I make further investigations. She will need to be searched by ladyfolk while she is detained. I will instruct them on what to look for."

Agnes was manacled and locked up in the church with the horses, while Hopkins and Sterne rode up to Worth Matravers, accompanied by five of Bingham's men. They soon found her cottage and made their way inside. They searched the downstairs and the upstairs and finally the garden, to the rear. As they prepared to leave, Daniel Spear confronted them and asked their business. He was dismayed when Hopkins told him that he was the witchfinder general and had evidence that Ages was, indeed, practising witchcraft.

"Ridiculous,' he said. "She is a harmless woman who has helped and healed many locals, as well as delivered all babies hereabouts. Besides, she makes a wonderful gin."

"The devil's brew and indeed she may die for it, my son, for you mistake the disguises of Satan. He may portray his followers as pure midwives, and what better trade to inflict evil from the very moment they are born. My son, we have evidence that cannot be doubted right here," Hopkins declared, lifting up his satchel. "We will try her tomorrow and she will burn if found guilty."

Daniel was speechless as the two men mounted their horses and rode off, back to Corffe.

The next day Daniel Spear and many others from the surrounding villages, as well as Corffe inhabitants who had been taking refuge with them, including William Harvey, travelled into the village to support Agnes.

When ten men escorted the accused from the church, back to the Ship Inn, she looked frightened and confused, and there were cries of "Let her go!" and "She is innocent!" from the crowd along the way. She was taken inside but the door was then bolted shut, barring anybody else from entering. Thirty armed guards were positioned in front of the inn and more than twice that number stationed in the market square to quell any trouble, should it arise.

Inside the inn was just the colonel, the witchfinder general and his aid, all seated at one end of the room on a pew from the church, with a table positioned in front of them to create some semblance of a courtroom. There were also four soldiers; two by the door and two either side of Agnes. This time she was not offered a seat. It was the witchfinder general, occupying the middle seat, who was clearly in charge of proceedings.

"Agnes Potter — I am the Witchfinder General appointed by Parliament to hunt out and eradicate witchcraft in this country. I have the authority to try and convict suspects without jury. My duty is to get to the truth quickly. We know that Rupert of the Rhine is indeed a dark prince and follower of Satan and has the power to work with demonic and supernatural forces that have been, perhaps, lying dormant within our country. Mr Sterne, here, and I have been able to uncover such sorcery and treachery on numerous occasions. We are trained in the law but now also experienced in how the black arts are used and folklore. We started this campaign in Norfolk and Cambridge and as we have eradicated the evil, the curses have been lifted, and the Parliamentary forces have prevailed. We are now skilled at identifying witches and sorcerers, and I am sure you are aware that this is a felony punishable by death."

Agnes gave out a small squeal.

"I will present you with the evidence that we have against you, Agnes Potter, and it is already compelling. I urge you to confess so that your suffering will be quick. Firstly, you have been stripped and searched by the miller's wife and this investigation found three teats on your body. This is evidence of devil's marks and it is widely known that witches have this third teat to feed blood to demons. What do you say to that, Agnes?"

"What she found is no more than a skin blemish and most women in Corffe would have them. Even Lady Bankes, sir."

This last point did not help Agnes's cause, and was greeted by a raised eyebrow from the Witchfinder.

"We expected you to deny it: all witches do. Nor are we surprised that Lady Bankes also has such a teat. Let us move on to more evidence that we unearthed in your cottage yesterday."

There was some activity in the market square of which Lady Bankes and Captain Cleall had clear visibility from the second tower.

"What do you think they're up to?" said Lady Bankes.

"It looks as though they're building some kind of maypole but clearly, as it's September, it's the wrong time of year for that. Maybe it is a Puritan ritual that we are not familiar with in these parts," the captain replied.

"Maybe they are going to stake more villagers to a pole to shield their attacks. Coke is a heartless brute. Those poor people who have been staked in their camp over the last few weeks in the summer heat... He would resort to anything." Mary's face showed her anger.

It was now mid-morning and the couple could see the increasing frenzy of activity in the square. A pole had indeed been erected and was now supported by stanchions from all sides. As the couple watched, a small platform was positioned at the bottom of the pole and then its purpose became self-evident as straw and timber were bundled around the platform. This was no maypole, nor another post to create a human shield, but a stake of execution. Some chairs were put in place, presumably for the dignitaries, as if there were anything dignified about what the couple feared was going to happen. They could make out Colonel Coke by his distinctive charcoal officer's jacket that had become so familiar to the couple, with its red ribbons denoting his rank on the arms. He took his seat with two others, not known to the onlookers. A commotion followed as some soldiers seemed to be dragging some poor woman into the market square, screaming and screaming to try and avoid her fate. But the soldier's power was too strong. She was biting and fighting like a trapped animal until one of the soldiers launched a punch, which instantly knocked her out. Her unconscious body was carried up to the scaffold and tied to the pole and it was when the soldiers stepped back to admire their work in stringing up their captive that Captain Cleall realised who it was.

"It's Agnes, my Lady."

"Oh, the poor thing... This cannot be happening. Is there nothing we can do?"

One of the dignitaries rose and said a few words against a backdrop of shouting from the local villagers at the periphery of the market square, which was ringed and largely occupied by soldiers. A torch was set to the straw, and flames instantly lapped up around the stage. Agnes regained consciousness and her screams permeated through the walls of the square and Castell. Mary buried her head into Captain Cleall's shoulder, and he turned his head away from the scene of horror.

As the summer months drifted, the besieged endured their locked-down life in the Castell. While there was sufficient food for several months, with careful rationing, and a plentiful supply of water from the wells, it was the mental and emotional strain of being stuck in a single place that was the challenge. Furthermore, at any point in time, there was the fear of being shot at or blasted by a cannon as a couple of times each day the Roundheads would send several rounds of fire at the parapets or into the outer bailey, at least hoping to kill a sheep or frighten the hens to stop them laying. To maintain the pressure on the inmates, musketeers were positioned around the Castell, hoping to take a shot at anybody who happened to be in view. Joseph Cobb had never recovered from the day of the first attack and walked around the Castell grounds in a daze, muttering to himself. Every cannon or musket shot sent him into a craze before he curled up on the floor, hands wrapped around his head. Mary had suggested that he should be released, but Captain Cleall hoped he would recover and was reluctant to give the enemy any intelligence into the situation inside the Castell walls, for he would inevitably be interrogated.

It was Camille who came to his rescue. She took Joseph aside and listened to his self-doubts and absolute fear. She realised he needed a purpose to keep him occupied. She suggested that he became the master baker for the Castell, for he had already provided the flour and grain. She agreed to also teach him how the French made bread. He took up the offer with some enthusiasm and while his new role did not stop his tremors and nightmares, it certainly helped him to cope with them and made him a better person.

At night and at random times, small groups of soldiers would attempt to climb the walls, using ladders, in vain attempts to bridge the defences. In response, Captain Cleall had to ensure that the guards were

311

vigilant, which meant a strict rota of watches. Even Lady Bankes took her share of the watch, recognising that staring into darkness in the early hours of the morning, expecting an attack at any time, was draining. If she took her turn, nobody could complain but in truth she found the days turning into weeks and months hard. She was used to a world which she could enjoy and wherein she could interact, writing to and receiving letters from her friends and family, hosting and enjoying entertainment, taking rides in the Dorsetshire countryside and enjoying its natural, seasonal cycle as well as the banter of her tenants. All of this had been taken away from her and she was left with a few servants and some mercenaries to defend her home and make a stand for the king. On some days it would seem that even the birds appeared to have deserted them in the Castell, which was being sucked dry of life. Povington was driving everybody mad as he was in a permanent state of edginess and became very picky, causing some very heated arguments with the cook, Camille and the other servants. He had aged noticeably since the siege began. Lady Bankes had relieved him of his duties for a few days but that only made things worse.

Lady Bankes knew that it was her principles that held the Castell defiant, for many of the defendants were not steadfast Royalists, and she even counted Sir John amongst them, for as his health declined his heart for the fight waned and he now spent much of each day in bed. She knew Captain Cleall was loyal to her but was contemptuous in his regard to the king. Captain Lawrence was ardently behind the cause, but even many of his men were hired hands and would easily switch sides for an extra shilling.

Captain Cleall's military training helped him through the summer months. He preoccupied himself with ensuring everything was prepared for all eventualities, thinking of the worst thing that could happen and then creating a plan to deal with it. This resulted in him forming taskforces of men to address these possibilities, which ranged from tunnelling under the walls, poisoning of the water supply, fireballs being propelled into the Castell and so on. These task forces kept many of the men occupied, especially as the solution typically resulted in an action plan that the captain would insist was drilled a couple of times per week, or required a significant amount of work, such as barrelling water from the wells.

The tunnelling was the first plan that needed to be enacted and it had been Captain Lawrence whose ingenuity had devised the solution to this threat. The idea was to re-purpose one of the more accurate culverin cannons, place it on the gantry that had been used to defend the Castell from the first attack, and angle it at such a degree that it could fire down onto the ground in front of wherever the tunnelling was taking place. The hope and expectation were that as the force of the charge blasted the ground, it would result in the collapse of the tunnel. It required careful planning and estimating the progress of the tunnel to fire at the right time and place. The first tunnel collapsed after three shots, and when a second one was started, it only took two shots to see the demise of that one. And that was the end of tunnelling by the Roundheads.

September rolled into October as the villages around Corffe brought in the harvest. There was no prospect of a harvest festival at the Castell this year for the villagers but worse still was that much of their produce had been confiscated by the Roundheads to feed the troops and horses. The trees in the surrounding woods transformed into a montage of autumnal colour and could be observed from the Castell but it felt like that was in a far-off land. Within the bubble of the Castell, time was trapped and the natural seasonal rhythm could barely be sensed. Tempers were fraught and despair reigned as people felt imprisoned; they were on a constant state of alert and yearned for family and loved ones. The melancholy fermented further as the nights drew in and the wind shifted to bring cold air from the north, on many days blasting the exposed Castell.

Boredom and anxiety were the day-to-day enemies as much as the four hundred Roundheads camped outside the Castell. And so Cleall had earlier devised a sophisticated rota of duties around the Castell, which involved everybody moving to a different post and activity four times a day. There were eleven towers to be manned around the perimeter, and duties that included attending the livestock, fetching water, logging, preparing food in the kitchen, cleaning the rooms and preparing fires in the main residences, washing clothes, cleaning and preparing cannons, muskets and ammunition. There were some high- risk tasks, such as manning the towers on the western side, because of the musketeers' sniping. Fortunately, the accuracy of muskets at a distance was poor but as a safeguard, Cleall devised the use of mirrors to enable the guards to see over the wall without showing their heads. The rota involved training for many people in different skills, which was part of the plan to keep them occupied, but it was also designed so that each and every one was interacting with different people as the day took them from post to post. There was a lot of resistance to the rota at first, as people objected to doing certain tasks but with Lady Bankes joining in within a few days, everybody could see the benefit. People started to build better relationships and the days passed by more swiftly. Within a few weeks, Lady Bankes knew not only the names of every single inmate, but much of their background. Joseph Cobb was blending English and French recipes for bread, and experimenting with different types, but the musket shots and cannon fire continued to have their toll on his mental health. He was often found talking to himself or in a state of uncontrollable tremors. One October night, a lobby of musket fire was heard from the parapets, near the Castell gate. The guards found a rope had been tethered to the wall, and in the morning a body was seen at the bottom. It was Joseph Cobb. He had tried to escape, but the Roundheads had shot him down before he had reached the ground, and now left his body to decay.

Coke was becoming ever more desperate for a breakthrough and ordered two cannons to be positioned just west of the Castell gate, so they could try to blast through the entrance. The gate was made of one-foot-deep oak wood, braced with heavy iron struts, and behind it was the portcullis. It was heavily fortified with the two towers either side. Cleall watched the Roundheads as they prepared the assault. He had the culverins in each tower, loaded and ready to respond, and felt almost sorry for the Roundhead gunners, sitting ducks at such close range with no defence. Before the first Roundhead gun could be fired, Cleall's musketeers started to take shots at the artillerymen, and it was not long before they found their targets; first one and then a second gunner being killed.

The tower shook as the first cannon came to life and blasted its ball just to the left of the door, but with little damage. Cleall ordered the culverins to respond, and they roared in reply. The culverins were not powerful cannons but very accurate, and one found its mark, hitting the Roundhead cannon just as it was about to fire. It struck the barrel, digging it into the ground as its fuse ignited, forcing the weapon to recoil rapidly backwards, running over two of its shell-shocked gunners, and firing wildly into the sky, the ball landing in the outer bailey, sending the chickens into a frenzy. Coke had seen enough. Another humiliation and he ordered the cannons back to Rooks Hill.

The ever-shortening days of November passed by as Sir John's health deteriorated. He was now permanently bedridden. Lady Bankes spent much of the time by his side, holding his hand as he dipped in and out of consciousness. Some days, he did seem to rally but with each recovery he would sink further and closer to the inevitable end. He was suffering but rarely complained and Lady Bankes admired his strength. On one of the days when he did rally, he requested to see Captain Cleall. The captain entered his room. He had not seen him for three weeks or more. Time itself was hard to track within the confines of the Castell, but he was shocked at how much Sir John had deteriorated. It was difficult to relate to the skeletal body laid before him, lost in his nightshift, his drawn and gaunt face devoid of the vivacious character he had come to know over the last ten years. Sir John had stirred at the opening of the door but still looked confused as the captain quietly entered.

"Ah, is that you, Captain Cleall?" he managed to say. The captain took his hand and replied affirmatively, comforting him with talk about the resilience of the Castell for the Royalist cause and the strength of Lady Bankes.

"Ah yes, my Mary. She has been wonderful to me throughout my life. Whenever I awake, she appears to be there. I could not have loved a better woman. But listen, Captain. I know she also has feelings for you and I appreciate the support and protection you provided her with when I was with the king. I just wanted to say I will not be long in this world and I would not want any thought of me stopping you from making an advance to her if you felt inclined to do so. Indeed, I would welcome it, as I know you will look after her and be strong for her. She takes so much on her shoulders and I fear for what will happen when I am gone. This country is in such a mess..." He sighed and then continued. "My senses are that the Parliamentary cause will prevail. There will be little clemency for Royalists. I hope that will not extend to wives of Royalists, but she has most probably done more for the king's cause than most men."

The captain smiled to his friend, with a knot in his stomach, and declared an oath to protect Lady Bankes, after which Sir John's strength failed him and he left consciousness again. A week later, he finally passed away and was buried in the inner bailey, following a service conducted by Captain Lawrence, whose main credentials were that his father had been a church minister, while Captain Cleall comforted Mary.

Following Sir John's death, Captain Cleall and Captain Lawrence reviewed the siege situation with Lady Bankes. They recommended a revised level of rationing, which amounted to a slice of bread, a slice of cheese and a vegetable or apple each day. Every other day, this would be supplemented with either an egg or some meat, courtesy of the three remaining pigs. The cook was doing her best, but spices had run out months ago, and she had stripped the Castell bare of parsley, mint and even nettles to flavour he dishes. There were just a few sacks of flour and salt remaining. Ale was rationed to a mug a day but water would be freely available. They calculated this ration would enable them to last for four more months. Captain Cleall then proposed that they asked the Roundheads to let them free some of the incarcerated; namely Povington and Camille, but also half a dozen men who were close to breaking point or had been injured. He felt that the Roundheads would allow this, viewing it as a small victory, and this would extend the rations for a further few weeks. Amongst the released men, one would be charged with going in search of help because, ultimately, that was what they needed. Lady Bankes listen to the plan and agreed to it, as long as they could have some rations for a Christmas festival. She was adamant that there would be some form of normality within the locked-down Castell.

She would miss Camille and even Povington, but this was not their war. Thus, the two captains set about putting the plan into action.

Povington was in tears when he listened to Lady Bankes suggesting he should leave the Castell but he knew it was the right thing for him to do. He was close to breaking point and was a burden, so he agreed to leave. Camille, however, refused outright. She would stay with her mistress to the end, or at least until her husband returned. For all she knew he was dead; in which case, there was nothing outside the Castell walls for her. Six men were also selected to leave: three locals who were desperate to be reunited with their families and three who were from Captain Lawrence's troop, two of whom were genuinely injured and a third whom they dressed as though he were injured. He was Sergeant Joseph Cox and Captain Lawrence confirmed to Cleall that he was a resourceful man who could be trusted. He would be the one to go for help, wherever it could be found, for nobody in the Castell had any idea of the events of the war.

Colonel Coke was intrigued by the request to release seven men. It was Cleall who had made the request under a flag of truce from the Castell gatehouse tower. Perhaps this was the first crack in the Royalist defence and if so, he should seize on it. Coke had been frustrated by the failed tunnelling exploit, and his men had also failed to construct an effective siege engine. He had news that Bingham's men had taken nearby Lulworth Castell. In truth, he knew that this was little more than a hunting lodge, but Parliamentary headquarters in London would not know that. They would just see one Castell in Dorsetshire being garrisoned by Parliamentary troops and advancing the Parliamentary line, while no progress was being made at Corffe. Lulworth Castell had given him a new source of lead for musket fire, as he had sent troops to strip the roof, but Bingham could even claim that he was provisioning Coke's force. At least, the release of seven men would be some good news to report to London. So he agreed to the request and the release would take place the next day at noon. However, time had already run out for Coke. That evening, Colonel Bingham arrived with two hundred men and orders from London. Bingham had been charged by Cromwell himself to conquer Corffe and relieve Coke from his duty. Coke was to take two hundred of his own men and go north to Bristol. Coke was livid. He had been stuck in this backwater in Dorsetshire and just as the cracks were starting to show, he was being relieved of his command.

Chapter XVII
The Homecoming

Lieutenant Tom Harvey was amongst Bingham's troops, returning to his home village of Corffe. He had left when not much more than a boy and returned not only as a man but an officer. The promised opportunity of enrolment with the Parliamentary forces had paid dividends but as he entered the market square of his beloved home village, he wondered at what cost. He was shocked by the devastation of the village. The church roof had been ransacked, as had many of the houses, with broken windows and roofs stripped of thatch. There were no villagers to be seen; just soldiers who showed little respect for the place. The market square was full of squalor and the cobbles had been stained by a big fire at some stage.

The Castell itself looked intact but its walls were pitted with cannon ball shots, and large sections of the parapets had been destroyed and replaced by wooden or makeshift stone infills. It was shut down with no signs of life. It was unreal. This was his home and a place he knew like the back of his hand. It had always been buzzing with life but it seemed totally foreign to him now. He dismounted and wandered through the village to take stock. His dismay was compounded when he entered the church and saw the devastation that Colonel Coke and his men had caused. He then found the women of the village locked away in a makeshift kitchen in the cottage nearest the camp, producing food for Coke's men.

"Tom! Thank God! You have returned!" cried his step-sister Beth, who looked tired and forlorn. His step-mother, Elisabeth, also rushed over, and a guard tried to halt her passage but Tom ordered him back.

"We were so worried that you had been killed."

"Are you kept here by Coke?" he asked, as he hugged Beth, looking around to see other faces he knew.

"Oh Tom, it is so good to see you. We have been trapped here since the siege began and have not been able to see your father or anybody," Elisabeth said, as she joined in the hug.

"I am so sorry. This is terrible. So you have no news of Camille or father?"

"Nothing, but tell us your news..." Beth responded.

"I will, in good time. Let me see what I can do to get you out of here and make it better for you all."

He then left, leaving behind some cheer and hope amongst the women.

Tom reported the destruction and the treatment of the village women to Colonel Bingham. It was common practice that locals would be requested to help the Parliamentary cause, and often pressure was put on them to do so, but it was for a short period of time and in a civil way, even resulting in payment. He had never experienced locals being imprisoned and made to work like slaves. He proposed that all the women be allowed to return to their folk at night and then asked to return on a rota basis to cook the meals, and that some compensation should be paid for their past and continuing work. Bingham was shocked, as well, and agreed immediately to the proposal to release them overnight and would carefully consider the question of compensation and payment. He followed Tom over and personally addressed the women, apologising for their treatment and advising them of their new arrangements. They were all overjoyed, with tears and cries of relief.

Tom requested leave to seek out his wife and father, and to escort Elisabeth and Beth home. But they found that their home had been ransacked, with no sign of anybody. They learnt from one of Coke's men that nearly all the villagers had left, apart from the miller and a few others. Tom found Josh Miller, who told him that his father was staying with his step-brother in Worth, so he found a horse that would carry both women, while he jumped on his own and they headed out of the village. It was dark by the time they arrived. Dismounting before his horse had come to a standstill, asking the women to wait, he rushed to his step-brother's door, knocked but simultaneously opened the door to find his step-brother and wife, and father all seated around a table, eating their evening meal in front of a raging fire.

"Tom!" they all shouted in unison, lighting up the room with the smiles on their face.

Daniel Spear, his step-brother, was the first to embrace him followed by Jane, Daniel's wife, and then finally his father; an embrace which was strong and warm, the like of which he had not known from his father before.

"I have another surprise. Come!" Tom led them outside, and there were more shouts of joy as they found Elizabeth and Beth. William Harvey rushed to them, and helped the two women dismount, embracing them both.

They all returned inside and divided up some of the helpings, pouring some mugs of ale for the new arrivals. Daniel was eager to hear all about Tom's exploits, and what the braiding on his jacket meant.

"I'm a Lieutenant," he said proudly, looking at his father. His father nodded and raised his mug but did not say anything. Tom had not seen them since he had left after being conscripted in Poole over two years ago and with Daniel badgering him, he had no option but to talk through everything that had happened to him since; his training, the Battle of Edge Hill and the loss of Francis, but he did not mention Captain Cleall's role. He told them about several skirmishes with Prince Rupert's men on the road back towards London, before being stationed in Salisbury for winter training and then marching across Wiltshire. He described the defeat and loss of so many comrades after the siege of Devizes, and then his time, over the last six months, fighting in Dorsetshire under the command of Colonel Bingham.

They all knew Bingham as the powerful and ambitious magistrate and alderman of Poole, and the man who had nearly hanged Francis Trew, and so were very surprised that Tom spoke of him which such respect. He said that he had been under the command of many officers, and Bingham was one of the best. He had mellowed with the war and taken his victories with dignity and respect for the defeated. He tried to heal the wounds and rebuild communities, driven by his Puritan values. This was in total contrast to Prince Rupert, who plundered and would kill even the sick and injured. Indeed, it was Bingham who had taken him under his wing after the victory at Blandford and he had made him a lieutenant. He had learnt a lot about the Puritan ways, as Bingham talked about recognising the values of hard work for the glory of God but, in truth, he had seen little glory in the last two years, for the horrors of war could not be exaggerated. Francis was just one of many friends and comrades he had buried during that time and there were others who had died without even the dignity of a burial. But he was so pleased to be here with family and was desperate to see Camille. He asked for news of her and what had happened to Corffe. It was his father who spoke, having listened to his son so far with barely a word.

"Son — I am sure from your stories and from what you have not told us that you have seen horrors and felt pain no man should endure. I was angry and upset when you left to go, because I was so scared to lose you and I have prayed for your safe return many times each and every day since. I can see now that from the experiences that you have endured that you are grown into a man, indeed an officer. I'm sure that you fought your battles with courage and bravery, as well as honour and respect in the hope of the better future you sought. Alas, very little of that has been shown here in Corffe. And I have prayed as vehemently for an end to this madness as I have done for your safe return. We have had our own share of horrors."

"Tell me more, father," asked Tom.

His father took another log to put on the fire and topped up the mugs with ale before he continued.

"Where do we begin? I guess, with Lady Bankes. One can only admire her strength of character as she fortified the Castell and proclaimed it for the king. She is adamant that he has a divine right to rule, and while her husband provided counsel to the monarch, she was left to defend her home. She called for volunteers to help her defend the Castell from her estate and throughout Dorsetshire. I could not accept her request. I felt like I was betraying her, and the Castell itself, but I had to think of Elizabeth and the family. I was also not convinced of the righteousness of her cause. I had heard a lot about the king's indifferent attitude to his subjects, and even worse stories about Prince Rupert. But frankly, even then, I was not convinced by the Parliamentary view of the situation, either. Lots of people in London have idealist views above their station, which just upset the establishment and are certainly not worth fighting for in my opinion. So I was left in the middle, wanting this all to go away so we could focus on growing crops and managing the estate. And I am no fighting man. I know nearly all there is to know about estates and managing them, but nothing about guns and battles. I had many sleepless nights — didn't I, Joanna — before I told Lady Bankes I could not defend the Castell."

"You certainly did, William," Joanna confirmed.

"Captain Cleall is with Lady Bankes, and he organised the defences and trained the recruits who did rise to her call, and she did pay them. Yes, the Parfitt Brothers, Alfred Smith, many good men are in the Castell defending it with her. As is your good wife. I spoke to her before the siege started and she was adamant that with you away, her loyalty must be with her mistress. I think she is as stubborn as Lady Bankes: there was no way of persuading her otherwise. God be my witness, I tried."

"I am sure you did, father. I understand," said Tom.

"But then the Roundheads came. They are led by Harry Coke — Colonel Coke, son of Sir John Coke. He has a lot of history with Corffe, and alas it is not good. He hates the village and has returned after so long to seek revenge. I last saw him at his father's funeral when he was a spoilt drunk with a chip on his shoulder, not knowing how to live up to his father's reputation. I have heard since that he went to London and relished in all the sins of that city; whoring, drinking and gambling. But then he converted to Puritanism and led a Puritan militia that would punish people for the very sins he had indulged in before. A poacher-turned gamekeeper, if ever there was one. And Corffe was in his sights when he arrived with five hundred men in June. He cleared the villagers out of their houses and recklessly devastated the Church. How can that be to the glory of God, my son?"

"I have seen it, father. I was almost sick with disgust."

"He has confiscated much of the harvest and produce of all the people around and so folk have barely anything to live on. He has recklessly cut down acres of woodland to provide firewood and building material. He has taken stone from the quarry and the catches from the fishermen of Swanage, all without recompense. Of course, he has been bombarding the Castell but from what we can gather, with little success. He lost a hundred men on his first attempt and then he started digging tunnels, conscripting some of the quarrymen from Worth, many of whom have been killed; old David Beasant, his son and Joshua Stone amongst them. He used villagers as human shields to stop Lady Bankes bombarding his positions."

"What do you mean?" Tom asked.

"We have all had turns being staked to the ground amongst his men, so that the Castell defenders would not fire their cannons on his troops," his father replied.

"That is savage."

"Yes — a whole day at a time with no food or water. Even the children. But the worst was just before Christmas. when he brought in a witchfinder from the east, and he made some trumped-up charge against Agnes, and found her guilty of witchcraft. They burned her in the market square."

Tom was speechless for a while. His father was right. Coke was even more barbaric and brutal than Prince Rupert, but Tom and Coke were fighting on the same side.

"I am truly shocked, Father. This was not what I had signed up for and I am truly sorry that such horror should be brought on my family, friends and home. The only saving grace is that Colonel Bingham has relieved Coke of his command, and I know that such atrocities will not happen any more. That is not to say there will not be further loss of life but I will do everything in my power to bring a peaceful and swift resolution to this siege, and then Corffe can rebuild and get back to some normality. I must get Camille out of the Castell, and the village must be given back to its residents. Tomorrow, I understand, some people in the Castell will be let out. I hope that will include Camille and that will be the start of the end."

But the next day, as the outer gate was opened, Tom's heart sank to see that Camille was not amongst those being let out as they scurried under the partially raised portcullis. Four were wearing dressings and were clearly injured, supported by the other three as they made their way to Tom and Captain Sydenham awaiting them on horseback. A dozen armed Roundheads gathered them up and they were about to depart, when Tom spotted Captain Cleall on one of the towers above the gateway.

"Captain!" Tom called. "Captain Cleall!" and he urged his horse a few steps closer to the gate. The captain looked down and recognised Tom.

"Do not shoot!" he ordered his troops manning the rampart. "Tom Harvey — why, is that you?"

"It is. Lieutenant Harvey now. How is Camille?"

"She is well. I would not have dreamt to be defending this Castell against you, Tom."

"It is not the first time we have faced each other, Captain. I was at Edgehill. I saw you charge a cannon through our ranks."

"Yes, I was there with John Bankes. I swore an oath to protect him."

"And in doing so, your cannon killed Francis Trew!" Tom shouted.

There was a silence for a few moments.

"That day I vowed to kill you the next time I set eyes on you," Tom continued. "But I have now seen enough bloodshed on all sides. I understand war and we are all casualties of it, whether we live or die, whether we are the victors or the defeated, and I have been both. We need to bring this siege to an end."

"You speak wisely, Tom, despite being still young in your years. You have grown up and I can understand why you have been made an officer. But there are atrocities that have occurred here in Corffe that cannot be justified. Your comrades burnt Agnes, Tom. What harm had she done to anybody? They have ransacked the village and even the church, yet purport to be doing God's will."

"You are right. I have heard of the atrocities that have occurred under the command of Colonel Coke. He is no longer in charge and will be leaving shortly. Colonel Bingham has taken command. Can you not free Camille? She is of no purpose to you."

"Yesterday, I was trying to persuade her to leave but she wanted to stay with Lady Bankes. Today, now you are here, I cannot let her go. She does have a purpose now." Cleall was thinking that a wife of an officer of the enemy, inside the Castell, would temper their aggression.

"I thought you might say that. Can I speak with Camille, then?"

"I am sure that would be possible. I will arrange for her to come down to the gate at sunrise tomorrow. Good luck, Tom. Lieutenant Harvey."

"Thank you, Captain," Tom replied.

"Tom — one more thing. Coke's men killed Joseph Cobb as he tried to escape from the Castell. Coke has refused to let the body be collected. I am sorry, Tom."

"Where is it?" Tom asked.

"Just beyond the second tower. I can guarantee your safe passage if you want to recover it."

Tom reined his horse around in the direction of the second tower and sure enough, there was a body at the bottom of the wall. As he got closer, he realised it had already decomposed into a skeleton. How could Coke have allowed this to happen? Poor Joseph.

He rode back to camp and requested permission from Colonel Bingham to recover the body; a wish that was granted. Riding back, he spotted Coke coming out of a tent, readying himself to depart.

"How could you leave a body decaying at the foot of the Castell? Have you no dignity, sir? And what you have done to the church is nothing short of sacrilege; not to mention how you have treated the women of this village. The quicker you get out of my shire, sir, the better. But Colonel Bingham and I will be reporting back to Cromwell and Essex what has gone on down here. I will ensure that every detail is documented. In my opinion, you have no right to command under Cromwell's flag, for you stand for everything we fight against. Good day, sir."

He reined his horse around before Coke could respond, for he was struggling to stop himself from dismounting and hitting the colonel. The only thing that stopped him was the need to keep a clear head to develop a plan that could rescue Camille. And now Joseph Cobb needed him. With three other men, he carried his friend into a musket box, which acted as a makeshift coffin, and placed it on a cart. He then followed the cart to the churchyard, and sent for Joseph's uncle, Josh Miller, and they buried the body.

"He looked up to you, Tom, and resented his decision not to follow you and Francis when you signed up. He decided to help defend the

Castell with Lady Bankes as some kind of recompense. But as we all know, he was not a strong boy. I fear for how he stood up to the bombarding of the Castell and then to be shot down and left to rot. What Christian person would let that happen? My poor boy..."

There was nothing Tom could say to Josh Miller. They both stood over the grave for some time. Another friend lost to this conflict: Francis, Jerome and now Joseph. He had to stop this. He had to get his other friends and Camille out of the Castell without any more loss of life. But how?

On returning to the camp, Tom and Captain Sydenham interrogated each of the released men, one by one. They wanted to find out what conditions were like in the Castell, their state of mind, and why they had been released. Gradually, they gathered a picture of a community of about seventy people under strict rations but following well-ordered routines and activities to conquer the oppression of the siege. Povington provided welcome news of Camille's good spirits, and Tom was counting down the time before he would see her. When they interrogated the man called Joseph Cox, there was something that did not seem right to Tom. Apparently, he had been injured from a cannon blast, but said that was a couple of months ago and he was nearly recovered. So why release him? The other two men who were injured clearly could not fight, but he was also in good spirits, unlike Povington or the rest of the men who had been released, who were desperate to see loved ones. But Joseph Cox appeared to have no reason to leave the Castell other than the injury. When Tom and Captain Sydenham reported back to the colonels, Tom raised his suspicions. It was agreed that the others could be released, but Cox would remain.

The next morning, the cocks crowed across Corffe to announce daybreak and time for Tom to get up. He had been lying awake for a couple of hours in anticipation of seeing Camille but also vexed by his predicament. How could he lead an assault on the Castell with his wife inside, as well as many of his friends? He would have to devise a plan to end the siege peacefully or to get the Castell to surrender, but how? Both sides were entrenched in their views.

He put aside the quandary as he got up and set off to the Castell. The morning sky reflected his mood, a confusion of pinks and purples in the east but dark clouds in the west and all combinations in between. He walked towards the gate house with no weapons and waving the white flag of peace. A stone's throw from the gate, he stopped and announced, to the guards above, his desire to see Camille. A short while later, there she was, as beautiful as ever, in a crimson dress with brown shawl. Her face lit up with a beaming smile when she saw her husband.

"Salut, mon chéri!" she cried. The couple began conversing in French, which allowed them some intimacy despite the distance and audience. Tom recapped his battles and the places he had seen, the friends he had made and lost, and how he had been made a lieutenant. Camille told him of the confinement in the Castell, how Povington had driven her mad but that Lady Bankes and Captain Cleall were in good spirits. She had been briefed by Captain Cleall not to say anything about Sir John Bankes, rations or the strength of force in the Castell.

"I need to get you out of there, my darling," Tom said. Camille sighed. "But not yet," he added, which disappointed her. "As soon as I have a plan, which I promise will be soon, my love."

Tom found Colonel Bingham tucking into a healthy breakfast as he returned to the camp.

"How is your wife? What did you find out, Lieutenant?" he asked, barely looking up from his pewter plate.

"She is well, thank you, Colonel, but I did not find out anything we do not already know."

"Just because your wife is inside does not mean we do not attack. After breakfast, I will be summoning the officers to devise a plan to do exactly that. I suggest you persuade her to plead with Lady Bankes to let her out as soon as possible."

Tom nodded, excused himself and walked back to the market square.

There must be a way to end this quickly and without loss of life, but how? Asking Camille to plead to leave the Castell was one option but the military men inside would not agree to that. Lady Bankes would want to keep her, as well, as she is most probably her only female company. Once again, Tom went through all the scenarios. The Royalists are starved out which could take many months and will result in hardship and risk to

328

Camille. The Roundheads breach the walls by force, which was unlikely, apparently; would cost a lot of lives and also put Camille's life at risk. Tunnelling had not worked but could be tried gain in a month or two: it was not possible with the winter rain. He had to get himself or some other sympathetic man inside to open the gates. Yes — that was it, but how?

Tom took another lap of the square, looking up at the Castell and he further pondered this cause of action. How to get sympathisers inside? Then it occurred to him. Camille was on the inside and perhaps she could help. Could he develop a plan that involved her and perhaps somebody else to assist them to get inside? Perhaps she could get a rope over the parapet, or something? That would put her at risk but she was at risk already. He did not like it but decided to develop it further after the meeting with Bingham and his fellow officers.

Between them, the officers explored all options and out of frustration concluded that a new offensive on the Castell was the best of a bad bunch. Tom pleaded for some time to develop an alternative plan, saying he believed he could persuade his wife to help them from the inside. Bingham gave him two weeks but told the officers to prepare and plan for an attack in the meantime.

The next day dragged for Tom. He realised he needed to speak to Camille to further develop a plan for any options he came up with, despite his knowledge of the Castell, always floundered on his lack of knowledge on the current situation behind the walls. The following day, he rose with some feelings of hope but that was dashed with his second distanced conversation with Camille. She used a nod and a cupped hand to her ear to indicate that somebody was listening. Tom guessed it was Captain Cleall, who spoke a good level of French. He could sense Camille's frustration, which matched his own. They agreed to talk again the next day.

Tom returned to the camp and went to see the captive, Cox. He had released the others but something about Cox had persuaded him to retain him a little longer. Could he learn anything more from a further interrogation? He found the prisoner still asleep in one of the tents, chained to the pole and guarded by two men. He decided to play a more conciliatory approach. Perhaps food and indeed ale would free the man's tongue. He woke him up and presented him with a slice of bread and a mug of ale. Cox looked at him suspiciously but within a few moments could not resist the offerings and was wolfing them down. Tom pulled up two stools for both of them and told him that he had just seen his wife, Camille, in the Castell which itself seemed to build a bridge. It appeared that Cox had liked Camille.

"Your wife is a fine lady, Lieutenant. She has charm that would bring a smile on to any man's face, and she nursed myself, Jack and Harrold. You ask them. They would say nothing but good words about Camille."

Tom had separated all the prisoners, so Cox was unaware that he had released the others.

"I am indeed very lucky to have married her. I would dearly love to see this siege end to be reunited with her," Tom said as he topped up Cox's mug and poured one for himself, pretending to drink more than he consumed. Cox's mug was topped up again and again and each time his tongue appeared to loosen. Before long, the two of them were chatting freely as if the war had ended and they were two mates in the tavern, after a hard day's toil in the field. Cox was downing three mugs to every one of Tom's, but it was not long before even Tom could detect the impact of the drink on his head. He invited the two guards to join them and the atmosphere became even more jovial. Tom then chose his moment and patted Cox on the shoulder.

"So how is that injury of yours, my friend?" he asked.

Cox laughed. It was almost a roar. "There is nothing wrong with me, my friend. But I fooled you, didn't I? It was just a ruse to get me out of the Castell so I could find and bring back reinforcements."

He laughed again, held up his mug in some kind of defiance, swigged another draft and then collapsed off his stool and onto the floor, with an almighty clamour as stool, mugs and ale went flying. Tom left him with the guards. He needed to get his mind into shape but he could already sense the kernel of a plan planted in his mind.

Back inside the Castell, Captain Cleall was hoping for Cox to return with reinforcements, for rations were now running low. He had just reduced everybody's daily allowance, which had resulted in a lot of grumbling by all, but it was necessary to stretch out the siege. They had been eating the chickens, which meant the egg supply was dwindling, and at most they had two months' supply of flour. He was running out of ideas, and while Cox's successful return was unlikely, each day he was storing more and more hope in it. But the reality was that Cleall had no idea if there were even any Royalists anywhere near Dorsetshire, and even if there were, would they be inclined to send reinforcements to Corffe, and if they were, what chance did they have of making it safely through the Parliamentary forces? But he had to remain positive for Lady Bankes' sake. Since Christmas and Sir John Bankes' death, they had remained close, sleeping together and providing emotional support. Yes, Captain Cleall realised he needed Lady Bankes as much as she needed him. They tried to be discreet, but as time went by, it was not just Camille who realised what was going on and there was growing resentment.

"My Lady, you said you would let me go if I changed my mind. Now Tom has returned, I would dearly love to be back with him, although I would very much regret leaving you. But I have not seen him for two years now," Camille said, as she brushed her Lady's hair.

"Camille, I know I said that, but unfortunately I cannot allow you to leave now. Both the captains say that you are too important for us to release you, as you being with us will reduce the threat of an attack. Tom is an officer and will be influencing Bingham's plans. I could not have foreseen this. I am truly sorry. But I have to think of the welfare of all the people in the Castell."

"So I cannot see my husband, but you are free to be comforted by your lover every night?" Camille snapped, standing back from Lady Bankes. "There are many people behind these walls who have wives on the other side and could not have foreseen being trapped in here for so long. We have to endure separation from our loved ones, while you are free to be with yours. One rule for the gentry and another for the rest of us. That is why my husband is fighting for the Parliamentarians, to be free from this unfairness. I hope he takes this Castell and gets the freedom he has been fighting for." Camille threw down the brush and stormed out of the room.

Lady Bankes was taken aback. She had not been expecting that. William Harvey had once told her that Camille may be small but she certainly could be fierce, something Tom had encountered on a few occasions, but Lady Bankes had not experienced anything like that, not from Camille or any servant. This was obviously an extreme situation but what could she do? She could order the captains to release her, but then what would be the impact on the others with loved ones outside? She even started to have doubts about whether the captains would comply with her order: they could take a military perspective overriding her views. She finished dressing and went to find Captain Cleall, who was in the hall, reviewing the rota. She told him what had happened.

"Well, my love, this makes things a lot more difficult, but we cannot let her go. We need to hold the line and stand firm. There is already disquiet amongst the ranks, given the reduced ration, and seeing the Roundhead reinforcements arrive. I suggest we get everybody together and Sydenham and I address everyone. If we do it in the outer bailey, a number of men can still guard the ramparts, while hearing what we say."

"And what will you say?"

"That we have come so far, and we should not give up now; that we have inflicted significant damage to the opposition, so much so that they are afraid to attack us; that we are expecting reinforcements, and our cause is worthy of sticking it out to the end. We should stay together and fight for it for as long as we are able to, but be honest that if reinforcements do not arrive, we cannot go on beyond two more months. That will give them an idea of time."

"I would also like to speak to them."

The predicament was explained and shared with Captain Lawrence, who agreed with the approach. When everybody was assembled, he delivered the main speech, calling for unity and more time. But it was not from his men that the first voice of discontent came, but Ned Parfitt, the man who had been first to sign up and whose loyalty Mary Bankes would not have dreamed would be in doubt.

"Captains. My Lady. The sacrifices that people have already made, putting themselves in danger and away from family and loved ones for months on end, are already immense. You are asking people to carry on. I ask to what end should we hold out?"

Lady Bankes looked at both captains and made it clear that she was going to respond.

"Ned, you are of course absolutely right. In different ways, we have all suffered and I am in awe at how you have all come through this for so long. I am so grateful and I am sure history will record it as the defining moment in this Castell's history. Why do I say that, Ned? Because we have witnessed the tyranny that rules outside of these walls. We have seen how our loved ones have been treated; we have seen the derogation of the house of God, and indeed the destruction of many of your own homes. We have heard the cries of Agnes on the stake, as the evil we fight sent, an innocent woman to death. And I am sure, when those reinforcements do arrive, they will bring with them more stories that will make our blood boil with rage. That is why we make the stand. That is our cause, Ned. We must fight this evil. We must rebuild Corffe. We must never let such atrocities occur again."

Ned's brother Jed started clapping, and people started joining him, until there was a sound of enthusiastic applause echoing around the walls of the outer bailey. But Captain Cleall noticed several had not joined in, including Camille, who looked stone-faced and stared at Lady Bankes with eyes that clearly defined her feelings. He would have to assign somebody in his rota to keep a watch on her.

Chapter XVIII
A Plan in Action

It was two weeks before Tom could put his plan into action. He had taken two days to persuade Colonel Bingham and the other officers that it was the right one to follow, in preference to an all-out attack. The other officers could see the merits of his plan but wanted it to be executed during the daytime, so that if it failed, they could use the chaos that would prevail for an all-out attack on the Castell. But Tom insisted on a night-time execution to enhance the chances of success. He finally convinced them but had to wait for sufficient time for the façade he was going to present to be real, but in the meantime, every night, at the witching hour, the Castell was bombarded with musket fire. This was part of the plan to tire the defendants and make them a little lax when the time came.

Cox had been easier to persuade than Tom's fellow officers. When he had sobered up, Tom showed him a rope with a noose ready to hang a spy or traitor, for that is what he had confessed in his drunken state. But Tom had outlined his plan and the role he wanted Cox to play as an alternative path for him. There was also a carrot of fifty shillings if he played his role correctly and an additional stick that Tom was holding in his hand: a cocked pistol that was poking into the back of the turncoat as they waited for the right time to execute the plan in the middle of the night, on February 12, 1646.

Tom, Cox and twenty-five men stood on Nine Barrow Down overlooking the Castell, the drizzle in the air keeping them alert as it gently blew in their faces. Tom could sense this was a critical moment in his life, as well as the history of the village. He had been over the plan countless times in his mind, as well as with his Roundhead officer colleagues. Had he thought through all the eventualities? What else could go wrong — other than, of course, he and Camille could get killed, not to mention many of his friends and villagers. The stakes were high. It was time to find out whether God favoured the Puritans and Roundheads that night and what would be the fate of the Castell and his home village.

Tom and Cox led the men down the hill and then up the steep hill, upon which rested the Castell walls. They had all been disguised to look like Royalists, with wigs for those who had Roundhead cuts and more extravagant collars and cloaks, but it was a thin veneer. The trump card was Cox, who was perspiring as he climbed the mound. A gentle prod from Tom's pistol helped him along his way and they soon reached the base of the tower in the middle of the eastern wall.

"Psst…" Tom tried to attract the attention of a guard, and it worked, for a head appeared over the parapet and looked down into the dark.

"What is that? Who is there?" he asked, anxiously.

Tom prodded Cox again.

"It is me, Sergeant Cox. I am returning with twenty-five men, loyal to the king."

They could hear the guard calling another to bring a torch, and moments later, two heads could be seen, waving a torch into the darkness, its flame revealing the silhouette of the men below.

"How do we know it is you?"

"Get Captain Lawrence. He will vouch for me," Cox replied.

The disguised Roundheads crouched at the base of the wall, waiting for a response. They all felt tense, hoping their deception would work. Thoughts flashed through Tom's mind, many asking the question what he was doing here, at midnight, trying to break into the very Castell that had been the bedrock of his life. The ideals of the Levellers, the values of the Puritans, the anger at the king, the deaths of Francis and Jerome… None of these seemed to justify this madness. There was only one motivation now and that was the safety of Camille. He prayed she would be asleep and this could all be over before she had been even disturbed. But then the doubts flooded his mind. Was the plan going to work? He again recalled Captain Cleall's words: 'It is a plan that gives you the edge in the confusion of battle, not the sword.' Tom was about to put that advice into action, first by creating the confusion and then by executing a plan to take advantage of it.

A commotion was heard above and then Captain Lawrence's head was seen, waving a flaming torch twenty-five feet above them.

"Is that you, Cox?" he asked, dampening his voice so they could just hear.

"It is, sir, and I have returned with twenty-five loyal men from Dorchester. There has been a heavy defeat there, sir, to Bingham's men, but I found these men sheltering in a barn near Whitchurch."

This was the tale that Tom had briefed him, and Cox recounted it well.

"We also have four sacks of flour," Cox continued, "plus plenty of muskets and shot." This was the carrot that Tom hoped would persuade the Royalists to open the gate.

"Good, Cox. You have done well. Are there any officers with you?" Lawrence asked.

This was a question Tom had not anticipated. He whispered "He has been wounded" in Cox's ear.

"There was a captain, sir, but he was badly wounded and we had to leave him behind. Can you open the gates, sir? I am afraid we will be spotted by the bloody Roundheads and turned into musket fodder."

Lawrence paused for a few seconds and Tom held his breath, before the captain finally replied.

"Yes — come around to the gate and remain in the shadows by the tower until the gates are opened."

Cox looked around to Tom, who returned a nod. He had played his role well, but Tom realised there was still a risk of him double-crossing him, so with a gentle prod he reminded him of the pistol in his back. The men made their way slowly around the base of the wall, towards the Castell gate, conscious of a couple of guards above, monitoring their progress, but at least they had no torches that could have given them away.

When they reached the side of the tower, above the gates, they all crouched down within the shadows of the wall and waited. The drizzle had stopped and the breeze died, as even nature seemed to be holding its breath to see how events unfolded. Then, there was the cranking sound of the portcullis being raised behind the gate, as the chains were winched up; a sound that reverberated around the Castell and into the walls. Tom had anticipated this and it was part of the plan. It was an eerie sound that seemed to go on forever, and the impatience of Lawrence above resulted in a raised voice before the sound halted. Some more muffled voices were heard behind the gates as bolts and latches were released, and then finally one of the doors creaked open.

A head, silhouetted by a torch behind, popped out and said, "Quick — this way" but before he could retract his head, the sound of musket fire rang out from the direction of the market square, and the shot sent splinters flying off the Castell gate. Cox and Tom were now running out of the shadows and towards the gate. More shots were heard from the town, and men shouting and sounding the alarm. The tower walls and the gate started to be peppered with shot but by now, Tom and Cox had made it to and through the gate. A man behind cried out in pain, and then another. The Royalists were now firing back at the Roundheads in the market square, with Captain Lawrence directing the response from above the towers, above the gate.

Tom looked back to see, as one of his men came holding a bloodied arm. There were twelve guards inside the gate with muskets loaded or swords drawn as a precautionary welcome by Lawrence, as well as two other men at the gate. But the guards were confused. Two greeted Cox; another four ran up the stairs to aid the response against the Roundheads, while two others went to the aid of the first and second wounded men who came through the gate. A further man went to help one of the arrivals who was struggling with a sack of flour, which had apparently been hit and was quickly losing its contents. This was the confusion that Tom had planned for. He pulled back his cloak and fired his own pistol at a guard who had stood his ground, and simultaneously drew a knife, which went into the belly of the one standing closest to him.

This was the sign his men needed. The two apparently injured men recovered instantly, and their swords gutted the men who had come to their aid. A knife slit the neck of the guard who had been trying to recover the precious flour, and knives also stabbed into the backs of the two men at the gate. A guard fired his musket at Tom, who saw him just in time and twisted his body, but not swiftly enough to stop some shot piercing his left shoulder. He winced in pain, but the adrenaline was now pumping and pushing him on. With his right arm, he thrust his sword into the chest of the guard who had fired at him, and he felt the blade sever the man's rib cage before slicing through internal organs. The guard opened his mouth to scream but it was already welling up with blood. The gate was now being opened wider and the rest of his men were pouring in with pistols blazing, and the remaining three guards in the gatehouse held up their hands in surrender.

The Royalists above were oblivious to what was happening in the arch of the gatehouse below, but Tom realised every second was precious now to ensure his plan would succeed. Blood was starting to seep through his left shoulder jacket, but there was no time for that. His next objective was to keep the gate open to allow the Roundheads in from outside, whilst also securing the inner gate to prevent reinforcements coming from the rest of the Castell.

If the Royalists held the inner gate, they could hold the keep, which was even more impregnable than the outer walls. He was to take ten men to the inner gate, while the remaining men would protect the outer gate. Everybody knew their roles as he had drilled the details into them repeatedly over the last few days. Pistols were hastily reloaded, then Tom took a deep breath and he and the nine others followed him, running up the hill and into the inner sanctum of the Castell, every step closer to his precious Camille.

A man shouted from the west tower. He had spotted them, but his voice was lost in the mayhem. He was expecting musket shot from the rear, for they would have been an easy target for anybody on the gate tower, but as he had hoped, it seemed they were all preoccupied with the shooting in front of them, for the Roundheads would now be storming the front gate. Within a moment, Tom had made his way to the inner gate. It was deserted and Tom dispatched men to secure front and rear. He looked back at the outer gate, and his elevated position gave him a good view of the battle below and how his plan was coming to fruition. Once again, Captain Cleall's words resonated in his head. He had planned his way into the Castell and he had planned the confusion with the Roundheads, poised to start firing on the outer gate as soon as the door creaked open, aiming high above Tom and his men's heads and the screams of his men reinforced by the red berry juice. He really liked the pierced flour sack as he was sure there would be one guard more focused on his belly than his orders.

All his men knew the plan and it had been meticulously executed. And now dozens of Roundheads were approaching the Castell gate under the protection of three canopies, while the Royalists were peppering the assault with musket fire. He could make out Captain Lawrence, directing proceedings from the tower above the gate. He must have realised, at that very moment, that something was not right and turned around and peered over the rear of the Castell gate-tower parapet. His face was met by a volley of musket fire, but he pulled back just in time. For a second, he did not move. Tom could almost hear the thoughts of dread that were going through his mind. He seemed to be looking straight at him over the outer bailey but he was confident that he could not be seen. Did he detect the feeling of defeat in his gut? He galvanised his thoughts and ordered half the men on the parapet to turn about and fire down at the gate house.

Tom's observation was broken by the sound of a pistol behind him, followed by two further shots in rapid succession. He turned round and rushed to the rear of the gatehouse. A group of ten, maybe a dozen, Royalists had been running towards the gate from the inner keep. His men had shot one, who was crouched down injured, but the rest had taken refuge in doorways either side.

"Shall I finish the bastard off, sir?" one of the men asked.

"No. Hold your fire. There have already been enough deaths. It appears our plan is working and as long as we hold this gate, then the rest of our forces will be with us shortly and I hope to secure a surrender with no more loss of life."

There was the outline of some heads tentatively peering from the shadowy doorways but no fire. They would have little to aim at from their position and time went by as the battle raged behind. Tom returned to see what was happening and was delighted to find Roundheads pouring into the Castell, and Captain Lawrence and the ten remaining guards surrendering. "Thank you, God," he said in his mind. Victory was now surely his to take, but it would be worthless without ensuring Camille's safety.

He returned to the rear and shouted. 'We have now three hundred men flooding through the outer gate and Captain Lawrence has surrendered! I suggest for your own lives, you do the same. You will be treated well and with respect. My name is Lieutenant Tom Harvey, and I am from Corffe. You have my word."

The wounded man looked up. Something about his outline reminded Tom of something but he could only make out his outline in the dark. His thoughts were interrupted by the sound of steps coming down the path from the keep and more figures approaching.

"Hold your fire, men," Tom ordered. "Do not approach any further. This is Lieutenant Tom Harvey. We have taken the outer bailey and now have three hundred men inside the Castell. Surrender and you have my word you will be treated fairly."

"Tom!" a woman's voice shrieked. It was Camille's.

Then another voice cried "James!" and the figure started running towards the wounded man on the ground. Tom recognised the distinctive frame of Lady Bankes, who knelt down to attend to the wounded man. Tom took a deep breath. He needed to secure a surrender and ceasefire.

"Lady Bankes. Will you surrender the Castell and prevent further bloodshed? Your cause is lost."

She was clearly focused on attending the wounded man and so Tom repeated his request. This time, she lifted her head and said, "I surrender."

The siege was over. Camille was safe. The plan had worked.

Tom tentatively moved out of the protection of the gate, followed by four of his men.

"Everybody, step out, drop your weapons and raise your hands."

Ten figures did that, and Tom's men rushed towards them with their pistols raised and rounded them up.

Camille rushed toward Tom.

"Mon chéri!" she cried and embraced him, before pulling back when she realised his shoulder was bleeding.

"It is nothing, Camille. The most important thing is you are safe and we are together," and they kissed. The sweetness of her lips sent a tingle throughout his body and he did not want this moment to end, but it was interrupted by Lady Bankes.

"Help me, Camille. The captain is badly hurt."

They both turned, and then rushed over to find Captain Cleall in her arms. He had been shot in the chest, and blood was oozing out of a musket-ball hole in his jacket and already pooling on the wet stone. His face was very pale and he was gasping for breath. Camille knelt down, ripped off a length of fabric from her skirt and started to wind it around the captain's chest. There were tears rolling down her face.

"I have lost my Castell, but I pray not my love" she muttered.

"We must get him inside," Camille said, but the captain shook his head.

"Too late," he managed to say, and then, "I am sorry, my Lady. I have failed to protect you." He took another deep breath. "Tom, promise me you will look after both of these ladies."

Tom nodded and said, "I will, of course. I will do everything I can to keep them both safe."

There appeared to be a hint of acknowledgement on the captain's face, but then his eyes glazed over and the life drained out of him. His body was still and he was no more.

"No, no, no, my darling… Do not leave me…" Lady Bankes burst into tears. Camille comforted her and Tom felt awkward, but there was some commotion behind him, and he turned to find Colonel Bingham at the gatehouse. He marched over to him, saluted and said "Siege over, sir. Lady Bankes has surrendered."

"Well done, Lieutenant. I trust your wife is safe? And where is Lady Bankes? I wish to see her."

"With respect, Colonel. She has just suffered the loss of a close friend. Could you kindly wait a moment?"

"Nonsense, where is she?" retorted Bingham, pushing Tom away and marching passed. Tom followed.

Lady Bankes saw him coming and took a very deep breath, which brought a veil of composure over her. She stood up and confronted Bingham, determined to be the Lady of the Castell, and hand it over with dignity. She stood and faced him, her eyes still watery, but her face solemn and steadfast.

"My Lady. I understand you have surrendered. And where is Sir John?"

"I have surrendered my Castell and my home, but my heart remains the king's. My poor husband's life was surrendered three months ago."

"I am sorry to hear that, my Lady, but under the circumstances it is better for him. You have certainly served your King well and beyond all call of duty. You have proved a more worthy opponent than most of his generals. Your men will be disarmed and imprisoned until the king surrenders, but we will not punish them. Your dead will be blessed and buried. You will be allowed to reside here under twenty-four-hour guard until I get confirmation from London concerning what should be done with you. But before you do that, there is one thing I need from you tonight. Would you excuse me."

He walked past Lady Bankes and into the inner keep with a guard of ten men.

"Excuse me for saying this. You are remarkable, my Lady," Tom said.

"Tom…" Camille exclaimed.

"I have known Captain Cleall all my life, my Lady. He was truly a great man and taught me so much — to hunt, to fight, to speak French and charm my wife, to be a man, to be straight and honest. He taught me how to win battles, and ironically it was one of his lessons that enabled us to take the Castell tonight. But there is no victory tonight. I am devastated that you have lost your home and now we have all lost a great friend. This war has no meaning to me whatsoever now. I only had one cause tonight and that was to rescue Camille, but I have seen too much death and lost too many friends now to believe in the cause that started me on this journey."

"And I feel very much the same, Tom," Lady Bankes said.

"Your son, John — I have news. We came close to killing each other on different occasions. But on each occasion, God intervened and made it so that we were both given the choice and opportunity not to. We were together six months ago, after a famous Royalist victory that almost saw the end of me. He is well, but as troubled as I am to understand the cause he is fighting for. I will do everything I can, my Lady, as a humble lieutenant but with some influence over the colonel, to ensure you are treated well."

"Thank you, Tom. I am sorry for what you have been through. In truth, I am myself questioning what I have been holding out for. Yes — the Castell and my home, but for what? It is only stone and many lives have been lost in defending and attacking it; people who should have been living together in peace. Captain Cleall was very dear to me. Indeed, I loved him. He was more of a foundation in my life than all this stone around me and now I have lost him. My beloved husband, Sir John, has also passed away and he, too, had lost heart in the Royalist cause. What do we have left to show for what we believed in? And what we believed in has barely shown us any cause to sacrifice what we have lost."

Just then Colonel Bingham and his men returned, carrying a large painting.

"My Lady, I have to relieve you of this burden. Ever since I first met you, the image of the Popist Queen has haunted me. She has left the country, which is a great relief, but tonight I will destroy and erase another memory of her."

Lady Bankes was about to speak again, with defiance, but Tom quickly intervened.

"The lady is tired and distressed, Colonel. I believe it is better to let her retire under my protection and we can determine the best course of action in the morning."

"Of course, Lieutenant. You should get that wound attended to. I would also like you to know I will be recommending you for promotion to captain, but we can discuss that then, as well."

"Thank you, Colonel, but I believe tonight is my last action in this war."

"We will see about that. I will leave you to safeguard Lady Bankes. I will round up the prisoners, the dead and wounded and post guards around the Castell. We can then enjoy a good bonfire for our Queen here," and with that Bingham and his men departed.

Tom called over two guards and ordered them to carry the captain's body inside. He followed them with a sombre Lady Bankes and Camille. Tom escorted Lady Bankes to her room and posted two guards on the door, and then Camille led Tom to her room. As she closed the door, he wanted to hug her but felt a fog come over him, a throbbing in his head and the pain in his shoulder intensify. The adrenaline that had kept him going was losing its effect, and his body was succumbing to the tiredness and injury. He collapsed on the bed in a state of semi-consciousness, but Camille came to his aid and set about attending to him as only she could. She removed his jacked and shift and cleaned the wound. There were two pellets buried in his shoulder which she knew had to be removed. She heated a knife on the fire and removed them with care and precision. Tom's face grimaced with pain but he was barely conscious. She then bandaged him with more strips from her skirt, and made him comfortable to sleep, before lying down next to him, wrapping an arm around his waist and praying for his recovery.

The morning light awoke them both. Tom was feeling much better and was just so happy to be with his wife. They had no desire to face the day, but just talked about how much they had missed each other and the trials and tribulations they had been through whilst apart. They promised never to leave each other and then made love with a tenderness that started to heal their pain of being parted for so long.

Chapter XIX
The Aftermath

Lady Bankes had not slept. She mourned the loss of Captain Cleall and yearned to be with her children. She had learnt that while her Castell was under siege, the Royalists had suffered a defeat at the Battle of Naseby, which had turned the tide against their cause. Apparently, defeat was now almost inevitable She worried about the future, less for herself and more for her children, if she were to be tried for treason. On many occasions, she had asked herself why she had taken the stand she had, and not just left the Castell and stayed with her children. She had had no news of them since they left eight months ago. Fears and regrets circled her mind, but the loss of Captain Cleall was almost overwhelming. She needed him now, more than ever.

Shortly after a cockerel from the village had declared dawn breaking, a flock of seagulls circled around the Castell and their calls of 'huoh-huoh-huoh' echoed around the stone walls. James had often remarked to her that the sound of seagulls was something that he found reassuring, and the more she listened to them, the more she convinced he was swooning with them. The birds were sending a message from her lover; a message of comfort and reassurance. He was still with her and even protecting her. She looked out of the window at the birds. The sky was in transition: a velvet dark to the west, but the sun was opening up over the horizon like a flower of fire above Nine Barrow Down, to the south-east. The clear sky was shades of pinks with blue in between. It was truly a wonderful dawn. The seagulls were circling above the Castell Gloriette in excitement, as though they had a mission to wake everybody up in a cacophony of squawking that pierced through the morning break. Lady Bankes managed a smile as a gentle breeze refreshed her face and she asked herself what Cleall would do if he were here. The answer came to her as if he were standing next to her. "Make a plan." The seagulls seemed to reinforce the message as 'huoh-huoh' started to sound like 'plan, plan'.

And so she did.

Camille had brought Tom some milk and fresh bread, baked that morning from the very flour that he had brought into the Castell as a diversionary tactic the night before. He wanted to get up but she insisted he continue to rest and should stay in bed until his wound had healed. He reluctantly agreed, and as she departed, he realised how tired, in fact, he was. He could not remember the last time he had slept well and the anxiety, stress and emotion of the previous night had amplified his fatigue. As Camille closed the door, he fell back into a deep sleep and it was lunchtime before he was woken again, this time by the colonel. After enquiring how he was, the colonel made a proposition to Tom.

"Tom — when you were explaining to me and my command how you planned to take the Castell, I recall you saying, 'A plan in the confusion of battle gives you more of an edge than a sword'. Well, I thought I would use your current confusion to give me an edge and so I have a plan that I would like to propose. Last night was a wonderful victory, Tom. We lost only two men, with only four more, including yourself, injured. Even on the Royalist side, just seven lost their lives. Never in history, I am sure, has any Castell been taken with so little loss of life. Just compare that with over a hundred lost lives when Coke made his attack and without any gain. This victory will be heralded throughout the land to both our credits. Yes, I will make sure your part is recognised as it should be."

"It was the Royalist Captain, who died last night, who told me about planning in the confusion of battle. He was a good man and taught me a lot. I am sure he did not realise what he taught me would result in his death."

"I am sorry, Tom."

Tom started to say something else, but the colonel shut him up before the words could be formed.

"Listen, Tom. I heard what you said last night about this being your last fight and I can understand why. Now I have met Camille, a lot of things make sense. God has provided you with a wonderful wife, Tom, and definitely somebody worth fighting for. And you have done more fighting for the Parliamentary cause than most, indeed more than anybody I know. You were at Edgehill when it all started and have seen great victories and suffered great losses. You have seen many comrades and friends die — including the captain last night. I am sure you have had doubts at times as to why we are doing this, what we are fighting for and whether it is worth it. The nation has been divided and ripped apart. But I am going to give you the chance to rebuild something and be a force for good, right here in Corffe. I want you to take the position of captain, and take command of Corffe and its garrison, the Castell, the village and the estate, and be its interim governor, until Parliament decides the cause of action. You will report to me, as I oversee the entire shire. The Puritan values will help guide us re-build these communities through peace and goodwill.

"Lady Bankes will be your ward and can remain here in the Castell but she must not leave until Parliament has decided what to do with her. In the meantime, there is the rebuilding of the village: the church, the tavern, the cottages. Coke seemed to have vented more anger and destruction on the village than the entire Castell. I understand your father was the Bankes' estate manager. I am sure he can help you. We need to secure this part of our nation as a place where Puritan values are understood and practised, where hard work can be rewarded, food provided and wealth created, all for the glory of God. The income from the estate will finance the parliamentary effort, and ultimately bring victory and peace to the whole nation. And of course, you will be paid an officer and governor's wage, as well, as a reward for the victory you have secured here. I believe we are paying Cox fifty shillings for his role: well, surely the mastermind behind the plan and the man who executed it should receive many times that sum. What do you say, Tom?"

Tom did not know what to say at first, this was more than he could wish for. But then he remembered something that had been concerning him while planning the Castell's capture.

"Thank you, Colonel. You have bestowed a great honour on me and there is nothing else I would want better than to rebuild the village. But one further request: the men of Corffe who are amongst the prisoners…

I know them all and there is not a Royalist amongst them, but they are loyal to the Castell and the Bankes. Can they be freed under my ward?"

"Always thinking of others first. Yes, I can agree to that. Cromwell and Essex are concerned only about the death of Sir John Bankes and the end to the siege. I honestly do not know what they will think about Lady Bankes. Only time will tell. But in the meantime, you need to rest, Tom. I need to prepare the men for departure. I am planning to leave tomorrow, and will take all the men with me, leaving fifty for you to garrison."

The following day, the first step of Mary's plan was put into action and it was the most painful: the burial of Captain Cleall. But until he had been buried, she knew she could not move on, so she arranged for him to be buried in the Castell, next to Sir John. Tom was well enough to get out of bed for it, and a small service was held under a couple of canopies that kept the morning drizzle at bay. Lady Bankes put on a brave face in front of many of the men who had stood strong with her behind the Castell walls over the last eight months; Ned Parfitt, Alfred Smith, Ralph Povington, Sergeant Cox, as well as the villagers from outside, including William Harvey and his family, and Josh Miller. The respect that Captain engendered across the community was clear to Tom and Camille, and as the vicar concluded the service, the strength of the "Amen" reinforced this. The singing of a familiar hymn seemed to blow away the cloud and drizzle, and a solitary seagull appeared to join in at the end with a 'huoah, huoah'. This made Mary look up and some of those who were there detected a smile on her face. Tom and Camille went to share their condolences with Mary at the end but found her not wanting any of it and ready for action.

"Tom — sorry, Captain Harvey, I understand that you are in charge of the Castell, the estate and my keep," she said.

It was the first time anybody had called him captain and it took Tom slightly aback.

"As you say, my Lady," he replied

"Firstly, I have two letters I need to send. The first is to Alice to inform her and my children that I am well but also of the death of their father. The second is to Sir John Borlase, her husband, who will be in

London. If I have any chance of not being tried for treason, I will need all the help I can get. Sir John is influential in the Parliamentary hierarchy and is my best hope. Speed is of the essence, as Bingham will be requesting orders. You are at liberty to read them before I seal them. But please grant me this request. I am desperate for news of my children."

"Of course, my Lady. I know the perfect man to get them dispatched."

"And secondly, if you are well enough, would you kindly escort me to the village? I want to see what Coke and his men did and provide some support to the villagers."

Camille gave Tom a grudging nod, accepting that even she could not stop Lady Mary and Tom when they were both set on something. Tom then had a quiet word with Sergeant Cox and handed him a purse, as well as the letters. The purse contained twenty-five shillings, half his reward, with the other half and an additional ten shillings waiting for him on his return, as long as he delivered the letters and returned back to Corffe with the Bankes family. The sergeant ran off immediately to get a horse and set off on his mission, while Lady Bankes, Tom, Camille and William Harvey waled down through the inner gate and into the outer bailey.

"We need to return this to a state of normality, bring back horses and animals and artisans to make good the damage to the Castell," Lady Bankes said, as the group made their way to the outer gate. There were still blood stains on the cobbles, but the stains on the village itself were far greater. Lady Bankes was moved to tears on several occasions as William and Tom showed the two ladies around the destruction that Coke had left behind, no more so than when she entered the church, stripped of its slates, its doors, pews and font. The building had been left to stable horses but had not been cleaned out and stank of dank, putrid straw.

"Religion and war seem to be inextricably linked. How can religious faith be the promotor of such evil? Coke has desecrated this place of peace and sanctity, and turned it into a shit house," Lady Bankes declared.

They found many of the villagers had started to return to their homes and were mending the damage the Roundheads had done inside, beginning the necessary repairs to roofs with fresh bundles of straw. Mary Bankes had brought a purse with her and gave each householder ten shillings to help them with their repairs. Each and every one of them was grateful: although they knew her stance had been the cause of their misery, they knew she was a good person who would not have wished any harm to them. News had spread of the loss of her husband and how she had protected the villagers within the Castell during the siege.

The following day, Camille and Mary Bankes were in what was left of the garden in the inner keep, stripped of anything that had been edible during the siege. It was in a sorry state. They sat on a bench and both women knew they had to reconcile from the last days of the siege.

"Camille, I am sorry we were not able to release you earlier so you could have been with Tom. If we had, perhaps life would be different now. Tom would have been less inclined to make his daring move, and instead we would still have been trapped in the Castell and no doubt under attack, and many could have lost their lives. I hope you understand."

"Maybe Tom would have lost his life in the attack and so it is me who should be apologising, my Lady. I prayed for Tom and myself to be reconciled and we are, thanks to God, but I did not realise at what cost to you, my Lady."

"Camille — on the night Tom launched the attack, the captain and I were in bed. We heard the firing, and the captain wanted to go out to find out what was happening. But we had been fired on at midnight for the last ten days or so, and each time he left me for no reason. But that night I wanted to cling onto him. Something inside me told me not to let him go, and so he stayed. Those few moments I will treasure for ever, but they were only moments for as we embraced, he still had an ear listening to the assault and realised that it was more intense that the previous nights. So he kissed me and left me and I followed shortly after, with you, to find him shot. I will never know if those precious moments would have resulted in a different outcome, had I not detained him or, indeed, had I been stronger and detained him for longer."

"I am sorry, my Lady, but at least you shared that time together in the siege. He was there to protect you and for no other reason. His love for you resulted in the ultimate sacrifice, but only in this world. I am sure you will be reunited in the next world. Tom told me that he had planned the shooting on the Castell at midnight on the previous nights to make the defendants complacent. His plan worked. But who taught him planning in such detail? It was Captain Cleall, of course."

Two weeks later, Cox returned with two carriages packed with the Bankes children. Alice and Sir John Borlase had also made the journey. Mary Bankes was overjoyed to see them all.

"We have been so worried about you, Ma," Alice said as she hugged her mother, but Lady Bankes was too overcome with emotion, to respond, not wanting to let Alice go.

"What has happened to my constituency?" Sir John Borlase asked. "I have spoken to Cromwell, when I was in London, making your case, my Lady. I journeyed to Oxford with Cox and wrote to him again. I am sure he will view my request sympathetically. And I am sorry to hear about Sir John and hope he passed away peacefully, without too much pain. He was truly a great man and one of the few positive influences on the king. Even Cromwell acknowledged this when I spoke to him and sent his condolences."

"Sergeant Cox told us about how Pa died. When he left Oxford, something inside me told me that I would not see him again. Where is he buried, Ma?" Alice said, welling up with tears, still in her embrace, which had now been joined by all the other children.

"Have you news of John, Alice?" Lady Bankes asked.

"Yes, Ma. He is well."

"Thank God."

"We have seen a lot of him as he has been garrisoned in Oxford. Fortunately, he was not at Naseby, but he has just headed west again. The king is in Wales, and I believe his brigade will be trying to connect with him. He is now a captain."

The Bankes trailed inside the Castell, catching up on events in Oxford and the development of the children as they walked. Eight months had seen them all grow and change, and they each had a story or two to tell their mother. Arabella was now talking and clung to her mother, fearful of being separated again but after a while, she found the prospect of running around the Castell with her siblings irresistible. Edward, Bridget and Ann ran around the hall with wooden hobby horses, the girls pretending to be princesses, while Edward rescued them from imaginary dragons. It was almost as though normality had been restored and Lady Bankes could forget, for a moment, the threat of the treason charge that she was facing and the traumatic months she had faced. She had stood strong for her family, their home and their future, and while she had missed her children more than she could describe, her spirit was renewed and strengthened with them around her.

Captain Harvey arrived and welcomed the Bankes family, embracing Alice.

"I understand you are governor of the Castell now, Tom," Alice said. "But that does not mean you can boss me around."

"I have never been, nor will ever be able to do that Alice — sorry, Lady Alice. I know the limits of my command."

"In which case, can I request, or even command you, to escort the Bankes family to Green Island tomorrow?"

Her request was greeted with cries of 'Yes!', 'Please, Tom!' and 'You must, Tom!' from all the children.

"It looks as if I have no option, my Lady. I will start preparing. We can take horses and a picnic," Tom replied.

The next day was a crisp but bright spring day, with all of nature alive and the birds singing as the horses set out from the Castell and over the Down in the direction of Studland and the island. Tom led the way with little Mary perched on the front of his saddle, followed by Lady Bankes, who had Arabella strapped to her, and the other young children were shared between Camille, Alice, John Borlase, Mary and Elizabeth. Ralph rode alone, and in no time at all had taken the lead, determined to show off his horsemanship.

"I am going to be in the cavalry, like my brother John," he declared, with a wooden sabre in his hand to prove his credentials. They soon found Tom's old rowing boat and emptied it of water before launching it and then Tom ferried the family across to the island in groups of five at a time.

"Colonel Bingham told me he camped on the island the night before his first attack on Corffe," Tom informed Mary, as he rowed her across the narrow strait of water that separated the island from the shore.

"Oh, really? That was a long time ago, or at least it seems it. I sent him away with a flea in his ear that day, for sure."

"Yes. I even heard about that in Bristol."

"If he ever knew it was just me, Captain Cleall, Camille, Ralph Povington, the cook and the maids behind the ramparts, he would die with embarrassment," Mary said, and they both laughed.

Laughter, indeed, was the order of the day; something that had been sparse for many months in both Corffe and Oxford, and the bonding of friends and family on the magical island provided relief from the anxiety that had overshadowed them for so long, and the pain of the loss of so many. This was the first time Tom had visited the island without Francis, and Studland had been a regular riding haunt for Mary and Captain Cleall. John Bankes loved his trips to Green Island and was still absent, but hopefully would be returning soon. Indeed, the day of play and laughter, of picnicking and being in the nature, provided the Bankes and the Harveys with a hope for a future where love and friendship would enable them to reconcile the past.

Bingham returned the following month with news from London. As he rode up to Corffe, he thought about how he would share the news with the two people who would be most impacted: Lady Bankes and Captain Tom Harvey. He had learnt a lot from the war and most probably the biggest lesson for him was that there were good and bad people on each side. If a new, better world was to be built out of this mess, then it was the good people who had to recognise their differences and build alliances to reconcile the terrible things that had occurred. It would not come from people like Coke or Prince Rupert, but people such as Lady Bankes and Tom Harvey.

The Battle of Naseby, when Oliver Cromwell's New Model Army had dealt the Royalists a massive defeat, had resulted in the momentum being with the Parliamentary forces. The training and discipline that Tom had demonstrated in Blandford was giving the Roundheads the upper hand, and the king had fled to Wales. There was still a lot to do, but Bingham was confident that the end was in sight and the prospect of building peace was now real and becoming ever more important.

Obviously, there was the question of the king and what should be done with him when he was finally captured but that, thankfully, was for others to consider.

He was surprising himself with the respect he now had for Mary Bankes; a woman he had despised for her aristocratic arrogance and what he believed were her Catholic sympathies. But Tom Harvey had assured him that her respect for the queen was purely as a woman; one who had come over to England as a young Catholic girl in a largely anti-Catholic royal court and to be queen of a country that was suspicious of the French and with a Parliament that was paranoid about Popist conspiracy plots. Yet she held her own. She played an active role in state affairs and influenced her husband, who respected and listened to her advice as much as any advisor, if not more. Bingham had not considered her from this perspective. She was just a Catholic and so, in his old book, should not be trusted. But perhaps he was wrong, as he had been about painting Lady Bankes with his aristocratic brush as one of those people who were born into wealth and did nothing in return to make God's world better. They just flaunted their wealth at social events and hunts on the backs of their tenants' hard work.

Tom Harvey had told him that nothing was further from the truth when it came to the Bankes. Sir John had been the champion of justice, and Lady Bankes cared deeply for the welfare of everybody in Corffe. His words were vindicated by the interrogation he conducted, alongside his officers, of the defendants of the Castell, the morning after the victory. He heard repeated stories of Lady Bankes leading by example, whether it concerned the chores around the Castell, taking turns on the watch on the towers, defending the Castell when it was attacked, nursing the wounded and even giving up her rations for the sick. She was still defiant at the moment of surrender, but one could only admire her for that, as well.

Then there was Tom, whom he now knew well and respected as a man who epitomised everything he stood for; a man who would have been his model son if God had blessed him with a child. Indeed, it felt as though he was becoming a surrogate son to him, and the victory he had masterminded over the Castell was truly God-inspired and given. This made the journey heavy, for the news he would be bringing would dismay both Tom and Lady Bankes.

Tom and Lady Bankes were waiting for him in the hall when he arrived, sitting in chairs either side of the fire. Tom immediately got up and saluted the colonel as he entered the room, and Lady Bankes gave him a respectful nod. How things had changed since he had first met her in this very room.

"I have news from London," he said, as he sat down on one of the two remaining chairs positioned around the fireplace. "I know neither of you are people who would want me to beat around the bush, so I will come out with it straight."

"Of course, Colonel," Mary said, the first time she had recognised his rank, as he unfolded a document.

"Let's start with the good news. Lady Bankes — you will not face any charges of treason."

She simply nodded, but both men could detect the relief on her face, although sensing she was waiting to hear the full verdict from Bingham.

"However, under the Act of Indemnity and Oblivion, all Bankes' property has been confiscated by Parliament."

"This is disgraceful. What have I done but to defend my home? What right have you got to just attack anybody and then confiscate their property when they defend their land? That amounts to theft and a breach of God's seventh commandment."

"I am just the messenger, Lady Bankes, but I will have to execute Parliament's wishes. I would suggest you lobby against this judgement, as I do confess that I have sympathy with your view. There are Royalists who have actively campaigned in aggressive ways to support the king and I believe this Act should be targeted at them."

"If I have no possessions, it will be hard for me to lobby and appeal, Colonel. I will need to hire a lawyer, at the very least."

"Tom will be charged with the process of disposition and I fear he will struggle to find many buyers quickly for many of the assets, although some disposition of assets will be essential or else Parliament could impose a less sympathetic Executor."

"Thank you for your counsel, Colonel," Lady Bankes said, recognising that his suggestion would alleviate the situation.

"But unfortunately, there is not much I can do about the third and final requirement. The House of Commons has voted on the demolition of the Castell by mining and explosives, and again I am going to have to ask Tom to execute this order."

Tom and Lady Bankes both looked at each other in horror. It was Tom who spoke first.

"Never. We cannot destroy this, Castell. It is the heart of this community. It is our home. Never."

"It is my home, Colonel," Mary pleaded. "It is where I have brought up my children. It is where my husband and Captain Cleall are buried. It is what I stood up for in the siege. I have defended my home and my penalty is its destruction."

"I understand everything you both say but many other Castells that have defended the Royalist cause throughout the kingdom have or are being slighted; Kenilworth, Pontefract, Sheffield. I can see no way to avoid this. All I can say is that I need to re-join Lord Essex, whose forces will be sweeping through Dorsetshire in the next few weeks. The king's forces are in disarray and I am hoping we will see the end of this madness in the near future. We can then start to rebuild. But you must write to me in the next two weeks and give me the assurance that plans are in place to slight the Castell, or I will have no choice but to impose on the Castell a command to get the job done. Tom — it will pain you grievously to do this but I am sure it will be better for you to do it, with Lady Mary and the villagers by your side, than an outsider. Think it through and be sure to write to me, with details of the plan. I am truly sorry for this news and believe me, I did challenge the order several times as I knew it would grieve you both. I know you are both strong and will come through this. I must now take my leave for I am needed in Dorchester. Good day."

"Yes, sir. And thank you, sir," Tom said, begrudgingly.

Tom escorted the colonel to his horse, and by the time he had returned, he found Lady Bankes already writing to Mr Pumphrey, her solicitor, about reversing the requisitioning order.

"Well, at least you will not be tried for treason, my Lady, but the Castell? I cannot comprehend it. What shall we do?" Tom sat down in despair.

"Well, it appears that you are going to have to do it, Tom. I think Colonel Bingham has a point: this will be like a family death and it is better that we involve all the members of the family. By that, I mean the household and the villagers, and that will also give you and me the strength to come to terms with it."

Lady Bankes and Tom gathered all the household and elders of the village, which included Will Harvey, together in the Castell hall the next day. Sir John Borlase and Alice were present, as well.

Tom spoke to the gathering first. "We have gathered you here today to share some bad news. The Castell will have to be destroyed by order of Parliament. The walls are to be mined or blown up."

The room filled immediately with shouts and cries of indignation.

"There is little we can do about it," Tom pleaded, trying to make himself heard over the clamour, "other than come to terms with it and work together to determine how best this can be done."

"So this is what your campaign for a better world has led us to, Captain Harvey," said Sam Ash, with some contempt in his voice.

"It is not possible. The Castell has been my life. Lady Bankes — stop this," Ralph Povington squealed.

"Tom, you know without a Castell the livelihood of all around will suffer," Tom's father added.

"And the likes of us, who stayed throughout the siege, will be the first to be out of work," Mary Hardy the cook shouted, to ensure she could be heard above the mayhem.

"Quiet, quiet!" Tom demanded, banging his fist on the table to bring matters to some order.

"Believe me, I know how you are all feeling," he continued. "And yes — please vent your anger on me, the Parliamentary cause, and this bloody war. I apologise, but if I had not gone to war to defend the rights of every one of us in this room, there would be some other man, like Coke, standing before you. No — in fact, he would already be setting the first charges. All I can say is that we, Lady Bankes and myself, believe it is best if we work this through together and somehow address all the issues you have raised, one by one. That means not shouting over each other, not blaming people, but coming to terms with the situation pragmatically."

"Well said, Tom." It was Lady Bankes who was standing up and speaking. "This is my home I will be losing, where half my children were born, and in which all have grown up and loved it. I will not only be losing this, but Parliament are requisitioning all my assets. I have also lost my husband, who is buried here. But I am not looking for sympathy; just understanding. We have all suffered a lot, and it would appear that we have no option but to face this new trauma in our lives, and it must be better to do this together, supporting each other and working out what we can salvage from this situation."

She sat down, and the room was silenced. People were reflecting on what she said and it was Sir John Borlase who was the first to say something.

"As the Member of Parliament for Corffe, I can make representations to Cromwell and the other leaders in Parliament. I know that there is little possibility to stop the slighting order for this is the way for many other Castells. Nonetheless, I will return to London at the end of this week and make representations. But if there are other ideas that you may have that will help reduce this act, and that need Parliamentary support, well — now is the time to come up with them."

"Sir John, my Lady — perhaps we can use some of the stone from the Castell to rebuild some of the homes we have lost, or even build new homes for a bigger and better village." William Harvey came up with this first suggestion.

"A wonderful idea, William," Mary replied.

"We could build a new market square, with new stones to replace the fire stains from Agnes' execution," William added.

"Do not forget the church. It could be rebuilt; maybe even extended so more people can come and worship in the village," Sam Ash jumped in.

"Yes, that would be a positive outcome. What do we need to do, Father Jerome?" Lady Bankes asked.

"Well, we will need a lot of God's grace and of course, manpower and money," Father Jerome responded. "But stone from the Castell would be a good start."

"Maybe I can ask Parliament for some money," Sir John suggested. "I know finances are tight, but Parliamentarians must think beyond the war to rebuild the nation. I could lead a campaign for such assistance when I return. I am not going to build up your hopes, but if we do not ask, we will not get anything."

Lady Bankes then spoke again. "In normal circumstances, I would have wanted to finance the rebuild but as I have told you, as I stand before you, I have no assets. But I have appealed against the requisition, and maybe this supports the case. Rather than take all my assets, some could be left for the village. I am also hopeful to retain some assets for my family and if so, I will need a new home and would want to bring my household with me wherever that is; perhaps in Studland or perhaps by the river at Wimborne, but here in Dorsetshire and on Bankes land, or the estate as it was."

The group disbanded, still with very heavy hearts, but at least they were talking about some of the ideas that would frame a world without a Castell. But as word spread about the impending tragedy that would fall on that community, everybody asked themselves and each other how could there be a Corffe without a Castell. It was left to Captain Tom Harvey to come up with the plan to take the Castell and its protection away and report back to Colonel Bingham. Besides the emotion, there was the practicality of demolishing a building that was built to be indestructible. It had just faced eight months of bombardment with hardly a scar to show for it.

April 1647

Mary looked down on the Castell from Nine Barrow Down, alongside her son, John Bankes. There was a fine drizzle in the air, and the breeze on the hillside blew it towards them. It was a grey day for a grim spectacle: the demolition of the Castell. There were small huddles of people dotted along the hillside ready to witness the event. John Bankes had a sling around his arm, for he had returned from the West Country after being injured in battle, being thrown from his horse as it reared up after a cannon shot exploded right in front of them. John had escaped with a broken arm and the realisation if he had been three or four yards ahead, he would have no longer been alive to tell the tale.

The Royalist cause was lost in England and John would be fighting no more. The Bankes had just learnt that the king had placed himself under the protection of the Scots in the north of England, but Sir John Borlase had written to them and told them that a Parliamentary negotiating team had already embarked from London to negotiate with the Scots to hand over the monarch. While there were still skirmishes here and there, and smaller country towns under siege, holding out for the king, with no monarch there was little to fight for. But after three years of fighting, John was glad of a respite, and even more pleased to return to Dorsetshire to see his mother and siblings, as well as Tom Harvey, in more civil circumstances. Both held the rank of captain, and they each had more than their fair share of war stories to tell, as well as reflecting on why and what they were fighting for; something that they had shared together on several occasions in the Ship Inn and Fox Tavern in Corffe over the last few weeks. Talking to his friend, who had been fighting on the other side, had brought clarity to John's own thinking and how wrong and misguided the war had been. Tom's words from their last visit echoed in his mind as the drizzle refreshed his face.

"John, it was Captain Cleall who had given me some advice which helped me on numerous occasions through this terrible time. He told me, 'In the confusion of battle—'"

"'A plan gives you more of an edge than the sword.'" John finished the line he, too, had heard the captain say so often, and the two captains laughed.

"Yes, the captain was a good man and a great instructor," Tom added and both men toasted his memory. "But what I realised was that all the planning had been for war and conflict and how to kill and maim fellow countrymen. Nobody had been planning how to reconcile people's views and build understanding and peace. Who was giving peace the edge?"

"You are so right, Tom. My father often spoke to me of such things, but as a young lieutenant eager to get onto the battlefield and prove myself, I did not understand what he was saying at the time. In hindsight, I believe he was a lone voice of reason in a wilderness as the nation divided. He always told me that there were three things to build nations: firstly, developing a common understanding of people from different creeds; secondly, tolerance and thirdly, leadership that could build on the first two. I fought for the king, mainly out of loyalty to my brigade, as well as my family. But I heard the king address his troops on several occasions, and it was all about him and nothing to do with the nation. My mother defended his divine right to rule, putting the Castell and many lives on the line. But I saw no Godly inspired leadership from the king I served, and my father frequently told me how he despaired at his arrogance and lack of empathy for both his Parliament and his people. He was certainly not one to plan for peace, as you say, Tom."

"Both sides were misguided, John, including myself. I went to war for a better world, a freer society, but not recognising the good I already had here, in Corffe. The Bankes family have always been good to Corffe and indeed the Cokes before them, yet I was blinded to this by the likes of Freeborn Lilburne. You counselled me wisely when we first heard him in London, but I ignored you, wrapped up in a desire for change. And so I found myself fighting alongside people like Harry Coke; men driven by greed and power. Could there be a worse character than Harry Coke?"

'Yes, he is certainly the black sheep in an otherwise good family. It was his brother George who fixed my arm in Oxford. You could not have met a better man and he despaired at his brother's actions. Of course, they were on different sides, as well."

"And now I have to destroy the Castell. Your home. Our home. And for what? I just pray that the nation can learn a lesson and the ruin will remind us of what happens when we have no leadership, no understanding and no tolerance. As Camille says we need a big dose of compassion and love to heal the wounds."

John's thoughts returned to the present. Today, he wanted to be with his mother to comfort her and share the pain of the culmination of an agonising time, which had seen the Bankes family stripped of their assets and most of their possessions sold, with the proceeds used to fund the Parliamentary campaign. Sir John Borlase had managed to safeguard ten per cent of the proceeds to fund the reconstruction of the village church, for which Lady Bankes had been very grateful. Tom had also directed much of the stone removed from the Castell to the church. The roof had already been repaired and a new aisle to the west of the naïve had emerged from foundations to head-height from Castell stone. Furthermore, Tom had allowed Sir John to purchase two cartloads of his mother's most precious possessions at a heavily discounted price. He had also allowed her and the family to live at a lodge house on the estate between Wimborne and Wareham. That was only until the appeal of the requisition of her assets had been concluded. Initially, Parliament had rejected her appeal, but with more lobbying by Sir John and Mr Pumphrey, it had been agreed, in February, that she could retain her estate but a very large fine would have to be paid over the next five years. With John's return, he would naturally take over the estate, and they had calculated that the rents from the tenants and income from the quarry would enable them to pay the fine and live a modest life for five years, after which time they could perhaps build a new home. At least, there was some light at the end of the tunnel and putting today behind them would take them further towards it.

Mary and John could now see Tom, down there in the inner bailey of the Castell, with his men, preparing the fuses. It was akin to watching a loved one being executed. The horror had to be endured for the comfort of the victim. In this case, the victim was made of stone, but it was still a beloved home and structure that had defined a community, full of character and the stage for countless memories.

It had taken Tom and his father, as well as quarrymen and artillery men with good knowledge of gunpowder, the full two weeks initially allowed by Colonel Bingham to develop the plan to slight the Castell. It had started to be executed the following week, but it had taken almost a year to put it in place and arrive at today for the first explosive demolition. A lot of the character of the Castell had already changed as it had been stripped naked of its fixtures and fittings, scarred by the tunnelling under its walls, as well as a process of chiselling fissures into its walls and removing stone blocks to weaken its structure. It looked in a sorry state as it awaited this final day of reckoning.

That morning, Tom had escorted Mary around the Castell grounds for one last time.

"As governor of the Castell, it is in my power to give these to you, Lady Bankes. There is no person who has given more to this Castell and you should be the custodian of the keys," Tom said, as they reached the outer gate. He handed her a large key ring containing all the keys of the Castell.

As Mary now stood waiting on Nine Barrow, she clutched the ring and vowed that they should remain with the Bankes family forever. Camille came up and joined Mary and John. She was no longer Mary's lady-in-waiting, for Mary could not afford her service, but nor did Camille need the work, given Tom's status as captain and governor of the Castell. But they both missed each other's company, and had met up regularly for tea, which Mary had found comforting and a great support.

"You are looking well, my dear," Mary said, as she arrived.

"Thank you, my Lady, and how are you on this sorry day?" Camille asked in a comforting voice, holding both of Mary's hands.

"It is going to be a hard day but we will get through it. But are you sure you do not have a fever, Camille? Your cheeks are very rosy."

"The truth is I am with child, my Lady," Camille responded with a joyous smile.

"Well, that is wonderful news. That is the tonic I needed to help me through today. I am so pleased for you. Tom must be delighted," Mary said, hugging Camille and welling up with emotion.

"That is the best news I have heard since the start of this wretched war. Congratulations, Camille," John said, giving her a welcoming kiss on the cheek.

"Yes, Tom is delighted and cannot wait to be a father. I only told him yesterday, as I thought it would help him through today, as well."

"Well, it looks as though it is about to happen. See... The men are running back into the outer bailey," John said.

The miniature forms could be seen running through the inner gate and Tom was easy to make out, directing proceedings. The last men had barely made it through the archway before the first rumble was heard from inside the keep; a sound that was soon muffled out by a gigantic boom that came from the same area, followed by a blast that ripped the heart out of the Castell near the bastion; stone and glass exploding into the air. Another boom from the rear of the gloriette, and a third and a fourth. The shockwave of the initial blast could be felt in the ground beneath their feet, as the explosion echoed around the hills as if the heavens were declaring their dismay with thunder. A ball of dust and cloud was now rising above the location of the first blast but was blown away by another boom a few yards away. This caused the whole side of the gloriette to fall like a deck of cards, crashing down, many blocks at a time, creating an even larger dust ball that mushroomed out of the debris. To the rear, another blast, and more of the Castell collapsed into oblivion, giving rise to another dust ball. Flames could be seen licking their way through the clouds, and adding a black smoke to the scene, rising into the sky, and the smell of sulphur hung heavy on the air.

The Castell was no more.

The audience watched in silence as the ruin emerged through the dust and smoke as a testimony to the destruction of a nation at war with itself. It would be a memorial for all time to a conflict that saw the death of more Englishmen as a proportion of the country than any other in its history, and the loss of Sir John Bankes, Captain Cleall, Francis Trew and Joseph Cobb. John, Mary and Camille on the Down, and Tom, in the outer bailey, watched with regret but the realisation that they needed to see through the smoke of devastation to a new world beyond, to a peace without a king, to new homes and to new family members, and Francis' dream of a better and fairer life.

Acknowledgements

A Nation in Ruins stays true to events and people as far as possible, with some variation to the timing of happenings and supplementary characters for literary effect. The Bankes' family names are real and the story is true to their historical record, but characters, relationships and specific events are fictional. The Harveys are entirely fictional. A Captain James Bond was an acquaintance of the Bankes and indeed, did hold out with Lady Bankes during the siege, but I have changed his name for obvious reasons, but there is a hint of the Ian Fleming character in the renamed Captain Cleall. John Bingham was a true character and an alderman of Poole, but most of his story in the book is fictional. Sir Edward Coke did own the Castell and his death and legacy are all historically correct. His son, Harry, did have gambling debts, but the rest of his character and the events associated with Corffe are all fictional, as are the events and roles related to his siblings. Humphrey Weld did acquire Lulworth Castell. The book is dotted with other historical characters, including Freeborn John Lilburn, John Milton, John Bunyan and Robert Boyle, all of whom are placed historically at the right time and location.

The battles of Edge Hill and Roundway Down were both landmarks within the English Civil War. There were skirmishes in Dorset, in and around Blandford, before Lord Essex did drive through the county, but the battle between Bingham and Seymour is fictional. However, all the events and timings relating to Corfe Castle are true to account and I would like to acknowledge Andrew Norman's *By Swords Divided*, a factual account of Corffe Castel during the Civil War, which provided a great reference. Wareham changed hands multiple times during the war, and my account covers just one of those but is not true to historic timing. Sir John Bankes did not return to the Castell before the siege but died in Oxford at the same time as depicted in the book. The exploits of the

Witchfinder General Hopkins and John Sterne were something that was true during this time, but these two characters were constrained to East Anglia, being responsible for the deaths of a hundred 'witches' during the Civil War. However, generally across the country there was suspicion of women who claimed to have 'the sight' or used herbs to heal, and many were tried and executed. The 'Putrid Throat' was an illness, fictionally named in Winston Graham's Poldark book as diphtheria, which was common at the time, and I have borrowed its name.

A big thank you to the National Trust, a wonderful organisation that looks after tirelessly the ruin of Corffe Castell, amongst so much of this nation's heritage. I have visited the Castell so many times and I am so grateful each time, for its sheer splendour, as well as the medieval events that are staged there, the informative volunteers and the cream teas in the café. It is a marvellous experience that I hope will be enjoyed by many more after reading this book. I would advocate a visit in spring, summer, autumn and winter to witness the reflection of the seasons on the ruin, and definitely at night at Xmas time when torches burn from its walls and you can sense the ghosts of this story passing through the stone walls.